AWAKENING

BOOK III

I. R. HARRIS

In honor of a mother's gift gone unfulfilled…

THE BOUND TRILOGY

To Ana, the Bonding ritual is a dangerous part of being human. She herself hasn't been chosen--yet. However, her dear friend Kai has, and on the surface he seems happy. However, Ana knows that Kai was lucky; his Bonder didn't make the choice to kill him. When it is her time, she might not be so fortunate. As it so happens, the choice to take Ana as a Bond was made years ago and her time is now. When Ana's peaceful life in Indonesia is suddenly intersected by a Bonder Demon named Nathanial, she is thrown into a roaring tempest of choices, of love, of ever changing loyalties, and of lies. She quickly realizes that loving someone is not the same as knowing them, and that having either of those things offers no guarantee that her heart will be protected or her life will be spared. For Ana, does being Bound mean to live in the absence of love, of autonomy, of trust or does it mean she will have to make the ultimate sacrifice in order to reclaim who she is and to save not only herself, but also the lives of those to which she is forever tied?

BOUND BOOK I

FALLEN BOOK II

AWAKENING BOOK III

Part I

Chapter One

Nathanial

My brother didn't know. I was keeping Patric out of my mind, my thoughts and my plans; he didn't know that I had been tracking her, following her every move, watching, waiting. He had been generous with her, allowing she and Lucie to go without him, to travel and relax and heal; he wanted her to be free, not to feel obligated to him or to what had transpired between them. The memory of being in that room the night I'd come to see her, to see my brother and finding them together, finding him with her, kissing and touching her when I'd told him to keep his hands off of her—it infuriated me. Watching him move his body with hers, seeing how gentle he was, how tender he'd become, how he'd taken advantage of the changes in her body since the attack by Carlo, of her sadness and grief, how he'd betrayed the knowledge that she was mine, she would always be mine—he made me sick. I wasn't upset with Ana, not after everything that I had made her endure, not after she had so unselfishly saved my life. I loved her even more, if that was possible. I understood. I knew that she was hurting, confused, exhausted, but I also knew she needed me, she wanted me, she loved me. I just needed to make her see, make her realize that we belonged together. I had a plan.

I watched the port where the boat was docked and saw Ana exit, carrying Lucie in her arms. Another couple they were traveling with also exited and together they gathered on the dock collecting their bags. The couple was older, maybe in their sixties and it was their

2

boat that Ana's Irish friend had offered to she and Lucie. Ana's traveling companions seemed totally enthralled with both Ana and Lucie and I could see just how much of a friendship they all had formed in the months they had traveled. We were in Mykonos, Greece, one of my favorite places and one that I had often spoken with Ana about, one that I had hoped to take her. I was feeling slightly guilty about leaving Micah, but since Carlo's death and Patric's willingness to concede various land agreements, most of the fighting in South America and in the States, had quelled. I wasn't worried. Patric was keeping himself busy tending to the business of Carlo's ranch, which I had discovered was now actually owned by my brother and he was constantly in meetings about the various components that made up the multimillion dollar enterprise...he wouldn't miss me.

Ana and her group moved down the dock and toward a small convoy of vehicles ready to take them to their accommodations. I already knew the house where they would be staying and I had planned to reveal myself to Ana as soon as possible. Greece was the last stop on their voyage and she and Lucie were scheduled to return to Ireland in a week and it was my hope that I could persuade her to leave Greece with me and start somewhere fresh, a place where we could create new memories and have the life together that we both deserved.

Ana

Catharine and Andrew had been two of the most glorious travel companions that I could have ever hoped for; to have them with us for

3

these last summer months made this entire journey what I had always hoped it would be. We'd been to Italy, Spain, France, Switzerland, Denmark and now Greece, our last stop before heading back to Ireland for a while. Actually, I wasn't exactly sure why I had scheduled us to return to Dublin after our trip, but for some reason, I felt that I needed to go back one more time before making any decisions about where I wanted my life to take me. I wasn't expecting to see Stephen again and Patric had offered the luxury of not pressuring me into having a relationship with him; he understood that the night we spent together before I left had been one of the most beautiful and sacred experiences of my life, but that I still needed to heal. We both now knew that we loved each other and I was starting to think that Carmen had been on to something when I spoke with her before she died. She believed that you most certainly could love more than one being, one soul, but that you ultimately had to decide who was the person who completed you in the most ways. For me, that was a challenge. Each person that I loved offered me something different, a unique combination of nourishment, of passion, love, desire, laughter, but sadly, none of them were able to offer me security. I had no idea if Patric would want to have a life with Lucie and me now, if he saw himself as a father or a partner. He was transitioning in so many ways and again, I felt as though our journeys were continuing to run parallel to each other, each of us trying to understand these new people that we'd become. Stephen was gone, I had no idea where he was and I was guessing that he preferred it that way. Then, there was Nathanial. I had not seen him before I left. I had wanted to talk to him, but for some reason, he'd been keeping his distance from me since I'd left Micah's house after my illness and returned to Patric. I got the feeling from him that he was not too pleased with the way my relationship to

4

his brother had developed. I wasn't Bound to Nathanial anymore; he was free and I was free and even though I still loved him, I had no idea where to go with that, he was so different to me now and really all I wanted was for us both to find some sense of peace with each other, some resolution to our relationship to one another. I just felt it was always a perpetual circle with Nathanial, like a revolving door and we were never on the same side at the same time; we were always off, passing each other as our lives continued to cycle around and around and yet…yet Nathanial would always be my gravitational pull. He was there constantly, knowing just how to move me, how to help me shape the sands that my waters caressed; he was inside of me, igniting my need for him and no matter how much I wanted to resist, I couldn't.

We arrived at Catharine and Andrew's vacation home and I started to unload everyone's suitcase. The house was situated in a nestled mountain community that overlooked the Mediterranean Sea, but unfortunately for me, those waters only served as a reminder of a person whose eyes reflected their exact color and shone just as brightly against the backdrop of a setting sun. I sighed and watched as Andrew hoisted Lucie up on his shoulders and carried her laughing, up the steep front walk. Catharine put her hand on my shoulder and smiled; I had told her some of what had happened between me and Patric and Nathanial, and I'd even felt comfortable enough with her friendship to talk about Stephen and about the baby we'd lost. Catharine too had miscarried a child and she understood the deep sense of loss and why, even now, I considered myself to be broken, to be unworthy somehow to bear any new life. It was so nice to feel safe when revealing my emotions and not feel guilty about trying to navigate my grieving process.

Lucie insisted that we wait to unpack and head straight to watch the sunset on the beach; she'd been obsessed with watching the sky change from painted fire to the quiet deep of twilight and almost every night for the last four months, we'd sit together just she and I and gaze out upon the horizon. I would notice every so often that Lucie would be staring at me, her eyes startling in their depth and I was beginning to wonder if she could read my thoughts, catch the tenor of my emotions, feel the struggles that I was experiencing. I never asked her what she was thinking, mainly out of fear—I was probably the worst person to be trying to raise a half-Vampire child; I wouldn't know how to help her navigate any of her special abilities as well as Carmen or Liam or even Stephen—I felt terrible that she was stuck with me. I smiled as I watched Lucie charge down to the shore, running at full speed down the beach. Catharine had gotten Lucie a tiny digital camera in Spain and she had yet to part with the thing. She'd snap pictures of everything and everybody and I couldn't help but think of Stephen; they shared the same enthusiasm and contemplative assessment of the world around them and I was glad that Lucie, for whatever reason, had managed to keep a bit of her uncle's influence with her. I took my place on a large rock and breathed in the salt air, my body shuddered and I tried not to cry. Even now, even though I knew that he was never coming for me or us, Stephen's face, his scent, his memory seemed so tied to me. It was odd, but sometimes I almost felt him in my blood, as if every part of who he was or is coursed through my veins. I would get these sudden surges of emotion that boiled up through my body; anger, despair, desire, confusion…they would all be there and yet none of them I could find a place for in my own mind. Yes, I had been experiencing some of those feelings for many months now, but never to the degree

6

that these harsh currents would create; they knocked the breath out of me. I exhaled and watched as the moon rose over the sea. It had to get better. People healed and recovered from much worse and I would make sure that I did too—for Lucie.

Catharine and I took Lucie to the outdoor market the next morning. It was a wonderful place for us to gather fresh food for our dinner tonight and as it turned out, also a very good environment for an aspiring photographer. I was having trouble keeping tabs on Lucie in the crowds, she kept darting everywhere. She was so fast and I thought I caught a glimpse of her little body blurring from one point to the next, she'd be shimmering soon I was sure. I never had to scold Lucie; she never whined and she always did what I asked of her, but now she was making me nervous. I left Catharine at one of the meat stands and moved quickly through the mass of people to catch Lucie. She was standing over near a large fountain, snapping pictures of the crowd. I grabbed her and swung her up on my hip.

"But Ana, I'm not done!" she said, whipping her head this way and that, her long curls swinging and sweeping across my face.

"Oh yes you are, young lady," I said, carrying her back to Catharine. "Lucie, I've told you, when we are in a crowded place, you need to stay with me at all times. I know you like to take pictures, but I can't have you leaving my side when we're in a place like this. Am I understood?" I said, putting her down and taking her hand. She stuck out her lip.

"You sound like daddy, Ana," she said, looking up at me. I glanced at her.

7

"Well, your daddy was a very smart person, wouldn't you agree?" I smiled and Catharine handed her a mango. Lucie smiled back at me and took her fruit. I hated that I had to use Liam's reference in the past tense; it made me gut-wrenchingly sad. I felt Lucie squeeze my hand and I almost gasped; the way she was staring at me, the way her eyes flashed as they scanned my face, it was as if she knew, as if she'd heard what I was thinking about Liam. I swallowed and forced myself to turn away from her gaze.

We returned to the house and I was somewhat grateful that Andrew had offered to take Lucie down to the beach while Catharine and I started assembling things for the meal. It wasn't that I didn't want to be around Lucie, it was just that having her look at me, watch me—it was unnerving. Andrew and Catharine were hosting several friends that had just arrived and we were preparing a rather large, traditional Greek meal. It was slightly laborious, but I was in need of the mental distraction. Catharine proved to be the best food prep companion. She was vivacious and funny and I could only hope that if I managed to live to be sixty, that I would be as stunningly beautiful in spirit and body, as she was. Both Catharine and Andrew were human, but most of their life's work was spent on trying to forge a better relationship between Vampires and humans. They were anthropologists who studied various coven dynamics and the very secret nature of Vampires and their special abilities. I couldn't help but think that Lucie must be quite a case study for them, as well as me I guessed. Andrew brought Lucie back from the beach and I left the kitchen to get her ready for dinner.

The meal itself was pleasant enough, we had several humans and two male Vampires and they were proving to make me ill at ease. With all of my experiences in the last two years, I wasn't beyond noticing their subtle observations of Lucie and me. They were watching us, watching us interact and their attention to Lucie was making me very uncomfortable. They were polite and interesting and they seemed very intrigued to learn about our travels over these last four months; they also looked very rough and rugged. Every time I would stand or sit back down, the one closest to me, the younger of the two, would glare at me. It was odd, but I was sure that's what he was doing. I racked my brain; did I know him? There was no way I *could* know him; these two were African in decent and I had yet to meet any African Vampires, I would have remembered. I tried to smile and push the mounting anxiety that was beginning to stir in my chest, aside. I was paranoid. I couldn't think of a single reason why any Vampire or Bonder would be after me, not now. Both Patric and Nathanial had assured me that the interest in my powers and my blood seemed to be waning after the death of Carlo, and the Bonders were all too grateful just to have a break in the fighting that they didn't seem particularly energized to try to take me out. I still had no idea how Carlo had died and every time I had tried to ask Patric or Nathanial about it, they would say it was a mystery to them as well—I wasn't buying it, but I also was trying very hard not to get sucked back into that world again; I desperately needed a new group of friends.

I carried Lucie upstairs and put her in her pajamas, tucking the blankets around her shoulders. I kissed her on the cheek and turned on the tiny nightlight by her bed.

"Ana?" Lucie spoke in the now darkened room.

"Yes baby?"

9

"Those men downstairs, why are they mad at you?" I froze.

"What do you mean Lucie?" I asked, my words coming slowly as I gripped the doorframe.

"They're upset; they were staring at you," she said quietly as I came to sit on her bed. Lucie was observant, clearly she had just noticed the one Vampire glaring at me. I couldn't see how one wouldn't notice—he wasn't trying to hide his emotions. I exhaled.

"Well, I'm not sure. Perhaps he was just having a bad day and he didn't like what we were serving this evening," I said, laughing lightly.

"Vampires don't eat," she said and even in the dark I could see her eyes searching my face. I swallowed.

"No they don't do they?" I replied, trying to calm my nerves. Lucie shifted to sit up.

"Did you do something to make them mad?" she asked, sweeping her hair behind her shoulder and putting her thumb in her mouth.

"No, I don't think so. I don't know them and they don't know me or us," I said weakly, my voice quiet and now sounding uncertain.

"Do you think they know daddy?" Something in my body suddenly shifted. They were African, South African to be exact. Liam and Carmen and Lucie were hiding in South Africa before they were killed. Patric thought that Carlo was responsible for killing Liam. Carlo was dead. Lucie was alive. No. No. There was no way that these two would be here for us, for Lucie—they were friends of Catharine and Andrew. I didn't know anything about how Carlo had died; I had no

10

part in his demise and I wasn't seeing the connection here, except that perhaps they wanted to finish the job, they wanted Lucie, but why? What could killing a little girl get them; they had already taken out one of the most powerful Vampires in Liam. Why would they want Lucie?

"Ana?" Lucie was staring at me.

"I'm not sure if they know your daddy Lucie; do they look familiar to you?" I asked her. Maybe she would remember seeing them at some point, seeing them around the house or the village where they were living. She shook her head "no". I sighed.

"But I saw uncle Stephen," Lucie murmured. My heart stopped.

"What?" I whispered.

"I saw uncle Stephen in their heads." She smiled at me. "I see him in yours too." Her voice was quiet. "And uncle Nathanial and uncle Patric too; their faces are in your brain!" She giggled and sucked on her thumb.

"Lucie, you saw uncle Stephen in their brain…in the minds of our guests tonight?" I asked, my heart had started again and now it was thundering in my chest. She nodded. "In them both?" I asked her, tying to frantically get my mind around what she was saying and what she appeared to now be able to do.

"No, just the one who was staring at you, the angry one," she said, her eyes beginning to close. I tried to breathe. What was going on? What did Stephen have to do with either of those two? I had no idea where Stephen was or what he was doing. I hadn't bothered to ask Patric or Nathanial because I felt it didn't matter. I assumed that he wasn't

11

coming for Lucie and that was that. I didn't need to know how he was spending his time—I could only imagine. I heard Lucie begin to snore. I rubbed my face. This wasn't good; it couldn't be good. We needed to leave—now. I thought about Patric and wondered if he would be able to help me piece this together or...I fingered the tiny phone that for some reason I still kept with me, the one with Liam's number and Stephen's. I wasn't sure what to do. I had the feeling that both Patric and Nathanial were keeping things from me, and that made trusting either of them a bit difficult. Still...Patric was connected and considered powerful across both Bonders and Vampires and he would be able to possibly make some inquires into what exactly had happened to Stephen and how in the world he would have associations with those two Vampires. I grabbed a piece of paper and wrote a quick note to Catharine and Andrew—I felt terrible and rude leaving without seeing them, but I had no choice. Catharine would understand. I grabbed my purse and pack from my room, grabbed Lucie's backpack and camera and pulled her gently from her bed. Holding her close, I thought of Patric and wrapped my body inwards around Lucie. A gust of wind shifted and we were gone.

Patric

That was odd. I had misplaced the map that I was keeping with all of Ana's routes sketched out, her itineraries and when they were scheduled to arrive at each location. I could of course just try to track them through my internal knowledge of Ana, but I kept the map just in case. I never misplaced things, especially things that were so important. I had been gone to the States for the last two weeks visiting several wineries that I was interested in buying and I had also been trying to contact Nathanial. I hadn't seen or spoken to him in almost four months. His attitude towards me before he disappeared, had been cold and distant and I was sure that he was seeing just how much I missed Ana, how she'd managed to infiltrate every thought that I had. I also hadn't gone out of my way to hide those images of her from him, so perhaps he was feeling a bit jealous. I didn't let him into the most intimate of my memories of her, of the night we'd spent together in the week before she'd left. That was sacred to me and he didn't need to know, not right now, not until Ana had had a chance to decide what she wanted, whom she wanted. I wasn't going to demand anything of her. Of course I hoped that in the end she would chose me, but I was willing to give her whatever leeway she needed to come to that realization herself. I began rifling through my desk searching for that damn map when a sudden scent moved across my face, my brother's scent. I picked up several pieces of paper on the top of the desk and sniffed. I frowned; Nathanial's fragrance was all over them. I swept the papers and books to the floor and bent my head close to the surface of the desk. Nathanial; his chemicals were in the wood. Had he been in my room? Surely I would have known. Why would he have come to my study? I sighed and put my hands on my hips. I was sure that I had kept the map on the…Christ. A sudden realization hit me. He had it. He had taken the schedule. He wanted to follow her. It all made sense now; his behavior towards me before we'd both said goodbye to Ana, his behavior towards me the week after she left and then he'd suddenly disappeared, even Micah hadn't known where he'd gone. He was tracking her and Lucie and thanks to my map, he

13

knew when and where they would be; their Bond was broken and he wouldn't be unable to track her mentally, but why would he bother? I rubbed my face. Yes, my brother was in love with Ana, yes he wanted to get her back, repair their relationship, but he also knew that she needed to heal, that she was trying to come to terms with the events of her life and he shouldn't, he wouldn't want to pressure her; it wouldn't serve his purposes very well. Ana wasn't one to appreciate individuals putting pressure on her to do anything; it would backfire on him. What was he thinking?

I sunk down on my couch, trying to reason through Nathanial's thought process. I started to sip my drink when a shot of cold air blew so forcefully through the room that the current took my glass right from my hands. I stood as I saw Ana and Lucie materialize in the air, Ana almost toppling over from the force of her shimmer. I caught her just as she leaned forward.

"Ana?" I was stunned and elated. I wasn't expecting her back until next week and even then she had not said whether or not she'd be returning to the ranch or to Dublin. Upon seeing her face, my joy moved quickly to panic. Something was wrong. She took Lucie and placed her gently on my bed, that girl could sleep through anything. Ana ran her fingers through her hair; she looked manic. "Ana!" I said, wanting her to come to me. "What's happened? What's wrong?" I asked, taking her hand and leading her back to the couch.

"I need you to help me Patric. We need to piece something together here..." She was staring at me and I could see images of people in her head, people that I didn't know. Was she remembering something from her night with Carlo? Had it finally happened?

14

"What Ana? What do we need to piece together?" I wasn't quite prepared to tell her everything that had transpired and I wasn't quite sure that I was the best one to tell her why Stephen had left and what Nathanial had proposed to him or that technically she now had both Stephen's blood and his venom in her system, even if her body had rejected the Change. Christ, it was too much.

"Liam, Patric. Liam's death; you told me that you thought Carlo was responsible for that?" She was staring at me. I nodded. "Carlo wanted Liam dead, he killed Liam and Carmen and tried to kill Lucie..." She was speaking so fast. "But Lucie somehow survived; I know Carlo. I know Stephen. Stephen knows Carlo. Stephen is Liam's brother..."

"Ana! What the hell are you talking about?" I turned her toward me. Her eyes found mine.

"Patric, where's Stephen? Do you know what's happened to him?" she asked, her eyes were moving so rapidly that I was starting to get dizzy. I held her hands, not really wanting to go there, but it seemed important.

"Ana, will you please tell me what's happened? Are you...were you attacked or something?" She looked ok physically. She shook her head.

"We were at dinner and there were these guests, these Vampire guests and one of them kept glaring at me and they both were watching me and Lucie and I didn't know them; I'd never seen them before..." She was breathing hard and I was trying to follow her train of thought. "Then Lucie said that she saw pictures of Stephen in his mind; the one who was glaring at me, she said she saw Stephen..."

15

"Wait, hold up," I said, rising from my seat. "Are you saying that Lucie could see what the other Vampires were thinking?" Ana nodded.

"She's half-Vampire Patric; I'm sure she has some extra abilities." She also stood, rubbing her temples.

"These other Vampires, what did they look like?" I asked, pacing.

"They were African, South African," she said, staring at me. My heart kicked up a notch. Jesus, what the fuck had Stephen done?

"Ana, did they see you leave? Do they know you've left Greece?" She shook her head.

"No. I told Catharine not to let her guests know that Lucie and I had to leave; I trust Catharine and Andrew, they wouldn't do anything to put us in jeopardy. Why Patrick? Do you know those Vampires?" She was studying me now, her eyes focusing on mine. He would have had to let something slip; there's no way they would know that she was responsible for Carlo's death, unless someone told them. My mind was racing. He wouldn't have done that to her. He wouldn't have sold her out, put her life at risk, put Lucie's life at risk…Stephen was a bit wrecked mentally, but he loved Ana, he loved her desperately and I couldn't let myself think that he would have wanted to cause her any intentional harm unless…

"Ana stay here please, I need to see Nathanial." I was trying to locate him in my mind, but he was shut down.

"Why? I want to come with you, I want to know what's going on!" Her voice rose.

"You need to stay with Lucie. You're safe here, I promise. Stay here until I get back." I didn't have time to argue with her so my tone was less than civil. Her eyes narrowed, but she sat down on the couch. I shimmered to Micah's hoping he would be able to get Nathanial back from wherever he was, trying to track Ana, I guessed.

Micah was in the middle of a meeting and I stood outside the door waiting to catch his eye. Immediately upon seeing me, his face shifted to what looked like fear; that was odd. He excused himself and met me in the hallway.

"Patric. What are you doing here? Are you alright?" His eyes searched mine and I could see pictures of both my brother and I painted against their clear turquoise depths.

"Micah, I need to know where Nathanial is, it's important," I said, walking down the hall and into the kitchen. My uncle sighed, his eyes turning sad.

"I wish I could tell you, but your brother did not leave me with any knowledge of his destination. I can only imagine that he went following after Ana." Micah looked at me, his stare penetrating. The clues finally fell into place. The missing map, the scent of him, his demeanor towards me; it wasn't just that he knew I wanted Ana, he'd *seen* us together. He'd known we spent the night with each other. He'd seen us in our most intimate moment and he snapped, chasing after her, following her every move, waiting for the right time to approach; god, he was obsessive. I shook my head.

"Micah, I can't really be worried about whether or not Nathanial is upset with me or if he's suddenly decided to turn into some

17

psychopathic stalker; we have a situation. Ana and Lucie are at the ranch and something's happened. I need to see Nathanial." My voice was stern and dark and I hoped that my uncle would be able to see past his desire to have his nephews reforge their relationship and just do as I asked. Micah nodded.

"I can try to summon him; that's all I can do at the moment. He's been quite protective of most of his thoughts of late." Micah eyed me; he knew. I sighed. My god since when was it a crime to have sex with someone that you loved? My uncle laughed quietly and closed his eyes. Nothing.

"What happened? I asked, wondering if the summoning had worked.

"Nothing; I've called him to come home. Now, we wait." Micah poured me a glass of wine and I began pacing around the kitchen. A blast of chilly air swept through the space and I turned to see my brother standing, his arms crossed and face looking furious. As soon as he saw me, his form began to fade and I lunged at him, grabbing his arm and pulling him back. Nathanial shoved me hard, sending me hurdling across the kitchen and out to the living room. It took every ounce of self-restraint I had, not to rip his head off.

"Nathanial." Micah stepped between us. "Your brother is here because something has happened with Ana. You need to listen to him please." Nathanial was breathing hard and his stance was rigid. I smirked at him.

"You didn't happen to notice that the woman and child you've been stalking, have suddenly left the area?" I said, straightening out my shirt and running my hands through my hair. Nathanial lunged again,

18

but this time I was ready for him and we collided in mid-air. I grabbed his shoulders and we flew across the room, shoving him against the wall. "You want to fight? Is that what you want? You want to fight?" He punched me in the stomach and my grip slackened. I growled and caught him around the legs as his back was turned, pining him to the ground.

"You son of a bitch!" Nathanial cursed at me as he punched me in the face. I struck the side of his head, slashing his flesh. He heaved me straight up in the air and grabbed me by the neck and slammed me down on the floor, shattering the boards. "She was mine! She *is* mine!" he yelled as he stood over me, his boot on my chest.

"You're sick!" I took his leg and swung it out to the side, spinning his body in mid-air and sending him soaring across the room. He crashed down onto the coffee table, his back smashing through the solid wood as if it were glass. I was on him in a heartbeat. His fist collided with my jaw and I heard it crack. I spit blood in his face as I brought my arm down over his windpipe, crushing his throat. Suddenly I was blasted off of him as Nathanial's body was jerked out from under me. He was thrown to the opposite side of the room and I couldn't move to charge after him. I was paralyzed. I saw my uncle move slowly into the center of the room, his eyes black and his hair blowing behind him, swirling in a nonexistent wind. He was huge and I felt a distinctive pulse of control and heat coming from his body. I had never seen my uncle display any of his more powerful demonic attributes and I could see why; Micah was terrifying.

"That's enough," he spoke, his voice unrecognizable. I felt chills break out on my skin. He waved his hand and the coffee table reassembled itself, as did the cracked floorboards and the broken stones in the wall. I noticed that we were no longer alone; Micah's entire meeting had now gathered and they were all staring at us. Micah turned to the group. "I apologize for my nephews' behavior this evening. Please forgive them and me for such blatant disrespect of your company. Let us reschedule our session for a later time." His tone was even and calm, but I could easily hear the undercurrent of disgust and anger that he was suppressing. The group disbanded leaving the three of us alone. He waved his hand again and Nathanial dropped to the ground, his hands on his knees. I still couldn't move. Micah came and stood in front of me, pacing. "I have never, in my entire existence, been more ashamed of my family than I am at this moment." Micah's voice was dark and his tone was fierce. "The two of you have done nothing to honor the memory of your mother or father and you continue to cause upheaval and distress amongst yourselves and towards others. You are both a disgrace." He looked between us. "You are children and you know nothing of the world; you know nothing of what it means to love. You know nothing of what it means to sacrifice, to fight or to die for what you know to be right and true. You are fools and every breath you take only serves to dishonor your sacred blood. Neither of you have proved deserving of Ana; neither of you have shown her the love and respect she deserves and neither of you have honored the destinies that your mother gave her life for. Ana's heart is not a pawn in your selfish games. She is a woman, a Human who has endured more loss and grief than anyone should have to bare. She is flawed and she is young, but she has constantly saved you both, never once expecting you to stay with her, never once thinking that her modes of action may cost her, her life. Always she has been there gambling away the sacredness of her soul to protect two individuals

20

who are soulless. I am sick at the very thought that Ana would even be with either of you, sick at the notion that she is grieving over you and now that I have seen such displays of disrespect and arrogance, I will do whatever I can to protect Ana from ever being subjected to the two of you for a very long time." I was dumbfounded. He couldn't keep us from Ana; we weren't children. Nathanial snorted. Micah rounded on me. "Don't test me Patric." Micah's eyes flashed and I suddenly felt very, very cold and I wondered if he knew, if my uncle had somehow gotten through my mental wall and had seen that I had yet again, let my ambitions rule over my love for Ana. I wasn't letting anything surface and I had hoped to just forget about the plan I had months ago to deal with Carlo. Ana was alive and we had shared the most special night of my life, I wasn't about to confess to my greed; not now, not ever. Micah turned toward me and his eyes narrowed. I bowed my head. "Now, I believe you needed your brother for something concerning Ana? I suggest you make it quick, my patience with the two of you has reached its limit." Micah waved his hand and my body released. I looked at Nathanial and exhaled.

"Do you have any idea where Stephen might be?" I asked, wiping the blood from my face and resetting my jaw. Nathanial crossed his arms over his chest.

"No. Why?" He leaned against the wall, his face now hidden in shadow.

"Because I think he may have gotten himself into a situation that has allowed for him to tell some very vengeful Vampires, that Ana was the one responsible for Carlo's death," I said, spitting a clot of blood from my mouth into my hand.

"Stephen wouldn't do that Patric. He knows Ana has Lucie; he wouldn't put either of their lives at risk." Nathanial's tone sounded flat and he was staring at me, even through the darkness I could see the glow from his eyes. I shook my head.

"What if he didn't have a choice?" I asked, matching his gaze.

"What do you mean?" Nathanial pushed himself off from the wall and stepped into the light from the moon.

"What if he's been captured, tortured and he's given her up? What if they were able to see into his mind, to know what he knows about her? He's been on a revenge bender over Liam and since doing what he had to do to Ana, I am quite sure he's not himself," I said, looking at Nathanial, thinking how similar the two of them actually were. My brother snarled. Micah interrupted.

"Patric, what's happened to Ana to make you think this?" he asked, his form still huge and menacing. I sighed and proceeded to tell them about the two Vampires who joined Ana at the house and how Lucie had seen Stephen's face in their minds and how Ana was almost close to piecing this all together. I was exhausted.

"What do you know about the South African covens?" Nathanial asked, moving to sit on the couch, blood now drying on his neck and the side of his face. I paced.

"Not much. The one coven that Liam was working with is pretty well respected and they liked Liam; I don't think even Carlo would have coerced them into killing Liam and his family. Saden runs the other coven and I don't know about him. He's young as far as coven leaders

22

go. I hear he's ambitious, somewhat fair as far as any agreements between Vampires and Bonders go and he's powerful, not someone who you would want to necessarily challenge or try to assassinate and I have no idea what his relationship to Carlo was, if they were close or if they were enemies; from the looks of things I would have to guess that they were close." I ran my fingers through my hair, thinking.

"And you think that Saden might have Stephen?" Micah asked, moving to stand in front of Nathanial. I shrugged.

"I have no idea. I just can't think of any other group that might have any ties with Stephen. He was headed to South Africa and who knows, maybe he managed to stir up some trouble. I mean even if Saden and Carlo weren't close, I'm not sure how favorably any coven would look upon a Human who is as powerful as Ana has become. She killed one of the most feared and skilled Vampires, even if his reign was a mere illusion. Most of the covens didn't know that and I wasn't inclined at the time to tell them." I exhaled.

"So Stephen might be in trouble," Nathanial spoke, his voice soft. I glanced at him; he couldn't possibly be feeling sympathy for that sorry sack of shit could he? Nathanial took a deep breath.

"Or he's totally gone off the deep end and has decided to sell Ana's life out to the highest bidder," I said bitterly, remembering the images that Ana had of finding Stephen's ring in the gambling pile.

"No, if it was just Ana maybe, but Stephen knows that Ana has Lucie in her care and not even the most wrecked Stephen would do anything to harm that little girl; he must be in trouble." Nathanial stood, his face lined with worry. I didn't like the thought that even if

Ana had not had Lucie with her, that Nathanial was under the impression that Stephen would want to harm Ana, I thought he loved her. He was the father of her child had she been able to keep it; why would he want to ever be in the world without her? Nathanial's eyes flashed. "Because he's a fool; he's selfish and tired and constantly at war with himself." Nathanial flung his arms in the air. "Because he's sick." He turned to stare at me, throwing my words back in my face.

"Fine, what do we do? Ana is much further along in her understanding of this issue, but she's asking about Stephen. What do you propose we tell her?" I said, breaking Nathanial's gaze on me.

"Bring her here Patric. She should know what's happening and we can devise a plan to help her and Stephen if need be," my uncle spoke from the window, his back to us. I sighed.

"Do you really think—" I started to speak.

"Bring-her-here," my uncle said, still not facing me. I glanced at Nathanial and raised my eyebrows. He nodded, but he also looked a bit awestruck at our uncle's sudden turn in temperament.

"I'll be back," I said quietly as I shimmered out of sight.

I landed back in my suite to find Ana sleeping in my bed with Lucie curled up beside her; my heart heaved. There was no way that I would let my uncle keep me from her, I needed her too much. I reached down and stroked her hair, not wanting to startle her. She opened her eyes.

"What happened to your face?" she murmured and I smiled.

"It's nothing," I said, letting my fingers trace along her cheek and over her lips. She sighed and for the second time this evening, my self-restraint was tested. I wanted her. "I hate to do this to you, but Micah thinks it would be better if you and Lucie came over to see him tonight. We need to discuss some things with you," I said, bending so I could kiss the top of her head. Nathanial could kill me; I didn't care. I loved Ana just as much as he did and she belonged to no one. She raised her head and our lips met.

"Hmm...sorry," she said, pulling away. I laughed softly and kissed her again.

"What are you sorry for?" My mouth moved against hers and hungrily, I tasted her.

"Umm...Patric?" she said, pushing me back a bit. I looked at her, wondering if I had over stepped the line. She was glancing over at Lucie. I had forgotten she was there.

"Woops," I said, helping Ana off the bed.

"Let me guess," she said, taking my hand. My body surged with the warmth from her touch. "Someone is after me again." She rolled her eyes. "I've done something to piss someone or some group off and now they've decided that the lives they are currently living are just too damn boring without some stupid human to go after." She sighed and laid her head on my shoulder. "What could I have possibly done Patric? I'm not that clever." She laughed, looking at our entwined fingers. I shook my head.

"Grab Lucie," I said, standing and pulling her up.

"You're not going to tell me?" she asked, gently lifting Lucie from my bed.

"I can tell you that one, you are not stupid and two, yes, you are that clever." I smirked and wrapped my arm around her waist, pulling them both close to me. Lucie murmured in her sleep and I swept us back to Peru.

Ana

I couldn't explain why, but I was really nervous having to see Nathanial. I hadn't spoken to him much before I'd left for my trip and after the last conversation I had with him, he seemed distant and dare I say cold. I felt weird thinking that he might be mad at me; I couldn't see any reason for it, even if he could read that Patric and I had...if he could see that Patric and I cared for each other, I hadn't done anything to him. I hadn't cheated on him or left him for someone else—he wasn't mine to leave. Ugh. I should have never come back here. I wasn't ready to face any of this again. The drama was too much, too overdone now.

"Ana." Patric was staring at me, his eyes seeing my thoughts. "He knows." I shook my head.

"Well, screw it! I'm a grown woman. I don't have to defend myself or my actions to him or anyone else for that matter." While looking at Patric, something occurred to me. "Is that how your face got like that? Did you and Nathanial fight?" I asked, as we stood outside the door. I

26

grabbed his shoulder. "Patric? Did you two fight about what happened between you and me?" Patric exhaled.

"Yes." He stared at me. Juveniles! Fucking Juveniles, I thought. Patric laughed darkly.

"You and Micah seem to be of one mind Ana," he said, and pushed opened the door. We walked down the hallway and I shifted Lucie from one hip to the other; she was snoring against my neck. Patric led us into the living room where Micah and Nathanial were sitting at the table, a bottle of wine between them. They weren't looking at each other. What the hell had happened here? Upon seeing us, Micah rose and came immediately over to me, grasping my free hand.

"Ana, I'm so happy that you've returned from your travels." I kissed his cheek. "I have Lucie's room all ready, why don't you put her down and come join us. Can I get you some tea?" he asked, his eyes shining, but I could distinctly make out a deep onyx tone to their coloring. I wondered if he'd been present when Patric and Nathanial had fought. I bet he was pissed. Micah laughed and winked at me. I put Lucie down and walked back out into the living room where Micah had set up my tea. I noticed that he had me as far away as possible from both Patric and Nathanial at the table. Nathanial was staring at me.

"So, what's up?" I asked, steeping my tea bag. They all looked at each other. "Anyone? Speak up," I said, watching each of them in turn. Nathanial started to talk, but Micah cut across him.

"Ana we think that Stephen may be in some sort of trouble; we're not exactly sure yet, but we fear he may have inadvertently put you and Lucie in danger," Micah said evenly and I heard Patric snort. Micah

27

shot him a look and immediately, Patric sunk lower in his chair. I sipped my tea.

"What kind of trouble do you think he's in? I mean, is it something that we can help with or…" I cut myself off as I saw Nathanial roll his eyes and glare at me. I crashed my teacup down on the coaster shattering it. That was it. "Do you have a problem with me Nathanial?" I leaned across the table. Patric laughed. I glared at him. "Shut it!" I said, turning back to Nathanial. "You have something you would like to say to me?" I said, standing now. I didn't come back here to be treated like this, not after everything I had let him hear about how I was feeling, about how I had asked him why he'd left me, why he didn't want to stay with me and work on things, not after I had let him see just how fractured I was after seeing him with *her*. I didn't deserve this. He turned away from me. "You're jealous is that it? You're jealous? Well that's just too damn bad! You don't get to be jealous you ungrateful bastard!" I was yelling at him. "You're mad at me? At Patric? Does it sicken you to know that we were together Nathanial? Does it make you sick? Well, fuck you! I don't care! At least I love your brother, at least I care about him and he cares about me. At least I didn't fuck the first thing that spread their legs for me!" Nathanial stood, his breath was coming in shallow bursts. "How dare you stand there and judge me; how dare you roll your eyes at my concern for Stephen you pathetic piece of shit. I saved your ass. I saved you and for what? To watch you judge me, to sit across from you and your anger, your jealousy? Well you know what Nathanial, the next time you decide to try and kill yourself don't look to me to help bring you back!" I threw the shards of my cup at his face.

"Ana!" Patric stood and was holding me back.

"GET THE FUCK OFF OF ME!" I shouted, sending him flying backward into the wall. I stormed down the hall, picked Lucie up from the bed and called for Micah. He came instantly. "I'm very sorry Micah. I don't mean to ever, ever disrespect you or your home or your family. I love you like a father, a brother. I know you need to speak with me so why don't we agree to meet tomorrow and just you and I will talk, ok?" I asked, hoisting Lucie up on my hip, breathing hard. "I'll be in Dublin, back in my old apartment; please come and I'll try to help you with anything you need," I said, my eyes full of tears. "I'm very sorry you had to see me like that." Micah smiled.

"Ana, I couldn't have said it any better my love." He kissed my cheek and I shimmered out of that wretched house.

Chapter Two

Ana

I was glad to be back someplace that had just been mine, someplace that I had taken control over, that was all me. The apartment was exactly the same; it looked frozen in time, even some of my clothes that I had decided not to pack when Liam was here, they were still strewn across my bed. I had organized a play date for Lucie with one of my neighbors and her little girl, just in case. If something happened to me while she was gone, then she might have a chance to get away, to escape; maybe Micah would be able to track her down.

I was waiting on Micah to arrive and I was trying to straighten up. I walked to the front door and stopped cold. Leaning against the brick wall was a covered canvas; a present that I had never opened. I reached to pull the delicate fabric, sliding it slowly off the frame. I gripped the side of the wall as the painting shone into the apartment. My face was reflected back to me except I didn't quite look right; I was much prettier in the painting, much more mystical looking. I was standing, my hair whipping behind me and Lucie was at my side holding my hand. The portrait was a nightscape with mountains in the background and a full moon rising. My eyes traveled up and I gasped. Hanging above my figure were the faces of each person that I had loved; Kai, Alec, Noni, Patric, Liam, Carmen, Micah, Nathanial and Stephen, all their gazes were turned outward, penetrating me, knowing me. I noticed that Stephen had painted my amulet in the most perfect way, giving it light and heat; I could feel it pulsing out, permeating the space where I stood. I looked at his face and I saw something shimmering around his neck. A thick sliver chain hung and at the center was his ring; the ring I had given him. I looked to Patric and there too was his amulet, melded to his skin. I turned to Nathanial and his shirt was open and gracing his chest was his mark, also shining through the very paint and fabric of the canvas. My eyes drifted once again to the somewhat familiar form of myself. I looked to my left hand. My ring shone bright around my finger and I could easily make out every single detail and carving in the band.

"What a truly beautiful representation of all the many lives that you have touched Ana." I whirled around to see Micah standing behind me, his gaze falling over the painting. "I think…" he paused looking at his nephews and then at Stephen's face, "I think I understand better, just how difficult it is for these beings to part with you. Stephen loves you very, very much Ana; perhaps this was his way of telling you that he too understands just what each of these souls mean to you. You are bound to us all." Micah turned his eyes to me. I swallowed, unable to wrap my mind or my heart around what Micah was saying.

"Micah, am I being hunted again?" I asked, taking his hand. "Are Lucie and I in danger?" Micah smiled and I followed as he walked gracefully into my living room.

"No Ana, I don't feel that you are," Micah said quietly, sitting on the sofa. I sighed.

"Then I don't understand. Those Vampires we met in Greece, they seemed to know me and Lucie saw Stephen in their minds; what do you think is going on?" Micah turned to me, his eyes clear.

31

"I think those individuals that you met, know Stephen and I think he's been working with them to help avenge his brother's death. I think that they have seen you in his mind; they saw Lucie…most Vampires, Ana, are not inclined to develop any relationships with Humans. They look upon such affections as weaknesses, distractions. It is my guess," Micah paused and I saw him look back toward the portrait near the door, "it is my guess, that since Stephen left, that his mind has been quite preoccupied about whether or not you died that night you fell ill; he doesn't know that you survived. Unfortunately one or both of my nephews made sure not to go out of their way to see to it that Stephen was made aware of your full recovery." He shook his head. "I don't think those guests were looking to harm you or Lucie; I just think that you provided them a justification for why Vampires should never be close to Humans. They recognized you from seeing Stephen's mind and I'm sure his occupations with you have made their business of revenge killing a bit difficult for their new recruit." It was my turn to shake my head.

"I'm sorry Micah, but I'm a bit slow." I laughed. "Why would Stephen not think that I would have survived my illness; I was just sick. I mean it was bad yes, Nathanial or Patric never once said that my life was in danger…" I looked at him, not wanting Micah to think I was stupid.

"Ana!" Micah laughed. "I most certainly would never think you were or are stupid. All the events that have befallen you in your life, I'm actually amazed at how well you've been able to assimilate and accept so much information, so much drama, if you will. You are not stupid, you've just been kept in the dark." He chuckled.

32

Over the next two hours, I sat spellbound as Micah recalled every event that happened on the night I went to dinner with Patric, about Carlo shape shifting, about me knowing that my rare blood types would kill any Vampire that was not my chosen mate or to whom I was not Bound; how I had threatened Carlo, how I had frightened him and how ultimately I killed him, but not before he'd bitten me, injected me with his venom and left me to die.

"But I didn't die," I said quietly, trying to absorb everything. "I'm alive." Micah stared at me, his eyes flashing bright as he held my gaze.

"Yes Ana, you did survive and that is because of a single act of courage, a single choice that someone did not want to make, not under such circumstances at any rate." Micah again stared at Stephen's painting. I held my breath. "Stephen saved you Ana; he completed the Change that Carlo left unfinished. He gave you both his blood and his venom—his life if you will, and he saved you, hoping to at least give you some semblance of an existence, even if that would be as a Vampire." I didn't exhale. Micah continued, sensing my next question. "You are not a Vampire Ana. We learned that apparently your blood tends to dilute any venom that enters your system, but not before it has an opportunity to heal you; it's remarkable really." Micah shook his head back and forth.

"How much blood do I have from Stephen?" I asked, thinking about those misplaced upsurges of emotion I had been experiencing over the last few months.

"Hmm…yes, that might explain some things," Micah murmured hearing my analysis. "You have quite a bit of blood from Stephen, Ana; it's necessary in order to make the transition. Technically, Stephen is your creator for all intents and purposes—he was the one to give you your Afterlife, had it stuck." Micah smiled at me. I finally exhaled.

"He was upset," I whispered. "That's why he left, he didn't want it to happen like that…he was upset." I was looking at the painting. "We had a plan, the two of us, for when I was ready…we had a plan." Micah took my hand, breaking my revelry.

"Ana, I think that Stephen may be a bit in over his head with his current…his current role," Micah said, staring hard at me. "I also think, and I can't be sure, but I think that Liam may be alive." I gasped.

"What?" I asked, standing. "We found their bodies in that wretched fire; me, Nathanial and Patric, we found them." Micah shook his head.

"You found bodies, charred bodies beyond recognition. Nathanial and Patric assumed that they were Liam and Carmen, but I happen to think otherwise." I was stunned.

"No Micah, it had to be them because Lucie was left; had they been able to escape they would have taken her with them. They wouldn't have left her to die in that fire." I shook my head.

"They may have not had a choice Ana," Micah said quietly. "I think Liam may be in trouble. I think he and possibly Carmen may have been taken. I think that Liam hedged his bets and they hid Lucie as best as they could before they were captured. I think Liam knew that upon hearing of their possible deaths, that you would come for Lucie; I think he knew, Ana." I froze, remembering the last conversation I had with Liam before he left me on Carlo's deck. I remembered him telling me that if I had to, I could shimmer, that someone's life may depend on me being able to call upon that power—he knew! "I don't think he anticipated what was to come Ana, but Liam is a planner and I would guess that he had some sort of plan ready to be executed the minute Carlo's cronies came for him. Liam is not one to shy away from a fight and I believe that he could have easily taken down those who were sent to kill him, however they must have threatened his family, they must have threatened Lucie. They must have made him feel that her life was in danger. I'm guessing he and Carmen negotiated for Lucie's life and now Liam and maybe Carmen, are being held somewhere." Micah stood and took a deep breath.

"And Stephen's been running around the globe killing Vampires trying to avenge Liam's death and he's making enemies," I said, my mind racing. Micah nodded. "Micah, can we be sure? I mean how can we be sure that Liam is in fact, alive?" I asked. Micah turned to me, his face solemn.

"I think Ana, this is where you will need to make a choice. I think that with the blood from Stephen, you now are able to better tap into your ability to channel him, to find his location and possibly the location of Liam, a skill that Stephen has lost as of late because in his mind and in his heart, he has deemed Liam to be dead. I think that you may be able to find Liam, with my help of course and possibly we may be able to devise a plan to get him out of whatever hell he and Carmen are experiencing. You may also be able to save Stephen from getting himself killed trying to avenge a death that never happened. It's up to you of course. You have a chance to start you life over again and to not get involved in the situation, to let things take their natural course. I feel that you are no longer in any danger and the possibilities for you are endless at this point. You don't need to help Stephen, but I'm guessing that your love for Liam and his family, is enough to guide you down the right path." Micah stared at me.

"Do Nathanial and Patric know any of this?" I could only imagine how Nathanial would react if he knew that I wanted to help Stephen. Micah waved his hand.

"No Ana, and I'm not inclined to tell either of them. They have betrayed each other and you. Both of them decided not to tell Stephen that you had lived, both of them were selfish in their love for you and I don't think either of my nephews need to be anywhere near you at this time." I smiled; he sounded so fatherly.

"Stephen could have come though, Micah. He could have checked on me at some point," I said quietly.

"Stephen is not without his mistakes in all of this Ana, but I am more inclined to give him a slight bit of leeway considering all that he was battling at the time, thinking his brother had died, thinking you were to die, having to change you in such a violent way, losing you and your baby; all of his decisions were coming back to have their debts paid and he was overwhelmed. Nathanial offered to step aside so that the two of you could be together Ana, but even that gesture had ulterior motives for my nephew. He was counting on you seeing Stephen as damaged beyond repair and he was counting on the fact that you would be so disgusted with him that you wouldn't even consider trying to repair your relationship. Nathanial's attempt at a noble gesture was not without its arrogance and selfish need to acquire your love again." Micah sounded disgusted. That much I had figured out, but I didn't know that Nathanial had gone to Stephen with such an offer to step aside. Jesus Christ.

"But Patric loves me Micah; *he* loves me." Micah smiled at me and took my hand.

"Yes Ana he does, but he is also driven by competition and his desire to take. He's angry with what Nathanial has made you endure and while I'm sure that Patric feels his intentions are well meaning, his constant need to hurt others, to get back at them for past wrongs is not beyond him, even these days. Taking you away from Nathanial is Patric's way of punishing Nathanial for his crimes against you—again, I do believe Patric does love you Ana, but the motivations that spur that love, are essentially selfish." Micah held my hands and stared deep into my eyes. I couldn't help but see a few similarities between Patric and Stephen. Micah laughed softly. "Yes, perhaps they do share some similar qualities, however I have always felt that Stephen has been one to try to work on reconciling those selfish tendencies. I know that Liam believed that Stephen truly wanted to be a better soul for you, one who was deserving of your love and who could acknowledge his past and all the mistakes that came with it. It's a struggle to try to learn about why we make some of the more destructive decisions in our lives, but just acknowledging that you need to make a journey in order to reconcile those past transgressions, I think shows quite a bit of resolve to fight for something that has changed the very course of your life, to prove that you are worthy and essentially unselfish in your ability to love." Micah winked at me and let my hands drop.

"What do we need to do?" I said, my own resolve to fight... surfacing.

"You mean to help then?" Micah asked, his eyes studying me.

"Of course; I love Liam and if he's alive, then I will do anything, anything to save him and Stephen too," I said quietly. Micah nodded.

"Good. I think the best place to start is to find Stephen, to let him know that his brother may still be alive. Having Stephen help us will be quite an asset. He's built up an arsenal of contacts and some very brutal fighters and we may need all of them."

"I'll go. I'll find him," I said.

"Ana, the group that Stephen has aligned himself to, are not your typical Vampires. They are all trained assassins, they hate Humans and they are brutal in how they live their lives. I don't want you thinking that Stephen is the same as you remember. He may be quite different in his appearance and his attitude towards you. I'm not sure he would be inclined to protect you should something happen." Micah seemed worried; I, surprisingly, was not.

"Can you take Lucie?" I asked, as I pulled my backpack out of the closet. I looked at Micah. He smiled and shook his head.

"Yes Ana, Lucie will be safe." I touched Micah on the shoulder.

"I can do this Micah. I can do this for me and Liam and Lucie and Stephen. After Carlo, after Devon and Alec and Andres, after fighting, after falling, after living and loving; I can do this—I will do this," I said, kissing him on the cheek. "We're agreed that Nathanial and Patric don't need to know right now?" I asked. Micah nodded. "Good. Now how can I contact you should I need to?" I asked, stuffing more clothes into my pack. Micah handed me yet another tiny phone and an envelope full of thousands of dollars. My eyes widened.

"Take these Ana. You may have quite a journey ahead as Stephen rarely stays in the same place for long." Micah grinned. "You call me as soon as you get to your first destination and from each destination after; do you understand?" He sounded so much like Liam. "Stephen is not the only one with connections who are trained to kill, so if you get yourself into trouble, you just need to summon me in your mind Ana; you have to concentrate though ok?"

"Got it!" I said, hoisting my pack on my shoulders. "I love you Micah," I said pulling him into a hug.

"And I you." He smiled. I closed my eyes, thought of Stephen and felt myself disappear, not knowing at all where I was going to land.

Stephen

I couldn't remember where I was, what city, what country; I lost track. Each lead I got only seemed to end some place dark, someplace where I'd stalked, murdered, fed and then did it all over again the next day. We had annihilated so many covens, so many of my own kind; all, we were told, had some part in the killing of my brother. I was running on adrenaline, on the high that came from feeding and destroying life; it propelled me to move forward, to keep moving, keep tracking and it kept me from thinking about Ana, about if she had survived or if she was now like me. So many times I had wanted to go to her, to see her just to check, but the last time I had tried to contact Nathanial he'd put me off, told me what happened to Ana was no longer my concern, that I had chosen to leave; I got the same from Patric. They didn't want me to know and I had accepted that because part of me thought they were right, so I left it alone.

I dumped the body I had been feeding upon, wiped my mouth and walked out from the alley. Times Square was lit...New York. I sighed. I couldn't remember where I'd come from before—where was the last place that I'd been. I waved my hand over my t-shirt, clearing the blood from the fabric and my skin and stepped out into the street. I was expected at a party. The group I was traveling with was not unlike Cillian and Eamonn in Dublin, with one very crucial exception, they hated Humans and always after stalking or seducing their prey, they killed them, usually leaving them to bleed to death alone in some godforsaken place. They were all brutal killers and I had learned quickly how to take out a dozen or so vampires in one sweeping motion, ripping their hearts from their chests with one wave of my hand and tearing through the still beating muscle with my fangs. I had very rarely ever used my teeth in such a way and they never seemed to surface, even during my feeding I could do what I needed to without bringing out that side of myself, but no longer. I noticed that anytime I became angry or if I was having sex and I was slightly aroused, they were out, razor sharp and ready to tear flesh, muscle and bone— ready to kill. Since leaving Ana, I had been mostly celibate, only engaging in sex when I had had a dream about her, when I saw her face, remembered kissing her, touching her; I had tried to recreate those feelings with someone else only to be left feeling depleted, sick and massively depressed. I knew that the brethren I was traveling with,

40

were not pleased with my memories of her; it made them angry and I was keeping myself as locked down as I could. I made my way to the bar and found the table near the back where I was expected. I ordered a scotch and slid into the seat. I was early.

Ana

So far I had landed in Ecuador, Chile, Brazil, some horrible club in Germany and I was back in Dublin. Every time I arrived some place new and I conjured Stephen's face or name in my head and heart, I was suddenly whipped away to a different location. It was as if he was moving so fast that my own ability to keep track of him was now going on autopilot, taking me wherever he currently was. I had been traveling for weeks and I had yet to gain any sense of where Stephen was. Micah was doing his best to help; he was much more skilled at tracking and shimmering than I was and together we'd been trying to gain a solid position on his whereabouts. Was he here? Could he be in Dublin? I actually was grateful to be able to return to my apartment and take a shower. I had called Micah as soon as I arrived and he seemed just as puzzled. I sat on my bed, hair wet and in my sweats trying to decide what to do. Suddenly I had an idea. I pulled on jeans and a tank, tied my hair back, grabbed my freshly repacked bag and left my apartment.

I made my way down to the club where Stephen used to play, Eamonn's club, and knocked on the door. *Please be here. Please be here.* I wasn't expecting Stephen to be around, but I was hoping that the one person who always seemed willing to help me, would be. The door opened and Cillian stood in front of me his eyes wide.

"Fuckin Christ! Ana! What the fuck are ya doin here? Last I heard ya were dead or somethin'; holy fuck!" Cillian really needed to work on getting a more diverse vocabulary. He laughed and pulled me inside.

"Listen Cillian, I need your help, it's really important. Can you focus for a minute?" He was looking me up and down and I watched as he licked his lips.

"Sure, sure Ana what do ya need?" he asked, guiding me over to a seat, his hand on my back.

"Do you have any idea of where Stephen might be?" I asked, moving away from him slightly. He stared at me, his grey eyes churning.

"Stephen? Wow, Ana dat guy's been gone for ages; da last I heard he's been traveling around da fucking globe slaughtering all sorts of covens and Humans. He's gotten himself shacked up with vampires 'dat even I wouldn't hang out wit." Cillian sipped his drink. "Hey weren't you living wit Carlo?" Cillian asked, his eyes roaming over my face and neck.

"It's a long story Cillian, another time maybe," I said feeling frustrated. "So you haven't had any contact with him at all; I mean he's not been back here?" I sat back against the booth. Cillian shook his head. "What about his house? Do you know if he's returned?" I was thinking that maybe he might have left something behind, something that would give me an idea about where he might be headed.

42

"Christ Ana, I have no fuckin clue. You can always check." Cillian frowned. "What's wrong?"

"I don't know," I whispered. I wasn't sure if I could trust Cillian at the moment. Reading my thoughts, Cillian put his hand over mine.

"Whatever you need Ana, I'll help ya," he said quietly. It was the most contemplative that I had ever seen Cillian capable of expressing; it suited him.

"Thanks Cillian and you can be sure that if I need you, I'll ask," I said, standing. I left Cillian and shimmered to Stephen's old house in Bray. It was locked up tight and I tried to shimmer inside, but for some reason, I was thrown back and I was sure that I wouldn't be able to actually shimmer through the door like Nathanial and Patric, so I broke a window in the back and climbed through. The lights weren't working so I had to stumble in the dark, pulling the curtains back trying to get whatever light from the moon, to shine into the rooms. The living room was dusty, but I could clearly make out the shattered pieces of a guitar lying on the floor. That was Stephen's favorite; Liam had given it to him. I sighed, picking up one of the pieces and turning it over in my hands. I glanced around the room, my eyes falling upon several large canvases erected against the wall. The paintings were all of me. I moved slowly toward the one closest to my position near the fireplace. The image was of me, curled up on the sofa, a cup of tea in my hand. I was wearing my worn sweats and favorite tank and I was reading. I reached to trace along the canvas. Next to that portrait was another one of me standing on the wet streets of Dublin in front of the Pennys, a hat pulled down of over my head and there were festival decorations and lights shining all around me. Behind those, another larger canvas and this time the depiction was of Stephen and me and we were dancing together at Eammon's club. It was on that first night he had asked me to go out, after he'd pulled me from the overlook in Idaho, after he'd fought together with Nathanial. I choked back a sob and his face swam before me and I was whipped away.

Stephen

We were scheduled to leave tomorrow for Mexico. Michael had heard that there was a coven loyal to Carlo and they most likely would have tried to help in the plan to kill Liam. I was ready to go now, but my group seemed to be a bit preoccupied with indulging their needs for the time being. I had fed just before arriving so the only thing that I cared remotely to bother with was sex. I pulled the girl that had been sitting with me most of the night and led her to a dark back room; it wasn't romantic or even clean for that matter… blood and semen were everywhere. She didn't seem to mind and neither did I. I felt my fangs engage and I pushed her down onto the mattress left on the floor.

Ana

I landed outside a very vile looking bar in New York, very vile. I could smell something dank and tinged with rust and what appeared to mimic the odor of semen. I gagged and tried to find a place on the door to grip that wasn't covered in blood. Jesus, he couldn't pick a bookstore to hang out in? I held my breath and opened the door. Thankfully, there were humans inside and all seemed to be relatively unharmed so I exhaled and scanned the room. I pulled my cap down, shielding my eyes and walked further into the space. I saw couples coming from down a dark hallway and my heart started to beat rapidly; he was probably with someone. I could do this. I could get past what he was doing and I could tell him what was going on. I could do this. Micah told me that he wasn't himself, that he may not even look like the Stephen I remembered, but he always would be Stephen; the one who created a child with me, who I wanted a life with, who at one time, had promised that we would find our way back to each other. I reached into my pocket and pulled out the ring he gave me and slid it on my finger and started down the hallway.

The smell from the outside of the club was now at full strength and I started breathing through my mouth. I had no idea which door to go into and the last thing I wanted to do was interrupt a feeding Vampire that I didn't know. I thought about Stephen, brought his face into my mind and my feet stopped walking outside the last door on the right. I pressed my ear to the wall and I heard growling and snarling and a woman moaning. I took a deep breath, waved my hand and swung the door open. The image was nightmarish and I had to stop myself from screaming. I had no idea if it was Stephen because all I could see was this demonic face with fangs, pale skin and eyes that were a sickly gold color, not bright and deep, but evil, with the pupils vertical and narrow. I was captivated in my fear and before I knew it, the Vampire was on me, hurdling me through the room and smashing my body

45

against the wall. I heard someone scream. Oddly, I stayed up against the wall, my body hovering off the ground just like it had done when I was practicing with Patric. I watched as this crazed being launched itself in the air, heading straight for me. I pushed myself off the wall at the last second and he crashed against the cement, cracking the stone. I landed on the ground, crouching. He lunged again, this time taking me by the hair and tossing me like a ragdoll out into the hallway. I held on, taking him with me. We rolled, crashing through the backdoor exit. He flipped over my body and I sprung up whirling to face him. I had no idea where any of my fighting tactics were coming from and I could only assume that between Patric and Stephen, I had managed to know intuitively, how to fight like a Vampire. I didn't miss a beat, jumping into the air and kicking the guy square in the chest. I heard a crunch as I leveled him to the ground, my boot over his heart. His fangs were out and his eyes were glowing. He lifted my foot, but I was ready and I swung my other leg around, easing myself into his flip, kicking him in the face as I turned over. He was gushing black blood and I saw something catch the light from around this neck. I let my attention slip just a fraction and he struck me across the face sending me crashing to the ground. He was on top of me. He had my hair in his hand and he snapped my neck back. This seemed oddly familiar. I heaved my hips in the air, but he had his legs hooked up under me in such a way that made it impossible for me to move from side to side. Definitely Stephen. I wrapped my legs around him and brought his body close down to mine, trying to use his own gravity as leverage. Something shiny caught my eye again as he decked me in the head. His ring. It was dangling on a chain around his neck. I spit blood in his face.

"STEPHEN!" I yelled! Finally launching myself upright and pushing him forcefully off to the side, my head bleeding. He growled and tackled me around the legs, but I flipped him over just as I hit the ground sending his back crunching against the pavement. I kicked him in the side of the head. "STEPHEN!" I yelled again. I grabbed him around the neck and pulled him to his feet; he was snarling and dripping blood. I choked him from the front and sent us flying through the air, pressing his back against the alley wall. I moved my hands so they were gripping his throat, my nails drawing blood. He was terrifying and Micah had no idea just how different he would actually look. I had never witnessed a Vampire in full form and I had to work very hard to quell the massive amount of fear that was now seeping into my bones. I had no idea that this is what Stephen and Liam, for that matter, actually were. He was snapping at my face and I pressed harder on his windpipe hearing him gurgle. I had him and he knew it. "Stephen! It's me! It's Ana!' I said to him, bringing my face close to his ear, trying to keep my neck away from his fangs. He growled and I shoved his head back against the wall, hard. "It's me! Jesus Christ! It's me!" I said, dropping us to the ground and letting him go. I was beside myself in fear and grief as I tried to hold myself together. He crouched and snarled at me, blood coming from his head and neck. I slid off my ring, his blood making my fingers slick. I held it up. "Look!' I shouted at him. "Look! It's my ring, it's the ring you gave me!" I said, walking slowly toward him, my own blood streaming down my face. "Look!" I stood in front of his body. He rose from his attack position and he loomed over me looking huge and as if he'd just been resurrected from Hell.

47

I rose myself slightly off the ground so we were level and I saw him cock his head to the side. "Look," I said, my voice soft. I moved closer to him holding the ring in my hand. I reached toward him and he growled. I breathed deep and took the chain from around his neck and held it up, my ring next to his. "Look Stephen." My voice and my hands were shaking and I was hoping beyond hope that he wouldn't kill me or that I wouldn't have to kill him. His body shuddered and he closed his eyes. I drifted back down to the earth, my head bowed, tasting my blood on my tongue and I slowly backed away from him. Perhaps I was too late. Perhaps he was already too far-gone for him to even know me anymore, for him to know us. I leaned back against the wall, breathing hard and watching him slowly approach me, his eyes still sick and his face contorted. He grabbed my throat and I felt him dig his hands into my flesh, making me bleed. I stared at him, stared at the eyes I didn't know, at the face that terrified me. I stared hard. His breath was shallow and I felt him tighten his grip. I could attack. I could continue to fight; I was waiting. I reached up and began tracing my fingers along his exposed fangs, feeling how slick they were, how sharp. He growled deeply and closed his eyes. Suddenly I felt his mouth begin to move and he was tracing his tongue over each of my fingers, caressing them. It was a familiar gesture and one he'd done many times before. He growled again and his grip on my throat released. I exhaled, but didn't pull away. He bit one of my fingers and began drawing my blood. The sudden surge of heat from his motion caught me off guard and I struggled against the wave of desire that he was creating. I swallowed, desperate not to fall apart. He closed his eyes and I watched as he continued to pull more of me into him, into his body and his soul. I could feel what he was feeling and I almost collapsed from the intensity. He was experiencing a deep anger and sadness, hunger and depression; he was aroused and full of love, so much so that it threatened to make my heart explode. I gasped and had to pull away; I had to break the connection, his emotions were overwhelming me and my mind. My soul and heart were struggling against both what he was feeling and what I was experiencing for myself. He opened his eyes. The seas had calmed. He stared at me, his marine blue eyes seeing everything, knowing everything with perfect clarity. Micah had said that Stephen was my creator for all intents and purposes, and in this moment, while we stared at each other, I hoped he would realize just how grateful I was to him for his courage and for his love. His eyes grew wide and suddenly, he shimmered us away.

We landed back in his old house in Bray, my hands still on his lips. His fangs were gone. He stared at me, his gaze intense.

"You're bleeding," he said quietly. I stepped away from him. I suddenly felt horrible, scared, drained and overwhelmed...I tried to collect myself, tried to remember why I was here. I needed to tell him, to let him know. "Ana?" He moved closer to me and I held out my hand; he stopped mid stride. I swallowed, feeling his confusion, his desperation to be next to me, and his fear of me seeing him in such a horrific state.

"It's ok. I'm ok," I said, turning around to stare at one of the canvases. I thought I was speaking more for my benefit than his. "It's ok," I whispered, reaching to touch my throat, feeling the blood and the flesh that he'd tried to tear. We had fought each other, my soul shuttered under the weight of that realization. I sighed, turning to look at him. His eyes were closed and he was breathing softly. I

49

gathered myself, but kept to my side of the space. I had no idea when or if he would be triggered into attack mode again; this was all so new to me and my guard was up. "I have to tell you something Stephen, something that Micah sent me to tell you; are you able to listen? I mean are you yourself enough to listen to me?" I watched him as he took a deep breath. His skin was still pale and his fists were clutched at his sides. He nodded once. "Stephen, Micah thinks that Liam and maybe Carmen are alive, that they might be in trouble, captured, that they negotiated for Lucie's life the night they were attacked and now they are in some sort of trouble..." I realized that I actually didn't have many details to give him and I hoped that he would believe me. "We need your help." I tried to move through everything that Micah had told me to say. "We, Micah and me, we need help trying to figure out who may have Liam, where he may be; Micah thinks that you've made some connections over these last months and that you can help us...if you...if you want." It would be weird if he didn't want to help, but what the hell did I know? Stephen was staring at me, his stance wide and his arms crossed over his chest in a very defensive posture.

"You're alive," he said, his jaw set. I looked to the side.

"Umm... yeah, but your brother Stephen, he may also be alive." Had he heard me?

"How long?" he asked me, his body rigid.

"How long what?" I asked, thinking that maybe he'd snapped or something.

50

"How long have you been recovered?" he said, his tone icy and I felt a flood of anger flash though my body, not from me, from him. He was pissed.

"Months I guess; four or five months." I guessed he was referring to my illness after Carlo. He closed his eyes and breathed out pinching the bridge of his nose.

"Months," his voice barely a whisper. "Months." He was staring at me.

"Yeah, listen Stephen, your brother, Liam, he may be alive and we—" He cut me off waving his hand and suddenly my voice became trapped in my throat. He silenced me.

"I spoke with them, with each of them. I asked them both if you were alive and they let me think…they let me wonder, they left me to conjure my own nightmares, my own hell of being in this world without you, of knowing that I may or may not have changed you, that you may or may not have survived. I stayed away and they shut me down from trying to sense you, trying to sense your presence; I stayed away thinking that they were right, that I should have left you there in that house, in their care. They intentionally misled me; they wanted to keep me from you, to keep me doubting myself and I let them." His voice was so black that the fear I was trying to quell, was now raging full on in my chest. I tried to clear my throat. Stephen turned his eyes to me and waved his hand; my voice was released.

"It's not important," I whispered, and that was wrong thing to say. He punched the wall shattering the wood and the concrete. I backtracked. "It's not important *right now*," I said, not moving. "Did you hear what I said about your brother Stephen; he needs us and we need you," I said, pleading with him. I was starting to think that coming to find Stephen first was not the best plan. "I can summon Micah; maybe you should talk to him… I'm not the best person…" I trailed off as I watched him cross the room and stand in front of me, his eyes roaming over my face.

"You're bleeding," he said again. I was now quite sure that Stephen, had in fact, snapped. He smirked at me and rolled his eyes. Yep, snapped. I pictured Micah's face in my head and began chanting his name in my mind; I needed some help. A blast of cold air rushed the room and Micah stood looking graceful and powerful, in front of us.

"Ana!" he said, moving to embrace me. I winced from the pressure of his hug and he pulled back, his eyes assessing my injuries. He rounded on Stephen. "Did you attack her?" He was standing toe to toe with Stephen, Micah looking large and frightening.

"Micah, it's fine; I'm fine. We had a little scuffle that's all," I said, moving to step between them. Stephen looked at me and I thought I saw him smile. I wondered if they had mental institutions for Vampires. Stephen chuckled softly and stepped away from Micah. "Micah, I don't think I'm doing a very good job explaining to Stephen exactly what you think has happened to Liam; I'm sucking at the moment as far as communicating details…" My voice shook and fell to a whisper. I was feeling exhausted and my head was pounding. "Can you catch him up please?" I asked, holding the side of my head. "I'm just going to clean my face." I moved down the hallway toward the bathroom, hoping that Micah would be able to make Stephen concentrate enough for him to understand what was being said. I closed the door and leaned against the sink surveying my face. Christ. I had a huge gash on the left side of my face stretching from my temple down to my jaw. My lip was split and swollen. There were slashes on my throat and my hips felt stiff. I lifted my shirt and unbuttoned my pants sliding them down to reveal deep red and purple blood-bruises spreading under my skin. The back of my neck hurt from when he'd pulled my hair back and my scalp felt tender; he'd pulled out some of my hair by the roots. I splashed water on my face and tried to remove the blood from the wounds. I felt dizzy. I stayed in the bathroom sinking down against the wall, my head bent towards my knees. He could have killed me. I closed my eyes, too exhausted to cry. As much as I loved Liam and would do anything to save him, this may not have been the best of plans. I had no idea how long I stayed in the bathroom; I couldn't get up, I didn't want to get up. I just kept picturing Stephen, his eyes a deep, sickly gold, his waxy skin and those fangs. Christ. My body shuddered.

"Ana." I raised my head, turning to look at the opened door. Stephen stood leaning against the doorframe. I put my head back on my knees.

"Are you going to help us or not?' I asked, not looking at him. I heard him move into the bathroom and slide down against the wall next to me.

"Yes," he said quietly. I nodded. "Where did you learn to fight like that?" he asked, and I felt him brush my hair back from my shoulders.

"Patric, and you I guess," I mumbled, keeping my head buried.

"Hmmm," he said, stroking my back; the touch was so familiar and my very core seemed to shutter and expand.

53

"You've always been better at ground fighting than me," I said, smiling despite my current emotional state. He laughed and it was a laugh that I knew, that I loved. I raised my head. Our eyes met and he surveyed my wounds.

"Jesus," he whispered shaking his head.

"You pulled out some of my hair," I said, my eyes narrowing. "I thought that only girls fought like that." I reached up to touch my scalp, wincing. He exhaled and I could feel his emotions; he was beyond feeling guilty. "I can sense what you are experiencing now," I said, as he stroked my face. "Everything that you feel, I feel it as well," I spoke, my voice stronger now.

"Is that right?" he said, his voice rough, quiet. I nodded. He studied me. "Let me clean those wounds." He rose from the ground and moved toward the medicine cabinet. I watched as he removed a bottle of alcohol and several cotton balls and then pulled me gently off the ground. He led me down to his room and I sat on the bed. "I'm sorry, this may sting a bit," he spoke as he pressed the cotton to my wound. It stung—a lot. I took a sharp breath in and he stopped to look at me. "Sorry," he whispered. I sighed and let him work tenderly over the gashes on my face. He wiped delicately over my throat and my lips and I could feel just how intensely he was battling wanting to be close to me. I suddenly thought about Patric and how we'd been together before I'd left for my trip and I wondered if Stephen would be mad. He pulled back staring. "No," he said quietly. "No. Ana, I'm not mad; you love him and he needed you and you needed him…" he trailed off as I bowed my head. He was holding my face in his hands, his eyes

54

blinding me with their clarity. He bent my head and kissed my forehead.

"I need you too Stephen; you saved my life. I'm sorry that you had to do that," I said, suddenly feeling horrible that he had to perform such an act. I cringed. He pulled away.

"Yes, well, I originally had a much more romantic scenario in mind for that event to occur." He chuckled.

"Oh yeah, like what kind of a scenario?" I asked, smiling. He laughed.

"Hmmm…well I know how partial you are to all things ocean and moon related. I was thinking I'd whisk you away to some secluded place where we could go about consummating our relationship on the beach under the stars perhaps." His lips curved up in a crooked smile. I frowned.

"I had always heard that doing it on the beach was kind of uncomfortable; you know with the sand getting everywhere." I laughed. His eyes widened. "And haven't we already consummated our relationship? Lots," I said snickering, feeling my own eyes flash. He cleared his throat and I remembered something that Patric had told me before I left. "Hey, you want to know something weird about me now?" I asked him, shifting to tuck my legs under my hips.

"More weird than you being able to fly through the air and kick my ass?" he asked, lying back on the bed, his arms under his head. I waved my hand.

"Whatever, that's nothing," I said, and he raised his eyebrows. "Patric thinks that because of you, now I seem to be able to send stalking signals out," I said, suddenly feeling embarrassed. Stephen turned to me, his face concerned.

"What do you mean? You're stalking Humans now?" He propped himself up on his elbows, his tone worried. I laughed nervously.

"You'd think that wouldn't you?" I said, meeting his eyes. "But I'm the exception to most rules as you already know." I leaned back letting my head rest against the mattress.

"I don't understand; who exactly are you stalking Ana?" He moved to turn on his stomach and I realized that I had been keeping him out of my head. He couldn't read my thoughts. I laughed.

"Vampires!" I said, tossing my head back and shaking my hair back and forth.

"What?" He was hovering so close to me now that I could feel the heat from his skin.

"Yep. I didn't know I was doing it, but Patric said that as soon as I woke up that I was releasing some sort of more potent version of my own scent—a predation scent and I had targeted him; he could feel it. He said he could feel that he wasn't able to have control over how close he wanted to get to me and that most of his abilities to dictate what he wanted were being overruled by what I wanted from him, not the other way around. He said it was a role reversal of sorts; the prey stalking the predator." I grinned. Stephen was leaning away from me and I could feel his confusion and a slight tenor of fear. "You don't have to freak out Stephen, I'm not going to attack you or anything," I said, feeling slightly abashed. He frowned.

"Why not?" he asked; it was my turn to express confusion.

"Why not what?" I asked, not following his question. He leaned back toward me, his eyes traveling up and down my body. His stare was making me feel self-conscious.

"Why aren't you trying to stalk me?" He was still frowning and a wave of desire and heat flooded through his body. He wanted me to stalk him?

"Umm… I'm not sure," I said. "I mean I don't really know how it works or if I even have control over it." Christ, I hoped that I did. He was staring at me.

"Try," he said, moving closer to me; he was freaking me out.

"What?" I said, leaning back from his body.

"Try. Channel your emotions and what you want and try to push them out toward me," he said, his eyes flashing and churning.

"Stephen, seriously, you and I just engaged in a horrific fight where you punched me in the side of the face!" I said. "I'm not sure this is the best time for me to be trying to…trying to…to seduce you." I laughed. "I'm pretty sure that most would classify what you did as a crime of female brutality or some form of domestic violence." Plus, I just wasn't sure how I was feeling about him at the moment. I was still angry for him showing up wrecked to get Lucie and of course there was still the whole issue of him leaving me in the hospital…it was a lot to reconcile. Stephen stared at me, his eyes finding mine and I sighed. I had missed him so much over these months and to be here with him now, back in his home; I really just wanted to spend some time catching up and

57

talking about Liam. I sat back on the bed and stared out the window at the moon. Stephen was quiet and still and I wondered if he had fallen into his evening trance. Lifetimes passed.

"Try," Stephen suddenly spoke in the darkness; his tone was deep and his eyes pieced through my mental resistance as he moved to look at me. I exhaled. I didn't even know how to go about doing this.

"Stephen this is not really appropriate; I mean you and I, we're...we're not..." I was struggling to express myself. All I kept picturing was us in the hospital and before the hospital when I was begging him not to leave me, when I was pleading for him to stay with me. My heart shuddered at the memories and I heard Stephen take a shaky breath.

"I know Ana," Stephen whispered in the darkness. "Try," he said, longing deep in his voice. Jesus. I sighed and tried to focus on him. I let my mind drift to all the images I had of being with him, of our most intimate moments, of how passionate he was, how much I liked when he was in control, how it felt to have him touch me and kiss me and how much I did love him, intensely and more deeply than I could have ever thought possible. My body churned and I felt my skin swell and some sort of flood of chemicals raced through my blood, their release I couldn't control. I could feel them; they moved swiftly, igniting every ounce of desire I had in my entire being. My eyes darkened and all I could see was Stephen. My vision was focused on just him, on his eyes, his throat and his body. I felt nothing else but desire and my mind was thinking nothing but how much I wanted him; I was pulsing inside of myself and I moved toward him. I was on fire.

"Jesus Christ," I heard him whisper, but he too was moving toward me. "Jesus." His body was trembling and I could feel his need for me crash over him. Suddenly, just before I lunged, he was blurring to the other side of the room, hovering above the ground a few feet, smirking. I took a deep breath and tried to come down from the high of such intense desire. I glared at him.

"What the hell Stephen?" I said, sitting back down on the bed. "I thought you said you wanted me to try. Why are you running away? I'm not going to hurt you," I said, but my voice sounded odd; it sounded sensual and dark. Perhaps I had not come down quite enough. I cleared my throat. "Seriously, please come back over, I'm not going to do anything to you." Nope, still not my voice. Shit! This was totally beyond me; I couldn't control what was happening. I heard him laugh as he walked slowly across the room. He moved to stand in front of me. He leaned over, his hands pressed on either side of my shoulders.

"Ana, I have no problem with what you are doing to me. Actually it's an extremely arousing experience to have my desires dictated to me; I like that surprisingly and I especially like it coming from you." He moved his face close to mine. We were in trouble. "Moreover, I like this side of you. I like what you make me want, the way you sound and," he took a deep breath in and growled low, "I love the way you smell; it's intoxicating and I would do whatever you wanted just to have your scent on my skin and to taste you in my mouth." That was it. I lunged at him and brought his body down hard upon mine, rolling so that I was on top. I tore his clothes, shredding them. He growled and ripped my shirt. I pulled him up and flung him against the wall holding him there, hovering above the ground. I tore his jeans and rose up level

59

with his body. He was staring at me, his eyes fierce. I was craving his blood; I could smell it, smell him. It was odd, that particular desire, but that's what I wanted. I had never bitten anyone before, not in the way I wanted to right now. I wasn't sure how to go about doing it. Stephen grabbed my head and pulled me close to his neck, his fragrance and the swell of his blood under his skin made me groan. He wanted me to do this. I was gasping and my mouth was watering and I had such a violent need to take him that I wasn't able to control myself any longer. "Do it!" Stephen breathed against my face. "I want you to Ana." He pressed my mouth to his throat and I wondered just how much of him wanted me to do this and how much it was coming from me. "Stop thinking and bite me for fuck sake!" He moaned and I dug my teeth deep into his flesh feeling the skin tear and the heated blood move over my lips and into my mouth. He gasped and came right there against the wall, thrusting and thrashing as I held him, helpless, in mid-air. I pressed my mouth harder against his neck drinking from him; the sweetness of his blood filling me with such pleasure that I shoved him inside of me, coming even before he could fully penetrate. He gasped and shoved himself deeper as he pressed my face forcefully against him. I sucked him harder and he came again, moaning in his release. I ground against him violently. "Go down!" He gasped. "I want you to go down on me." He groaned and he pulled me away from his throat and shoved my head down between his legs. I ran my tongue over his groin tracing up and down and taking him in my mouth. I pulled and sucked hard letting him climax in my mouth. "Ana! I want you to bite me, do it!" He was gasping and I was savoring his taste. I swallowed greedily, urgently, feeling his delicious heat scorch my throat. He shoved my head back toward the pulse in his groin. "Do it, I want to feel you take from me. God please, I want to come with you biting me, please Ana!"

60

He was begging me and I loved it; I wanted him to beg for some reason. I bit down hard, feeling the pressure from his pulse explode in my mouth, but I waited to tear his flesh. I wanted to hear him ask me again. He gasped. "Please Ana, I want this, I want you, I need to come, I want to come, fucking do it!" he shouted and I ripped his flesh, puncturing the vein. I felt him heave and he snarled violently and I sucked as hard as I could, he growled and I drank, climaxing over and over again, gasping and panting as I continued to pull his very life into my body. He yanked my face away, blood dripping from my mouth. "I want to fuck you Ana; that's what I want. I want us to fuck, now!" He lurched forward sending us crashing to the floor. He drilled himself inside of me and I thrust against him. His fangs were out and he slammed me over and over on the ground. "My turn," he hissed and his eyes changed color; they glowed bright silver, not the sickly gold he'd displayed before and the pupils went vertical. This time I wasn't frightened, this time I wanted him like this. I pressed my teeth to his throat and pulled from his veins, at the same time I felt him plunge his teeth into my neck. I gasped, unable to control my desire. He thrust inside of me as he drank the blood from my throat. "I want you Ana, I want you to come for me, in me, in my mouth." His voice was dark and deadly and his mouth was dripping with my blood. I smiled at him and started lapping up the blood that was now spilling down his chest. His eyes were burning and his fangs were slick with dark red. He moved down my stomach and he growled. He forced my legs apart and bit down on each of my inner thighs drinking the blood from both wounds. He took me between his lips and I groaned loudly as he pressed his tongue and his fangs into my flesh, biting down hard.

61

"Christ!" I screamed out as I felt the blood begin to flow and my desire release.

"God, you taste so good! I want more!" He snarled and he pulled and tugged and sucked. This is what I wanted from him, this is what I had been willing him to do; I needed this. "What do you need Ana?" he growled his eyes penetrating me. "What do you want me to do to you?" He brought his face to mine, his lips glistening. He thrust himself inside me, making me moan. He did it again, his eyes watching me move. "Do you want me to fuck you?" he asked, his voice sinister; I loved it.

"Yes!" I growled back.

"Yes what?" He shoved himself deeper inside. "Yes what Ana?" he breathed.

"Yes I want you to fuck me Stephen!" I snarled at him pressing his body deeper into mine. He laughed and suddenly I was spinning him on his back. I mounted him and shoved him inside making him groan. He spread my legs pressing his hands into the bite marks. I came, writhing up and down upon him. He pressed again and I released again, feeling as if I was drowning in my pleasure.

"You want more?" he said, pushing violently against me.

"Yes!" I growled and started riding his hips.

"Christ that feels so good!" He pressed and I thrust and we climaxed, almost brutally, together. I wasn't nearly done. I pushed harder and faster and he groaned and gasped as I moved him rapidly against me. He dug his fingers into my wounds and I screamed as I exploded and ignited, my orgasm shattering my bones in its release. He was still coming when I rolled off of him and I moved to taste him, wanting to heighten his pleasure. "Ana, god what are you doing to me?" He started to thrust in my mouth and I pushed him further "Ana!" He yelled and he came again and I laughed, collapsing on the floor next to him. Yep, totally out of my control.

Chapter Three

Stephen

I was lying in bed watching Ana. I had never seen her sleep so deeply before. I was confused. She wasn't a vampire but her actions last night were anything but Human. Her blood tasted Human and she felt like she always had, her skin soft and her body strong; she was beyond my comprehension. I was hoping she would explain. I stroked her hair as I scanned over her face. I had dreamt of this moment, fantasized about it, grieved over it, cried over losing it; now here I was, here we both were, lying together. My body shook with the love I felt for her. I wanted to tell her that I loved her, that I needed her to be with me. I felt inadequate, unable to express the depth of my feelings, the depth of my complete inability to be without her beside me. I was bound to her in my own way, not with metal or stone, but in my complete love for her. Our blood ran together, side-by-side with all the rest in her heart, but I knew there was more; we had created life. Our joining had been enough to heal Ana's body to a certain extent and I wondered what the chances were for us now that she had my venom in her system, at least I thought she did.

I wrapped my arm around her and felt her breathing. She was dreaming. I saw pictures in her mind, pictures of my brother and some of Lucie. I could see that they had been on a trip somewhere; she and Lucie went together on a boat. I saw an image of my face move in her dream, the painting I had given her swirling and shifting. She'd opened it, finally. I saw a fight she apparently had with Nathanial. I saw her

64

throwing shards of glass or porcelain at his face and shoving Patric away as he tried to hold her back. I wondered what happened. I saw her apartment in Dublin and I saw Micah hugging her, talking to her. I saw her putting on her backpack and I saw her in Brazil, in Germany, in Ecuador, all the places I had been; she'd been looking for me. I saw her standing outside the bar in New York, trying not to gag. I watched as she pulled open the door, her eyes searching for me. I saw her walk down the hallway and I felt her body tense in my arms. I saw her press her ear to the door listening and then opening the door with a wave of her hand. Her mind brought me into focus, blood covering my face, my whole being transformed. She was terrified. She jerked as her dream showed me launching myself at her, throwing her against the wall, a hit that would have killed any other Human. I shuddered as the scene of our fight played out in her mind; it was brutal and horrendous and utterly terrifying. I saw her show me her ring and I felt myself gasp; I didn't remember that. I watched as she lifted the chain from around my neck and held up the thick silver band. I touched my neck and found her gift hanging solidly around my throat; it felt hot. I traced my hand down the length of her arm finding her fingers. She was wearing her band and I shuddered again, another image of me strangling her, blood seeping through my fingers as I pressed against her windpipe. She startled and sat up in bed gasping and crying.

"Stephen?" she said, clutching her chest. I sat up and rubbed her back.

"I'm here Ana, it's ok, I'm here," I said, gently pulling her back down into my arms. She looked at me as if not believing that I was really there. I touched her lips and smiled. "It's ok," I whispered, staring at her. I wiped the tears from her cheeks and ran my hand up and down her back, stroking her softly. She wrapped her arm around my chest and I felt as though every force was pulling from the center of the earth, holding her to me and me to her. She fell back to sleep and I heard my phone buzz. It was Micah. I tried to speak softly. "Micah, what have you learned?" I asked, wondering if all this business about my brother was just a ruse; I couldn't let myself believe it.

"Stephen, I think South Africa will be your best bet. I think that your brother may be with Saden and his coven." Saden. I didn't know much about him. I hadn't had any dealings with him and the only person that I knew who had ever been with him for a certain period of time was Cillian. "Yes, you and Ana may want to talk to Cillian before you depart." Wait what? Ana wasn't coming with me, no way. I heard Micah laugh softly. "Clearly you two delayed catching up on everything that Ana has been able to learn about herself. Trust me Stephen, you don't want to go up against any coven, any coven, without Ana by your side." I glanced at the woman lying on my chest and frowned. "When you get to South Africa you need to head to Soweto township and find Masakeng bar. Kendrick should be there; he's a very good friend of mine and he'll be waiting for you. He has accommodations and he knows the lay of the land. Tell me the instant you arrive so I can notify him, and Stephen," Micah paused and I held my breath, "you need to listen, listen to Ana and listen to your brother should you find him; while you are quite skilled in many areas, Ana and Liam are both masters at diplomacy. Ana was able to frighten Carlo and even though he managed to get his teeth into her, he lost that fight. You need to trust her and trust your brother, am I understood?" His tone was low and chilling. Again, I looked at Ana; she seemed so peaceful and calm. Micah laughed. "Isn't that the case with the deadliest of predators; you underestimate just what they are capable of accomplishing... Ana is no different."

"Ok Micah, we'll call you when we arrive. Are you sure that Ana is up for this?" I was worried that she might not be prepared for what we were going to have to do; whatever that was, I had no fucking idea.

"Ana will be fine Stephen; you should know that when I asked if she would help you and Liam, she didn't hesitate. She can do this and she will be a great help to both you and your brother I think. Summon me should you need anything at all." I sighed.

"Thanks."

"Goodbye Stephen; take care of her please." I was thinking that it was most likely that Ana would have to take care of me. "I meant her heart; I believe that it is you that she wants, but she's terrified and feeling guilty and thanks to my nephews, she's feeling a bit on edge with her emotions. I don't think she trusts herself to know what's best for her anymore... I meant take care of her heart."

"Yes," I choked and Micah hung up the phone. I got up hoping not to wake her; I was stunned. I had no idea what had happened to Ana since I left her that night and I was hoping she would feel comfortable enough to tell me. I ran to the store, realizing that I had no food in the house and I was sure that it had been quite a while since Ana had eaten; if I wasn't counting the blood she'd gotten from me. I smirked to myself and shook my head. I set about making her an omelet and coffee. I turned up the stereo a bit and tried to think about what in the world my brother would be doing with Saden.

"Hey," Ana spoke from the kitchen door. She was wearing a t-shirt of mine. She looked sleepy. Her left eye was a bit bruised and I frowned. She was right; people would think that I beat her, which I guess I actually had. "Don't worry about it." She waved her hand, apparently sensing the tenor of my concern. "Anyone who asks, you just say that I beat the crap out of you first." She smiled and walked into the kitchen. Suddenly I felt very aware of what she and I had done last night, the way we'd been with each other, the things that we'd said in the heat of our intimacy. Our actions had been like nothing that we had ever experienced together and suddenly I felt aroused and shy. I felt myself blush. Weird.

"Are you blushing?" Ana gasped as she drank her coffee. "No frickin way!" She moved to stand in front of me, her eyes scanning over my face. I smiled at her and she came to put her arms around my waist. "You're not embarrassed are you? Not you, not the guy who's been with thousands of women, who engages in bondage rituals, who likes to feed on women when he's having sex." She wasn't making me feel better. She laughed and kissed me. "I love that you are embarrassed; that's too funny!" she said sitting down at the table. I set her plate down in front of her and glared. "I'm sorry, really I am; it's not funny, it's sweet," she said, as she studied me over her mug. "If you want, we can put a moratorium on any intimate relations until you are feeling a bit more comfortable in your sexual personalities." She laughed, choking on her coffee. Wait, she'd wanted to be with me more than just last night? I couldn't afford to get my hopes up.

"I think you and I tried that once before and we failed miserably did we not?" I said, pulling out a chair and watching her eat. She shrugged. "May I ask you something?" I wasn't sure if this was the appropriate time but...

"Anything," she said, eating her eggs. "These are so good! Thanks!" She smiled at me. I laughed.

"Why are you not a vampire?" I asked, frowning as I watched her eat so fast that it was dizzying. "Slow down, you're going to get sick." I reached to touch her arm. She laughed and nodded.

"I'm hungry man, I've been running on adrenaline for weeks!" she said putting her fork down. "What? Oh, the Vampire thing, right. Ok, so apparently because I have something around ten different blood types in my system, they somehow let my body utilize the venom to heal me but not to change me. No one really understands how that happens, but that's what Dr. Connelly thought. He thinks that my blood neutralizes whatever properties make the venom initiate the change from human to Vampire, but keeps the properties that allow venom to heal the body, make it strong or whatever," she said. "May I have some more?" She looked at me. I was still frowning as another thought filled my mind, a memory.

"You were so angry with me when Nathanial brought me back to Peru to get Lucie," I said quietly as I cracked more eggs and put some potatoes in the pan.

"Yes I was. You were drunk and wrecked and in no shape to be anything to anyone at that moment much less a surrogate father," she said, her voice commanding a sense of truth and conviction. "I was also angry with you for what I found when I came to Belfast; that was my fault. I took my emotions out on you. I was hurt and devastated and I didn't want to see you." I kept my back to her, remembering how I had taken off her ring in a drunken stupor, feeling broken and shattered; it was a horrible, horrible mistake. Cillian was so pissed at me for that, he didn't speak to me for weeks.

"So, you slept with Patric again," I said. We might as well get everything out there. She choked and stared at me, surprised at my bluntness. "What about Nathanial?" I said. I hadn't seen him in her mind except during her dream when they were having a fight.

"Stephen!" she said, and I turned around to face her. "God, what is with you? NO! I did not sleep with Nathanial and what happened between Patric and myself happened between two people who love each other. It wasn't like I spread my legs for some random stranger." She glared at me. "Not like you," I heard her mumble under her breath. I sighed putting down her plate. "Thanks," she said, not looking at me. "I mean," she put her fork down, her eyes raging, "you don't hear me asking you who the whore was you were fucking last night when I found you, do you?" It was odd to hear Ana curse; she was always so articulate and diplomatic. I must have pissed her off or she'd been hanging out with Patric too much.

"I've never loved any of those women Ana; none of them I have ever been in love with. I don't think it's quite the same thing as hearing that you made love to someone who you actually *do* love," I said quietly. "Those women were a means to an end, where as Patric, he would offer you his life; he would offer you anything you wanted if you just chose to be with him. It's not the same," I said, eyeing her.

70

"What's the right thing to say Stephen? I don't know what you want to hear." She ran her fingers through her hair, sighing. "You know all of this already, we've already been down this road. You know everything about how I feel. What-do-you-want-me-to-say?" I knew what I wanted her to say, but she wasn't ready; she didn't trust herself yet to tell me, to ask me and she didn't trust me yet either. I would wait; I trusted Micah and he knew her, he understood her history, her decisions and her love. I trusted him and I trusted myself enough to know that when she was ready, I would be there, ready to offer her the life that I had promised, the life that even Nathanial knew I could give her; I would be ready. I leaned forward and kissed her gently on her cut lip. She kissed me back, more forcefully than I had done her and I laughed. Both of our emotions were all over the place. I didn't care.

"We need to meet with Cillian," I murmured as she wound her hands around my neck. I felt myself begin to lift her up and I slid the plates off the table, pushing her up on the surface. How was it possible that one person could be so passionate, so sexual, every time we were together? It was as if her desire and her sensuality got stronger every day. I shoved her shirt up over her hips and spread her legs as I kissed down her stomach. She groaned as I felt her arousal spreading like lava over my mouth.

"Are you...do you need... are you hungry?" She gasped as I traced my lips back and forth between her legs, tasting how sweet and rich she was; I felt high and nourished all at once. I tongued her forcefully, my arousal commanding my body and I laughed as she climaxed, groaning and grunting in her complete need to be satisfied.

"Actually no, *that's* all I wanted," I said, breathless, moving back up to kiss her chest and finally her mouth. She had no idea what it did to me to pleasure her; it was more than arousing, it was addictive and I could spend hours watching her come by my hand or my mouth or whatever else I wanted to use to make her feel good. "Go get dressed and I'll clean up," I said, biting her gently on the neck. She stared at me.

"You know, I could make you do what I want now," she said, sliding herself off the table and I suddenly caught her scent, her predation scent and I felt my mind begin to drift and haze. I cleared my throat; holy shit she was good at doing that.

"Ana, you could do that before you became whatever it is you are now." I laughed as I took a step back from her; her eyes had turned hypnotic. "Seriously, Ana. I promised Micah that we would meet with Cillian today." I cleared my throat again and shook my head. She tossed her hair and sauntered from the room; she actually sauntered!

****

We arrived at the club thirty minutes later after having to return to New York to locate Ana's backpack. I found it in the back room where I'd attacked her. Jesus, our relationship would be so fucked if it didn't work so damn well and feel so damn good. She was wiping off the material and glaring at me.

"Christ Stephen! There's like blood and semen all over this thing! Gross!" she said. "Can't you wave your hand and clean it up or something?" she asked, holding out the pack to me. In her defense, it was pretty gross. I cringed and ran my hand over the canvas material wiping it clean. "Thank you!" she said, pulling a small bottle of perfume out of a pocket and spraying it lightly.

"What's that for?" I said as I knocked on the club door.

"It smells like other people." She raised her eyebrows. I smirked and shook my head. The door opened and Cillian popped his head out.

"Holy fuckin' shit Stephen! First Ana, now you; what da fuck is goin' on?" I turned to look at Ana. She'd been to see Cillian? She shrugged. "Whoa! Ana; ya're back!" Cillian craned his neck out the door to look at her. "What da fuck happened to yer face, love?" I shoved past him pulling Ana with me.

"It's nothing Cillian, just a little brawl," Ana said, taking my hand.

"What'd da oter guy look like?" Cillian was staring at her.

"You're looking at him," I growled.

"No shit! No way! You two? No fuckin' way! You fought! Christ! Who won?" Cillian was staring at Ana with such awe it was making me uncomfortable and if I was being honest, proud. She'd finally stood her ground against me. It had taken her long enough.

"It was a draw," Ana said, sliding into the booth and putting her pack down. She stared at me and smiled.

"Man, I bet she totally kicked yer ass up and down da fuckin' street!" Cillian sat down next to Ana naturally, and I moved to sit across from them. "Of course it would have been different if ya were in full out vamp mode I guess." Cillian looked at me. "No way she would have been able ta get a punch in!" he said. I stared at him, my eyes falling flat. "NO WAY!" Cillian practically jumped from his seat. "YOU VAMPED OUT ON HER! Oh Christ!" He was looking back and forth between Ana and me, his hair whipping from side to side. "No fangs dough; dere's no way." He looked at Ana and she looked at me. "FUCK NO!" Cillian slapped Ana so hard on the back that she lurched forward in her seat.

"Jesus Cillian, calm the fuck down will you?" I said, reaching to take Ana's hand in mine. "We need your help," I said, watching Ana. She seemed to be thinking about something and I was wondering if she regretted being intimate with me again; maybe it was too soon.

"What do ya need?" he said, sipping his drink and watching Ana out of the corner of his eye. I sighed.

"What can you tell us about Saden, Cillian? You hung with his coven for awhile didn't you?" I asked, motioning for the server. Ana eyed me and I ordered us both ginger ales. She smiled.

"Saden, wow, yeah I did hang wit him fer about a year." Cillian sat back putting his arm on the spine of the booth. "Why, what do ya want wit him?"

"We think that my brother might be with him," I said. Cillian spat his drink out, spraying me in the face with scotch. Ana handed me a tissue from her pack. I wiped my face.

74

"Liam? Are ya tellin' me dat Liam is alive?" Cillian finished his drink and called for another.

"We don't know for sure, but it appears that my brother may have been able to negotiate for his daughter's life and now he's hold up with Saden; we don't know..." I said, my chest feeling tight. I missed my brother. I felt Ana reach under the table and rub my knee. I squeezed her hand.

"Well man, if he's wit Saden den he's probably pretty damn screwed." My heart sunk.

"Why Cillian?" Ana spoke for me. Cillian shook his head.

"Saden is one fierce vamp. He's young as far as our kind go, only 150 years or so, but he relishes every part of our species—every part." Cillian looked at Ana. "He likes trainin', fightin' and he loves being a predator. He's brutally violent, addicted ta sex and blood and enjoys instigatin' chaos. It's like dealin' wit an insane teenager." Cillian laughed.

"What about powers?" Ana asked. "Can he do anything special?" I knew she was thinking about Carlo's illusionary trick with her and with Patric. Cillian shook his head.

"Special? Special...hmm... He can make ya want him," Cillian said, sipping his drink and I saw Ana frown.

"Uh...what do you mean?" She was staring at me, her eyes narrowing. Cillian laughed.

"Not sexually, not fer males at least; females are a different story. He makes ya want ta be in his presence. You want to participate in da fightin' and da violence. He loves pittin' vamps against each oter, his own little version of da UFC." He looked at me. "Ya start ta forget where ya're and what ya're doin', who ya're doin'; it's like bein' on a year-long bender, at least it was fer me."

"He let you leave?" Ana was asking all the right questions. I was surprised and impressed.

"Yeah; he likes ta keep up a rotation of guys and gals, he gets bored easily and has a short attention span. Leavin' isn't a problem unless ya have somethin' he wants." Cillian stared at Ana.

"Like what?" She stared back, holding his gaze. Cillian cleared his throat.

"Like skills dat he can learn from. He knows he's young and he doesn't have da worldly experience dat most of us have and he sees da tings some of us are able ta do, above and beyond da normal talents." Cillian's eyes grew dark as they roamed over Ana's face.

"Cillian!" I cut across his trance.

"Sorry man, she just smells really good." I turned to Ana. Was she releasing her scent to him? She'd have to learn to better control herself. She shook her head and rolled her eyes at me. I relaxed a bit.

"So why would Liam be in trouble? Does Saden know how powerful he is?" Ana asked and Cillian nodded his head.

"Who doesn't know how powerful Liam is?" Cillian replied. Ana frowned.

"Do you think he knows that Carlo is dead?" Ana asked and for the second time, Cillian spit his drink across the table.

"Whoa! What da fuck? Carlo Rios is dead?" Cillian stared at Ana and she stared at me.

"You didn't know?" she asked him. "How could you not know?" He shrugged.

"We hear rumors, kinda like wit Liam I guess," he said, turning to me.

"So there's a chance he doesn't know that Carlo is dead?" she said quietly.

"Always a chance. Who's runnin' da show in South America?"

"Patric Arias," Ana said, and Cillian choked again. "Are you guys living under a rock or something; what kind of Vampires are you?" Ana turned toward him exasperated. "Yes Patric's alive. Carlo is dead. Now, is there anyway that you can find out if the coven in South Africa knows of Carlo's death?" she commanded of Cillian and I could see his arousal rise to the surface. He enjoyed domineering women. I sighed and kicked him under the table. He laughed.

"Yeah, I can do a little recon fer ya, but tell me sometin'; who killed Carlo?" Cillian looked at me and I nodded toward Ana. "HOLY SHIT!" Cillian grabbed Ana and pulled her toward him. "DERE'S NO WAY ANA, NO FUCKIN' WAY!" He was tousling her hair. Then he looked at me. "Why didn't ya tell me? We're supposed ta be like broters; I tell ya everyting." He actually sounded hurt. I exhaled.

"Cillian," Ana pulled herself from his hold and smoothed her hair, "would you be in any danger if you checked this out for us? I don't want your life at risk." Ana focused on him and he smiled at her.

"I'll be fine Ana, but yer concern fer my safety is positively arousin'." I kicked him in the groin. He winced. "You two stayin' around here fer a bit?" he asked, breathless. Ana looked at me, I shrugged.

"We'll be in Bray, Cillian, come find us as soon as you know something." Ana stood and slid out of the booth letting Cillian by; she hugged him and his eyes flashed. Christ, she was going to get herself in so much trouble. He shimmered out of the club. I looked at Ana and stood standing to face her.

"I should call Micah don't you think?" I asked as we left. Ana sighed and turned her face to the sky, the rain falling gently on her skin.

"Yeah, let's call him. He'll want to know what we found out about Saden." She started walking.

"What *you* found out about Saden," I corrected her. "I didn't ask a damn thing." I laughed and took her hand.

"I know. What's with you? Losing your edge as a stealth assassin? I thought you were supposed to be a high ranking Vampire; you kinda suck at interrogations." I pulled her against me and held her close.

"Do you really want to challenge my rank and just how I came to be so feared, Ana?" I growled gently into her ear. "Besides, I was trained to kill first and ask questions later; questions aren't my forte." I held her in a soft chokehold and kissed her cheek. I loved having her so close.

"Hey," she said, turning to face me, her eyes serious. "I just want you to know, that if Liam is alive, we'll find him Stephen and we'll fight to bring him home for you and for Lucie," she said, standing to study me. I matched her gaze, believing every word she said.

"I know Ana. Thank you," I said quietly. Her eyes traveled down the length of my body, stopping at my left hand. She smiled.

"You're wearing your ring," she whispered. I raised my hand to look at the band of silver. "Do you like it?" she asked. "It looks nice on you and it seems that Liam got your size right." She was pleased. I grinned at her.

"I love it Ana. I loved it when you first gave it to me and I love it now." I stared at her hard, wondering if I should say it, if it was too soon for us, for her. I still had questions about what she was feeling for me and Nathanial and Patric; I didn't want to overwhelm her.

"I'm glad Stephen," she said, as she started to walk. I sighed, wondering if she would be ready to talk to me. We made it back to my house and I started a kettle of tea and called Micah. Ana sat on the couch next to me, biting her lip. I pressed my finger to her mouth to keep her from making her lips bleed, not that I would have minded. "Let me talk to him," she whispered as I listened to Micah's contemplations about Saden.

"Micah, Ana wants to speak with you. Hold on." I handed the phone to her and watched as her posture suddenly became erect.

"Hi Micah. How's Lucie?" There was a pause and I saw Ana's eyes shift to me. She was still keeping me out; something I also wanted to discuss with her. "I see. And what's his problem?" She sounded agitated. "They don't know right?" she asked and I only assumed she was referring to Nathanial and Patric. She laughed. "Well that was predictable I suppose. Are you ok there with Lucie?" She looked back to me and I studied her. "Hmmm…do you think he'll figure it out?" she asked, starting to bite her lip again. "No Micah, I wouldn't dare underestimate your abilities to divert attention." She laughed again. "But Patric is not one to be kept in the dark for long and neither is Nathanial; I'm happy to help if need be," she said. "Oh I don't know, throw another tea cup at him I guess." She smiled. "Ok. We'll call you as soon as Cillian gets back and if any of that information leads you somewhere, let us know. Love you Micah." She ended the call and sighed. I moved to start a fire.

"How's Lucie?" I asked; it was an innocent enough question and I truly wanted to know.

"She's good. She's happy," she spoke quietly and I sensed she was thinking about something again. "She's with Micah mainly." She looked at me.

"Why?" I asked, moving to sit down next to her.

"Because Nathanial left. He and Patric aren't speaking anymore and he became angry when he thought that Micah was hiding something from him. He's pretty perceptive." She chuckled.

"What happened with Patric?" I was fishing and she knew it. She studied me intently, searching my face and my eyes wondering how

80

much she could trust me with, wondering what it would be that she would say that would make me abandon any chance at restoring our life together; I could see this in her eyes. "Ana, you can tell me; it's ok now, really," I said, touching her face. She exhaled heavily.

"They fought again, about me, over me, who deserves me, who doesn't; I don't know," she said, leaning back against the couch. "They fought and Nathanial left."

"Hmmm…and you fought with Nathanial as well no?" I asked and her eyes widened, but she nodded. "Over what?" I held her hand, tracing my finger along her wrist.

"Over you. Over the fact that I had wanted to help you first before asking why they thought my life was at risk again. I put you first and Nathanial rolled his eyes at me and I lost it," she said, staring at my finger on her arm. "I told him that the next time he needs his life saved not to call me for help," she said. "It wasn't very nice, but he wasn't being very kind either, not after everything I had helped him with; he was being cruel and not choosing to understand me and he was pissed that I was with Patric." She looked away.

"Ahhh…yes Patric. Where are we falling on him again?" I said, turning her face back towards me.

"Nowhere Stephen, we're falling nowhere. I love him and he loves me and we shared a very intimate evening and then I come to find out that both he and Nathanial kept you from knowing whether or not I had survived after you…after you tried to change me and well, I've just had enough of the two of them." Her eyes were angry. I sat back and surveyed her, thinking and taking a chance.

"And what about us Ana; where do you fall when it comes to us?" I had to know. It was killing me having her here back with me and not knowing if she still loved me, if I was a part of her heart that she'd given unselfishly to so many others. She took a deep breath. Suddenly a burst of air swirled around us and Cillian was standing in the room, his hair looking windswept.

"Cheers mates! How are ye?" he asked, collapsing in the chair.

"Cillian that was fast!" Ana sat up. He winked at her.

"Well love, I can go slow if ya like dat better," he chortled.

"Cillian!" I growled at him and he laughed. Ana was shaking her head.

"What did you find out?" she asked, curling up on the sofa.

"Well lots actually," he said, leaning forward. "It appears dat da South African covens have heard da rumors dat Carlo was killed, but it appears dat Patric has managed to convince everyone dat it was he who took Carlo out and not you Ana," Cillian said, his face flush as he stared at her. Christ, I was going to have to keep him behind some sort of barricade. "He knows nothin' about ya or what ya can do but he's a fan of Stephen!" Cillian looked at me.

"What do you mean he's a fan?" I asked, my tone wary.

"He's seen ya fight man; he's seen ya fight in da ring and he's all about ya!" Cillian laughed and I saw Ana stare at me.

"What about my brother; do you know if he's with Saden?" I asked, not wanting to explain how I came to learn such a brutal fighting style to Ana. She didn't know that Carlo had taught me most of what I knew and the rest apparently came very naturally to me.

"Yeah; well I couldn't come out and ask da bretren, but dey did say dat Saden has a new advisor, someone who's helpin' him wit his fightin' business and his oter ventures; he owns a ton of shit, horses and football teams and wineries. His relationship wit Carlo helped him make contacts wit various capitalistic high rollers; he also owns several escort clubs. I could only assume dat his new advisor would be Liam. Saden's not stupid. He knows power and influence when he sees it and your broter is da crown jewel." Cillian sat back. "Liam kept his life and da life of his little girl by agreein' ta help Saden expand his influence. Like I said, Saden's young and he tends ta make some stupid and reckless decisions. I'm sure havin' someone like Liam by his side has only served ta channel his love of learnin' tings from people or vampires. Liam has a lot ta teach." Cillian stood. "I've got ta get ta da club mates, serious date and what not. But if ye need more, ya know where ta find me." He winked again at Ana, snapped his fingers and disappeared.

Ana

Stephen and I were back at my apartment and I was trying to repack for South Africa. We were leaving tomorrow. Stephen had been staring at me the whole day and I knew he was waiting for me to answer his question about how I felt about him and us. I wasn't ready to respond just yet; for some reason I was feeling cautious in revealing

83

just how devastated I was when we were in the hospital and just how much I had grieved over losing the baby and I how I wished he would have been there to help me, to help us. Then there was the whole Belfast fiasco and it was as if the wound would scab and then it would be torn off, leaving it opened and exposed to the infections of sadness and hurt and anger all over again.

"You know you're keeping me out," he spoke quietly from the bed. He was watching me as I assembled some of my clothes.

"I know," I said, not looking at him.

"Why?" He sounded sad and I exhaled slowly.

"Protective mechanism I guess," I spoke honestly.

"You don't trust me," he stated, his eyes closed. I frowned.

"I don't really trust anyone right now Stephen and I haven't for a while now, including myself." I snapped my pack shut and sat on the bed.

"What is it that you don't trust in yourself Ana?" he asked me the question I didn't want to answer; he was asking me if I still loved him. I took his hand and pressed it over my heart.

"I can't answer that right now," I whispered, hoping he would understand. I could answer it though; I could have answered it months ago and I could have answered it when we were in the hospital and I think I could have answered it the first night when we were in the alley about to be attacked; I had fallen in love with him. Those nights that he'd watch me paint, those times when he would sing to me and play his guitar, those times when we'd drive around in his car just laughing and talking about nothing at all. I didn't know it then of course. It was a slow and tender process, a journey just like everything else in my life, but I had let him in and I had let myself heal from Nathanial and I had loved Stephen, been ready to have a life with him, to let Nathanial go and then…then Stephen left me; he couldn't accept my love for Nathanial, that we would always be a part of each other. Stephen chose not to accept me even though I had promised him that I loved him, even though I wanted to have a family with him—he left me, alone and scared just like Nathanial had done. Stephen sat up, his eyes dark and panic flooded my heart. Had my guard slipped? Had he heard?

"Yes Ana, I heard and you're right and you don't have to answer me right now—or ever if that's what you decide," he said softly. "But I love you…and I can never make up for hurting you like I did; there's nothing that I can offer you or say to you that will make those choices I made, ok; they weren't right. I understand if I'm too late, if the chance for us is over." He was staring at me, his eyes brimming with emotion. "I just ask that you try to forgive me, that you not cast me from your life, that you let me still know you." I fingered my amulet as he spoke. All I could do was nod, thinking.

Stephen made me breakfast the next morning and I was glad that he didn't seem to be upset; our conversation last night was a bit awkward. I had asked him to stay. I wanted to be with him and he seemed content to just lie beside me and talk until I fell asleep. I wasn't quite ready to engage in a steady intimate relationship with him; the last night we'd spend together seemed to be just something that we both needed to do. Plus, he'd baited me a bit with my predation issue. Regardless, I was still immensely attracted to Stephen. I missed him, I missed his touch, I missed his fire and the way he made me feel…this was going to be hard.

He called Micah this morning to let him know that we were ready to leave for Soweto and so Micah could notify his friend Kendrick, that we were coming. I wasn't as nervous as I thought I would be or as I probably should be; I thought after Carlo, nothing seemed that intimidating anymore. Stephen grabbed our packs and I quickly scanned his hand; he was still wearing his ring. I swallowed, feeling a bit better. He noticed me staring and shook his head.

"It's not going anywhere Ana," he said, adjusting the straps of my backpack. I nodded and he wrapped his arm around my waist, pulling me close. "Ready?" I gave him the thumbs up sign, he laughed and together we faded away. Stephen had, by far, the most violent shimmer so when we landed outside in the street, I toppled forward having lost my balance during the blast of air and space. He reached out and grabbed the side of my pack pulling me back up towards him just before I hit the ground. I glared at him. "Sorry," he smirked, "but in my defense, I haven't been used to traveling with a partner. I forget that it's hard on Humans to shimmer." I turned my back, but I could tell he was smirking. I rounded on him.

"It's not *hard* on Humans you dope; it's hard when the individual who is transporting us is sloppy and distracted!" I said, knowing that right before we left the apartment, Stephen was thinking about whether or not he should try to kiss me. He laughed and pulled me close to him, taking my face in his hands.

"Hmmm…you're right, I was distracted, but again, I don't really think that's my fault love. You seem to be having difficulty controlling your ability to attract your prey." He laughed and bent his head to kiss me on the cheek. I hadn't known that I was doing anything to affect him; I didn't feel myself get amped up like I did the night we were together. He studied me. "It doesn't always have to be that violent; your desires wax and wane and the way you attract your prey also waxes and wanes, it can be subtle," he said and I saw his eyes lose focus a bit. He cleared his throat and shook his head. "Like that!" He laughed and stepped way from me. He turned around and began surveying the city. "Let's see, I have no idea where we are. I've never been here before…" he murmured. I rolled my eyes and pulled out the map I'd gotten of Soweto the day before. It had a list of all the streets and various landmarks and I scanned over the entries looking for Masakeng Bar. According to the map, we were on the opposite side from where we needed to be. I stepped in front of Stephen and waved the map at him.

"This way," I said, taking his hand and pulling him forward. He chuckled.

"A map, what a novel idea!" He looked at me and winked. We didn't really have a plan to find Liam. Micah recommended that we wait until we spoke with Kendrick before we decided what to do. Apparently, Kendrick was a Demon, who like Patric, had also undergone the Change necessary to become half-Vampire. He was well connected, well respected and he and Micah had known each other for several centuries and Micah trusted him implicitly. It took us an hour to get down to the other side of the township, mainly because Stephen kept stopping to ask if he could buy me things from the various shops and open-air tents. We were in front of a guitar shop when a thought occurred to me.

"Hey," I said, looking at him.

"What?" he replied, eyeing a very beautiful jet, black acoustic guitar in the window.

"Umm...did you...did you eat before we came?" I asked, hearing the oddity of the question, but I couldn't remember if he'd gone out before we left. I was sleeping so deeply these days, I'd never know if he'd managed to take care of his needs, so to speak. He chuckled.

"I'm good Ana," he said, staring at me. I was trying not to contemplate just how he went about feeding; it was making me uncomfortable to think about him with other women and I hoped that maybe perhaps he could leave out the whole sex part when it came to satisfying his hunger. We started walking.

"Are you asking me to be celibate?" He held my hand. "Because that would indicate that you and I are involved in some sort of monogamous relationship." He smiled down at me. I narrowed my eyes at him.

"I was simply asking out of concern," I said.

"No, you were specifically trying not to think about me having sex with other women; you were thinking that you would prefer for me to eliminate the whole sex part of my feeding ritual, were you not?" He was looking straight ahead. Frick! He was reading my mind again. I saw the bar across the street and I started to take off across the road, but Stephen pulled my hand, stopping me. "Were you not?" he asked me again. His eyes were lighter and clearer today. They reminded me of those brochures you get for some tropical island and they show you the best pictures of the sea, sparkling blue-green. He laughed softly still holding my hand and my gaze.

"Yes, yes!" I said. "That's what I was thinking. Now can we go please?" I said, turning away from him and he smirked. The bar was packed and I checked my watch, six in the evening on a Friday. The music was nice and upbeat and there were a ton of tables with people crowded around drinking and eating. If we weren't here on a rescue mission, I might actually let myself enjoy the atmosphere. "Do you know what he looks like?" I was standing next to Stephen watching him scanning the space.

"Nope," he said, smiling.

"Well, do you know what time he was expecting us?"

"Nope." I rolled my eyes.

"Seriously Stephen, perhaps you should consider reentering the realm of teaching again; you suck at this!" I said, staring at him. He laughed.

"Ana? Stephen?" A strong male voice came from behind and I turned to see who I could only assume was Kendrick. He was stunning of course, with long, neatly woven dreadlocks that hung to his waist. He was tall, about the same height as Stephen and his very dark skin and sky blue eyes made a very mystical contrast. He was muscular and his stance spoke to someone who commanded attention and respect. He suddenly laughed and stared at me. "Why thank you Ana; what a wonderful and kind assessment of me," he said, taking my hand and grasping it in his own. His accent sounded Jamaican. "Right you are!" he said, turning to lead us to a small deck where three chairs and drinks were already set. He pulled out my seat and motioned for Stephen to sit next to me. "So, so, how are we?" he asked, pouring a carafe of something that looked like tea.

"We're good, how are you?" I asked him, nodding as he handed me my glass. Kendrick smiled.

"I'm well Ana. I'm well and I'm happy to finally be able to help my friend Micah. He's managed to do so much for me and my family for so many years and I have never felt that I have given him much in return." He shook his head. I touched his arm.

"Micah is not one to expect anything in return for his kindness Kendrick and the fact that he speaks so highly of you and your relationship, says that Micah values you for just who you are, not for what you can give to him." I said, smiling. Kendrick's eyes flashed and widened.

"My goodness Ana, Micah was right about you. We've just met and already I feel as though I have a greater appreciation for myself than I did before." He studied me. I shook my head.

"It's the truth Kendrick." I sipped my drink and I saw Stephen staring at me.

"Well, then I hope I have proven worthy of such truths. I'm here to help you, so let me tell you what I know." He leaned forward and I saw Stephen's body tense. "Your brother and sister in-law are alive."

Stephen exhaled. "They are unharmed and I would venture to guess as far as what could have happened, relatively well taken care of. Liam is of course an asset and his power and reputation have managed to give him quite a role in Saden's coven." So Liam was with Saden, I looked at Stephen; he was rubbing his face. "Liam has been working closely with Saden, offering him guidance on his various business investments and helping him to organize and run his coven effectively; the group is a bit rogue in their behavior and Saden is not the most effective leader." I thought about Cillian's description of Saden behaving like a violent teenager. Kendrick laughed. "Yes, that would be a very apt description Ana, very apt indeed."

"How would you recommend we proceed?" Stephen asked, sitting back in his chair looking extremely powerful, his muscles flexed and his eyes dark. "I'm guessing that my brother has made some sort of arrangement with Saden; he keeps his life and Carmen's and they stay with the new coven?" Stephen's voice was low. Kendrick nodded.

"Yes. Apparently, Saden decided to go after Liam with a bit of a push from Carlo. Saden likes to please and prove himself and Carlo's influence and power were attractive to him. However, Saden is not known for his ability to organize the murder of a powerful vampire such as Liam and his group of assassins that he sent, failed to listen to his orders to just kill your brother; they attacked Carmen and they attempted to attack the little girl, but they underestimated Liam's powers and he managed to kill most of the twelve that were sent. However, two individuals did get a hold of both Carmen and the girl and threatened to take their lives right there. Liam had no choice but to negotiate his way out of such a horrendous situation. He managed to convince the two vampires to take him and Carmen to Saden and to let the girl go. Saden was beside himself having Liam in his presence and having him offer to aid him, it was the jackpot as far as Saden was concerned. Of course, Saden also realized that Carlo had basically instructed him to kill Liam and he had not managed to do so; Saden is a bit of a coward so when rumors came that Carlo was dead, Saden was able to relax and enjoy having so much power at his side." Kendrick looked at me. "We hear that Patric Arias is now in charge of the South American covens; is this true?" I nodded. "Well, Saden really has no more business with those covens and I'm pretty sure that he and Patric have never met, so he knows nothing about you Ana or that you were ever at Carlo's ranch. We keep to ourselves a bit here; it's a populated country, a big continent, there's plenty of our own chaos that we deal with on a daily basis." He smiled and reached into his breast pocket withdrawing what appeared to be a pair to tickets. "These are for tonight. Saden has an underground fighting ring; it makes millions and it's very well received. It's mostly vampires, but he realizes that there is a certain Human audience that appreciates violence and he has slackened his low tolerance for the species and allowed for them to watch and bet. The fights are not between Humans and vampires, they are between vampires only." Kendrick turned to Stephen. "I'm not sure that Ana should attend Stephen; does she know?" They were having a silent conversation about something while Kendrick was speaking out loud.

"Would she be in danger if she came?" Stephen asked.

"No. There will be plenty of Humans there; she will be fine. Saden does not know that you are here and arriving this evening to one of his fights, will for sure get his attention. He's a big fan of yours I hear." Kendrick laughed. That was the second time I heard someone say that about Stephen, what the hell kind of fighter was he? Kendrick looked at Stephen and back to me. "She has no idea does she?" He smiled and shook his head. I glared at Stephen; he should tell me things. "I think the best way to proceed is to let Saden come to you, let him enjoy your presence and use his enthusiasm to get him to invite you to the house. I'm sure that won't be an issue. That way you can get a better idea of what sort of arrangement he has with Liam and you can assure him that you are not there to try to take Liam away, and that you were always under the impression that your brother was presumed dead, but that you can see that he is well and happy." Kendrick poured another glass of tea.

"What about Ana; he's not a fan of Humans, how will she be received if we go the house?" Stephen seemed worried. Kendrick stared at me.

"I think…I think that Ana will prove very intriguing to Saden. I think her relationship to you will be a bit baffling to him, but he knows very little about love and sacrifice; he's young and unfocused. He's not aware of anything that Ana can do." Kendrick's eyes found mine. I guessed Micah must have told him about my ability with fire and possibly about my rare blood types. "Hmmm…yes he mentioned those things to me. Saden likes to learn; he enjoys seeing what others are capable of and challenging himself to acquire such talents for himself. I would keep your powers to yourself for the time being, although they may prove a useful bargaining tool for you in the future. Saden has never known a Human to have abilities that far exceed what any Demon or vampire can possibly display and neither have I!" Kendrick chuckled. I thought that description of what I could do was a bit off; I was still Human and I was quite sure that I wouldn't be much of a match against that many Vampires or Demons in most situations; I had just gotten lucky so far.

Stephen snorted and frowned at me. "The fights begin at eleven; if you would prefer that I accompany you instead of Ana, please call me and I will be happy to do so." Kendrick wrote his number on the back of one of tickets and I was wondering just why neither of them seemed to think that I should be attending these fights. "Here too is the address of the guest house that I have you arranged for you. My brother and his wife are traveling abroad and they have offered you their accommodations. I think that you should find everything that you need but if not, please let me know." He winked and stood. "I am also in contact with Micah and I have made him aware of your arrangements for this evening. He's asked that you call once you have returned from the event this evening." Stephen nodded and stood extending his hand.

"Thank you Kendrick; you've been most helpful and we are grateful." I stood as well.

"Of course Stephen. I'm here for whatever you need. Please contact me as well when you have returned tonight and we can make a plan for whatever is to come next. I promised Micah that I would keep you safe and that I would guide you as much as possible through whatever offerings Saden makes. I have known him since his inception as a vampire and I can assure you, he will not want to harm either of you while you are here." Kendrick nodded to me and I stepped forward to give him a hug. "Well that was quite nice; thank you Ana!" He laughed and hugged me back. "I'll look forward to hearing from you tonight." He turned and melted back into the crowd.

Chapter Four

Nathanial

I knew that Micah had been hiding something from me; I sensed it deep in his mind, something about Ana. I combed through her apartment, pulling out clothes and thumbing through papers she had on the kitchen table. A large painting hung on the wall by her bed and I stared at my own face and my brother's looking down on me as I tossed her belongings about the room. I found a man's shirt on the bed and I placed it to my nose. Stephen. I tossed it aside wondering what she was doing back in Dublin and why she was with him again. We had worked hard at avoiding his calls and summons about Ana and both Patric and I had agreed not to tell him any information about her condition after Carlo's death. Perhaps that shirt was from an earlier time. I tried to calm myself and not let my imagination fuel my anger. I needed to focus. I grabbed her laptop off the kitchen table and opened the screen. A map of South Africa flooded the window and I scrolled through the site. She'd been researching the country and the various townships, but why? Micah had assured me that our theories about Vampires in South Africa being after her, were unfounded and I believed him, yet I knew that he was keeping me out of his mind, there was information he didn't want me to know. I checked the date for when she'd searched for this particular site and saw it was just yesterday. Was she still here? I had already been to Stephen's and found nothing except a few items of her clothing. Again, I told myself that those could have been from some point earlier in their time together; it didn't mean anything. My brother had taken the stand of letting Ana go, letting her live her life and he was hoping that she would eventually come to her senses and choose him to be with, but he was content to let her be; he wasn't scared of losing her, of not being able to have her with him. He was under the impression that no matter what Ana decided to do with her life, that he would always be a part of her in some capacity. I was not willing to subscribe to such stupidity. Ana and I belonged together and I would make her see that; she would come to understand just how much she needed me and I how I knew her, how I could please her. She would realize that everything she could ever want, I was willing to give to her.

I stood, pacing around the room, my eyes retuning to the canvas near her bed. I faced the painting and traced my fingers over her face, touching her lips and her cheeks. He had painted this I was sure and I found myself glaring at the image of his face, the ring she'd given him hanging like a curse around his throat. Anger surged in my blood and I gripped the painting, tearing it into pieces

Stephen

I was in no way comfortable having Ana attend these fights this evening. She didn't know how vampires killed one another and I was sure that neither Patric nor Nathanial had spoken to her about how we'd finished what she'd started with Carlo. Kendrick had spoken to me silently about this underground ring and it was brutal to the ultimate degree—they fought to kill. I had participated in such a venture before I had come to train with Carlo. I was new to my

Afterlife and wanted to test my powers. Liam had been the one to lower the hammer on me when he found out, proceeding to show me just how violent vampires could be when pushed. He scared the shit out of me and I stopped fighting in those rings. I had however, been undefeated, a point that didn't seem to impress Liam in the slightest.

I was currently surveying our living arrangements. The house was small, but cozy and looked as though it was used as a hostel of some sorts. There were various beds arranged in the different rooms and several bathrooms scattered over the three floors with two kitchens, one on the first floor and one on the second. I climbed the stairs to find Ana, who was trying to figure out which room was ours. She was standing in the doorframe of a bedroom. I peered over her shoulder.

"Well, clearly they don't anticipate couples sleeping here." She laughed. I could see one single bed in the room and an adjoining door with an additional single bed. The furniture looked to be bolted to the floor. There was a huge bathroom connecting the two rooms. I hadn't noticed any other sleeping arrangements that would allow Ana and me to share a bed. That sucked. She threw her pack on the bed and sat down. "So, what's up with this fight this evening; why were the two of you so concerned about me going?" She had her hands behind her, pressing her palms into the mattress. I went to sit beside her.

"These fights are not what you are used to seeing Ana," I said quietly but sternly. I wanted her to understand what it was that I was saying. "They are between vampires and the little display you had the pleasure of experiencing with me the night that I attacked you, that's the tame side of things." I raised my eyebrows at her.

"Ok, so they're brutal. How brutal?" I shook my head.

"No Ana, they're not just brutal; what happens at these fights, it's beyond most people's comprehension and I was stunned to hear that any Human would want to watch such acts of violence." She stared at me.

"You mean they're fighting to kill each other," she said, resting her head back on the bed.

"That's saying it diplomatically." I watched her chest rise and fall as she breathed.

"So what, do they decapitate each other or something?" She turned to look at me.

"Sometimes, but that's pretty mundane." I leaned onto my arm, my body facing her. She sighed.

"Well, can you tell me when not to look or something? I mean you've fought before right? Apparently you're quite the guy in the ring." She smiled. I shook my head.

"I guess I can tell you, but things happen pretty fast. I might not see it coming myself Ana." I moved to run my fingers over her stomach; I couldn't help myself. She looked at me, her eyes darkening.

"Well I'm not staying here. I'm going with you, so I guess you'll just have to do your best to anticipate what's happening." She exhaled and I slid her shirt up gently, wanting to feel her skin. I let my scent release, beating her to the punch. I wanted her. She stared at me. "I thought we decided not to engage in such criminal acts until you felt more comfortable with your sexual aggressiveness." She laughed softly, but I could see my affect on her desire beginning to rise.

"Oh, I'm comfortable, especially when I'm the one in control," I whispered, watching her breath coming in more shallow beats.

"You didn't seem to mind me having control the other night. In fact, I distinctly remember you begging me to do certain things to you." Her tone turned sensual and suddenly I could smell her fragrance. I laughed and scanned the room. I didn't think that Kendrick's family would appreciate us destroying their home to fuel our more violent sexual appetites.

"And what did you think about that? Did you like me telling you what to do, begging you?" My own tone suddenly turned rough and I felt my teeth elongate and become slick with my desire. I bent my face over her and my eyes shifted; I felt the pupils contract and change and the colors in the room became deeper and clearer. She studied me, biting her lip. She traced her fingers over my exposed fangs and I tilted my head back, letting her run her hands over my throat.

"I enjoy you when you're like this," she said, pulling her mouth to my throat, her own teeth grazing along my flesh. They felt sharp.

"One of us is going to have to surrender control here, otherwise it could get very, very rough." I growled and pinned her hands over her head. Clearly I wanted the dominating role this time. I rather enjoyed that side to myself and I'd never been with anyone that I cared enough about, to have it displayed. In some ways, Ana was a blank slate, sexually; she'd only gotten so far in her experimentations, even with me and I couldn't help but be enchanted with the idea of introducing her to some more adventurous forays. Many times, I had fantasized about Ana and myself having a bit of a Dominant/submissive relationship, but only sometimes and only with her understanding that she was still in control over herself and not in any way, a victim. The notion of teaching her things, showing her what she might like and enjoy, it made me deliriously happy and aroused; we just had a few hurdles left, a few more bricks in the wall that needed to come down and then maybe, maybe she would be ready. I turned my attention back to her.

"I know," she purred, answering my previous musings and flipped me on my back in one motion. I growled loudly and grabbed her hair, pulling her head back exposing her neck. I could smell both of our scents in the air, but Ana's seemed the more dominant, not surprising considering where she was now sitting. My mind darkened and the only thing that I seemed to be able to think about was pleasuring her; not that that was unusual for me, but I actually felt a deep commanding desire to do whatever she wanted, to make her come as powerfully as I could and watch while it happened. I pushed her up and moved so that she was on her hands and knees. I pushed her jeans down spreading her legs. I slid under her, positioning myself so that her groin was directly over my mouth and her arms were over my head. She tossed her hair and head back and I traced my tongue between her legs, feeling her heat, her liquid fire. She was already quite aroused. She widened her hips allowing for me to suck more of her, which I gladly did. My own body heaved with passion and I grew hard; I started to thrust my hips. She was moaning and I snarled as I watched her face and her body experiencing me. I loved tasting her like this; it made her so wet and so aroused and I enjoyed fucking her with my tongue. She was gasping, her body quivering each time I penetrated. I sucked the tip of her most sensitive area, flicking and swirling my tongue, letting her writhe against my lips. She groaned loudly as I grabbed her hips and pulled her back and forth against my mouth. God I loved this spot; it was so sweet and I could tease her with my tongue, licking and sucking harder and softer until she was begging me to finish her off. I was pulsing hard and my thighs were contracting with my need to come. Watching her move and groan was captivating and my body responded making me thrust fast. The pulse in her groin was thundering next to me and I smelled her blood. She was still Human to me and the desire to drink from her was running along side my desire to have her come in my mouth. I wanted them both. I felt my fangs seek her flesh, but I didn't want to move from giving her what she wanted. I snarled and bit her, lapping up the blood as it trickled down from between her legs. I put my entire mouth over her and pulled, hard. She screamed out and spread her legs wider, now fully on her knees. She was caressing herself, running her hands over her breasts and through her hair. Jesus; I couldn't tear my eyes from watching her. Some very heated desires were surfacing and I suddenly knew what I wanted to watch. I released the more potent version of my scent and waited for it to hit her. She groaned.

"What do you want Stephen? Anything." she whispered, my lips still taking blood from her. I growled and pushed her down on her back; she was still writhing as I kept my hand between her legs.

"Anything?" My tone was hypnotic and I could see that my eyes were affecting her, commanding her.

"Yes," she said, touching my hand as I pushed my fingers deep inside. She moaned. I took her hand and guided it down replacing mine. She gasped as she felt herself.

"I want to watch Ana. I want to watch you come without me," I said, moving her hand for her. I shifted to the side and started kissing her stomach and breasts, pressing her hand so she knew not to stop. I removed my clothes and ran myself up and down her body, as she massaged herself. I was so hard at this point that my release was sure to be violent. I put myself in her mouth and watched as she both sucked on me and aroused herself. I growled, thrusting as deeply as I could . I didn't want her to be distracted so I rolled to the side and let my eyes roam over her body as she opened her legs. I could see everything and I spread my own legs letting my body react to the visual. I groaned and contracted my stomach muscles, listening to the sounds of her as she massaged herself. She was too good. She knew her body and knew what I would want to hear and see. My legs stiffened as I watched her fingers caress rapidly over the spot I had bitten, she was releasing more blood. I pushed up and let myself release as I watched her, my eyes never leaving her body. I came again, the force of the action pushing me back against the mattress. She screamed and moaned and I saw her body tremble and her legs contract and I snarled watching her orgasm, I kept her hand between her thighs and started to move it rapidly for her. I wanted to watch again.

"Faster Ana." I gasped. "I want you to scream." I growled and pushed her hand away, taking over. My need for her was too great. I moved deeply and quickly as her breath heaved and my own body surged ready to penetrate her. I was on my knees as she remained under me

102

and I began to run myself over her, touching and teasing with the very tip of myself. I was pulsing forcefully and I ached, the pain fueling my orgasm.

"Stephen," she gasped and I watched as she started to pull me into her, moving me expertly and making me tremble. I pushed myself away from her; I still wanted to see her climax without me, she was so sensual and her groans were making me so aroused. I put her hands back down between her legs and stood over her, watching and keeping my scent releasing so she would do what I wanted.

"Deeper Ana, go deeper," I commanded as she moved her fingers around herself, and I laughed and snarled. She gasped and my eyes took in her body as she led it to peak and heave and finally come. She screamed out again and I growled low as I listened to her pant and slow her rocking body. I closed my eyes and breathed deep, smelling her release and her blood. I lunged, wanting to feel how wet she was; I shoved myself between her legs, empting myself as I grunted and thrashed back and forth. I groaned softly, withdrawing slowly from her. I moved my hands over her body, calming her and letting her come down slowly. She was breathing hard. I crashed down beside her on my side and watched as her nervous system steadied.

"You hypnotized me," she whispered, licking her lips. "You've never done that before." She turned to look at me. I stroked her hair, the images of what I just witnessed filling my mind. We needed to do that more often.

"I'm sorry, did you not like that?" I asked, bending close to her, feeling my teeth return to normal. I kissed her deeply. "Because for me, well, that was quite a fantasy of mine." I laughed and ran my tongue over her bottom lip.

"I like it better when you do it." She smiled at me. "It's more fun." She rolled over on her stomach. I laughed and ran my finger down the length of her spine. She groaned.

"What?" I said, watching her. Her eyes closed.

"I can still smell you." She bit her lip.

"Woops, sorry!" I said, and quickly gathered myself, restricting my scent.

"So that was new for us," she said, grinning. "Are you going to blush over that as well or are you feeling more comfortable asking for what you want now?" She smirked at me.

"Hmmm…if you'll agree to do that every time we're together, I'll be as comfortable as you want," I said, pressing my lips to her ear.

"Every time? Won't you get a bit bored; I mean once you've seen it doesn't it lose its erotic charm?" She frowned.

"Not at all. Besides, I can think of several more ways to experience you like that and not be on the bed." I bit her earlobe thinking of watching her in the shower, watching her with her legs spread, bound and tied, watching her sitting in my chair at home. I could come up with dozens of scenarios that would make me very, very turned on and then of course there was the whole anal sex thing. We hadn't even dared to approach that, but I bet with a little coaching, Ana would find just how deeply pleasurable it could be. I glanced at my watch and noticed it was already ten. "We need to get ready to go," I said, feeling disappointed and slightly anxious as Ana rolled and sat up.

"Umm...can you clean this up?" she asked, motioning to the bloodied and wet bedspread. I grinned at her and waved my hand making any evidence of our coupling, disappear. "Excellent." She hopped off the bed and started pulling out a long sleeve shirt and a pair of jeans from her pack.

"Are you sure you want to go?" I asked, searching through my own bag for a change of clothes. I couldn't help but watch as she slid up a new pair of underwear and fastened a very nice black bra around her chest. Christ. Was it possible that I was ready to have her again? Could I already be that turned on? I needed to get myself under control. It had always been like that with Ana though, from the first time I had felt her skin at the concert we'd been to, since the night at the club when she'd first offered me her blood; always, I was desiring her, wanting to pleasure her, needing her. I cleared my throat and forced myself to concentrate on getting dressed.

We arrived just before eleven to what looked like a giant pyramid shaped warehouse. There were hundreds of cars in the open field and tons of Humans pouring into the base of the structure, Ana looked at me.

"Are you ever going to tell me what kind of fighter you used to be or still are?" she asked as I took her hand.

"No," I said, smiling slightly.

"Great. So along with your new Vamped out sexual behavior, you've suddenly decided to stop communicating. Do they go hand in hand or something?" We approached the doors and I handed her one of the tickets. I felt slightly amped up, like I used to get before my own fights, but I was also on edge. I wondered if Liam would be here. We filtered through with the crowd into a large concourse where tons of liquor and food was being sold. I couldn't remember the last time that Ana had eaten; we didn't get food while we were with Kendrick, she must be starving. I looked at her.

"Are you hungry?" I asked frowning.

"Nah. I brought a banana," she said, patting her pack. That wasn't exactly what I considered a substantial dinner. I'd have to do better making sure she ate tomorrow. I took her hand and searched the concourse for our seats. They turned out to be on the very top, which for a vampire fight was the prime location considering our ability to fly through the air. We were also up close, the first level near the ring; that was not necessarily such a good place to be as you couldn't avoid seeing any of the action. I sighed, my body tensing. I led Ana into our row. We were the only two seats, with no one on either side of us. I also could see the entire arena, not just a coincidence on Kendrick's part I was sure. I scanned the place quickly looking for Liam; I could see every face in the crowd perfectly.

"Hey, do you know what Saden looks like?" Ana turned to me. I turned around in my seat to look behind me.

"No," I said frowning.

"Well maybe he'll have some sort of entourage." She settled back in her seat and took out a baggie with some pretzels and a banana. She should eat now rather than during the fight. I was really not happy to have her here. This was one of the worst possible arrangements for her to be in. I didn't want her to see exactly what kind of being I truly was, a being that I had chosen to become. I was afraid she may look at me differently and not in a good way. Music began blaring from loud speakers and a line of scantily clad Human women came walking into the ring, Ana leaned over to me. "Now I see what the draw is." She munched on her food and smiled. I shook my head. I turned to look back behind me again and then to the side. No Liam. "Relax, we'll find him," Ana whispered. "Besides, you don't know if Saden's already spotted you; don't look so nervous," she said, keeping her eyes forward. She was right. I needed to calm down. "You wanna pretzel?" She smiled and squeezed my hand. I would marry her tonight if that wouldn't totally freak her out. She was my best friend and I loved her more than my own existence.

The announcer arrived and we listened to the introductions of the fighters. I knew one; I had fought him myself once. I'd kicked his ass. More music and then the bell rang. I watched as the competitors launched themselves in the air, ready to go.

Ana

I really didn't want to watch the fight, so I tried to keep my attention on the crowd. I couldn't see as well as Stephen, but I figured that if

Liam was anywhere near us, I might be able to spot him. Stephen was leaning far in his seat and it appeared that he was actually enjoying himself. Perhaps I did not want to know about his past as a fighter; it was just enough to be able to wrap my head around a Stephen with fangs. The music was so loud that it competed with the cheers from the crowd and it made it hard to decipher what was happening with the fight if you weren't inclined actually watch. I took to studying Stephen for a bit. His hair was longer and he was keeping it tied back in a thick ponytail at the base of his neck. His highlights glistened even under unflattering florescent lighting. He'd been pale when I first stumbled upon him, but over the last week his normal burnished glow had returned and it was richer in tone making his eyes dazzle against his darker skin. He looked more rugged and a bit rougher around the edges than usual, which was saying a lot considering that Stephen was usually quite rugged already. I thought about the painting he'd done for me, and just how he'd actually depicted my image. It really didn't look anything like me and I was sure that he was being generous with my physicality. I started to feel somewhat bummed out. I couldn't believe that I had ever been comfortable enough with him to let him see me naked. Maybe I shouldn't be doing that for a while. I frowned, thinking about all the intimate things we'd experienced together and just how battered and scared my body was now; it wasn't a pretty sight I was sure, and all those girls out there near the ring didn't have any scars, at least none that I could see…ugh, I was so gross. Stephen turned to look at me, his eyes dark, he looked mad.

"I swear to god Ana, if you ever keep me from being with you, from touching you; if you ever prevent us from being intimate because you have such a distorted perception of yourself, I will haul your ass into

counseling so fast you won't even have time to take a single breath."
His voice was low, but I could actually hear him perfectly over the
insanely pounding music. "You are the most beautiful, stunning, exotic
creature that I have ever known and had we not had to come to this
place tonight, I would have been quite pleased to show you just what
you do to me by being exactly who you are, scars and all." He
sounded like he was scolding me and I was trying not to laugh. "I don't
see a single thing about this discussion that's remotely humorous
young lady." Young lady? I burst out laughing. Unfortunately, my
gaze turned toward the ring and that's when I saw it. I screamed as I
watched one of the fighters hold down the other in mid-air, right next
to us, reach to his opponent's chest and rip his still beating heart right
through his sternum. Black blood sprayed everywhere and before
Stephen could force me into his chest, I saw the fighter hold the heart
up and plunge his fangs deep into the still beating muscle. The
defeated player exploded in a shower of blood and bones, his brain
seeping from his skull before erupting into a blast of fire and smoke. I
puked and the crowd cheered. "Ana!" Stephen was leaning forward
in his seat, his hand on my back. "Jesus Christ." He sounded upset; I
hoped not with me. He sighed loudly.

"Napkin," I called to him. "In my pack." He grabbed my bag from the
back of the chair and I heard him rifling through the pockets. He
handed me a tissue and I wiped my mouth, trying to steady my
breathing. I felt utterly terrified. Was this who Stephen was? Was Liam
like this too? Carmen? I was overwhelmed. I sat up slowly. Stephen
was staring at me, his gaze intent and he studied me deeply, reading
my fear.

"You're frightened," he said quietly. Someone suddenly appeared behind him and I looked away from Stephen to the Vampire who had joined our seats.

"Excuse me. Mr. Byrne? If you wouldn't mind coming with me, Mr. Vale would like a moment." Stephen stood and offered me his hand. "I'm sorry, not the Human, just you. You'll be back before the next fight begins; she's fine here." The Vampire looked at me and I nodded. Stephen looked torn.

"It's fine Stephen. I'm fine," I said, quietly, trying to quell so many different kinds of fear at once. He bent to kiss me on the cheek and he whispered in my ear.

"I love you Ana and I don't want you to be frightened by me ever. I'm sorry you had to see that. Stay put please." I nodded and tried to swallow feeling slightly shell shocked.

Nathanial

I had waited at her apartment for hours; she wasn't coming back and I could only assume that she'd left Ireland. The only lead I had was the site she'd pulled up on South Africa and I was debating if I should try to track her there or if I should just continue to wait for her to return. I was sure that she'd probably told Micah of her whereabouts; she'd want to keep tabs on Lucie and would want to help should Lucie need her. I started to think.

Stephen

Christ, Ana was terrified of me now. I knew it. I knew she shouldn't have come. This was horrible. One of my worst nightmares was to have her afraid of me, afraid of being close to me, afraid of what I was, what I could become if necessary. I felt sick. The escort led me to the opposite side of the arena from Ana and I turned to look for her. I could see her perfectly. She was sitting in my seat and she'd pulled out a book.

"Mr. Byrne?" The escort touched my shoulder and I continued to follow him down to the lowest row. There was an entire group of people and vampires sitting in every seat down the aisle; they were drinking and eating and women were everywhere. I scanned down the row and there, sitting in the last seat looking as calm and strong as he ever did, was Liam. He turned and our eyes locked and I saw shock and terror move over his face.

"Stephen Byrne!" someone shouted and pulled on my shoulder. I shifted my gaze to who I could only assume was Saden. "Christ, I can't believe you're here. I've been a big fan of yours man, big fan!" I shut my mind and surveyed him closely. He was slightly shorter than me, muscular, very tan, with blond hair that was cut in a similar fashion to my own. He had dark green eyes and a dazzling smile. Something about him reminded me of a surfer, someone who you would see out in the States or in Australia. His clothing reflected my assessment. He was wearing distressed jeans, various leather bracelets and a loose white shirt opened at the throat revealing a hemp type necklace that held a single stone of turquoise. His enthusiasm reminded me of Cillian. "I can't fucking believe it man, sit down and have a drink. What do you want?" he asked, motioning for a bikini-clad woman to come over.

"Scotch," I said, thinking that Ana wouldn't mind considering the circumstances.

"Of course scotch; of course!" he chortled, turning to face me. "Man! What are you doing here? I can't believe that you've come here to my little arena. Tell me please!" He sipped his beer. I was an excellent liar, another skill that Ana had yet to see me utilize.

"My girlfriend was out on a bit of a voyage and I asked her to come and meet me here. I've been underground as of late and I had heard that my brother might have been residing here. I haven't spoken to him in a very long time." That was a bit of a risk, to talk about Liam, but I wanted to gage his reaction.

"NO FUCKIN WAY!" Saden slapped me on the back. "Your brother is here! He's here right now!" Not quite what I was expecting. Saden stood up. "Liam! Liam get the hell over here, you are not going to believe this!" Saden was just shy of jumping up and down and I was starting to see why Cillian had compared him to a teenager. I was not quick to forget that Cillian had also said Saden was a very violent vampire, one who liked to instigate chaos. I watched my brother stand and make his way down the aisle, moving gracefully and full of power. I looked back to Saden and I could see how much in awe he was of Liam.

112

"Stephen." Liam smiled at me, but I could tell that he was pissed and surprised.

"Man! How long has it been since you've seen each other?" Saden asked, and I sensed an undercurrent that he was fishing for information. I answered quickly.

"Years," I said, gazing at Liam. "It's been years. I had been hearing rumors that you might have been killed." I searched his face. He looked mentally stable at least.

"That's right man! Carlo Rios wanted him taken out, but we managed to strike up a deal of sorts!" Saden was staring at Liam. "But he's not dead! No way!" So that was the story he was using, that he had protected my brother from Carlo. That made sense; it made Saden seem more powerful and more in control, especially against someone such as Carlo. "Stephen, are you still fighting?" Saden asked as he handed me my drink and motioned for Liam to sit down. I sipped from my glass, the scotch burning my throat; it was beyond strong.

"Not so much anymore. I've taken up some different outlets I guess you could say." I looked at Saden and he shook his head.

"Man you were the best. When I saw you in New York, you were the best." He turned to another of his guests and spoke. "This guy could tear the heart out before the other dude even saw it coming; the thing would still be attached and Stephen would just hold him there letting him see what was about to happen. Amazing shit!" Saden smiled at me and I tried not to gag. Liam was staring at me. That was information that Ana never needed to know. "So, I'm having a big blowout tomorrow man, at the house; you need to come! People will totally fucking trip if you show up! Is your girlfriend with you? You should bring her for sure! Human or vamp?" he asked me.

"What?" I didn't know what he was asking me.

"Your girlfriend! Is she Human or vamp?" He was smiling at me over his beer.

"Human," I said, not quite sure if that was the most accurate description for Ana as of late.

"Jesus Christ! No way! Not me man. I can only fuck'em and suck'em; I can't commit to them!" Well this should be a fun party, I thought sarcastically. Ana was sure to never speak to me again after this entire trip. "But if you like her, then she must be hot." Saden was continuing to speak. "I'm right outside of Soweto, just a few miles from here actually; you won't be able to miss the place. Nine tomorrow! Man I can't believe that you're here. Good shit man, good shit."

"Saden, would you mind if I spoke with my brother for a moment?" My voice was even, but I really wasn't asking him and he knew it.

"Sure, sure man, catch up. I don't need him!" He laughed, but I could see him watching me as I stood. I shook his hand. "Tomorrow night!" I nodded and moved down the aisle with Liam behind me. He was going to kill me, I was sure. Christ, there was so much he didn't know, about Ana, about her blood, about Carlo, and about me, and what I had to do to save her. I sighed. He touched me on the shoulder and instantly we were swept away from the crowd. We landed outside. He turned to face me and I was ready for him, ready to defend why I was here, but upon seeing his face, upon realizing that my brother, my only family, was still alive, I reached to embrace him. I was twelve again and I wanted things to be ok, I wanted to protect him like he'd protected me for our entire existence, both human and otherwise.

"Stephen," Liam spoke softly, pulling me gently back, the rush of emotion bringing tears to my eyes. He shook his head and held my face. "Stop now. It's ok. I'm ok," he said sighing. "Is Ana with you?" He sounded slightly shocked. I nodded. "Do I even want to know what the two of you are doing here?" he asked, but immediately his eyes became worried and I saw that he was thinking about Lucie.

"Lucie's fine Liam; she's with Micah." He nodded and started pacing. I was about to elaborate when he cut me off.

"We don't have time for details Stephen. Why are you here?" I thought that was kind of a stupid question.

"Micah sent us. Well, he actually sent Ana and he asked me to come along. He never suspected that you were killed and he thought you might be in trouble," I said, watching him move back and forth in front of me. "Liam, what are you doing with this idiot; you could totally take him out, he's a child!" I said, wondering exactly was going on here. Liam waved his hand.

"I don't have time right now Stephen." He was thinking. "Micah sent you?" he asked.

"Yeah," I replied. Liam shook his head.

"Have you spoken to him since you've arrived?"

"We've spoken to his friend Kendrick and we're supposed to call Micah when we get back tonight," I said, holding his shoulder.

"Kendrick! My god he had quite a few of his bases covered didn't he?" Liam said. I could feel my agitation beginning to rise.

"Liam! Are you in trouble?" I asked, turning him toward me. "And where's Carmen?" Liam waved me off gently.

"Carmen is fine Stephen; she's back at the house. I'm fine as well, all things considered." He looked at me. "How's Ana? No, never mind, we don't have time and I want to make sure that you are able to tell me everything about her and Carlo. You'll need to come tomorrow, both of you, but you need to keep Ana with you at all times—all times." He looked at me, sensing my hesitation at wanting to bring her at all.

"I'm pretty sure that after tonight, Ana won't want to be anywhere near me again," I mumbled. Liam held my shoulders.

"She saw did she?" He searched my face.

"She threw up." I shook my head.

"Ana is a remarkable being Stephen and she has loved you in spite of your worse attributes that you have allowed to surface. She'll understand, but this might be an opportune time to allow her to know you a bit more," he said. Even with his current situation, Liam was still able to guide me, to give solace, to be my brother. "Always Stephen." He smiled at me. "Make sure you tell Micah that I appreciate all of his efforts," Liam said as we walked back toward the entrance. We moved back up to the concourse.

"Hey," I called after him. He turned. "This summer Ana took Lucie on a boat and they apparently had quite the journey; Italy, Spain, Greece…they spent almost the entire summer together," I said grinning. Liam closed his eyes.

"Tell Ana that I look forward to thanking her for saving my daughter a second time in both of their short lives." He waved and shimmered back to Saden.

I made my way back to Ana, hoping that she wouldn't still be too freaked out. The second fight was about to start and I wanted to get out of there as soon as possible. I saw her reading and I went to stand behind her bending my head to her ear. "Let's go," I whispered and she jumped. I stood and removed her pack from off the seat and waited for her. She wasn't looking at me. I led us outside and gently touched her shoulder shimmering us away. We arrived back to the house and immediately Ana went upstairs. She didn't speak. She was upset, but not about what she saw tonight; she was upset about something that I never thought about, something that I never even contemplated because it didn't matter to me. I exhaled and climbed the stairs. Her door was closed so I went around to my side and stretched out on the bed. She'd shut the adjoining door and I could hear her crying. I wished she would talk to me. I could reassure her, tell her that it didn't matter; it would never matter. I heard the water running in the bathroom and listened as she rifled through her pack for her toiletries, brushing her teeth and washing her face. I smiled; I loved that she was Human. To me she was like a superhero, my superhero. The door slid open and she stood in the frame wearing one of my long sleeve shirts and her sweats. I sat up and stared at her.

"May I come in?" she asked. I laughed. She was an incredibly silly superhero.

"Of course," I said, shifting on the bed. She scooted herself next to me and laid her head on my chest. Immediately I relaxed; she wasn't frightened anymore, not about me at least.

"I'm going to die," she said quietly. "And you're not, unless someone rips your heart out apparently," she said. "You even tried to change me and my stupid blood wouldn't even let you do that." She sounded so sad. I smoothed her hair. "It's like I can't do anything right; I can't even be a Vampire or a mother…"She was staring at her ring. I breathed deeply and bent my head to her ear.

"None of those things have anything to do with who you are as a soul in this world Ana, and none of those things matter in the slightest when it comes to how I feel about you or how Patric and Nathanial, Micah and Liam, Kai or your Noni, feel about you. Do you think that makes us love you any less? Do you think it makes me not want to be with you? Your life transcends blood Ana, it transcends flesh and bone and metal and jewels. It's your heart and your soul that all of us long to be close to. It's your passion and your conviction and your internal power. It's your willingness to believe in other people's capacity to redeem themselves and it is your love that transcends any physical ability that you may or may not have." She hugged me.

"Thank you Stephen; you are very kind." She smiled up at me and I rolled my eyes.

"You didn't believe a word I said did you?" I frowned at her. She laughed.

"Some," she said, pressing her face into my chest and breathing deeply. "Did you see Liam?" she asked, moving so that she was lying next to me. I sighed.

"Yes. He looks better than I expected. Shit!" I leaned forward pushing her off the bed accidently. "Oh Ana! I'm sorry!" I said, grabbing her arm and catching her before she landed on the ground.

"No worries!" She stood and crawled back onto the mattress.

"I forgot to call Kendrick and Micah," I said, pulling out my phone. I dialed Micah's number. He answered on the first ring.

"Stephen," he spoke into the phone, but suddenly I heard his voice in my head. *Nathanial is here and he's not quite himself. If you have located Liam just answer yes and I will call you in the morning.* The voice faded and I felt chills up my spine.

"Yes," I answered and then the phone went dead. I held it in my hands staring.

"Stephen? What is it?" Ana stood in front of me.

"It wasn't a good time to talk," I said quietly. "Something about Nathanial not being himself." I looked at her. She frowned.

"Well that seems about right. He doesn't want Nathanial or Patric to know what we're doing so maybe Micah thinks that Nathanial is suspicious or something." She shrugged.

"Maybe," I said, but there was an undercurrent of distress in Micah's tone and I wondered just what was happening with Nathanial yet again

119

and why wouldn't Micah want Nathanial or Patric to know about Liam or where Ana and I were? I was beginning to feel slightly on edge. Upon calling Kendrick, he'd advised us to stick with the original story that Liam and I had been out of touch for a very long time; that meant that Ana would have to pretend to not know Liam that well and that she'd agreed to meet here during her travels. I was recounting all of this as I watched her dress for the party later the next evening.

"Stephen, I got it," she said, pulling on her jeans. She'd seemed to be feeling a bit better about the events that transpired last night and her mind apparently was on Liam. "Do you honestly think that you and Liam will be able to catch up? I mean, won't people be able to listen to you even if you don't speak to one another?" She flipped her head over, shaking out her curls. I slid on my boots.

"Liam and I are well versed in communicating with walls fully in tact," I replied. It was one of the first skills that Liam showed me how to manipulate and apparently, the closer the siblings, the easier and more powerful the mental connection could be. I stood and watched as Ana put on some very scandalous lipstick; it stained her lips with the faintest blush of deep red tint and it served to make her look as if she had just come from feeding on something or someone. I wanted to bite her. After what she'd seen last night, I had been very, very cautious about instigating any intimacies with her, especially the ones that we both seemed to be partial to currently. I caught her staring at me sometimes when she thought I wasn't paying attention and I could see the images of the fight rush her memory. She was trying to reconcile the many sides of myself she kept of me in her mind; they seemed to be contradicting themselves to her.

"So what's this Saden like?" she asked, shutting the light in the bathroom and grabbing her purse. I exhaled.

"Think Cillian on heroine and crack and then think about a sixteen year old guy; hormonal, violent and reckless." I smiled at her and touched her cheek, the heat from her skin making my body tremble.

"Awesome. So what's the plan?" she asked, stepping away from me and out into the hall. I sighed, feeling slightly frustrated at our lack of physicality with one another.

"I don't have a plan," I said, laughing darkly. "I'm not sure exactly what Liam wants to do and honestly, he doesn't seem to be in any particular danger. I mean, I don't think this is what he'd hoped he'd be doing and certainly, I'm sure that he doesn't want Carmen in this situation, but he seems relatively calm considering his circumstances." I sighed longingly as I reached to stroke down Ana's arm. She felt a bit disconnected from me at the moment.

"But he's afraid that Saden might come for Lucie if he tries to leave or tries to kill Saden? That's why he's stayed as long as he has? I mean they must have some sort of knife over his head otherwise I don't care how jacked up on heroine or crack Saden is, I'm quite sure that your brother could annihilate him in one breath." She made a good point; him staying must have something to do with Lucie. I nodded to her and took her hand in mine as we left the house.

Chapter Five

Nathanial

Ana would come for Lucie. She would stop everything and leave everyone she was with for that little girl. Of course I would never harm Lucie; I wasn't so far gone that I would ever consider imploring such means to acquire what I wanted, still, I wasn't beyond using their relationship... Ana needed to listen. She needed to hear me and hear what I had to say; I would make her understand.

Ana

Stephen and I arrived at Saden's to a large crowd of mostly Vampires and a few humans. There was a DJ, a pool, various fountains of champagne, a full bar and catered trays of food. It wasn't a bad way to spend an evening if we weren't there to try and rescue Liam. I was still feeling a bit overwhelmed from seeing the fight and I was working very hard to wrap my head around who Stephen actually was; a Vampire with the capacity and the inclination to be excessively brutal and violent. He turned to stare at me, hearing my thoughts and I smiled at him. I didn't want him to feel bad; it was just one of many sides to who he was. He stopped to touch my face and hold my gaze.

"Holy shit man, this must be her!" A voice suddenly broke through our connection and I turned to see a guy that looked to have come from some sort of beach photo shoot, move powerfully through the crowd toward us. Stephen took my hand and I was glad; I hated when we weren't touching. The guy froze upon seeing me and I suddenly became very, very tense. His body went rigid and Stephen immediately stepped in front of me. "Jesus Christ; you smell…your scent…it's…" the guy continued to speak, his eyes dark as he started to move toward me.

"Saden!" Liam's voice sounded clear and forceful through the music and the crowd. Saden swallowed and shook his head; our eyes met. Liam came to stand beside him. "Your company is needed outside, potential investors I think, best not to keep them waiting," Liam spoke and touched Saden on the shoulder. Saden's eyes were still locked with mine and I was wondering just how much strength it was taking for him not to attack me. I squeezed Stephen's hand. Saden nodded and reluctantly turned away from me. I exhaled and looked at Liam. "Well Ana, it appears you've made some changes since I left you at Carlo's." He raised his eyebrows at me. What changes? He didn't know anything about what had happened with Carlo and me or with what Stephen had done.

"Your scent, love." Stephen turned to me and I noticed that like Saden, Stephen's eyes had turned a deeper shade of blue. I frowned. "You're releasing it," he said quietly to me. Frick!

"God, I'm so sorry. I didn't even know it…" I had been thinking about Stephen and touching him; I wasn't trying to attract Saden. I trailed off, staring at Liam. "I'm sorry," I said. I wanted to hug Liam, to tell him everything and that I tried not to let him down; I tried to make him proud. I had tried.

123

"Ana." Liam stared at me and his eyes flashed in understanding. "I have a place arranged for us to talk, shall we?" he asked, pointing inside the house. I saw Stephen frown. "Perhaps 'talk' isn't the right word." Liam laughed softly and we followed him up a spiral staircase to a large living room. I glanced down to see Saden watching me as I ascended the stairs. Once again, our gazes locked and he licked his lips. Christ. Liam motioned for me to sit on the couch and he and Stephen moved next to another bar, pouring two glasses of scotch. Liam waved his hand and a large black door slid shut, closing us into the room. "What would you like Ana?" Liam asked me. I was anxious and really not in the mood to eat or drink anything at the moment. I was however, wondering if I was going to make it out of this place without having to fend off another attack on my blood. Exhaustion started to seep into my bones and as much as I wanted to know what happened to Liam and Carmen, a mounting panic attack was beginning to rise in my chest. Between that stupid fight, finding Liam, and now Saden with his bloodlust, I was starting to think that Micah might actually be trying to get me committed to some mental institution.

"I'm fine Liam, thank you." I remembered that I was supposed to be distant from Liam, act as if we didn't really know each other just in case someone had managed to listen to our interactions. "Um…I think I'll just sit outside for awhile and let you two catch up." I knew that Stephen would be replaying various images of the last several months; images that I, myself didn't have. If it wasn't for Micah I would have stayed ignorant of the fact that Stephen had tried to save me and that Carlo actually bit me. I heard a bottle drop to the floor and I looked up to see Liam staring at me, his eyes wide. I sighed, stood and

124

slid open the door to the deck outside and sank into one of the plush couches wondering if I was ever going to have a life worth living, a life that was full of normal things like maybe a boyfriend who I could cook dinner with, or girlfriends that I could talk to on the phone or over coffee. I wondered if I would ever work in a job that I loved or maybe get married some day or just live with someone who wasn't my assassin or my Bond. I wanted to buy a house, something small with a front porch and a deck and hardwood floors and fireplaces. I wanted my wolves back. I wanted to row on a lake. I wanted to go out dancing and drinking a bit. I wanted to curl up on a Friday night and make pizza and drink a beer and have someone to kiss and hold on the couch. I sighed, feeling heavy and drawn as if I was walking through water with weights tied to my limbs, trying to fight against the currents of my life.

The world didn't feel right for me. I didn't belong in this place and I didn't belong with Vampires or Demons; I didn't belong Bonded or Bound. I didn't even know who I was anymore, not that I ever knew really, but I knew what I enjoyed, what made me happy and they were all simple things, uncomplicated things; not money or cars or clothes or fame… I wanted calm. I wanted peace in my heart and my soul and I felt that I had run out of time, that my life was spinning so rapidly out of control that I no longer could provide myself with the opportunities to have any of those things that I desired, that I was running on empty and had been for over two years and maybe even before then. My heart was in so many pieces that it resembled dust and shadows. I had fallen apart and reassembled so many times that each time I fell, a part of me didn't awake; a part of me died and I only had so many parts left with life in them to awaken. When was the next time going to be the last time? I exhaled and closed my eyes.

"Ana? Would mind coming back inside?" I jumped. I must have zoned out. Stephen was standing in the shadows and I wondered how long he'd been there, listening. It didn't matter. Liam was standing by the fire, his back to me. I could hear the music coming from downstairs and people laughing. They seemed normal, happy.

"I'm sorry Ana," Liam choked on his words and I saw his body tremble slightly, still not turning toward me. I had no idea what he was apologizing for and I guessed he couldn't say. I wasn't as versed at keeping what other people said out loud, behind my wall; it was harder for me and it would be risky to talk to me too much.

"You don't have to apologize for anything Liam. It's ok. I'm ok," I said quietly, hoping that he would know that I wasn't angry with him for leaving me at that stupid ranch and that I was so happy that he and Carmen were alive, that Lucie had her parents. There was a knock on the door and suddenly it slid back, heavy and ominous in its girth. Saden was standing there, a drink in his hand. His eyes went to me.

"Catching up?" he said, winking and moving into the room toward the bar. Stephen was right; Saden did resemble Cillian in his twitchy energy. "Stephen, I've got a world-class training facility in Soweto, right in the township. You should come and check it out tomorrow." Saden sipped his drink, his eyes catching me in their emerald green light. "Ana, are you a fan of Mixed Marital Arts?" Saden asked, leaning casually against the bar.

"Yes," I said, watching him.

"As a spectator or a participant; you look fit." His eyes traced over my exposed arms and shoulders and down to my legs. I was standing next to Liam and I distinctly felt some weird kinetic energy move between us; it made me feel strong.

"Both," I said, tossing my hair back and widening my stance, crossing my arms in front of me and meeting his gaze. Saden swallowed and grinned.

"No shit. You ever fought this guy?" He motioned toward Stephen, clearly thinking that he was being witty.

"I have." My tone was even and Saden's eyes widened.

"In the ring?" He looked between Stephen and me.

"No, in an alley in New York City," I replied, not taking my eyes from his face.

"What? Wait; you fought each other in an alley; like what, did he attack you or something?" Saden laughed… he *was* young I thought.

"Yes." He stopped mid-sip and stared at me.

"No. No fucking way. But aren't you two together or something?" he asked and I could see his face begin to flush with excitement.

"Every couple has their ups and downs Saden." I cocked my head to the side staring back at him. He turned to Stephen.

"You attacked your girlfriend? Holy shit man, that's really brutal, but it's good shit though. I don't know any Humans or that many vamps, who would even dare to go up against Stephen; he's the worst kind of violent!" He laughed. What did that mean? "You should come tomorrow as well Ana; maybe we can spar a little bit?" He winked and I finally saw Stephen move into the light; he'd been watching me.

"I'm not sure that's the best idea for Ana, Saden. Despite her innate ability to fight me off, she's still Human and I don't want her getting hurt." Stephen moved to stand next to me, sliding his arm around my waist. Saden smirked and took a step closer to me, his eyes shining.

"Perhaps we should let Ana decide what's best for her, you know feminist power and all that. What would you enjoy Ana? Do you want to come check out where the big boys play?" He raised his chin. "We don't usually let the girls in, but I'll make an exception just for you. What do you say?" I stepped toward him, the toe of my boot aligned with his.

"We'll be there," I said, smirking slightly. I never really smirked, but for some reason it seemed appropriate. Saden's eyes grew dark and I saw fire ignite in his gaze.

"Good," he murmured. "I like a woman who speaks for herself," he said as he reached to touch my arm. I heard Liam clear his throat and Saden stepped back, smiling.

"I think that Ana and Stephen should be going for the evening; they've had a very long couple of days," Liam spoke, walking to stand on the other side of me.

"Sure. I'm glad you came and I'm very glad to have met you Ana. I'm always fascinated when one of our kind seems to think that one of your kind is special enough not to be treated like a whore; it's extraordinary really." Saden looked me over and suddenly a deep rumble erupted from my chest and my soul. I growled ferociously. Everyone in the room stopped breathing. I took a step forward, blackness swimming before my eyes. Saden's eyes widened and I could see a brief glimmer of fear pass over his face.

"Let's go." Stephen took me by the elbow and pulled me out from the room. He shimmered us rather forcefully back to the guesthouse and I knew immediately that he was angry. "What the hell do you think you're doing Ana?" He rounded on me as I tried to get my bearings from the sudden force of air to my lungs.

"I didn't mean to growl at him; he pissed me off! He was basically calling me a whore Stephen and by the way, thanks for not sticking up for me!" I said, turning to meet his stare.

"I'm not talking about your growling, although that's an entirely separate issue; you didn't give me chance to respond, *by the way*!" He fed my words back. "I'm talking about your inability to resist being baited into grappling with vampires. Who do you think you are Ana? You're not immortal!" His voice rose.

"Oh I know Stephen; I'm not that lucky to be able to rip hearts from chests and tear them open with my teeth; how disappointing for me. Perhaps I'll get to learn from someone who is seen as 'the worst kind of violent'. Maybe you can teach a weak human some new tricks!" I yelled, walking up the stairs.

"Don't walk away Ana; we're not done with this conversation." He caught the bedroom door just as I tried to shut it. I flung myself on the bed and untied my boots. "You have no idea what goes on in these training sessions Ana. The limited time that you've spent with me

129

or even Patric for that matter, has not in any way, shape or form, prepared you for what you've now gotten yourself into." He glared at me.

"Oh, so fighting Devon and Alec, having Nathanial almost kill me, almost being raped by Andres, battling with Carlo, fighting you; none of that could have prepared me for some stupid workout session with a bunch of hormone induced Vampires?" I said, peeling off my clothes and putting on my sweats and tank. Stephen was pinching the bridge of his nose.

"No," he said, moving to sit on the bed. I stood before him, defiant.

"Why?" I asked, "What's the problem?"

"The problem is Ana, that you are Human. The problem is that you seem to have this inexplicable blood type that attracts even the most seasoned vampires and makes them want to abandon all sense of restraint to get even within a few yards of you! The problem is that what you saw from me in that alley was only the tip of the iceberg when vampires are allowed to explore their deepest most sinister natures unchecked and unchallenged. Having your blood, your scent in an enclosed space with male vampires who are unleashed, is the perfect storm for one or more of them to attack you. They won't be able to resist and you won't be able to fight them off without revealing your powers with fire," he said, staring at me.

"I'm just going to be with Saden," I said, Stephen's concern for my life was making me feel bad about fighting with him; he was very kind. He sighed.

"I'm not kind Ana, I'm selfish and I would rather keep you and your blood with me for as long as you want to stay, than have to fight off a half a dozen blood crazed vampires as they tried to feed from you!" He was annoyed. I didn't really have anything left to say except the main reason why I wanted to go.

"I don't want to be away from you," I said quietly. For some reason, I had this odd feeling that my time with Stephen was running down, that just like everything in my life, our relationship was held together by threads and they were fraying, unraveling. He wasn't really mine to keep because I couldn't stay with him the way I wanted. I wasn't like him and our differences, the fact that he was immortal and I would never be, were impossible to reconcile, impossible to bring together in some sort of fusion that would hold the whole quilt together. I exhaled.

"Ana." Stephen was staring at me, his eyes full of emotion. I waved my hand.

"Don't worry about it Stephen, it's just the way I'm thinking at the moment. I'm sorry I've gotten myself into a dangerous situation, but I think it will be ok. I promise not make you have to save my life again. I think since Carlo, you have enough humanitarian credits to last you several Afterlives." I laughed bleakly and pushed my hair back out of my face.

"Hmmm…" Stephen's eyes were churning and I could see the tides moving swiftly back and forth in their depths. "You know you never answered my question," he said, staring hard at my face.

"What question?" He always asked so many.

"About where you fell on how I fit into your life, about how you were feeling about us; Cillian interrupted us if you remember." His tone was contemplative. "I suppose after hearing how you feel about the issue of immortality, maybe I already have my answer." He sat very still, watching and waiting.

"Honestly Stephen, I would have to say that I'm probably not the best person for you or anyone for that matter, at least other than a human guy. My compatibility to beings other than my own kind, doesn't seem to be the most conducive to any semblance of normalcy, however you want to define that," I said, sitting down next to him on the bed.

"That's not what I asked you," he said, lying back and staring up at the ceiling. I swallowed. I wasn't ready for this discussion.

"Ok. Ok, well, I'm scared Stephen and confused." My voice was shaking. "I've come to understand, to some degree, why you felt that we shouldn't be together when I was in the hospital, but the very thought of you making a decision that essentially said you didn't want to be with me because I had loved other people, because other people would always be part of my life; that you left me when I was at my very worst, scared and confused…it was devastating. I tried to be ok with what you wanted. I tried to accept what you were saying and agree with you, but that's not at all how I felt and I think you knew that." My sentences and my thoughts were running together now and the crushing sadness that I had felt after waking up from my surgery came flooding back. "And then when I came to find you to tell you about Liam the first time; what I saw, what I found, it all started to make sense. You didn't want to be with me at all. You didn't love me and you wanted to forget me, forget us, so I tried to come to terms

132

with that idea. I tried to let you go because that's clearly what you wanted." I worried the silver band on my finger, turning it around and around. I glanced at Stephen, his eyes were closed and it didn't sound like he was breathing. "So, here we are and Nathanial is still in my life and now so is Patric, and I'm pretty sure that neither of them are going anywhere anytime soon, even if they are angry with me and even if I'm still pissed at them. Granted, Nathanial and I aren't in the best of places with each other, even after I saved his life, but still, he's a part of me…" I thought about the last argument I'd had with Nathanial, how angry I was with him, how angry I still was with him. "I needed you Stephen; I needed you to tell me it was ok, that losing something that wasn't really mine to lose in the first place, wasn't my fault. I needed a partner and I needed the man that I loved and you left me," I said quietly. I had always thought of Stephen as a man, especially after that first night when he'd asked to Change me, when he cried about Laura, about what he'd lost in his life—he was a man. No matter what I knew him to be now, no matter how violent his true nature; to me, he was a man, he was human and for a brief moment in time, he was the father of our child.

"Ana," Stephen spoke quietly. "Are you still in love with me?" His eyes were still closed, but he was breathing now albeit rather shallowly. I didn't have to think.

"Yes." My heart collapsed and surged at the same time and fear enveloped me; fear of losing him, fear of him not understanding, fear of finally having come to understand that Stephen was the soul that I wanted. I wanted his heart and yet I knew that there probably would never be a place for us to exist together. What kind of life could we possibly have when he would continue to thrive, and I would eventually wither away, only to be lost to him forever? It really wasn't the best plan, even if with Nathanial's blood in my system, my life expectancy was way shorter than Stephen's and clearly I didn't have the capabilities to be Changed. I couldn't win. Perhaps it had to be enough for him to know that I did love him, that I would be with him if I could, but I wasn't the best choice for his existence. Stephen deserved to have someone who could live out their life with him, to always be by his side, to give him what I could not. I patted him on the leg and stood, knowing that he had heard my thoughts. "I'll be ready to go in the morning," I said, opening the door. He didn't respond so I left quietly, not looking back.

Stephen

She loved me. That's all that mattered; it was the only thing that mattered now. She wanted me. She wanted my heart and my soul and I would give them both to her. I didn't care about my immortality. I didn't care that she wasn't like me. I wanted all the same things she wanted. I wanted a house with a porch. I wanted dogs or wolves as Ana had. I wanted to make dinner with her and be there when she came home from work. I wanted to go on trips together that didn't involve rescue missions and bloodthirsty vampires and I wanted to watch movies and laugh and hold her. I wanted all of those things and I didn't care now about Nathanial or Patric. She would be with me if she wasn't so scared of losing me or of her dying and leaving me behind. She was more like me than she thought and now with my blood in her system, she would live beyond anything that she realized; she'd be like Lucie or something close. Maybe she could be Changed now, we didn't know. She was so different after I had saved her; her body was different… maybe there was still a chance. It really didn't matter either way for me. Before I could even let myself be happy with what I knew, I had to get Ana through today first. Her display last night had Saden's hackles raised and he was wondering what kind of Human Ana actually was. He was intrigued just like everyone was when it came to Ana and who she was. It went beyond just a hunger for her blood; they were intrigued by her personality, her spirit, her heart.

I came downstairs to find her eating a bowl of cereal and drinking coffee. I pulled out a chair and stared at her.

"Are there going to be people pulling out hearts today or is it just a normal training type thing?" she asked, avoiding my gaze. I reached to take her chin, turning her face toward mine.

"No hearts today," I said, watching the depths of her eyes. She was sad and anxious.

"It doesn't seem as if Liam is in any hurry to leave. What do you think is going on?" She looked down, moving her face from my hand. She was thinking about what would happen when we finally left this place; if we would be able to bring Liam and Carmen home to Lucie and she was thinking about how to brace herself when we parted. She was thinking that our time together was coming to an end, that we didn't have any other options except to go our separate ways. She was wrong.

"I don't know," I said, leaning back in my chair. "I'm thinking that I'm going to have to offer Saden something, an exchange of sorts. Liam wouldn't want me to do that, but I'm quite sure that he also doesn't want to leave Lucie without her parents." I sighed.

"What sort of exchange?" Ana eyed me; she was frowning. I had an idea, but I wasn't ready for Ana to know just yet, it would terrify her. I shrugged.

"I don't know yet. I'll have a better idea of what interests him after today I think," I said, hating having to lie to her. Her eyes narrowed and I thought for a brief moment that she might have been able to see what I was thinking.

"You interest him," she said, sipping her coffee. I smiled.

"So do you," I replied. She rolled her eyes and stood to put her bowl in the sink.

"Yeah, but I'm pretty sure that his room isn't decorated with full size posters of me; he's like a teenage girl who has gotten a crush on their favorite celebrity." She smirked. I laughed.

"Hmm…I wouldn't mind having a few life size posters of you in my room." I chuckled, watching her.

"Let's get this over with shall we?" She grabbed her purse, but stopped suddenly.

"What?" I asked, trying to get into her head; she was blocking me.

"You haven't…um, you haven't fed since we've been here. Aren't you getting hungry or something?" She stared at me, her eyes wide. I cleared my throat. I was hungry, very, very hungry—for her.

"Yeah, I guess I am." I sighed, knowing that she probably wasn't in the mood to indulge me per our conversation last night and I really didn't have the right to ask her, not yet at least.

"So what do we do?" She cringed thinking about how I normally went about satisfying my hunger. It didn't have to be that way; I could get what I needed without being with another woman and I didn't want to be with any more women. I wanted Ana. "Wait!" She made me jump. "Hang on!" She flew past me and sprinted up the stairs returning with her backpack. She pulled out clothes and baggies of pretzels and then surfaced, revealing two large vials of blood. My eyes widened.

"Why do you have blood in your pack? I asked; she was so wonderfully weird.

"No, it's ok, it's my blood," she said smiling; yeah, she was weird.

"Again, I ask, why do you have blood in your luggage?" I smiled and cocked my head. She laughed and handed me one of the vials.

"Just in case. You know, just in case you needed it or Liam needed it; I don't think it would kill him because I care about him; I love him so he would be protected, I think. Anyway, now you won't have to terrorize some innocent human in a dark alley somewhere." She nodded, thrusting the vial at me. "Here. Will it be enough?" She seemed concerned. I laughed again and took the vial. I shook my head.

137

"Yes Ana, it will be enough." She was always so worried about never being enough; not even in her offering of her blood did she feel that it would be what anyone needed or wanted. I started to wonder just how she managed to get her blood into the vials. Had she cut herself? It was a ton of blood that she was carrying and the very thought of Ana slitting her wrist or something was making me upset. "How did you get this? I asked, unscrewing the top of the tube, her scent knocking the breath out of me.

"Micah helped me," she said, waiting for me to drink. "I mean, he showed me how to do it so I didn't harm myself." She smiled and I gazed at her in awe. I swallowed her blood in one swig, immediately feeling the overwhelming strength and power that her unique composition offered to me. Unfortunately for her, along with the enhanced power came such an intense arousal and desire that was unique to only our pairing. I was her creator by all standards, and having her blood to nourish me only served to provide that much more of an attraction to her than I already experienced. I moved, pulling her toward me and kissing her deeply, my tongue relished the combination of the taste of her mouth with the flavoring of her blood. I thrust between her lips wanting her to feel what I so desperately needed. I started walking her backward, finding the counter and placing my hands on either side of her hips, then gripping the stone and moaning. She was kissing me back, moving her mouth passionately and holding my face in her hands.

"Maybe we can be a little late," I breathed as I started to unzip her shorts.

"Good idea," she whispered and I tore her shirt off and lifted us in the air heading for the wall.

After buying Ana some new workout clothes, we arrived to the training center. I was beyond amped for various reasons. I loved fighting and it was something that I hadn't allowed myself to participate in while I was with Liam, so I was excited to get back into the ring. I was also worried about Ana being here. I had no idea what Saden had in mind when it came to her and I could only go off what I had managed to see in his mind from last night; it wasn't gentlemanly. Music was blaring from the building and I felt a sudden surge of energy flow through my body. Ana pulled opened the door to the huge dome and we stepped inside. The facility was the size of at least five American football fields with a retractable roof, state of the art practice ring and weight area for the Humans who liked to grapple, and stadium seating for spectators who were invited to watch. I hoped that I could just leave Ana with Liam in the seats and she could observe. There was no way I was going to get that lucky. Grappling and air fights were already in practice and I motioned for Ana to sit next to me while we waited for Saden. I saw my brother down on the floor talking with several Human businessmen who I could only assume were possible investors of Saden's fight club.

"Well, well, well!" Saden suddenly appeared behind us, smiling broadly. "I can see that I didn't scare you off! Man, I'm so glad that you're here Stephen; I can't wait to introduce you to the team, they are going to fucking flip!" he said, slapping me on the back. He turned to Ana and bent his head close to her ear. I struggled not to attack. "You and me have a very special day planned while your boyfriend gets to relish in the glory of being one of the best fighters around.

139

What do you think?" He held his face close to hers, but Ana's body was relaxed and she smiled.

"Sounds good," she said, turning to face him, their lips almost touching. She was insane, but I could see that Saden was trying to swallow; she'd thrown him off with her accessibility, so maybe she wasn't insane, maybe she was just really, really smart. He wasn't used to going toe-to-toe with Humans. He had no idea just what he was getting with Ana. He pulled back first and turned to me, his eyes wide. "Come on down to the floor man." His eyes were still on Ana who had turned back to watching Liam. I leaned over and kissed her gently on the mouth and whispered in her ear.

"Whatever you need to do, do it Ana. I'm not sure that he wouldn't try to attack you, so if you need to use your fire, then use it and don't think about anything but defending yourself; do you understand me?" I said, speaking so low that I knew Saden wouldn't hear. She moved her head to kiss me.

"Yes," she murmured. I touched her cheek, hoping for Saden's sake, it wouldn't come to that. If he took even a single drop of her blood, he would be done long before I could get to him and finish him off; Ana would melt him from the inside. I stood.

"I'll be right back." Saden winked at Ana. She nodded and waved as we walked down onto the floor. Liam saw us approach and I could see him scanning the seats for Ana. I motioned and he looked over my shoulder and nodded. He immediately broke up his discussion and went to go and sit with her. He wanted to talk to her while Saden was occupied. I watched as he moved down the aisle and put his hand on

Ana's shoulder; she jumped. I sighed, hoping this day was not going to end in some giant explosion. Saden yelled at me and I jogged over to meet his team.

Ana

"Hi Liam." I was so glad to see him that I had to just stare into his face for a few moments. He and Carmen were alive and that meant Lucie would have her parents back. Liam smiled, but then his face turned serious.

"I need to give you some instructions Ana," he said, his eyes watching Stephen on the floor. I nodded. "Saden is not so different from Carlo in his never ending quest to acquire things. For Saden, that usually falls to acquiring knowledge about things he can then learn to adapt for himself. Unlike Carlo, he knows nothing about you or what you are capable of. He has no knowledge of your rare blood, or of your ability with fire or any of your very non-Human attributes, but he does suspect you are different, unique. He's also not terribly fond of your relationship with Stephen; he views you as substandard and not worthy to be partnering with one of our species. He's inclined to let it go with Stephen because he idealizes him and because he's under the impression that he's using you for sex and for blood, that there's no love between the two of you." Liam was speaking very slowly and his body was tense. "He also doesn't know you can fight and it would stun him to see just what a worthy opponent you have become. My brother, when he is fully immersed in his most violent nature, shall we

141

say, is not someone that even *I* would consider taking on. Stephen is an unusually gifted fighter and his abilities are really unparalleled; he doesn't actually even know how good he his. What he showed me of your fight, what he allowed for me to see, I was in awe Ana. He should have killed you. You should be dead." We were both watching Stephen as he shook hands with various other Vampires that had flown down to the ground to meet him. I swallowed, remembering. "Saden is wanting to test you, test his suspicions about you. You will need to show him just what he's up against without using your ability to blow things up." I turned to look at him and I lowered my voice.

"But Stephen just told me that he wasn't sure if Saden would try to attack me, that I should use whatever I needed to in order to defend myself," I said, not looking at him. I saw him shake his head.

"My brother loves you Ana and having you here is beyond terrifying for him. Saden will not attack you; he wouldn't dream of harming Stephen, someone who is his idol, who has come to his home with his chosen mate. He wouldn't dream of doing anything that would make Stephen angry—ever, with the possible exception of taking you on in a sparing match. Liam chuckled darkly. "Saden is powerful and violent, but he's also young and easily intimidated. His lack of knowledge about his own species and his reckless behavior have gotten him into quite a few unpleasant situations and he's always on edge wondering if someone is going to try to usurp his rule. Attacking the mate of someone so feared and respected as Stephen, would only serve to make Saden look even more immature and stupid." Liam's tone was disgusted.

"I don't really know how to fight that well Liam. I mean, what happened between me and Stephen, it was a fluke thing really. I got lucky and he actually got me in a position where I'm pretty sure if I hadn't managed to break through something in his mind, he would have most certainly killed me." I frowned.

"No Ana, there was nothing about your abilities that night that were remotely a fluke; you have something that even I can't figure out, a knowledge of yourself, a willingness to fight for what and who you love, a strength that came from your experiences of never being protected when you were a child, a conviction to persevere and find courage to survive against incredible odds. Perhaps even more stunning is that you have not once been bitter or cruel to those around you. You have devoted your life to helping others, to loving even those who are undeserving of that love and you have only served to enhance the very power that comes from your breath, your spirit, your heart. You don't need fire or rare blood to access those things Ana, they are yours by being exactly who you are." He turned to look at me and I smiled at him.

"You are always so kind to me Liam; you and Micah, you both seem to think that it's a good thing that I was born," I said quietly. Liam met my eyes and he studied me.

"Ana, your awakening into this world from your birth, has managed to save the only person that I could not." He turned to look at Stephen as he rose off the ground sparing with another fighter. I shook my head.

"So what do you want me to do with Saden if I can't use fire?" I asked, wondering how much I was going to get my ass kicked. Liam laughed.

"I want you to beat the shit out of him Ana. I want you to show him no mercy, despite your ability to always be inclined to do so; I want you to show him just how wrong he is about Humans, about women and then we'll figure out how to get Carmen and me the hell out of here!" He grinned and stood. I was surprised that Liam hadn't already thought of a plan for himself. "Well, I had a few things in the works, but it seems that Micah was a couple of steps ahead of me this time." He winked and held out his hand, pulling me from my seat.

Stephen

I had been messing around with the team for over an hour and lost track of Ana. When I last saw her, she and Liam were sitting together talking and now I didn't see her or Liam or Saden anywhere. It felt good to flex my mental and physical muscles a bit and Saden's assortment of fighters seemed to be top notch. I was also glad that they all were relatively preoccupied with beating the shit out of each other to notice Ana or catch her scent. I took a seat in the stands and focused on watching a pairing of fighters who'd just taken to the air to work on flying drills.

"I know what you're planning to do and Ana won't be happy Stephen," Liam spoke as he took a seat next to me. I stared at him. Christ, was I that transparent? "No, but I know you, and I know your mind perhaps even better than you do; it's an interesting bargaining tool and one that will most certainly work, but at what cost?" I turned away from him.

"You're not staying here Liam and neither is Carmen; Lucie needs you," I said quietly.

"And what of Ana? Do you think she'll be willing to just leave you here?" he said watching me.

"Ana will understand. She loves you and she wants Lucie to have her father," I said firmly. "She'll understand."

"And what if you're killed? Do you think she'll understand then Stephen? What of the life that you want to give her? What about your dreams of marrying her? Are you so willing to sacrifice yourself and the happiness that you have been searching for in order to save me?"

"Yes," I said, not looking at him. He shook his head.

"Well then, I guess I misunderstood. I guess that I misread your heart when it was shattering in that hospital the day you lost your child. I guess I've been reading you wrong from the first moment you ever met Ana in West Papua to the time she came to you for help. I must not be as accurate as I thought," he said solemnly.

"She'll understand," I said again.

"Of course she will, that's Ana. She would always understand you putting me first or even you putting yourself first as you have done in the past. She'll understand because that is what she expects Stephen, because she loves Lucie more than herself, because she loves me and Carmen more than she loves herself and because she loves you more than she loves herself." He sounded angry. I sighed and looked out on to the mats; Ana and Saden were walking to the middle and I gripped Liam's leg as my body tensed.

"What is she doing out there?" I looked to Liam. "I thought you would have come up with some way to keep her out of this mess Liam. If she fights him then he's bound to discover her talent with fire if he gets to close to wining!" I looked as the members of the team descended mid-flight to watch Ana and Saden on the ground. This wasn't good; if she started sweating just a little bit, they would be out of control.

"They've been ordered not to attack Stephen, Ana's fine," Liam said, leaning forward in his seat.

"That's what you said about Andres, Liam," I huffed.

"That's true and that was my mistake, but Saden has investors here and having his team display unruly behavior could cost him millions, so it's not a good plan if they want to live," Liam said flatly. I shook my head. He'd clearly gotten stupider since living with Saden. Liam laughed.

"At least I didn't attack the woman that I love." He looked at me smirking. "*That* was stupid." He motioned for me to watch the center of the floor where a small crowd had gathered. I wanted to throw up. Saden was talking to Ana and he was smirking. I watched as he grasped her hands in his and she nodded. I couldn't get a read on what he was thinking, but just having him touch her was enough to make me want to launch myself out onto the floor between them. She pulled a hair band off from around her wrist and proceeded to tie back her curls, a long, coppery plait cascading down over her shoulder. Saden reached out and swept her hair so that it was behind her and I heard Ana laugh; it was a dark and hollow laugh and one that I had never heard from her before. I stiffened.

"Relax Stephen, Ana has this," Liam spoke softly and I turned in my seat glaring at him. I heard Saden laugh out loud and I whirled around to watch as he stepped back a few paces from Ana, turning his back to her. Ana stood, her hands at her sides looking as if she was just hanging out, waiting for the bus. Christ, I was going to have to watch the love of my life get the snot beaten out of her.

"Watch," Liam spoke again, his posture poised and alert. "I'm not going to let him harm her Stephen." I held my breath. Suddenly Saden launched himself in the air heading straight for Ana. Just before he collided with her on the ground, she moved making him hit the mat with such force that he rolled and crashed into the back wall over a hundred feet away; at least I though she moved, she looked like she was standing in the same place she started. The team on the ground laughed and cheered as Saden stood, looking slightly dazed, but smirking and I thought I heard him mumble the word "whore". He nodded to Ana and walked to meet her, his fighting position up and ready. She mimicked him. He swung at her jaw and she crouched, ducking the swipe. He came from the other side, aiming high this time and she ducked again. Again and again he tried to hook her and every time she lowered herself making him miss the connection with her head. He stood back. I wished he were wearing gloves; he was coming at her with bare fists. Immediately he tried to punch her and she raised her arm blocking his strike forcefully. He leaned, trying to hit her in the stomach and she stopped his fist in her palm taking his arm,

147

pulling him toward her and spinning him in the air, leveling him to the ground. She was moving so aggressively; she seemed violent and angry, I was stunned. More cheers as Saden sprung back onto his feet, this time he wasn't smiling. Ana nodded to him and they stepped back into the center of the mat. Quickly, before she had a chance to turn, I saw him rise off the ground and try to sweep kick her in the knees. She turned, grabbed his foot and flipped him in the air sending him soaring clear across the gym. He flew back and tackled her around the waist sending them both crashing to the ground. I jumped from my seat, but Liam pulled me back. I shook him off and sprinted down to the floor. He had her on the ground! Liam was behind me in an instant, his hand blocking me from moving forward to help her.

"Wait," Liam whispered. I was beside myself as Saden hooked his legs under Ana and started to punch her in the face. I growled. Suddenly their positions switched and Ana was on top. It happened so quickly. She had him pinned and I saw her rear back and strike her fist into his temple, a gush of black blood began to seep down his face and I heard him snarl and try to throw her off. He connected with her jaw, but she hung on and struck the open wound for the second time with more blood spilling from Saden's head. He bucked and she flipped over his head, rolling and leaping to her feet. She wasn't bleeding thank god. Then the oddest thing happened. I watched Ana's eyes darken and I saw her take a step forward, her hair suddenly coming undone and blowing back behind her. The air shifted and no one moved or spoke. I was waiting for the fire, but it never came. Instead, I saw Saden suddenly become immobile; he stood still, fear spreading over his face. Ana continued to step forward so that now there was about twenty feet between them. She waved her hand and Saden's

148

body was violently jerked to the side sending him colliding against the wall where he was hovering, his back pushed against the siding. Ana walked casually over and stood looking up at him. I couldn't move; I had no idea that Ana could immobilize her enemies much less control their movements at will. Saden's head was snapped back as Ana looked on, her body calm. I heard him snarl and then Ana raised him higher in the air. He was snapping and growling so loudly that it was starting to drown out the music. Saden's fangs were out and his eyes were a fierce yellow, he was in full attack mode except he couldn't attack, he was paralyzed. Ana sent him to the very top of the building then she dropped him, fast. Just before he hit the ground she caught him by the hair and pushed him, stomach down, onto the mat; she mounted him from behind and wrapped her arm around his throat crushing his windpipe.

"Tap out!" she yelled and Saden snarled. "Tap out you sick son-of-a- bitch!" Her voice was so low, but it chilled me to the bone; I had never heard her speak in such a tone before. She pulled back further on his head and pushed down harder on his throat. He tried to spin her off, but she wasn't moving. "You want to see just how inhuman I can be?" She pulled more and I thought I heard a crack in Saden's neck. "You think I'm weak? You think I'm scared of you?" She jumped off and stood up. "Well get up then you pathetic motherfucker! Get up!" I was aghast; I didn't know this Ana. She was brutal and violent and I could see malice in her eyes. I could feel her anger, her pain; it was overwhelming to watch. Saden tried to stand and she came down knee first on his back, leveling him in one motion. "GET UP!" she screamed. "You thought you'd teach me a lesson? Thought you would show your team how to take down a woman? A human? GET

THE FUCK UP AND FIGHT YOU COWARD!" I was gripping Liam's shoulder, I was in total disbelief; Ana was scaring the shit out of me. Saden moved to his knees, bleeding and somewhat broken. She stood over him; she'd won and she knew it, anything more would just be out of sheer violence and brutality to execute. I was about to call it when Liam grabbed my arm. I stood, stunned as I watched what was about to happen. Ana reared up and spun to her left, bringing her right leg up and kicking Saden in the side of the head, spraying all of us with his blood. "That's for calling me a whore," she said quietly, bending her face to his ear. She spit on him and stepped over his body, leaving me absolutely dumbfounded by the woman now facing me.

Chapter Six

Ana

I was trying to stop shaking. The hot water from the shower was somewhat helpful, but I was having difficulty getting my body to calm down. I had lost it somewhat with Saden, although Liam seemed to think that I had done just what he'd asked; I had shown Saden what I was capable of, *without* using fire. I pushed my hair back and let the water run down my back; I was sore already. Stephen hadn't said a word to me the whole day and I couldn't tell if he was angry or proud or uncomfortable with my own display of merciless behavior; I just didn't know. His emotions seemed all over the place. Saden had left immediately upon being defeated, but apparently he'd invited us to dinner this evening, a peace offering of sorts—what a douche. I turned off the shower and wrapped a towel around my body and my hair. I sat on my bed and listened. I didn't hear anything from Stephen's side and I wasn't sure if he was even in the house. He'd shimmered us away shortly after I had spoken with Liam and he stayed downstairs when I went to clean up. I found some moisturizer and a small hairdryer in one of the drawers and I went about fixing my hair and getting dressed. I figured that I would just roam around in the town for a while until we had to be at Saden's; I needed to ease my mind a bit.

Stephen was nowhere to be found so I left the house and headed into the main part of the Soweto. I walked up and down the streets passing Masakeng Bar and the music shop we'd stopped by when we'd first arrived. The black acoustic guitar was still in the window. I opened the door and walked in. Thirty minutes later, I came out carrying the instrument in its leather case. I had wondered how Stephen's favorite guitar had become shattered and destroyed when I found it at his home. I hoped he hadn't done it himself, that would be upsetting. I checked my watch, six thirty. I sighed and started to walk back down the street toward the house. I arrived to an empty residence and wondered if Stephen would come back and get me to go to Saden's; I didn't exactly want to arrive unescorted. I put the guitar on his bed and brushed my teeth and fixed my hair.

"Hey." I turned to see Stephen leaning in the frame staring at me, his eyes bright and clear as he took me in.

"Hi!" I said smiling and moving toward him. "Where've you been?" I asked, touching his hand gently. He watched as I hesitantly took his fingers and weaved them around my own.

"With Liam," he said, suddenly looking away from me, his tone soft.

"Is he ok?" I asked, worried that my aggressiveness with Saden might have gotten Liam in trouble. Stephen chuckled.

"He's fine Ana, a bit in awe of you, a bit confused at just how you are able to fight better than almost any other vampire he's seen, but he's fine." Stephen smiled and pulled me out from the bathroom.

"Not better than you." I laughed, wrapping my arms around his neck needing to be close to him.

"I'm not so sure," he said, his eyes flashing as we stared at each other.

"I got you something," I said, pulling back and moving to open the adjoining room. I picked up the guitar and brought it to him, hoping he wouldn't pull the same crap he did when I first had given him his ring. Hopefully, he'd want to play the damn thing. His eyes widened and he raised his eyebrows.

"What's this?" he asked, eyeing the black leather case.

"It's for you!" I laughed. "I don't play a single instrument so clearly it's not for me," I said putting it on the bed. He moved to unclip the chrome clasps and lifted the top of the case up. Black velvet held the guitar snug and it gleamed, even in the dim light of the room. I would have bought it even not being able to play because it was so pretty. Stephen laughed, but he was staring at me. "I noticed that the guitar Liam got for you, the one he bought for your birthday; I noticed that it somehow got smashed up." I eyed him, my own eyebrows raised now.

"Yeah I guess it did," he said quietly, his fingers tracing over the face of the instrument. He wasn't going to tell me how, I assumed… I exhaled softly.

"Well, you need another acoustic. You have an electric; I'm guessing that one is still in tact, but every guitar player should have at least two guitars right?" I said, sitting on the bed. I suddenly felt rather stupid for getting this for him. He probably would want to buy his own guitar, something that met his preferences for how he played. "Umm…the guy said it was really special, some kind of South African brand that only the best players here use…" I whispered, my embarrassment beginning to surface. "But I can bring it back and you can exchange it for something else." I rifled through my purse and showed him the receipt. He shook his head and suddenly Christmas night with the stupid ring, came flooding back. I should just stop buying things for Stephen; it never went like I hoped.

"We need to go." He looked at me and I swallowed hard; I knew that tone. I felt like I was more prepared this time for the ending of our journey together. I had tried to resolve things in my mind and my heart. I knew that once we came back, once we had Liam and Carmen safe and back with Lucie, that Stephen and I would have to part. It would be best. Still, looking at him, hearing his voice, I felt myself begin to gasp and I swallowed again, not wanting to cry, not wanting to beg him again to stay with me. I nodded and moved out into the hallway.

We arrived back at Saden's, this time the house was quiet and cozy, transformed to its more laid back décor. No fountains, no huge DJ booth, no loud music; it seemed normal. Liam greeted us and I could see that he was reading my mood, seeing how I was trying to hold the broken pieces of myself together just a little longer. He looked to Stephen and I saw them communicate. I sighed and stepped away from them both and into the living room. Saden descended the spiral staircase and I watched as his eyes darkened upon seeing me. I guessed he was still pretty pissed at me for kicking his ass. His face was somewhat healed, but I still could make out a slight pink scar near his temple where I'd struck him. I smiled to myself.

"Ana," Saden greeted me, but kept his distance. "Stephen! So glad you're here man. I told everyone what we talked about and they are beyond psyched! I can't fucking believe it!" He went and put his arm around Stephen's shoulder. I wondered what he was talking about. "Of course, I'll hate to lose this guy and his gorgeous wife, but really, it's an offer I can't refuse!" He was pointing to Liam and suddenly my heart sunk. Stephen had negotiated a deal without me? Liam and Carmen were free to go? What the fuck just happened? I looked to Stephen; he was looking down. "Let's get some drinks and celebrate shall we?" Saden snapped his fingers and a man appeared with a silver tray of four glasses of champagne. I couldn't move from the couch and my throat was suddenly very dry. Saden handed me a glass and winked. He held up his own flute. "To new beginnings, new opportunities and to having my idol honor me by offering his extreme talents to my team; to our newest fighter!" Saden raised his glass and my heart stopped.

"NO!" I shouted, rising off the couch. Looking at Stephen. "NO!" Saden stared at me, shocked at the violence of my sudden outburst.

"Ana." Liam stepped forward holding out his hand to me. I jerked away.

"No; take me instead! I can fight! You've seen it! TAKE ME!" I shouted. Saden's eyes widened and he stepped back a few paces.

"Ana!" Liam's voice broke through my fury and my desperation. I was staring at Stephen.

"You'll die!" I said, reaching for him. "You'll die and I'll lose you and Liam will lose you!" I was grasping his shirt. There had to be another way, something else that we could offer—anything else. I turned to Saden, but before I could even tell him about my powers, Liam cut me off hearing what I was about to say out loud.

155

"Ana, we've already reached a deal; what's done is done now. You need to calm down." He stared at me; he was worried that my temper might give me away, that I might just blow the fucking house up. I wanted them to take me. I didn't care about getting my heart ripped out; it was already broken, shattered. I didn't care!

"Ana." Stephen had heard me and he was moving to stand next to me.

"No," I said, my voice weak and I collapsed against his chest. "Please," I begged him, but I knew it was pointless; it was over. I pulled away and ran out of the house stopping in the drive to heave, my hands on my knees. I gasped and cried and screamed, finally collapsing into the grass and pressing my palms into the soil. I felt a hand touch my back. I lifted my head up to see Carmen standing above me, she was crying. I reached for her and she knelt beside me in the grass and held me as my entire world crashed and burned around me.

Stephen

It would take a bit of time before Liam and Carmen could return to Peru for Lucie. Liam was heavily involved in running most of Saden's larger business ventures and part of the deal was that he would ensure that Saden could have someone who would continue to assist him with his investments. I had to stay and I couldn't escort Ana back to Dublin, if that was in fact, where she would be going. She was wrecked and falling apart. I had never seen her in such a state and it made me sick in my heart to see her desperation, her grief. I couldn't tell her anything that would calm her down; I couldn't promise her that I would survive. I didn't know that for sure. I was fairly confident that a six month stint with Saden would be manageable. I had no intention of getting myself killed in the ring, but there was no way that I could guarantee that that wouldn't happen. I was also slightly stunned that she had offered her life for mine, that she'd volunteered to put her life on the line so that mine would be safe. I was in awe and I was starting to believe that she was actually in love with me. Besides Liam, no one had ever offered their own life to save mine and continuously, Ana had made that declaration. I watched as she packed up her things. She was crying and I moved to touch her shoulder.

"Try to be safe ok?" she choked, stepping away from me. "Try to stay safe." Her eyes spilled over with tears and I felt my own cascade begin to stream down my face. I nodded and reached for her again. "If I was good for you Stephen, if I wasn't such a mess and I was more like you, I would want to be with you." She gasped. "I love you and I forgive you; I know that that night in the hospital you were trying to do what you thought was best. I know that you loved me, that you still love me. I would choose you!" Her body shook and I pulled her close holding her.

"You are my blood, my breath and my life Ana," I said, kissing her cheeks and her lips, the salt from our tears stinging my mouth. She kissed me back and I could feel her desperation. We moved together as I wrapped my arms around her waist and she held my face in her hands. I swept her up into my chest and laid her gently on the bed. I slowly lifted her shirt over her head letting her hair fall over her chest and down her back. There was nothing violent in our coupling this time, nothing dark or chemical, only the purest of love and passion. I

157

held her close, our eyes never leaving each other's faces as our bodies merged. I gripped her hands, and pressed them against my own as I moved gently inside of her. The world shifted and blurred and together we remained, locked in our perfect fit; a fit that healed, that created life, that awakened the man that I once was. I whispered her name. I told her that I loved her and that I never stopped loving her and I never would.

I awoke from my meditative state, to an empty bed. Ana had gone. My chest heaved and I let the tears come, let my heart break, let the scent of her linger on my skin. I promised myself that if I could make it out of here alive, that I would go to her and ask her to marry me. I would tell her that she didn't need to be like me and that I didn't care and that we could share a beautiful life together, that I would give her everything she deserved and then some; I wanted her for forever—no matter how long that would be.

Ana

I didn't know what else to do except go to Micah's. I guessed I could have called, but I needed to see him. I needed to see someone who understood and I wanted to hug Lucie, say goodbye. First, I stopped back in my apartment in Dublin to try to get myself together. I needed a shower and a change of clothes and I needed to regroup; I was a mess. I arrived back home and immediately started to sob violently. Stephen's scent was everywhere and I found one of his shirts on my bed; actually I found a lot of clothes on my bed, they were strewn everywhere. I was sure that I didn't leave my apartment in such a mess. I scanned the room and saw that several of my papers and printouts of maps were also tossed about, scattered haphazardly as if someone had been moving very quickly, searching for something. I frowned. Maybe Micah had been here; maybe he needed to come to check up on something. My eyes darted back and forth and I returned to my bed, picking up one of Stephen's shirts and I held it tenderly to my face. I turned to look at the painting and I gasped. The canvas had been torn, shredded, and pieces of the wood backing were heaped in splinters on the ground. I walked slowly over to the remains and traced my fingers along the now defaced images. Chills broke out on my skin. Someone had been here; someone had been in my apartment looking for things, looking for me and they were angry. I felt violated and unsafe. Quickly, I began pulling clothes and shoes out from closest and stuffing them in my pack. I grabbed my laptop and crammed it into its case, slinging it over my shoulder. My passport was still in my purse along with the cash and the phones from both Micah and Liam. I took one more look around, shut the lights and shimmered away.

Nathanial

I had heard the conversation. My uncle had clearly underestimated my abilities to permeate his mental walls. I had heard him speaking with Liam; Liam who I had thought I had found dead. Ana and Stephen had been in South Africa trying to negotiate for Liam's release and apparently they had been successful. Stephen was to stay and fight in some ridiculous fight club and Liam and Carmen would be returning in a few weeks to get Lucie. I didn't have much time. I knew that Ana had left, but Liam was unsure of where she would be going next, but I could track her easy enough; it would just take a bit longer now that we weren't Bound. My heart hurt at the very thought. I had a different plan in the works and one that would most certainly make my uncle and Ana very disappointed in me, but I was desperate and needed to do this. I wasn't going to hurt her. I was just going to use her as bait. I would never harm Lucie because Ana loved her so much.

Ana

I had no idea where to go. Ireland felt unsafe and Indonesia probably wasn't the best plan right now. Peru and Argentina were out—Idaho seemed like the safest bet, at least just to get my feet under me and make a plan. I was assuming that Nathanial wouldn't be in Idaho, but I had no idea and really didn't care at this point. Noni's house was the only place that I wanted to be at the moment. The house looked the same, untouched and unharmed. I was grateful. I walked inside and sighed. It was clean and I could only guess that the elders were making sure that they kept the place in good condition. I threw my pack on the kitchen table and collapsed into a chair, exhausted. I slept horribly that night. I kept waking up thinking that someone was in the house and I had nightmares about Stephen having his heart ripped out of his chest. I awoke in the morning having sobbed most of the

160

night into my pillow. The same scenario continued to repeat itself over the next four weeks and I could feel that my nerves were shot. I tried to stay busy thinking about where to go and what to do next.

The elders that I had seen around town were very excited to have me back and they offered me various jobs that they needed assistance executing. They were rebuilding the summer campsite where the fire and the attacks had happened and they were hoping to turn it into a place to serve some of the poorer kids in the community. They wanted it to have horses, hiking, canoeing and art; it was a nice distraction and I was happy to help. I didn't feel completely safe here, but it was better than Dublin at the moment. It was bizarre working back on the same piece of land where so much had happened, particularly between Nathanial and me and I could feel the memories try to push their way back into my heart and my mind. I was done with Nathanial, at least as far as wanting to be in any sort of romantic relationship. He would always be part of me and I could only hope that we might find a comfortable place to exist with each other as friends. I wanted to be with Stephen, but since that was unlikely, I was going to have to be ok with being on my own for a while, until I felt ready to move forward in a life with someone else. Although to be honest, I didn't want to be with anyone else if I couldn't be with Stephen—so being alone was looking more and more like the only option. The back of neck suddenly grew warm; it was the first time, in I didn't know how many months, that I had even felt my mark at all. I ran my fingers along the metal and stone, feeling the small eye at the center; I wondered if it had finally settled on a color.

Nathanial

I sat in the dark waiting for my uncle and Lucie to return. I truly hated to do this to him, but once he understood that I had no other options, he would forgive me. I would give him the choice first and if he didn't do as I asked, then I would have to default to using Lucie. I hoped it wouldn't have to come to that. A gust of wind blew through the room and I heard Micah and Lucie laughing in the kitchen. I waited.

Ana

I thought about calling Liam, just to see when he was scheduled to depart from South Africa and I wanted to ask about Stephen. Calling him directly would be just too hard, too painful. I took out the tiny phones and laid them side-by-side on the kitchen table. I wondered if Micah knew that I had returned; it had been so long since we'd spoken... I really should call him first.

Nathanial

I watched as Micah approached the living room turning on the lights. When his eyes found mine, I could see immediately that he knew that I figured him out, that I knew where Ana had been and what she'd been

162

doing and who she'd been with. I held out his phone, the one he used for private conversations. "Call her," I said, calmly.

"And just what would you like for me to say my son?" Micah stood before me, his arms behind his back. I rose from my seat.

"You are to tell her that Lucie has fallen ill and that you need her to return immediately," I said, crossing my arms over my chest.

"And when she realizes that it was a trick to get her here, that you tricked her, played on her emotions for Lucie, just what do you expect her to do Nathanial?" My uncle was standing very still, but my body was beginning to tremble.

"That's none of your concern Micah. This is between Ana and me; it doesn't involve you," I said, my voice shaking.

"Oh I think it does Nathanial, particularly if you are planning on causing Ana any harm, emotionally or otherwise." His eyes turned dark and I felt a chill of air blow past my face, shaking me mentally. I fought back.

"Call her," I said, grabbing his hand and thrusting the phone into his palm.

"No," he said, staring at me. I growled.

"Micah, don't make me do this!" I shouted. His eyes narrowed and I shut him out. "Call her now and tell her to come here," I said again.

"No." Micah turned to leave the room and I grabbed his shoulder spinning him forcefully around.

"Call her or I will kill Lucie!" I spat, my heart pounding and my blood racing. Micah's eyes grew wide, disbelief spreading across his face. He stepped back from me. "Do it!" Something in my tone and my words made me think of my brother. Micah shook his head and started to wave his hand, but I shoved him backwards into the wall, paralyzing him. I went down the hall and scooped up Lucie from her highchair and carried her, crying back down the hall. "Call Ana now," I said, holding Lucie close. My uncle stared at me, his eyes seeing into my soul. I moved Lucie to the ground with my hands holding her head. "Call now!" Lucie was screaming and I couldn't hear myself think. My uncle looked at me, closed his eyes and nodded.

Ana

I decided to wait until after dinner to call Micah. I wasn't prepared to talk just yet about what had happened with Stephen and Liam, although I was pretty sure he already knew. I poured a ginger ale into a glass and took my plate into the living room and curled up on the couch. Suddenly, I heard one of the phones spring to life as it buzzed on the coffee table. It was Micah's. I sighed and picked it up.

Nathanial

I stood holding Lucie as my uncle dialed the number, my heart racing.

164

Ana

"Hi Micah," I said, putting down my drink and plate.

"Ana, I need you to come home please." Micah's voice sounded tight and rough and I frowned.

"Why? Is something wrong with Lucie?" I asked, sitting up on the edge of the couch.

"Yes," he said, his voice barely a whisper. I felt cold.

"What's wrong Micah?" I asked, moving into my room to find my pack.

"She's ill." What was with these short answers? I held my breath.

"I'm on my way," I said, hanging up the phone. I frowned; I had never known Lucie to become sick, not even when we were on the boat for four months, she was never seasick, never a cold or a sniffle. This was odd. I thought of Liam for a moment and I made the decision to call him before departing for Peru. I picked up the phone and pressed the first button—the one for Liam. He answered immediately.

"Ana? What's wrong?" He sounded very anxious. I didn't want to worry him further.

"Umm…well I just spoke with Micah, Liam and he told me to come to Peru, that Lucie was feeling a bit sick." I wanted to minimize things until I had a chance to check her out myself. "I'm sure she's fine, but I just wanted you to know that I'm going to check up on her and I'll call you as soon I lay eyes on her," I said. There was silence.

"Ana where are you?" Liam asked.

"Idaho," I said, pulling on my jeans.

"You didn't return to Dublin?" he asked, he seemed to be thinking about something.

"Uh...well yeah I did but..." I sighed.

"But what Ana?" Liam's tone was stern.

"But it looked like someone had been in my apartment; they pulled a ton of my clothes and papers out and they...they..." I couldn't say it.

"Ana?" Liam's tone softened. I swallowed.

"They destroyed the painting that Stephen made for me; they tore it to pieces," I said, feeling overwhelmed again by sadness. Silence.

"I see," Liam finally said.

"Listen Liam, I don't want you to worry about Lucie; I'm sure it's nothing. She's probably just feeling sad about you and kids get sick over things all the time," I replied, hosting my pack on my shoulders.

"I'm sure you are quite right Ana." Liam's tone was very low.

"Um...how's Stephen?" I asked, not wanting to sound desperate.

"He's healthy Ana and safe. He'll be beside himself that he wasn't here when you called though; I'm sure he'll want to take my head off for not coming to get him as soon as I heard your voice." Liam laughed softly.

"That's ok. I don't want to bother him." I bit my lip. "Listen, I will call you as soon as I get to Micah's and see Lucie ok?" I said, grabbing my purse.

"Yes Ana, I'll be waiting." I sighed.

"Tell Stephen...tell him..." I choked

"I will tell him," Liam said and I swallowed hard and ended the call.

Nathanial

I kept Micah paralyzed and he wasn't about to attack me while I was holding Lucie. I just had to wait for Ana; she would be coming any minute now I was sure and then all of this madness could stop. We would be together and that would be it. My uncle watched as I paced the floor muttering to myself. He was in a chair, frozen. I had also paralyzed Lucie, putting her to sleep on the couch; she didn't feel a thing.

Ana

I hit the floor hard and had to brace myself against the wall. I had been distracted by my conversation with Liam and my focus prevented me from shimmering with ease. I steadied myself and headed down into the living room. The fireplace was lit. I stepped into the room and saw Nathanial pacing and Micah looking oddly still in a chair. Lucie appeared to be sleeping on the couch. Nathanial turned to look at me, and my eyes narrowed—he looked manic; his eyes were spinning wildly and his face was flush. I turned to Micah.

"Micah, what's going on with Lucie?" I said, moving over to the couch.

"She's feeling a bit under the weather," Nathanial said, standing over me. I stroked her hair.

"Micah?" I asked again, ignoring Nathanial. Micah didn't answer. His eyes were closed. Something was wrong. I turned to look at Lucie again and shook her gently. She didn't move. I shook her a second time and still she didn't move. I bent my head close to her mouth and I could feel the heat from her breath. She was alive. Why wasn't she moving?

"MICAH!" I said forcefully, moving over to stand in front of him. I reached to touch him, but I was met with some sort of resistance. I rounded and stared at Nathanial.

"Micah and I aren't seeing eye-to-eye right now Ana; it's best that he remain a silent party for the time being." Nathanial's voice sounded off and his body was rigid.

"What the hell Nathanial? What did you do to him?" I turned back to Micah and saw that his eyes were now open and he was staring at me.

"Nothing, he's fine and so is Lucie, Ana." Nathanial had moved toward me and suddenly I felt very tense. Everything about this scene was making me nervous. I shut down my mental dialogue. "It won't work

Ana." Nathanial stared at me, his eyes black. "For some reason since my little resurrection, my powers seem to be amplified and your wall is no longer effective so don't bother." He was annoyed and his tone reflected his emotions. I took a deep breath and tried to calm myself.

"Nathanial, what's going on?" I asked, moving a step back from him.

"I want to talk to you Ana, that's all," he said, his voice quiet, but shaky. I frowned.

"About what?" I said, crossing the room and sitting on the couch with Lucie.

"Everything," he said, watching me as I stroked her hair wondering what he'd done to her. "I said she's fine Ana!' he snapped and I studied him. "I'm sorry." He collected himself, my eyes narrowed as I stood to face him.

"Well, I don't really know what that includes Nathanial," I said, cocking my head. He exhaled and started pacing around the room.

"I'm not mad at you Ana; I'm not mad at you for sleeping with Patric. You made a mistake. You thought you loved him and he manipulated you when you were vulnerable and weak; you made a mistake and I'm not mad." He was speaking quickly and I watched as his form started to blur from one end of the room to the other.

"I do love Patric, Nathanial; that's something that you've always known." He rounded on me and suddenly he was only inches from my face, breathing hard.

"No! You didn't hear me; you're not listening to me. He manipulated you. He's always manipulated you from the first time you met; he used you then and now…you have no idea what he's done Ana." I felt the heat from his breath on my mouth and there was a tinge of bitterness to his normal scent. He stood back and glared at me. I was trying not to make any mental assessments of him or about what he'd said about Patric; my survival mode was kicking in. I looked at Micah and I could see that he was watching us, following our movements. I tried to calm my fear over what was happening. "No, Ana no." Nathanial's tone suddenly turned soft and he approached me again and stroked my face, his touch burning my skin. "I don't want you to be afraid of me, I would never want you to be afraid…" He looked into my eyes and I swallowed. I couldn't follow the sudden changes in his mood; they were throwing me.

"That's what you want to talk about Nathanial, Patric?" I asked, stepping back a few feet. His eyes flashed at my sudden movement and he reached to grab my arm pulling me back forcefully into him. "Nathanial!" I said; he was hurting me.

"You used to like when I was rough with you Ana, remember? You used to like when I controlled you." He was searching my face and I could feel a surge of heat coming off his body. His fingers were digging into my flesh, into his scar on my wrist and the pressure was shooting pain up and down my arm. I yanked myself away.

"You never physically hurt me Nathanial!" I said, my tone angry now. What the hell was wrong with him? He laughed darkly.

"I suppose after being with this new Patric that you like things gentle now. Is that it? You want your desires to be treated with tenderness Ana? I'm just not sure that after making the rounds so many times that you get to be so choosy." He glared at me and I gasped. His words tore through my heart. He shook his head and again his tone turned soft. "I'm sorry Ana, that was cruel. I didn't mean to say that to you. I can be gentle too; I can be whatever you want." He moved back toward me and my eyes widened. It was Nathanial. He had been the one to come to my apartment. He'd gone through my things, he'd destroyed my painting from Stephen; it had been him because he'd snapped. Suddenly Nathanial's fingers were grabbing me around the throat and he pushed me back against the wall. I was choking. I tried to fight him off, but he shot a pain through my head that leveled me mentally and physically. "It doesn't have to be like this Ana. We can be together and have the life that we were supposed to have. We can get married. It doesn't have to be this way." He brought his mouth to mine and forced my lips to part. He didn't taste right; he tasted bitter and full of acid and bile. He pushed himself harder against me and I tried to turn my head away, but he crushed down further on my throat. My head was splitting open. "Kiss me!" he growled, forcing his tongue so far down my throat that I started to gag. "Looks like you're out of practice." He snarled and started to move his mouth down my neck. His teeth grazed my flesh and again I tried to push him off. I felt him tear the skin and blood started to trickle down my throat. "Remember Ana? Remember when we first did this, when we first took each other like this? Remember how it felt, how much you wanted me? It can be like that again, it can be like that always." His tongue was tracing over the now burning wound he'd created. I wasn't sure why it was burning, it never had with Nathanial and I could only guess it had something to

171

do with what was happening to him now; how he'd changed. "Shut up Ana," he said quietly. "Shut up and let me help you remember." His tone turned dark and he sent another searing pain into my head. I gasped, trying not to throw up.

Stephen

I had cursed Liam out so hard that I was close to pummeling him. She had called and I had missed her. I had wanted to call since she'd left, but I didn't want to bother her; I thought that maybe she needed some time to relax a bit without me begging her to stay with me, to wait for me when I was finished with this insanity. Actually, the arrangement could have been much, much worse; aside from being away from Ana, I was getting in some good training time and Saden seemed more than pleased with our situation. Liam was scheduled to leave at the end of the week and I was glad that he and Carmen could get out of this place and be with Lucie. I had yet to fight and Liam promised that he would be there when that time came, just in case. I would want Ana to hear it from him first. I was sitting in the conference room waiting for a meeting to start about new recruits when my brother came in looking distressed.

"Has Ana called you?" he asked, standing over me, his eyes flashing.

"No, why? I asked, looking up at him. He rubbed his chin

"I don't understand. I spoke to her over three hours ago. She should have made it to Peru by now and seen Lucie." He seemed to be talking to himself.

"Have you called Micah?" I asked, taking out my phone. Liam nodded.

"No answer," he said and we stared at each other. That was unlike Micah not to answer his phone. Saden entered the room and looked at Liam, reading our concern.

"What's up?" he said, spinning around in his seat. Liam shook his head.

"It's nothing Saden. My little girl wasn't feeling too well today and we're waiting to hear how she's doing." Liam's tone was calm on the surface, but worry was seeping into his mind, worry for Ana and for Lucie. Saden shrugged.

"I didn't think vampires could get sick, even half ones," he said, pouring three glasses of scotch. Liam looked at me. "I mean I'd always heard that once we get venom in our system, we're basically immune to everything; being half I'm guessing that she could probably live forever or something," he said, slamming back his drink. I suddenly thought about Ana and smiled, but I noticed Liam tense.

"Yes Saden, you're right, vampires don't get sick," he said quietly and I saw fear move over his face, then I could feel it. It pulsed cold and deep across the table and I shuddered.

Ana

Nathanial was pushing himself against me, his hips grinding so hard into my own that my bones were beginning to hurt. I couldn't focus on fighting. Somehow he knew how to make me defenseless. "You used to like that Ana, being defenseless against what I wanted from you, against what you wanted from me; you used to like it when I held you like this." He was breathing hard. I was so confused. What had happened? Why was Nathanial behaving like this? This wasn't him. This wasn't the person that I had saved and loved. What was wrong? He shot another stabbing pain into my head cutting off my internal questions. My stomach heaved and I pushed my face away in time for me to throw up. I felt his grip slacken just a fraction and I lunged, pushing him back against the opposite wall and trying to grab Lucie. He was on me, jerking my hair and body over the couch toward him. I grabbed his arm, pulling him toward me and flipping him back. He was up in an instant and just as I started to shimmer, he grabbed my neck and I took him with me.

Stephen

I was watching Liam when a shot of cold and hot air came pulsing into the room and the table where we were sitting, suddenly shattered into a million pieces throwing me backward in my chair. I leapt up in time to see Ana hurdling into the rubble with Nathanial on top of her. She flung him off and he came whizzing by me. I jumped to my feet and ran up the wall, landing on top of him as he lunged for her. She was trying to move the shards glass and wood off of her legs. Liam was already in the air pulling her out from the rubble. I grabbed Nathanial around the neck, but he flipped so forcefully that I lost my grip and he crashed down grasping Ana's leg as he fell, pulling her with him. He rolled and pinned her down striking her across the face. I tackled him from behind snapping his head back, but again, he grabbed Ana, taking her with him as I flung his body across the room. They landed, crashing through the wall and as I jumped through the hole, I heard Ana scream. It was blood curdling and my heart seized.

Patric

I stood in the shadows watching my brother lose himself—he was gone, fallen. I moved quietly behind Stephen. I had gone to see Micah and found him paralyzed. He'd shown me everything.

Stephen

I halted midstride. Nathanial had Ana on her knees and was grasping the back of her neck; blood was streaming down over her shoulders. He had her mark. She was crying and screaming as he pulled and twisted her metal tattoo.

175

"Don't move," he said quietly. "Don't move or I will kill her, then she will belong to no one." He pulled and she screamed again. I put my hands up. I was fighting both shock and utter despair—what happened to him? I watched as more blood came pouring out of Ana; she was gasping. "See Ana, I'm making your choice very easy for you." He was talking to her and I saw Saden and Liam out of the corner of my eye. Saden looked tense. The blood, Ana's blood, it was spilling out everywhere now. "What do you want to do Ana?" Nathanial had her head pulled back and I noticed that her throat was also bleeding. Jesus Christ, Nathanial was going to kill Ana. I didn't recognize the being standing in front of me; this was not Nathanial. "It's me or no one. Not that hard is it?" he snarled and I saw him twist his hand; she screamed and gasped. My soul shattered. A blur shot from the side and I saw Saden launch himself into the air crashing down upon Nathanial trying to get to Ana. I didn't hesitate. I ran at Nathanial and dragged his body off of Ana shouting to Liam. I punched Nathanial in the head knocking his body across the room. I heard a snap and smelled melting flesh and I turned to see my brother standing over Saden, holding his decapitated head in his hand and his chest split open. Nathanial was down and I ran to Ana. She was trying to stand when suddenly I saw my brother's body jerked sideways and come crashing down against the wall. Nathanial stood in front me and I waved my hand, but he blocked me and I saw him lunge and grab Ana by the hair as he sliced across my stomach with something sharp. He'd stabbed me.

My brother was going to kill her. He had her mark in his hand and he was going to kill her. I stepped out from the room and faced him. Stephen was leaning against the wall, his blood streaking and dripping down the white paint. Ana was facing me and her eyes were closed.

"Nathanial," I said, taking a step toward him.

"Don't come near me Patric." He pulled a bit on Ana and she gasped. I walked slowly forward. "You're a traitor. You betrayed me," he said. My brother was crying, Ana's blood streaming down his hand.

"Well then, this is between you and me isn't it?" I said, taking another step forward. He shook his head. "You and me Nathanial. Brothers. We should be able to talk about this, heal." I moved again and he glared at me.

"Stop! Stop moving Patric or she's dead." He pushed her, bending her head forward, twisting the Bond and Ana threw up. I nodded. I had to hurry. Stephen was severely injured and possibly Liam, and if Ana lost too much blood, she would be lost as well.

"What do you want Nathanial?" I asked, moving subtly to the side. He gasped.

"I want you to leave us alone. I want you and Stephen to let Ana and me be together and stop trying to confuse her. She loves me and she wants me." He was crying and growling as more blood continued to spill from Ana's mark.

177

"Fine. Stephen and I will step aside, but you have to let Ana go; you're killing her Nathanial, is that what you want? You want to kill Ana?" I asked. He shook his head "no" and I moved forward a bit more, but suddenly I saw him pull back and I heard a god awful tearing of flesh and Ana screamed. I didn't have to think; I blasted my brother with fire, sending him flying backward in a storm of blue flames.

Chapter Seven

Patric

I iam, Micah and I were working furiously trying to save everyone; Nathanial, Stephen and Ana, all were mortally wounded and all were hovering on the brink of death. I could smell it. It hung in the air like a bitter and dense fog threatening to consume the souls of whoever decided to give up first. It was waiting. Between all of them, Ana and Nathanial were the worst. Nathanial had managed to detach most of her imprint and she was all but lost. She was cold, she'd lost so much blood and her heart, emotionally, was torn by his act; they went together, Bonds; what you did to one physically, effected the person mentally. It shut them down, quieting their will to fight, to hold on and Ana was fading fast. Stephen had been stabbed by a metal shank and he too had lost a ton of blood and he was hanging in the balance. Upon rallying from Nathanial's blow, Liam had immediately given Stephen some of his own blood and that's probably why we didn't loose him right there at the fight.

My brother was a different story. I had hit him with fire, *my* fire. He was my brother and I had tried to kill him. I had no other choice. I couldn't allow for him to take Ana's life. I moved over him, pouring my own blood and Micah's blood, the blood he shared with my mother, down his throat. He wasn't breathing and his eyes were open and still. I wasn't sure what was worse, having him live and know just how close he came to killing the woman he loved or having my brother die, existing in the world without him. At this point, I just couldn't say. I walked down the hall to check on Stephen. An odd thing had occurred between us when I arrived to the fight. He'd been up against the wall bleeding out and I could read every thought he had in his mind, every feeling that was coursing through his body and his soul; they were all of Ana, of how much he loved her, of how much he wanted to trade his life for hers, how much he wanted to give her, to show her, to experience with her. The amount of emotion pouring from him in that moment was excruciatingly painful in it's intensity. I had never felt anything to such an extent from anyone before, not even Nathanial. Stephen had begged for his own death if she would be spared and I knew in that instant, that he is what she needed. I loved Ana and I would always love her; we were Bound in a different way than she and Nathanial and she and Stephen. I wanted her to be happy and to have the life she wanted, even if that meant not being with her. She was that important to me. At least that is how I was feeling currently; I'd been known to change to my mind.

Liam was holding his brother's hand and I cocked my head. It was an interesting scenario, both of us fighting for our brothers; both of us giving our own blood, hoping they each would survive. The difference was that *my* brother had tried to kill *his* brother and yet Liam was fighting for them both. Stephen was breathing now, albeit shallowly. He was sweating and his skin was ashen. I looked at Liam and could see the deep sense of despair in his whole being; he was devastated.

"How's Nathanial?" he asked, not taking his eyes off of Stephen. I sighed and sat down on the edge of the bed.

"Not good. It doesn't look good." My chest ached. The fog seemed to be getting denser and smell of death more rancid.

"Patric, I don't know what to say to you. I want to offer you my thanks for doing what you did, for saving Ana from what was a certain death and for helping me to try to save my brother, but I also know that the decision you had to make, the choice you made; I don't know if I could have done the same in that moment. I'm so very sorry that things had to come to this; a brother should never have to make such a choice." He looked at me and I bowed my head. I didn't know how things got so out of control with Nathanial, how he'd lost himself so much that he saw no other option than to take Ana's life away, to take Stephen's and possibly Liam's; that wasn't my brother that I fought, it was a shadow, a ghost of a man and a being that no one knew. Stephen stirred and Liam startled, his eyes roaming over his brother.

"Ana," Stephen whispered and I moved beside Liam. "Ana." Stephen was trying to open his eyes.

"Stephen." Liam bent his head close and held his brother's face in his hands. The gesture was so tender and so intimate that it made my heart throb. I swallowed and ran my hands over his body, trying to cool him. Stephen turned his head and this time we saw his eyes. They were startling in their clarity and they pierced through every wall that I had ever built. I saw oceans appear and I watched, spellbound as the tides moved across in their depths, shifting and pulling back and forth. "Where's Ana?" His voice was soft, but he seemed alert. I looked at Liam. I didn't know what to say.

"Ana's been hurt Stephen. She's been injured severely." Liam stared at his brother, their eyes searching each other. Stephen nodded.

"Is she dead?" he asked as a single tear slid from his eye down his pale cheek.

"No," Liam said, wiping Stephen's face gently. "No she's not dead." I exited the room quietly and went further down the hall to Ana's room. I exhaled and opened the door. She was struggling, her breath coming in short bursts and she was crying. It was an odd thing to witness; she was hanging onto the edge of a cliff. I could see her fighting against the odds, against the damage that Nathanial had inflicted. I could see this was her chance, her chance to finally understand just how important her life truly was, how much I needed her, how much Stephen loved her, how much she had changed the very core of all of us—permanently. She said she had nothing left, nothing left to lose and now she had to make a choice. Did she fight for her life, fight for everything that she was and everything that she could be or did she fall, did she let go and leave us forever? She was shaking and her body was cold. I rested beside her and held her face, wiping her tears. I sat with her until Liam came in. He stared at her and went to sit on the bed taking her hand in his. I saw Micah go down the hall to Nathanial's room carrying a damp cloth soaked with herbs. I moved from Ana's side. Liam nodded and he took my place as I followed my uncle into my brother's room.

"He's not fighting Patric," Micah said, his eyes desperate. "He's giving up." I turned to look at Nathanial. His eyes were dark, no stars visible in their depths. The fog was the deepest in his room; it was waiting for him. I heard my uncle start to sob and then I became angry. I shook Nathanial, pounding him on the chest. He didn't move, he didn't respond. I rested my head on his chest listening. Nothing. I bent my lips to his ear and whispered.

"Ana's alive Nathanial and she's fighting; she's trying to hang on." I pulled away and watched. Nothing. I sighed. I wasn't ready to give up, not yet. I would fight for him even if he didn't care anymore, even if he had given up, I would fight for my brother, fight for the being I knew him to be. He wasn't a shadow; he was my flesh and blood, my twin. I put my head in my hands and exhaled, rubbing my face. I left the room and returned to Stephen. He was breathing steadily now and I gently pulled back his covers to look at his wound. Vampires had the capacity to heal quickly from bodily trauma, but a metal shank was our or rather their Achilles heel. I pulled up the blood soaked gauze and stared in awe at the gash along Stephen's stomach. It had pulled together and while the skin was still damaged from the slice, the major part of the wound was now a thick, pink line that resembled a surgery scar.

"How's it look?" Stephen's eyes were opened and he was staring at me.

"Not bad," I said, rummaging through my bag for some fresh bandages.

"Ana?" He breathed and his body shuddered from the movement. I looked at him.

"I don't know yet Stephen," I spoke quietly as I removed his old gauze and set about cleaning his wounds. He winced as I swabbed an herbal mixture over his skin.

"Nathanial?" Stephen turned his head toward me as I pressed gently down on his abdomen. I swallowed and shook my head, lowering my eyes. Stephen raised his arm and placed his hand on my shoulder. I applied a clean muslin cloth on his stomach and waved my hand, letting the medicine-coated underside penetrate into his skin.

"This should help with your own body's healing abilities and with the pain," I said, closing up my bag. He was looking better every minute and I breathed in a slightly tenuous relief. One out of three was not good enough.

"I want to see her," Stephen said, staring at me with those oceans in his eyes again. I shook my head.

"You're not strong enough Stephen. You need to rest." He turned his head slowly from side to side.

"No. I need to see her Patric." His voice was strong and I felt his conviction not only in his words, but I felt it in my own heart. "Help me," he said as he tried to raise himself off of the pillows. I walked and swung his arm around my shoulder and helped him bring his legs to the floor. He leaned on me as I gently pulled him to his feet. He gasped as he tried to rise up and he had to sit back down. I sighed and stared at him. This was a bad idea. "I'm ok. Let's try again." He looked at me and I nodded. I felt a sudden surge of strength in his body and he pulled himself to standing on his own. He wrapped his arm around my shoulder and together we walked out of his room and down the hall to Ana.

Stephen

I wasn't allowing myself to remember anything that had happened; the images, the sounds, they were just too close. I leaned on Patric as he opened the door to Ana's room. My brother was sitting on her bed holding her hand and he turned to stare at me, his eyes wide and full of relief. Our gazes locked and the private conversation they exchanged spoke of love, sacrifice, friendship and family. I swallowed back my tears as Patric helped me to Ana's side. I lowered myself onto the bed and grasped her other hand as my brother and Patric drifted silently from the room. I gasped, sobbing and I placed my head on her chest, listening to her heart. The beats were irregular and there were long pauses in between where there were no heartbeats, no breath. I reached to smooth her hair and caress her cheeks, they were wet from her tears and I held my face close, breathing her in. Her body was cold. I couldn't speak, my throat was closed and my mind wouldn't allow words to flow. All I could do was hold her. I pressed my face back down on her chest and tucked my arms under her shoulders and pulled her as close as possible.

"Stephen." Patric had moved next to Ana and he was watching me. "You need to go back to bed; you're not healed." I shook my head and held her tighter. He sighed as he sunk down into the chair and put his chin in his palms, thinking, watching.

"What?" I said, raising my head slightly to look at him.

185

"It's as if they're connected," he murmured, his eyes flashing as he focused on Ana. I wiped the tears from my face and sat up, wincing from the movement.

"Who's connected?" I asked, touching Ana's lips.

"My brother's life and hers; it's as if she knows he's not fighting. Her body knows that her Bond is ready to give up." He leaned forward, studying Ana.

"But their Bond was broken; they're not Bound anymore," I whispered, not understanding. Patric shook his head.

"Their Bond still remains Stephen. Ana was the only one of the two to emotionally disconnect from Nathanial, but he's never let her go; he didn't agree to the severance of their thread, it was one sided. I think his mental and physical bonds to her are still there and he knows her life is in danger and vice versa, and I can't tell if she's fighting; I can't tell if she's trying to hold on." His voice sounded urgent and I watched as he bent his face close to hers and studied her. It was odd to see Patric so emotionally invested in someone; it went against the very nature that I had always seen him display and it was a bit unsettling. He laughed softly. "Hmm...yes I guess I am emotionally invested in Ana, but I don't think that I am the best choice for her. I struggle too much with my own desires and ambitions and while I love her and while I would give my very soul to keep her in this world, I can't seem to come to her in the absence of selfishness. I wanted her because I love her, yes, but I also wanted her because I didn't want her to be with you or with my brother... not the best foundations for a stable relationship." He touched her cheek. "She deserves someone who is above using her heart as a pawn, good intentions or not." He stared at me and his eyes surged.

"She loves you," I said quietly. He nodded.

"Yes, she does and I don't deserve it. She loves you too Stephen; she's chosen you." I stared at him. I hadn't really believed Ana when she said she wanted to be with me because she also thought that she wasn't right for me because she was Human; she felt it better to go our separate ways. Patric waved his hand. "As smart as Ana is, she also has great difficulty putting things in perspective. She tends to see things as these vast challenges that she couldn't possibly be able to conquer and yet time and time again, there is evidence of the contrary." I smiled; Patric knew Ana well. He smiled back. "The challenges that she sees for the two of you are inconsequential. She's scared and whether or not she knows it, she's looking for an excuse to keep herself safe, to keep her heart safe." He smoothed her hair. "Look," he said gently turning Ana's head to the side and sweeping her hair back from her neck. I leaned over and saw her metal tattoo. I gasped. Patric's stone was there, but instead of running directly through the eye in the center, it was now entwined with her own symbol; a solid turquoise thread woven around glistening silver. The eye in the center was a clear marine blue and I could see the ocean moving deep within. I stared at Patric, not believing. "See," he said, meeting my gaze, his eyes fierce. "She wants you, her heart wants you Stephen." I bowed my head and sobbed.

I sat watching my brother as he remained still. I held his hand
wondering how things had gone so horribly, horribly wrong for him,
how he'd lost himself so much. I knew that he loved Ana, that she was
his life and his heart and losing her was devastating, but what he'd
allowed himself to do, where he took his mind and his soul; he'd
painted himself black. The fog was still lingering over him and I choked
on the scent, my brother's fading scent. Suddenly a thought occurred
to me, a thought that was both desperate and risky, but that just
might work. I bolted from the room and found Liam who was sitting
with Micah. Our eyes met and Liam rose from his seat.

"Patric, that's a very serious decision," Liam spoke quietly. "It may kill
him." He stared at me. I shook my head.

"He's dying anyway," I whispered. "He's dying and he shouldn't." My
chest heaved. "I need time, we need time to fix things between us; we
have a second chance and I need him. I need my family, my brother... I
need him to survive," I said, tears brimming in my eyes. "Please." Liam
turned to Micah and I saw my uncle nod. Liam exhaled.

"If you can live with the consequences Patric; if you fully understand
what you are asking, if you understand that my actions may kill your
brother, if you understand that he may not be the person you
remember for a very long time. If you can live with those things, then
yes, I will help you." Liam put his hand on my shoulder and I nodded.
"I'll need to speak with Stephen," Liam said and walked out of the
room.

Stephen

I was staring at my brother, my eyes wide. This was unbelievable.

"Stephen, put yourself in Patric's shoes; he loves his brother and is desperate to save his life. I would be doing whatever I had the power to do to save you and I know that you would do the same for me; there is no difference here between all of us." I couldn't help but see a few differences. My brother hadn't almost murdered the woman that I love, my brother hadn't cheated, lied, manipulated, hurt, devastated, wrecked so many lives and so many hearts; there was a difference. Liam stared at me. "And what of your own sins Stephen, the ones you committed before you were Changed; did I not forgive you? Did I not take you back into my heart? Did I not continue to protect you, love you, call you my brother?" We stared at each other and I bowed my head. "Saving Nathanial may mean saving Ana as well, we don't know," he said quietly, taking her other hand. His eyes narrowed as he looked at me. "Surely after all of this you wouldn't be worried? Surely after everything you now know about how Ana feels, you wouldn't be apprehensive about saving Nathanial because you are scared that Ana may find her way to back to him? Surely my own brother would not dishonor the love that he's been lucky to experience from such an incredible soul, because he is jealous." Liam's eyes grew dark as he searched my heart.

"No Liam," I spoke honestly. "I just wonder if he dies during the transition, does Ana die too? Is it worth the risk?" I said, staring back at her face.

"Yes," he said, rising from the bed. "I don't think that Ana is ready to leave this world, ready to leave you and I think," he touched her face, "I think she knows that you are waiting for her, but beyond that, she would want us to save him Stephen; Ana would want us to save Nathanial." I sighed. Of course she would. Liam nodded and left the room.

I decided to stay with Ana while my brother and Patric dealt with Nathanial. It wouldn't be a pleasant thing to watch and I really didn't have the strength to grapple with what would be happening in that room. I was feeling stronger by the day and I could now lie fully next to Ana without my stomach heaving in pain. I pulled her close and sang quietly in her ear and I felt her breathe. I thought about how I wanted to ask her to marry me, where we would be, what I would say. I pictured us driving around to look at houses to buy and where we would end up living. Ana loved Ireland and I would be quite content returning to the place of my family. I thought about the holidays we would have with my brother and Carmen and Lucie and shopping and taking Ana out dancing and going to concerts and traveling. I conjured images of kissing her and holding her and listening as she whispered my name in the dark. I thought about the child we had conceived and I wondered if we would try again; if she would want to try again. I jumped as a gut-wrenching scream penetrated my mind and the air shifted around me. Nathanial. Ana's body began shaking and I sat up staring at her. Another scream from down the hall and I heard Ana gasp, her body going rigid. I held her close. I could hear Nathanial as he writhed in pain as my brother's venom entered his bloodstream. His body was dying, mostly. He was a Bonder, a Demon by blood so he would become more like Patric; he would be half. Of course I could see in my brother's mind just how uncertain he was at exactly how Nathanial would handle the Change, being so near death for his Bonder life might make him more vampire and less Demon, if he managed to survive—we just didn't know. Ana was shaking uncontrollably now and she was sweating. I couldn't help but notice how she was all of a sudden reacting to what was happening to Nathanial, or so it seemed. I heard a door open and shut, another deafening scream, then silence. The only good thing about Nathanial being close to death was that he most likely wouldn't remember what was happening; if he survived, he wouldn't be able to recall the pain, the ice and the fire. He wouldn't be able to recall feeling his organs detach and reassemble, he wouldn't notice his skin cracking and bleeding out his old blood then healing new and regenerated and most likely, he wouldn't remember Ana. He wouldn't remember any of their time together. He wouldn't remember their Bond and he wouldn't remember trying to kill her. Nathanial's memory would be wiped clean and he would have to work very hard at recalling any knowledge of his past life and sometimes, that life is lost forever. I shuddered. The door opened and Liam came into the room. He looked weak and sad; he hated Changing people. He'd only done it a handful of times and only under the direst of circumstances or if they could argue a case for it and that was rare.

"How is he?" I asked, looking at Ana. She'd gone still. Liam shook his head.

"I don't know, he was so close to death; I have no idea how he's going to respond. It will take a few days..." His eyes went to Ana. "Is she breathing?" he asked, frowning and coming to stand next to her.

"Yes," I said, watching her chest rise and fall. "And she's stopped shaking and sweating," I said, sweeping her hair back from her forehead. Liam nodded, bending close to her face. He pulled back up then bent back down. "What?" I asked suddenly on edge.

"Don't you smell that?" he said, staring at me. I frowned; I didn't smell anything. I shook my head. "Here, bend you head near her mouth." He motioned for me to move closer. I leaned my nose and lips close to hers. I felt her breath on my mouth and I swallowed, tasting her, tasting her scent! It was diluted and weak, but it was there. I looked at Liam and he nodded and smiled. I kept my face close to hers, breathing and drinking her in. I hugged her close, not letting myself feel too much hope. Immediately Liam left the room and headed down the hall to Nathanial's. I held my breath. A heart beat later, he returned and nodded. I exhaled. He might pull through.

Ana

My dreams were so dark, full of blood and fire and pain. I was crying in all of them, crying and falling over the edge of a cliff through fog. I could see Liam and Patric, their faces solemn. I saw Alec, his green eyes shimmering then turning black. I saw Kai, his arms outstretched, reaching for me as I fell. I saw Lucie's face and heard her call my name. I turned over and saw Nathanial; we were falling side-by-side and I tried to touch him, tried to reach for his hand. I saw Noni and she was smiling, but her eyes were fierce. She was talking to me, telling me it was ok to look down now, that there was nothing to be afraid of anymore. I did. I looked down and saw Stephen waiting, hovering over the spinning earth, his arms ready to catch me and his eyes sparkling as he watched me falling closer. My body tensed and I slowed my fall, holding Stephen off. I wasn't ready. What if he stepped away? What if he changed his mind? What if I was just too broken to care anymore? Our gazes locked and I felt myself begin to pick up speed. I looked to the side and saw Nathanial staying with me, staying by my side. Who was going to catch him? I found Stephen again and he was staring up at me, watching. Fire ignited around him and he stepped out through the flames, arms outstretched. My Noni's voice shattered through my fear. *You are ready my bambina, my most precious gift, my heart. Look down now and fall; I promise that you will awaken and so will he.* I looked back at Nathanial once, then released my hold on myself and plummeted to the earth screaming.

Stephen

Ana jolted and released a blood-curdling scream and I flew off the bed, my heart freezing. Liam, Patric and Micah all came rushing into the room as Ana continued to scream, her body heaving and writhing and lifting into the air. Patric rushed to her side and pulled her back down to the bed, holding her close to him. Liam stood next to me, his arms wrapped around my shoulders. I watched as Ana gasped once, exhaled, then opened her eyes and whispered my name. The world stopped when I heard her speak and I cried out and ran to her side.

Patric nodded and moved so that I could take his place. I pressed her to my chest, cradling her head against me.

"Stephen?" she whispered again

"I'm here love, I'm here," I said, kissing her cheeks as my tears melted into her skin.

"You caught me," she said, her breath shallow as she tried to inhale.

"What?" I asked, my joy clearly not allowing for me to hear her accurately.

"I fell and you caught me; you were waiting for me to say it was ok. I fell." She closed her eyes and licked her lips. I glanced up at Patric and he shook his head.

"Ana, we need to check you over." Patric was stepping back over to me and he reached for her hand. I stood and laid her back against the pillows. I watched as Liam, Micah and Patric worked over every part of her body, checking her movements, listening to her heart, testing her reflexes, asking her questions about where she thought she was and what was the last thing she remembered. I held my breath as that last question hung in the air. We waited. She sighed and closed her eyes.

"Patric. I remember seeing Patric." She opened her eyes and turned toward him, reaching to take his hand. He smiled at her. "And Nathanial," she said quietly, holding his gaze, "he was going to kill me. I felt him grab my mark and he pulled..." She shook her head and started to breathe quickly.

"Shhh Ana, it's ok." Patric stroked her face. "It's ok now." She nodded and took a shaky breath in.

"Perhaps we should let her rest now," Liam said, looking at both Patric and Micah. They nodded.

"Nathanial?" Ana turned to Patric. "Did anyone catch him…?" Her voice faded and her eyes closed. Patric touched her lips and sighed. "Nathanial?" she asked again, but then she started breathing deeply, falling asleep. Patric turned to me.

"Stay with her. We still won't know anything for a few days as far as Nathanial is concerned and you need to rest as well." He walked out to the hallway.

"Should we tell her anything?" I asked, leaning in the doorway. Patric shook his head and turned to Liam.

"Not right now. If she asks just tell her that he's been injured and we are working to save him. She's been traumatized enough," Liam said as he sighed and held my gaze. I nodded and walked back into the room.

Patric

Ana had survived. She'd fought for herself and she'd survived. My heart was almost repaired, almost. For four nights I sat by my brother's side, watching, waiting to see if he would awaken. I knew he might not remember me and I knew that he would most likely not remember Ana. It was a heavy price to pay, but worth it if I could still have my brother. No matter what state he would be in, I would help him heal. I would help him to remember me and remember our mother and how much his strength reminded me of our father. It might take lifetimes, but he could do it if he wanted.

It was after midnight on the fifth night when I was awoken from my trance by a sudden gust of cold air filtering into the room. I looked around, but no one was there. I turned to my brother and his eyes were opened. I gasped. I heard a rumble of thunder from somewhere in the distance and I watched as lightening crashed against the dark night skies. Nathanial breathed out and I could smell his fragrance permeate the room. Another flash of lightening and just in the brief amount of light from the storm, I saw my brother's eyes had changed. Gone were the deep midnight blue and silver shade he'd always carried; now they were light blue with the deep brown center he'd gotten when Ana had saved him last. He wasn't moving, so I gently opened the buttons on his shirt. His chest was smooth and strong and his mark was gone; no imprint of metal, nothing of me or our mother remained melded into his skin. I pulled back. I had been young when I had asked to be Changed so I had not had the opportunity to develop my own imprint. The amulet that my mother had given me before she died became my own version of those marks and when I had taken Ana's blood the first time, the necklace became burned into my flesh. She was my Bond. From the looks of things, my brother appeared to have forsaken all of his demonic blood and was perhaps, now, a vampire in the fullest form. I didn't know. I called for Liam. "His mark is gone," I said, pulling back Nathanial's shirt to show Liam and Stephen, who had come to help.

"Hmm... and his eyes have changed as well, yes?" Liam asked me. I nodded. I noticed Stephen staring at me.

"What?" I asked, my tone sharp.

"Your eye color, have you always had that particular shade?" Stephen asked me and his gaze was intent.

"Yes. It's my mother's eye color and Micah's too. I kept it even after I was Changed," I said, turning to look at my brother. Stephen and Liam looked at each other.

"It appears that Nathanial is no longer a Bonder Patric; had he retained any of his own bloodline like you, his eyes would have remained the same. He's a full vampire now," Liam said quietly. I sighed; we'd done it. We saved Nathanial and I didn't care what he was. He was alive and as far as I was concerned, that was all that mattered. I heard Nathanial breathe in loudly and then exhale and we all turned to stare. He was looking back at us, eyes wide.

"Nathanial?" I reached to touch his hand and he jerked away from me.

"He's confused," Liam said. It will take him a bit to get his bearings; the world looks bit different right now, but that will fade. He'll regain his focus." Liam stood in front of Nathanial and I saw their eyes meet and I also saw what looked like recognition sweep over my brother's face.

"He knows you?" I asked, staring at Liam.

197

"It appears so, but I don't know in what capacity. He might not realize that I'm his creator. It's hard to tell." Liam surveyed Nathanial. "Nathanial? Do you know who I am?" Liam's voice was clear and commanding and even I found myself standing a bit straighter at his inflection. My brother cocked his head and nodded.

"Yes," he replied and his voice was strong and deep. It was mostly the voice I remembered, but there was a definite change; the tone was fiercer somehow. Liam motioned towards me.

"Do you know who this is?" Liam asked and I stiffened as Nathanial's eyes focused deeply on my own.

"We're related." He nodded to me and I exhaled. His choice of wording was odd, but at least he knew that we were of the same family. Liam went to stand next to Stephen.

"And him? Do you know this person Nathanial?" Liam watched as Nathanial sat up straighter leaning over to study Stephen.

"No," he said quietly as he fell back against his pillows. I looked at Liam.

"Perhaps it has something to do with the fact that we both gave him our blood; that your blood was the last thing that entered his system before mine and before his Change took place…I can't say for sure," Liam muttered.

"Does it matter?" my brother spoke softly and I turned to stare at him.

"No, it doesn't I guess," Liam spoke, moving to sit on the bed. "How do you feel Nathanial?"

"Tired, exhausted, but fine." He stared at Liam and I could see his mind trying to process the scene in the room. Liam nodded and patted his leg.

"Good. You need to rest and we'll talk more in the morning alright?" He stood and motioned for Stephen and me to follow. I turned to look back at Nathanial; he was watching me. I nodded to him and sighed, shutting the door. Liam leaned up against the wall as Micah appeared by his side. "We'll need to keep Ana away from him. He'll be hungry and thirsty by tomorrow and he'll be able to smell her blood from his room." Liam looked at me. We were all currently at the ranch in Argentina.

"I'll keep him here with me," I said, knowing that I could help him as much as he needed and that Liam would be available if something came up. Liam nodded.

"And I'll take Ana back to Ireland," Stephen spoke quietly. "If that's ok?" He turned his gaze to me and I smiled.

"I think that would be good for her," I said, feeling somewhat sad to have her away from me. Stephen laughed quietly.

"You can come by anytime Patric. After everything you've done as of late, I'd be a fool to try to keep you and Ana from seeing each other." He shook my hand and hugged me. I smirked at him.

"You sure?" I said, as he turned to walk backwards down the hall.

"I think I can handle you." He laughed and opened the door to Ana's room.

Stephen

Ana was awake when I came back to sit with her. She was staring out the window watching the lightening and rain. She pulled back the covers for me and I lay down beside her, snuggling myself close to her body.

"You should be sleeping," I murmured in her ear. "You need to rest." She sighed.

"I'm ok. I can't sleep," she said quietly.

"Patric says you can go home tomorrow if you want?" I tensed a bit. I wasn't sure if she wanted to even come home with me or if she was still thinking that we shouldn't be together. I held my breath waiting.

"Hmm…that sounds good, but I don't know where to go," she said quietly. "Where's home?" She sounded distant.

"With me Ana; if you want, home can be with me," I said, my heart trembling in my chest. She rolled over on her back.

"Are you free? I mean, you don't have to fight anymore?" she asked. I frowned. I guessed her memory was a bit hazy. My brother had killed Saden; we were all free to go.

"No Ana, I don't have to fight. I'm free and Liam and Carmen are free and Lucie's been dying to see you; they both have," I said, touching her face.

"Where are they?" she asked, staring at me, her eyes deep and soulful.

"They're at my mother's home in Belfast." I moved to caress her lips. She sighed.

"That sounds nice; if you don't mind, I mean." She looked down and I laughed.

"Nah. I don't mind. I just love you more than anything in this whole world and would never imagine taking another breath without having you by my side," I said, bending to kiss her gently on the mouth. Suddenly Ana grabbed me and pulled me on top of her, kissing me so passionately that I couldn't breathe. "Whoa! Hang on," I said, laughing and pulling away. "I'm not sure that's the best idea right now. You still have a long road of recovery ahead…we should probably slow down a bit!" I chuckled.

"I don't care. I love you and I want you," she said, pulling me back down toward her. I stared.

"You love me," I stated, watching her face. She nodded

"Of course." She laughed and kissed me gently. "Of course I love you." I studied her.

"And you want to be with me?" I asked, not sure I was reading her thoughts right.

"Yes," she replied, touching my face.

"And what of your issues with my immortality? Those seemed to be holding you back before." I rolled off of her and onto my side.

"It doesn't matter," she whispered, stroking my hair. "If you don't care then I don't care." She smiled. "Do you care?" she asked, bowing her head. "Or maybe you're still not in the right place for us; maybe you still need some time?" She glanced at the ring on my finger. I shifted so that I could bring her face close to mine.

"I don't need any time Ana and no I don't care at all about your lack of immortality. I want you and I want your heart and I don't care who else comes along with that as long as you want to be with me." I kissed her.

"Good! So it's settled then; we go back to Ireland and I can recuperate a bit." She cringed.

"What?" I asked, thinking that she might be hurting.

"Stephen, Nathanial destroyed the painting you made for me; that beautiful painting, its broken and torn." She shook her head and I saw tears falling down her cheeks

"Ahhh…well that sucks. Lucky for you, I can make you another one in no time; I'm just that gifted." I laughed softly and wiped her eyes. "It's ok Ana. He didn't mean it." I truly didn't think he did, which was surprising considering how I was feeling about Nathanial over these last months.

"Stephen? What happened to him? Where is he?" she asked, her eyes still brimming with tears. I sighed, not knowing where to go with this or what to tell her. The door opened and my brother drifted into the room. I couldn't help but think that he'd been listening to our conversation and I was actually grateful for his eavesdropping on this one occasion. Liam laughed and came to sit in the chair next to Ana.

"So we leave tomorrow then?" He looked at her, his eyes thoughtful. She nodded. "Good. Lucie will be thrilled." He was studying her, studying her emotions. "Ana, Nathanial was injured severely. In order to save him, we had to make a very serious decision." Liam paused watching her. She nodded. "It's important that you understand that the Nathanial you knew, the Nathanial you loved before all that happened; he is no more. He was very, very ill when he attacked you, this I think you have understood. He wasn't himself, but even *that* Nathanial is no longer. He does not know you. He does not know that the two of you were Bonded. He does not know about anything that has transpired between the two of you in your entire relationship. You are a stranger to him now. He will not remember loving you or you loving him." I thought that my brother was sounding a bit harsh and I glared at him, but he ignored me. Ana swallowed and I could see her mind trying to process what Liam was saying.

"Why?" she whispered. Liam looked at me, then back at Ana.

"Because in order to save his life, we had to Change him. Nathanial is a vampire in our fullest form." Liam's tone was even and he was studying Ana. I felt her hold her breath.

203

"You mean…you mean…" She was struggling and I hoped that she wouldn't loose it. She took a deep breath and exhaled loudly. "He's a Vampire?" Liam nodded. "You mean he's like Patric," she stated looking at me. I cleared my throat and pressed my lips together.

"No Ana. Nathanial is not like Patric. He was essentially dead when we initiated his transition; his Bonder bloodline was dead and he came into his Afterlife without that being part of his make up. He's now like Stephen and me," Liam spoke quietly but firmly. "Patric was very much alive when he asked to be Changed and he was fully a Bonder in his blood; that bloodline stayed with him during his Change even though his body essentially was killed and reawakened. His blood had not died prior to his transformation." This was a lot to take in and to understand and I was thinking that perhaps we should have waited until a later time to discuss the details.

"So our whole lives together have been wiped from his memory?" She sounded sad.

"Yes," My brother replied.

"He won't remember trying to kill me?" she asked, sighing.

"No."

"Wow, I wish I didn't remember that." She laughed gently and stared at me. I smiled at her. "Well, what's going to happen to him now?" She turned toward Liam.

"He's going to stay here with Patric. He knows that they are related, but he's struggling to understand in what capacity. It will take some time for him to adjust and he needs to learn how to navigate the world in his new form. He needs to heal." Liam's tone turned soft and he reached to touch Ana's hand. "You won't be able to see him Ana, not for awhile, not until he can learn to be around Humans without attacking. She swallowed and nodded.

"Will he be happy?" she asked. God, she was such an incredible person, much better than me.

"Well, that's up to him isn't it?" My brother smiled at her. "Just like it's up to you and to me and to Stephen how much we allow ourselves to experience happiness. The same will hold true for Nathanial."

"And Patric's ok taking care of him?" She seemed concerned.

"Yeah, I'm ok with it." Patric was standing in the door. "He doesn't seem to remember just how much I can kick his ass, but I'll help him." He laughed as he walked into the room. Ana didn't laugh and she was watching Patric. His eyes were bright and they flashed as he took her in. Liam caught my eye and he motioned for me to get up. I nodded, kissing Ana on the cheek and touching Patric gently on the shoulder as Liam and I left the room.

Ana

I reached up my arms toward Patric and pulled him into a hug. I sobbed violently against his chest.

"Shh… Ana. It's fine. It's ok. Don't cry." He held my face in my hands and wiped my tears. He hugged me close and together we cried just like we'd done the last night we'd spent together here. I didn't need to say anything and neither did Patric. We understood what we were to each other, what we would always be to each other. I felt my amulet grow warm as I clung to him, as I kissed him softly, wanting him to feel what I was feeling…love, friendship, gratitude, devotion, forgiveness and redemption. "Yes Ana," he whispered, kissing me back. "Always." My throat surged with intense heat and I felt my skin sink, the metal from my necklace forging itself into my flesh. I gasped as the back of my neck also ignited and I reached to touch my mark; it was gone. I looked down to see a thread of turquoise stone woven around each emblem of my necklace and one tiny jewel that sat in the center. I looked at Patric and reached to unbutton his shirt revealing his own amulet. They were the same now; his was mine and mine was his. They were forged out of our own Bond, our own love that had grown and changed and shifted. He hugged me and kissed me and we held each other as the world spun madly on around us.

Chapter Eight

Ana

It had been almost two months since I'd returned to Ireland with Stephen. Physically, I felt pretty good considering how close to death I had been. Emotionally, I was a tad bit unhinged. The whole thing with Nathanial was proving a bit difficult to grapple with and not just the fact that he was now a Vampire, but also everything that he had done to me; he'd wanted to kill me. It was hard to reconcile when I would ponder our journey together. I didn't think I could have ever anticipated that it would have resolved itself in such a violent manner. Plus, it wasn't like I could ever talk to him about it—he didn't remember me, or anything about our relationship. In a way I felt like he'd gotten off easy; he didn't have to atone for anything, feel anything, and I did. He could experience new dreams while I still was battling old nightmares and trying to heal old wounds. He'd gotten closure in a way and I just had to accept that he was no longer a part of my life, at least not in the same capacity.

Stephen was tremendously supportive. He was moving very slowly with me, and his tolerance for my contemplative moods over these last months, was a true testament to his love and capacity for patience. He would ask me questions, sometimes gauging if my memories were in tact. I was actually remembering more prior to the fight with Nathanial, but there were gaps. I remembered going back to Idaho after hearing that Stephen was staying with Saden. I remembered Micah calling me and I vaguely remembered phoning Liam to tell him that I thought

Lucie was sick. After that though, things became a bit dim. Currently, I was at a coffee shop in Dublin waiting on Stephen; he'd been at Eamonn's club rehearsing for a show tonight. I sipped my tea and stared out at the rain wondering how Nathanial was doing today. I had called Patric once a week, every week since returning to Ireland and again, Stephen never seemed to mind and he always gave me privacy; it was almost as if he actually trusted me. I smiled and watched as he crossed the street, turning up the collar on his trench coat. He took my breath away; I loved him so much. He waved at me from the window and winked. I pushed my newspaper to the side and turned to greet him as he sank down into the booth. "Hey," I said, leaning across the table and kissing him gently.

"Mmm…hey to you." He kissed me back, much more passionately than I did him and I laughed. He pulled back and held my hand, running his thumb over my ring. It was odd, but since I'd been recovering, my sudden upsurge of Vampire-like physicality, had dropped off. I could tell that I wasn't releasing my scent and I couldn't help but wonder if it had something to do with my emotional wellbeing. Stephen smiled. "Give it time, love. You need to be patient with yourself." His eyes flashed and I sighed, missing that side of me. Stephen laughed and I shook my head. Stephen and I had not been intimate since returning. It wasn't that I didn't want to, it was just that for some reason I had these urges to hold him as close as possible, to keep him next to me and to feel him breathe. I felt myself blush as I noticed him staring intently and I bowed my head. He must be so frustrated. He chuckled softly. "Ana, I will wait for as long as you want. I'm not in any hurry." Maybe he wasn't in a hurry but I sure was. He laughed loudly and messed my hair.

208

Stephen left me at the café and returned to the club to get ready for the show. I wasn't quite in the mood to be out this evening so I returned to the house, took a shower and cooked myself some dinner. I was curled up on the couch reading when a blast of air shot through the room and I tensed to see who was arriving. It was Liam. He, Carmen and Lucie were living in Belfast at another family house. They were in the process of buying a home up near Howth and they were waiting for all the paperwork to go through. I'd always found it funny that Vampires had to wait for their real estate papers to clear. I was pretty sure that Liam was paying for the whole thing in cash; he didn't need a loan. Liam laughed as he sat down next to me on the couch.

"What, no date with my brother this evening?" He turned to me. I shook my head.

"Nah, I've not been the best company lately." I smiled weakly. "I think I might be a buzz-kill," I said, playing with my ring. Liam stared at me, his eyes seeing into my thoughts.

"Hmmm…do you want to talk about anything?" Liam studied me.

"My powers don't seem to be working again," I mumbled, looking down.

"And why do you think that is?" Liam asked as he raised my chin.

"Because I'm sad and upset and angry and confused," I said, feeling my heart start to race.

"And what or who are you upset and angry with Ana?" I didn't hesitate.

"Nathanial!" I said, exasperated. "He doesn't have to apologize for anything Liam; you let him get off scot-free and he will never, ever remember hurting me or Patric or Micah or even Lucie for that matter. You gave him a fresh start, a free pass; he doesn't remember anything! He doesn't remember a single event in our lives together and not just the bad stuff, but the good stuff too. It's as if he never existed and neither did I for that time, not in his mind!" I noticed that I was yelling and breathing really hard.

"So perhaps it is me that you are harboring some resentment towards?" Liam leaned forward, his eyes watching me and his tone calm.

"No Liam! I'm not mad at you or resentful towards you. You were just doing what you could to save him. I know Patric asked you. There's no blame there. I'm sorry. I didn't mean to make you think that I was angry about what you chose to do. I would have wanted you to save him." My voice became quiet. "I'm just...I'm just frustrated is all," I said, sighing and collapsing on the couch next to him. "I'm sorry," I said, feeling my heartbeats slow.

"There's nothing that you need to apologize for Ana. You have every right, every right to feel frustrated and angry and also sad. No one would fault you for experiencing any of those emotions. What's happened to Nathanial, it most certainly affects you; there's no way that it could not." Liam took my hand. "Do you think if you saw Nathanial, if you were able to face him as he is now and not as he was, not as you remember him to be; do you think that may help you have the closure you deserve?" I swallowed.

"Maybe," I whispered; I hadn't thought about seeing him. Patric and I had talked about him and how he was doing, but I never thought to ask if I could come back to the ranch and see Nathanial.

"Well, you think about it Ana. I know that Lucie would love a trip to see Micah and perhaps the two of us could escort you there if you so wished." Liam smiled at me.

"What about Stephen? I asked, feeling a slight pang of guilt and fear filter through my chest.

"What about him? Stephen's fine Ana. He's well aware of just what a tremendous upheaval these last few months, hell these last few years, have been for you. There is no reason on earth that you should be feeling guilty or afraid of how my brother will respond should you want to visit with Nathanial." Liam's tone was calm and reassuring. I leaned my head on his shoulder.

"I'll think about it," I said. "Hey!" I shot my head up. "What are we going to do for Stephen's birthday?" I asked. His birthday was also in October, three weeks before mine. Liam laughed.

"Which birthday?" Liam asked smiling.

"Human," I said, definitely human.

"Hmmm…I don't think that we've ever celebrated his birthday since his Change. He's never been inclined to celebrate before," Liam spoke quietly letting his eyes find mine. "But now he has so much to honor now, perhaps we should plan something then yes? Maybe we can do a joint party. Your birthday is on Halloween?"

"Yeah, that sounds great; let's do that!" I was feeling less numb. Liam patted my leg and stood. "Hey, did you come here for something?" I felt bad that we had spent the last half-hour with me yelling and ranting at him; he probably had just wanted to say "hi".

"I was just thinking about you and I thought I would check in. Also…" he fished into his coat pocket and pulled out a piece of construction paper, "this is for you. Lucie said that you would know what she was trying to convey." Liam smiled and I took the yellow piece of paper from him. I exhaled, seeing a very detailed picture of Lucie and I on the beach and we were sitting side-by-side on a rock. She had painted one of the many glorious sunsets we'd taken to watching on our trip and I gasped as I looked closer at the horizon. There were faces in the sky. She'd painted Stephen, Liam and Carmen, Nathanial, Patric and Micah, all watching over us as we stared out at the sea. The similarities between Lucie's painting and the one that Stephen had done were overwhelming. I glanced at Liam and he smiled. "I guess she was right." Liam laughed and so did I.

Stephen

I thought the whole idea of a joint birthday was insane. I had never celebrated my birth and really I thought that out of the two of us, it was Ana's birthday that we should be celebrating. But between Liam, Carmen, Cillian, my band mates and god knew who else was involved, I wasn't given much of a choice. Actually, I was so happy to have Ana even *want* to celebrate with me. I was still slightly in awe that she had chosen to be with me, that she wanted us to be together. I knew that Liam had offered to take her to see Nathanial. He thought it might help her in coming to terms with what had transpired between them. I was fine with that. Whatever she needed to do to heal, I was on board. We'd been working on getting her powers back this week. She was frustrated that they seemed to diminish whenever she was feeling weakened emotionally. It was normal. Ana was still a Human as crazy powerful as she was; she was not like me and could not control how her powers were affected, at least not yet.

"So the party is going to be at Liam's new home; do you have any human friends that I should email directions to?" She was trying to distract me, I had asked her to light the fireplace. She was on her computer pretending not to acknowledge what I was trying to do. I stared at her, my hands on my hips. She sighed, but got up and walked over to the mantel. She was muttering under her breath about me probably being a hard ass professor and that's why I wasn't teaching anymore. I laughed.

"You do realize that I never actually taught anything. That was just a cover we used for Patric and that whole fiasco down in West Papua. I don't know the first thing about the environmental sciences." I walked and put my arms around her waist. She turned to glare at me.

"Figures," she muttered.

"Try," I whispered in her ear. She tensed and waved her hand. Nothing.

"See. It's pointless." She stepped away from my grasp, but I pulled her back.

"Try again," I said, holding her hand and turning her to face the fireplace. She took a deep breath and waved her hand again; this time tiny blue embers ignited at the base of the logs. "See. It's still there, you just need to regain your confidence." I kissed her cheek. "Now, how about some dinner?" I asked and pulled her into the kitchen. I turned on the stereo and pulled her close. She laughed and wound her arms around my neck. "Will there be dancing at this party?" I twirled her, catching her around the waist.

"For sure," she said as we held each other close, moving slowly to the music. She pressed her forehead to mine and sighed.

"You know what I think?" I whispered.

"What?" Her eyes were closed.

"I think you should personally invite Patric to the party and Micah too." I said, hoping that I hadn't made her upset. She pulled back to stare at me, her eyes wide.

"You mean I should go in person; I should see Nathanial," she stated.

"Yes." I hugged her close and kissed her cheek. "Liam will go with you. He wants to go."

"What about you? You don't want to go?" She put her head on my shoulder.

"I think this is something you have to do without me Ana, but I'll be here when you get back," I murmured, smoothing her hair.

"You promise?" She swallowed hard. I listened to her thoughts and I could see her picturing us in the hospital on the night she'd had her surgery. I had wounded her severely. My body shook, seeing us through her memories.

"Ana, I will always be here. It's ok now; we're ok now." I didn't know what else to say. I didn't know how to make her understand, to trust in my love for her. It would take time and time we had. She nodded.

"Ok, but when I get back, you and I are having sex! This is getting ridiculous now!" She laughed and I kissed her.

"You won't hear any complaints from me love." I smirked and danced with her until she became too hungry to keep moving.

Ana

Micah had invited me, Liam and Lucie to come to his home in Peru and we were set to leave in an hour. I wanted to throw up. This felt so weird, going to see someone that I knew, but who didn't know me, someone that I had shared intimacies with, someone who I had asked to marry me; it was like if your partner or husband suddenly had amnesia and came home not knowing anything about your life together. A wave of panic shot through my body and I sat down on the bed trying to collect myself.

Patric

I was nervous. Micah had called earlier in the week to tell me that Liam, Ana and Lucie, were coming to visit him and that Ana may want to see Nathanial. That should be interesting, I thought. Nathanial had no clue about who she was. He had started to remember bits and pieces of our time together as children and he knew my mother's quilt. I had shown him old sketches of our family and he could pick out various members of our kin by name. He was quiet and contemplative and he would stare at me quite a bit and I could see that he was trying to remember what he knew about me. He was working with me in the vineyard, and with the horses. I wanted to keep him as relaxed and occupied as possible and let his mind heal. Nathanial's feeding was proving an entirely different challenge. I actually didn't need to feed as regularly as full vampires and I could go a month or longer without craving Human blood. Nathanial was beating my record. He'd showed no interest in blood, not even when I'd offered it to him in a chalice. I wasn't about to suggest that he try and take it the way the rest of the species did; I didn't want to overwhelm him. He didn't seem too affected by his lack of meeting his needs, but I was for sure going to ask Liam about it when he came.

I was sitting at my desk looking at some of my stocks when Nathanial came drifting into the room. He was so quiet and not his usually commanding presence. He was still strong, but now there was a grace and elegance to the way he moved, almost like a dancer, fluid and powerful without brawn or bravado; it was hard to get used to. He came to the front of the desk and picked up a framed picture of Ana and Lucie; they were on the boat smiling and waving for the camera. Ana was holding Lucie on her hip with her hair loose and flowing behind her. Her smile was broad and she looked happy and beautiful. He picked up another picture, this one of Ana on a horse, Bastion, her favorite of all the stallions. She was wearing a cowboy hat and sitting tall and stunning atop the saddle. The last picture on my desk was one of Ana and me. Esther had taken it just before we'd left for our dinner in Buenos Aries, the night Carlo was killed. We were standing together on the deck of the guesthouse holding each other close and staring into each other's eyes. She was touching my face as the sunset blazed on the horizon.

"She's very beautiful," Nathanial said, gazing at the last photo. I smiled; Ana would beg to differ. Nathanial frowned reading my thoughts. "Why?" He looked at me and I sighed.

"Because Ana is very, very crazy," I said, staring at him as he stared at her. It was so odd, him not remembering.

"Is she Human?" he asked, examining the picture closely.

"Mostly." I laughed and gazed at the image of her and Lucie.

"Do you love her?" He glanced at me, his eyes bright. The shade was so startling and unfamiliar that it always threw me a bit when he looked at me.

"I do, yes," I said, my voice soft.

"Why aren't you with her?" he asked, still staring at me. I cleared my throat.

"It's a long story. Let's just say that I'm not the best choice as far as boyfriends go; we're friends and we love each other, that's enough," I said, knowing those words were true. "But she's coming here," I said, leaning back in my chair putting my hands behind my head. "They'll be here tomorrow and you can meet her," I said, watching him. "You should really try to feed a bit Nathanial before she comes; I'd like for Ana to come back and if you try to attack her, I'm sure she won't want to return." I laughed softly. He stared at me.

"I'm not hungry," he said, replacing the photo to the desk. I sighed. It was like having a picky child in the house. Nathanial laughed and smiled at me. "I promise that I won't attack the woman you love." He grinned as I darkened my mind from his infiltrations. He had no idea how bizarre his choice of words was; he had in fact attacked and almost killed Ana and he had no memory of doing so. This was going to be a very odd visit.

Ana

Lucie and I were in the back yard and she was riding on Micah's horse that she'd named Betsy. The horse was a male, but Lucie said that males could have girl names and who was I to argue. I was leading her around and around the sprawling acreage.

"Ana, are we going to see uncle Nathanial and uncle Patric tomorrow?" Nathanial didn't remember Lucie and Liam had explained to Lucie that Nathanial was more like her, but that he had been very ill and lost some of his memories. She didn't seem too concerned.

"Yep. Are you excited?" I asked, looking back to see her. She let one of the reins fall and gave me the "thumbs up" sign. "Good deal," I said.

"Are you excited?" Lucie's tone was contemplative and I knew that she could sense my anxiety.

"Yes. I'm excited," I replied, my tone cautious.

"But you're nervous too," she stated and I shook my head. It was like having a mini Stephen or Liam by my side.

"I'm a bit nervous." I led us back to the barn and helped her climb down. She wrapped her arms around me and nuzzled my cheek.

"They're just bad dreams Ana; mommy tells me that it's just your mind trying to work things out. Your dreams are just bad ones, you're safe." She stared at me and I stopped breathing. How had she known? Had she seen images of my nightmares in my mind? I had been recalling them so much lately; they were always there. "Uncle Nathanial would never hurt you; he loves you," she said, playing with my hair and my chest heaved.

Patric

I was pacing the deck waiting for them to arrive. I was slightly freaked out, which was unusual for me and I kept fingering my amulet.

219

"Quit pacing Patric. Why are you so nervous?" Nathanial was sitting at the table playing with the plates Esther had set out for Ana and Lucie. She'd made them their favorite lunch; black beans and rice with sweet potato fries and I couldn't get Nathanial to stop fingering the food. "Sorry," he said, dropping a potato back down onto the plate. I asked him, begged him to try a bit of blood that I had stored this morning, and again just an hour ago he'd refused. "I'm not—"

"Hungry. I know." I cut him off, running my fingers through my hair. I felt a rush of air and suddenly Liam, Lucie and Ana were standing on the deck.

Ana

I was staring at Patric and just like I had done the first time I had seen him at Carlo's, I ran into his arms, hugging him. Lucie screamed and laughed and bolted from Liam's side and ran to him as well, trying to hold us both in her small arms. Patric swept her up and threw her in the air launching her higher than any human child would be capable of going. She laughed and fell straight back into his arms. Patric put his arm around me and held Lucie on his hip.

"Uncle Nathanial!" Lucie twisted so fast that she dropped to the deck sprinting. I whirled, and out of nowhere, my arm shot out with lightening speed catching her elbow and pulling her back in one motion. Liam was at my side.

"LUCIE AMELIA BYRNE! What did I tell you about charging away from people who are holding you?" Liam took Lucie into his arms and stepped back a few feet.

"Sorry daddy." Lucie kissed his cheeks and I could see Liam sigh. I stared at Patric who was glancing over my shoulder. I closed my eyes and slowly turned around. There, Nathanial sat, still and quiet watching all of us. He looked the same, but different. I could tell by his posture that something was off; well not off I guessed, maybe "new" would be the better word. He was staring at all of us so intently and his posture was erect, but casual like Stephen's had always been. The sun was making a glare on his face so I couldn't see what his eyes looked like; I hoped they were the same. I felt Patric wind his fingers in mine and I let him lead me over to the table, Liam and Lucie in tow. Nathanial stood as we approached and I noticed how graceful his movements were. I swallowed and bowed my head.

"Nathanial, this is Ana." Patric stared at me, then at his brother.

"Ana." I heard Nathanial's voice, but it wasn't the same. It was deep, like a bass, clear and strong. He said my name, but it wasn't him saying it, it was a stranger. My throat constricted. I raised my head and stared at him. I took a sharp breath in as I saw his eyes. They were clear, light blue, like the furthest part of a horizon. In the center was a deep brown shade that shone out in bronze and copper and I could see tiny flecks of gold along the rims. I saw him tense as the wind shifted. Patric stepped back and took me with him. "I'm not going to hurt her," Nathanial spoke and his voice was soft, but I could see fire ignite behind his eyes. "It's nice to meet you Ana." He extended his hand. This was too much. I couldn't do this. My face flushed and I felt

221

tears begin to prick the corners of my eyes. They fell before I had a chance to wipe them away. I was holding Nathanial's hand and crying. "What's wrong?" he asked, alarmed. "Why are you crying?" Patric looked at me and sighed.

"I'm sorry…I can't do this…it's just too hard—I can't!" I pulled away and ran into the house. I shut the bathroom door, panicking. What if Nathanial had seen my mind? What if he saw the images I had conjured of him, of us? Liam told me before we'd arrived to close my mind, but I was so emotional I wasn't sure how effective I had been. I gripped the sink and choked and sobbed, feeling overwhelmed. My emotions were like rolling thunder, deep and violent and moving swiftly through my mind. Everything was coming back; every kiss, every touch, every laugh, every hurt, every image of us together was breaking through and I couldn't stop them. I gasped, the air leaving my lungs. I heaved, hyperventilating. I wanted to scream, but I had no voice. I gagged, spitting into the sink then collapsing to the ground, I shook violently. I wrapped my arms around my knees and tried to breathe, but there was no breath, no life in me. Lifetimes passed and I sat rocking, seeing fire and blood behind my eyes. I saw Nathanial dying, I saw him waiting for me by my car as I left school, I saw my wedding dress and his mother's quilt, I saw him in a kitchen fixing dinner, I saw him bending to pick up folders that I had dropped and our hands touching, I saw pale blue eyes staring at me as he shook my hand, not knowing me, not loving me; forgetting me. I started shaking again and the tears cascaded down my cheeks, burning me with their heat. No strings were left now for Nathanial and me; no threads, no bonds, no friendship, no love—there were only memories, my memories and they would fade and who I was with him, to him, would also disappear.

I pulled myself up, my knees shaking. My face was raw and my chest was aching. I splashed water over my eyes and ran my fingers through my hair. Noni would want me to be strong, she wouldn't want me run away no matter how hurt, no matter how devastated I was, she'd want me to stand, she'd want me to be strong. I blew my nose and took a deep breath opening the bathroom door. I returned to the deck and watched as Patric stood as I came over to the table. I couldn't look at Nathanial, but I felt his eyes on me.

"Ana, are you alright?" Patric held my hand.

"I'm sorry, please forgive me." I stared at him and he touched my face. I sniffed softly and turned to Liam. "I should go, but you and Lucie stay." I tried to breathe. "Patric, Stephen and I are having a birthday party in two weeks. It would mean a lot to both of us if you came to celebrate with us, but I understand if you…if you can't or don't want to." I choked. I looked past him to the mountains, not seeing, the tears filling my eyes. "Nathanial is also welcome." I bowed my head stepping back from the group. I lifted my head and my hair began to swirl around my shoulders; I turned once and saw Nathanial staring at me, our eyes met. I thought I saw a quick flash of silver as our gazes locked, and then I disappeared.

Stephen

Ana had been locked down for days since returning from Patric's. In fact, I actually hadn't seen her this whole week. She'd called me to say

223

that she was leaving Dublin for a few days and that she loved me, she didn't tell me why she was going or where she was going. I was waiting for Liam and I was worried. I poured a drink, my hands shaking.

"Stephen." My brother suddenly appeared at my side touching my shoulder.

"Hey," I said, sipping my drink and feeling slightly numb. I handed Liam a glass and sunk down into my sofa. "What happened Liam?" I asked softly.

"It went as I expected. Ana was overwhelmed, her memories came rushing back; she had no control over them. Nathanial looks very different. He sounds different and having to introduce them as strangers, well it was devastating for her." Liam sat down next to me.

"Did he see what she was experiencing?" I thought that might make for quite a challenge for Patric to have to explain how Nathanial and Ana knew each other.

"I don't think so. He's actually quite talented at only letting others see what he wants, but from what I could tell, no, he didn't see anything." Liam sipped his drink and turned to me. "Her blood is a different story." He laid his head back on the sofa.

"Why?" Nathanial was just going to have to learn to control his urges. Liam shook his head.

"That's just it. He hasn't had any urges to feed, not for months now. Patric's been trying to get him to try various methods but he refuses. He's not weakened apparently and seems to be coping quite well

224

when he's around the Humans on the ranch." I didn't like where this was headed.

"So, what's Ana got to do with his lack of affinity for blood?" I said darkly. Liam's eyes found mine. "Let me guess; upon meeting Ana, upon catching her scent, suddenly Nathanial's natural urges have decided to surface. Suddenly he's decided that he wants to indulge his hungers with the woman I love!" I threw my hands up. This was just fucking ridiculous.

"Stephen calm down please." Liam leaned forward and put his drink down. I glared at him. "Ana is not in any danger of being stalked by Nathanial; he has no such inclinations I can assure you." How did he know? He'd just gotten through telling me how skilled Nathanial was at hiding things; how could he be sure? "Because I am and while Nathanial may be versed at mental games, I am much better and much more experienced and I can promise you, that Nathanial will not be coming for Ana." Liam studied me. "Now," he continued and I exhaled and turned my back to him, not wanting him to go on, but he did anyway, "there seems to be some sort of familiarity with her scent that he experienced, something that triggered him to wonder about her. He's curious that is all and as you well know, Nathanial has no control over when or if any of his memories of his past life surface. Patric is doing a very good job at trying to keep details when he does remember or ask, to a minimum and so have I. Nathanial trusts us and he's accepting of our explanations; you have nothing to worry about." Liam stood. "As your brother, I would highly recommend that you not spend any more of your time and energy worrying about Nathanial; you've spent long enough having had him affect your behavior and your relationship. Ana needs your support and your love and that is

225

where your focus should be. This is very hard for her to understand, she is experiencing a grieving process of sorts; in her mind, it is as if Nathanial has died and she needs time to move through that grief. Allow her to do so please." Liam put his hand on my shoulder. "We have invited both Patric and Nathanial to your party next week," I rolled my eyes, "we have invited them both; Patric is important to Ana and you owe him quite a bit as well Stephen." Liam's tone was stern and I looked away. "Good. Now Ana is in Idaho and I expect that she will be retuning this evening. Do not make me come back here and find her upset over you as well. Am I understood?" I stared at him. "Stephen?"

"Yes! Fine! I won't upset her. I'm not a child Liam; I can handle my own relationship," I said, defiant.

"We'll see." He nodded and I growled low. He laughed and disappeared.

Ana

I wasn't going to drag Stephen down this road with Nathanial again; he didn't deserve that and I wasn't inclined to travel that path either. I loved Stephen and I wanted him to know that I was committed to him, that I was ready for us to start our life together now. I had to close the door; I had to walk away. Nathanial was gone and he wasn't coming back, at least not in the way I knew him to be. I did have a chance to start over again; Stephen was offering me that opportunity and I was ready to take it. Maybe it wasn't the same as erasing my memories and forgetting I even knew Nathanial, but perhaps that was a good thing. Perhaps it would only serve to make me that much more resilient and strong. Perhaps it would allow for me to heal and to keep the parts of him that I loved, close. It would be up to me to decide how to remember my time with Nathanial and it didn't have to be painful. I took a deep breath and shimmered back to Stephen, back to the soul that I loved and who loved me. I was ready. I had to be ready.

Patric

I was buttoning my shirt and trying to find the card that I had gotten to go with Ana's gift. Jesus, I needed to be better organized. I had called her almost every day since the whole visit fiasco; I was extremely worried about her. She'd insisted that she was fine and that she would personally come and kick my ass if I didn't show up. Nathanial was coming as well. I took a deep breath. Liam had called to tell me that apparently Ana's scent was somehow familiar to Nathanial and for the last two weeks Nathanial had been asking me questions about her. Where was she from? How long had she been living in Ireland? What did she do for a living? How was it that she could shimmer and be a Human? I did the best I could to keep my answers minimal, but he wasn't satisfied with minimal these days and he still wasn't feeding. I had put my foot down this evening. Which was a bit of a role reversal for us. Nathanial had always been the voice of reason in our relationship, even growing up he'd be the one I was always the

227

most worried about disappointing or making angry. I told him that he couldn't come if he didn't satisfy his needs before we left. There were going to be a ton of Humans at this party and I didn't think having him attack anyone on Ana and Stephen's birthday, was the best present. Only when I had told him that he wouldn't be able to accept Ana's invitation, did he reluctantly feed and it was the bare minimum from my own personal storage supply. I found the card and her present and turned to put on my coat.

"What did you get her?" Nathanial ghosted into my room, looking more and more like a vampire every day. He used to prefer the traditional Bonder style of casual Bohemian dress, but over the last month and half, he began to resemble more of the rugged and rough look of his species, stubble and all. I had gotten Ana a first edition of *The Catcher in the Rye*. It was actually one of the first to enter into publication when Salinger wrote the book. Her mother used to read it to her when she was young, before she'd been given up and it was one of the most precious memories that Ana had of their time together. Ana's copy had been burned in the fire with Devon and Alec and I was sure that she hadn't bothered to replace it. I had gotten Stephen a collection of signed Led Zeppelin albums from their original studio recordings in London.

"A book," I said, eyeing a delicately wrapped box that my brother was holding. I didn't know that he'd gotten Ana a gift. "What did you get her?" I asked, slipping on my boots.

"I made her something," he said quietly. I stared at him.

"What?"

228

"A bracelet." He tucked the box into his coat pocket as I looked at him slightly stunned. Our mother used to make jewelry; she'd made my amulet. Ana liked handmade things.

"That sounds nice. She'll love it," I said, standing and feeling slightly contemplative over my brother's gesture. He nodded. "Ready?"

Ana

"Stephen, we're going to be late!" I gasped as he kissed down my neck. We'd been trying to get out of the house for the last hour.

"I don't care." His voice was rough. "Do you realize that every time this week that we have been in the middle of something, that my niece has managed to interrupt us and then my brother has to come and fetch her and by that time, the intimacy of the moment has passed?" He pinned me down on the floor and moved his body so that he was gently hovering over me. Since I'd gotten back from Idaho this week, Lucie had suddenly developed the ability to shimmer and had taken to popping in and out of our house at the most inopportune times. Stephen and I still hadn't had sex and he was getting pissed, not at me, at his four-year-old niece—I thought it was quite funny. "Ana, there is nothing funny about getting me so turned on that it takes me hours just to be able to appear in public and then not be able to satisfy my desires from that turn on; explain please where the humor is in that?" He kissed down my throat and I felt him slide his hand up under my skirt. I half laughed and half moaned. I had forgotten just

229

how passionate we were together. Also since returning, I noticed some of my abilities had resurfaced. I could light the fireplace and it appeared that my sexual aggressiveness that I had been missing, returned in full force. I wasn't sure if my power to fight as well as Stephen was still around, and I wasn't inclined to have it tested any time soon. Stephen groaned. "You do know that your internal monologue is distracting me; I would tell you to shut it, but I also am not inclined to test your fighting abilities at this time." He smirked and rolled off in a huff. "This is all your fault you know. This party was your idea and if there were not at least a hundred people waiting for us to arrive, I would bind you to the floor right now and not let you back up until next week, or next year." He pulled me up and I held him around the waist.

"Tell you what," I said, suddenly feeling my scent hormones push forward. Stephen's eyes darkened and he started to kiss me uncontrollably. "Hang on." I laughed pushing him back. "I promise that after this evening, if you dance and hang out with your friends and have a normal birthday and if you have fun, I will surrender all control to you," I said, biting him gently on the neck. I knew Stephen had some dominant tendencies when it came to sex, nothing violent, he just liked controlling our intimacies a bit. He stared at me, his eyes returning to their normal clarity.

"All control?" he asked, eyeing me warily.

"Yep. All control," I said, grabbing his coat and holding it out for him to put on. He slid his arms into the sleeves and turned around to stare at me.

"Hmm…that means I have the entire evening to plan just what I want to do with you." He winked and we shimmered away to Liam's.

I couldn't believe what Liam and Carmen had done with the house; it was spectacular. The large deck overlooked the sea and it was ablaze with candles and tiny torches, the same ones they had leading up to the house. A fire pit was down below on the bottom level of the deck, close to the shore and they situated decorative heaters on both levels filling the space with comfortable warmth. String lights hung expertly on the awnings and along the railings of the deck and the smell of the grill wafted in the air. I was stunned. I dropped Stephen's hand and went to run and kiss Carmen. She was standing with Liam and talking to Cillian.

"My goodness Ana! Thank you!" Carmen laughed as I pulled her close.

"No, thank *you*!" I said, holding her face in my hands. "Everything is beautiful Carmen. I don't know what to say; there are no words!" She was tearing up and so was I. Suddenly Cillian grabbed me around the back and picked me straight up in the air. I saw Stephen shake his head and laugh as Cillian twirled me around, eventually putting me back down, but not letting me go.

"Hey love!" Cillian said as he pulled a thin red box from a table full of presents. "Dis is from me." He winked and looked at Stephen who raised his eyebrows.

"Wow, thanks Cillian," I said, eyeing the box; it looked familiar. "You didn't have to get me anything," I said, smiling.

"Well actually it's fer bot of ye; if ya get my drift!" He slapped Stephen on the back making him spill his drink. Stephen came and took the box from me.

"Perhaps we should open this later," he said and I nodded. I recognized the packaging now. It was from Liam and Carmen's adult store. Stephen put the box back on the table and took my hand. He bent his head close to my ear. "Patric and Nathanial are here." I swallowed. I was ready. I could do this. I scanned the crowd and saw Patric and Nathanial talking with several Vampire friends of Liam's. I caught Patric's eye and waved. He smiled and excused himself and he and Nathanial moved through the crowd toward me. I looked back to find Stephen, but he wasn't there. I frowned and turned to my right. He was standing with Liam and Carmen and one of his friends. He nodded and I saw his eyes twinkle. I took another deep breath.

"Ana." Patric hugged me and I held him close. He was safe for me; he knew me, he would always remember. "Happy birthday." He kissed my cheek gently. "You look stunning." He smiled stepping back to admire my outfit I guessed.

"Thanks, so do you!" I said. He laughed and I saw Nathanial come to his side staring at me.

"Happy birthday Ana," Nathanial spoke in his unfamiliar voice. I put up my wall and steadied my emotions.

"Thank you Nathanial; I'm so glad that you both came," I said, turning back to Patric. I was that afraid if I stared too long at Nathanial's strange new eyes, I would start to cry again. Suddenly Cillian came from nowhere and playfully tackled Patric almost to the ground. The force of his collision sent me lurching forward into Nathanial who reached to catch both me, and my drink with one hand. He pulled me toward him and we stood facing each other, his arms wrapped around my waist. His scent hit me; it wasn't his Bonder scent, it was his predation chemicals and they were strong. I cleared my throat and stepped back smoothing my skirt.

"Are you alright?" he asked, his eyes thoughtful and intent.

"Um... yeah, I'm used to Cillian's expressive behavior," I said and watched as Cillian and Patric laughed and drank. I turned to see Stephen. He was staring at Nathanial.

"You have a lot of friends." Nathanial smiled gently at me and turned to lean against the railing of the deck.

"Nah, they're mostly Stephen's," I said, trying to calm my breathing. It was odd having such a mundane conversation with him; it felt out of place.

"You were sad the last time we met. Are you feeling better?" he asked me, his eyes flashing as he gazed at my face. I was slightly transfixed by both his question and his stare. I swallowed and cleared my throat again.

"Yeah, I'm ok. It's very kind of you to ask, thank you." I sounded like a robot. He cocked his head to the side.

"You can keep me out," he said, not shifting his eyes away from me. "Your mind, it's keeping me from reading you." He moved a bit closer to me, his eyes roaming over my face. An image of us in my kitchen on that first day we'd ever met, rushed into my memory. He'd told me that my ability to keep others out was a weapon, just like his ability to sense emotions and desires; he said we were alike in that way.

"I'm kind of a private person," I whispered, forcing myself to look away.

"You let my brother in," he stated. It wasn't said in any jealous sort of way, not like maybe Nathanial would have been in the past; he was saying it as if he was trying to riddle something out in his head.

"I know Patric," I said, meeting his gaze and feeling the truth of my words. He searched my face and I felt him try to penetrate my thoughts; that was familiar.

"Ah...so it's a trust issue then. You trust my brother because you know him." He studied me. "You're important to him. He talks about you all the time." Nathanial laughed and turned to stare out at the ocean, his hair blowing back over his shoulders.

"He's come a long way and he's helped me quite a bit in our journeys together." I fingered my amulet. Nathanial glanced sideways at me, his eyes pulsing and I caught a wave of his scent on the wind. Patric was going to have to help him get that under control. I was too sad and too scared to even be affected by it right now so I inhaled and tried not look at him.

"Do you think you could trust me?" He reached to bring my chin up and then thought better of it and pulled his hand away. My eyes grew wide. He shook his head. "I feel a bit lost..." He turned to gaze at the moon. "Like I'm missing something, something very important, something that I need," he whispered. "You're very loved; I can see it.

People gravitate towards you; you make them feel important, cared for." He wasn't looking at me and I swallowed, trying to quell the rise of tears in my throat. "My brother feels better about himself when he thinks about you; you make him smile." Nathanial looked back down at me, his face was solemn.

"You make him smile too," I said, allowing myself to glance at him. "He loves you." I smiled gently at him. "You just have to give yourself some time Nathanial. You need to learn how to move in the world as you are now and you will; with Patric's help and Liam's, you won't be lost forever." My voice shook and I blinked back tears. He cocked his head again.

"Why do you cry when we talk?" he asked, looking puzzled. "Should I know you?" he asked and my head snapped up.

"Nathanial." Patric was suddenly at his side and his eyes were flashing. He'd been listening. "Ana, Stephen is wanting a dance I think, and so is Cillian. You've failed to mention in any of our conversations just what kind of crowd you are associating with these days." He laughed and touched me on the nose. I rolled my eyes trying to steady the rise of emotions that had just surfaced.

"They're your crowd too you know!" I said, hugging him. "And what about you? Don't I get a dance with you?" I said, grinning.

"Apparently I have to take a number, but I'm not prone to playing by the rules, so yes, a dance sooner than later I think." Patric winked and I nodded to Nathanial who just stared at me. I turned to find Stephen.

Patric

I looked at my brother. I had heard their entire conversation and I was slightly in awe of how kind and supportive Ana was being. For all intents and purposes, Nathanial had betrayed her so much that really, he didn't deserve that kind of compassion, but I could see her trying to reconcile him in her mind; she was trying to let the old Nathanial go. She didn't want to hold anger and bitterness against the being that he was now. She was a better spirit than I. I still had episodes when I became very angry with my brother for what he did to Ana and to my uncle; for forcing me to have to make the worst kind of choice and there were times when I wished he did remember, that he could see just how much pain and devastation he caused. I sighed. It didn't matter now. We had a chance to start over again and for my mother, I had promised that I would make sure that we took advantage of such a chance, that everything that had transpired between us, would be forgotten and we could start anew, as brothers, as twins.

"Patric, do I know Ana?" Nathanial looked at me, his eyes probing my mind. I cleared my throat and noticed Liam staring; I knew that he'd heard the question. He nodded and I took a deep breath.

"Yes, from a long time ago," I said, grabbing a beer from a tray and watching Ana and Cillian dance. I was thinking how Stephen was going to kick his ass if Cillian held her any closer. I shook my head.

"From before I was Changed?" Nathanial followed my gaze and I could feel a surge of heat coming from his body as he watched Ana.

"Yes," I said, turning my back on the crowd and staring out at the dark cliffs and turbulent sea. Nathanial was still watching her and I began to grow uneasy; I didn't want to recount their relationship. Liam and I had agreed to tell Nathanial that he and Ana had been friends at one point and that was all.

"Is that why she gets upset whenever we talk? Because she knew me before?" His voice was soft.

"I guess. Ana gets attached to her relationships and it's hard for her to adjust sometimes when those relationships change," I said, staring back at her as she was standing with Stephen, his arms around her waist.

"What changed?" Nathanial pressed.

"Well, you became a vampire for one." I laughed darkly, but immediately I could see his next question and I wasn't prepared to discuss just where that question was bound to take us. "Did you give Ana her present?" I asked, blatantly changing the subject. He frowned and stared at me, clearly frustrated with my refusal to indulge his queries.

"No." He stared at me then back at Ana.

"Well why don't you do that and we'll get out of here," I said, patting him on the shoulder.

"I'm not ready to leave Patric." My brother crossed his arms in front of his chest and for a split second I could see Nathanial the Demon, suddenly resurrected. I exhaled. He wasn't being defiant; his tone was calm and somewhat sad. I knew he was agitated with the gaps in his memory. It was a difficult process to learn about old relationships and having to face people who had known you before, but had no idea who you were now. It was an odd feeling.

"Ok, you just tell me when you're ready," I said, walking back into the crowd.

Stephen

"Ok, on a scale of one to ten, how well am I doing in showing how much fun I'm having?" Ana and I were dancing; the first after Cillian had commandeered her for ten dances already. Our favorite song was playing, the song that always played somehow when we were together. She pulled me close and kissed me softly.

"No talking," she murmured, her mouth moving slowly against mine. I trembled. She pressed her forehead to mine and we stood close, our bodies gently pressed together in our perfect fit. I had seen her talking to Nathanial and I heard most of their conversation, enough to know just how incredibly compassionate Ana was and just how difficult it was for her to stand next to him, with him not knowing her anymore. He was struggling with things, just like most of us in our species. The first year was extremely difficult, between the memory gaps and then the flashes of memory that sometimes returned, then the bloodlust and learning to feed, the hormones one experienced when one wanted to lure prey; it was overwhelming. "You're thinking too much." Ana buried her head on my shoulder and laughed. "I can feel your body tense. That lowers your score you know." She looked up at me and smiled.

"Well, I definitely don't want to do that now do I?" I lifted her face and ran my finger down her throat, rubbing my thumb over the pulse in her neck. Her heat was incredible.

"Hey! Did you see that stash of presents we got? Patric got you an entire record collection!" Her eyes were bright. I had to admit, Patric's gift was pretty spectacular and I was looking forward to playing through the albums with the guitar that Ana bought me in South Africa. "I got you something too, but it's not nearly as cool." She frowned and then smiled.

"How about you just promise to wear whatever it is in that box from Cillian and we'll call it even." I pulled her close and ran my tongue slowly over her ear. It was her turn to tremble. I wondered how pissed Carmen would be if Ana and I had sex in their new home, probably pretty pissed.

"That's a given; I'll wear whatever you want," she whispered as I ran my hands under her shirt and down her back. I bet if we made it quick, Carmen would never know.

"Ana," I murmured and Ana gasped as I let my hands start to superheat her blood.

"Stephen." She groaned softly and I pressed my lips into her throat. Honestly, I wasn't beyond taking her right there on the deck. I wanted her so badly, my body was beginning to ache with my need for her. I whispered her name again, running my hand discreetly up her thigh and under her skirt. I slid my finger deep inside and moaned as I felt Ana dig her nails into my back. The pain was orgasmic and I wanted her to press harder into my flesh; I wanted to come. I couldn't wait any longer. Nobody would miss us, not for a few moments or hours or days. I shimmered us back home and as we landed, Ana started to peel my clothes off. We were moving so fast, tearing fabric and crashing against the walls, knocking pictures to the ground. She seemed ready and her body was responding. Her scent released and so did mine. The combination of hormones and fragrance seemed to just amplify our passion and make us hungrier for each other. I was trying to keep my full vampire mode from surfacing. I didn't want to return Ana to the party freshly bleeding. That was a bit of a challenge. It had been two months since I'd tasted her, since I had her blood and her body and my more aggressive nature wasn't allowing for me to go slow. I felt my fangs engage. I was going to have to bite her somewhere that wasn't visible. I had no problem with that. I released more of my scent letting it dominate her own and I hoisted her up around my waist and lowered us the floor.

Ana

Ok, so no actual sex took place. Apparently Stephen's hunger was the more dominant participant in our coupling this time. He'd wanted my blood, a lot and he was having a difficult time pulling away in order to go any further. He was veracious in his need and having me submit to his hunger seemed to prove just as erotic for both of us than

240

actually engaging in sex. It was such a pleasurable experience for me that I didn't want him to stop. He was taking from me in a different way; Stephen as a fully engaged Vampire allowed for him to penetrate my flesh deeper and my orgasms were so powerful and so intense that I hoped he would be that way every time. It also felt wonderful to be close to him like that again. I had missed our intimacies and our connection. No one had appeared to notice our absence and the party was in full swing when we returned. The deck was overflowing with people and it seemed that the numbers of Vampires that were now attending, had doubled. I was in the kitchen having left Stephen with Cillian drinking and behaving like teenagers. Stephen was slightly manic after he'd gotten my blood and his energy level was amped. I rummaged in the fridge and fished out a ginger ale.

"Ana?" I jumped and smacked my head on the base of the freezer. "Oh! I'm so sorry! Are you alright?" I turned to see Nathanial standing behind me. I rubbed my head and stepped back a few paces to lean against the counter. He stooped to pick up my runaway can and set in on the counter next to me.

"No problem," I said, trying to smile at him. I hoped he wasn't going to be asking me any more questions this evening. I would implode for sure.

"Is your head ok?" he asked and again I saw him move to reach for me, but he retracted.

"It's fine. I'm a tad jumpy Nathanial. A bit of PTSD I think." I laughed, but it was true. I replaced the ginger ale with another one and grabbed a glass from the cabinet. "Are you having a nice time?" God, this was so awkward. He was leaning against the island across from me, his palms pressed against the marble countertop.

"I am actually. I'm having a very nice time Ana." He smiled at me and I swallowed my drink loudly. He was staring so intently that I was just waiting for him to figure it out, waiting for him to remember and then for the whole world to come crashing down upon us. He was making me nervous. "I got you something," he said, moving toward me. He was holding a beautifully wrapped box in his hand. The last gift he'd given me was his mother's quilt, but of course I'd given it back.

"You didn't have to get me anything Nathanial." My voice was shaky and I tried to concentrate on the music outside.

"It's your birthday Ana, you should have gifts to celebrate this day." His tone was soft and he was looking down at the box. He held it out for me.

"Thank you Nathanial, this is really kind." I took the box and held it in my hand not sure if I even wanted to open it, if I had the courage to open it. He was looking at me, waiting. "Oh, you want me to open it now?" I asked. He nodded and his eyes grew a shade darker as our gazes met. Well, shit. I cleared my throat and began to untie the dark silver ribbon. I lifted the midnight blue box and my heart froze. A hand carved metal bracelet sat on a satin pillow and the pattern was the exact symbol of my very first imprint, the one that I had received at the beach the first night that Nathanial and I had slept together. It was exactly the same, midnight blue and silver with his stars and his symbols entwined with mine; no turquoise stone, no eye, just the emblem of our original forged Bond. All the air left my lungs and the bracelet fell from my fingers as I collapsed to the ground.

Chapter Nine

Ana

Patric, Liam, Micah and Stephen were all at Liam's house arguing over exactly what may or may not be happening with Nathanial. I was curled up on the couch next to Stephen, the bracelet of my mark sitting on the coffee table like some murder weapon that no one wanted to touch.

"He has to know!" Stephen was leaning forward, his face flushed. "He has to know and he's trying to fuck with her; he's trying to make her think he's forgotten everything and he hasn't. Instead, it appears that he's turned into an even bigger psychopath than before!"

"STEPHEN!" Liam scolded loudly. "That's enough." I pulled Stephen back and rubbed his back. He turned to look at me.

"I'm sorry Ana," he whispered. I nodded. I was too exhausted to be really upset about anything. It had been a week since the party and Nathanial hadn't seemed to acknowledge that he knew what the bracelet symbolized. Liam had questioned him, Micah had questioned him, Patric had questioned him. Stephen had wanted to question him, but Liam threw down the hammer on that idea. Nathanial had claimed that the image had come to him in a dream. He didn't recall anything about Bonding or metal tattoos or me; he just thought that I would have liked the pattern. It seemed plausible enough to me and I thought we were wasting energy on trying to decipher what, if anything, were the intentions behind the gift. "No way," Stephen mumbled under his breath, hearing my thoughts. I shrugged.

"I don't think he knows about his Bond to Ana; I have seen into his mind Liam and there's nothing that would indicate that he knows her or that he remembers ever having Chosen her to mark," Patric said and he turned to smile at me as if apologizing for having to drive home those points yet again. "I don't think that there's anything sinister behind the gesture." Patric stood and walked to pour everyone drinks. I sat watching a storm roll in over the sea, thinking.

"What makes you so sure that he's not faking Patric? Nathanial has fooled all of us before and now with his new skills, his new insights as a vampire; how do we know that he's not managed to manipulate you or us all over again? Given his history, you have to acknowledge that it's a possibility, that he's fooled you and Liam, that he's just that good." Stephen stood and took his drink. I turned back to the window. No one spoke.

"Call his bluff," I whispered, not turning away from the growing storm.

"What?" Stephen touched my shoulder, but I didn't turn to face him.

"Call his bluff; if he's faking he won't be able to keep his guard up around me. He'll cave if I tell him everything, if I go to him and tell him, show him everything. If he's trying to manipulate us, he won't be expecting that and especially not from me. And if he's telling the truth then the worst that can happen is that he feels bad about things, regretful maybe, but really it doesn't matter if he knows; it doesn't change anything," I said, finally turning from the window to stare at

Stephen. "It won't change a thing for me or for us. We start over and move forward, we heal," I said, picking up the bracelet.

"NO!" Stephen shook his head. "We're not offering you up as bait Ana; we have no idea who we're dealing with here. If he is faking, then if you go to him and you reveal just how hurt you were, how hurt you still are, he could harm you again; he may want to harm you…" Stephen sounded desperate. I took his hand.

"Stephen." Liam was staring at me.

"NO!" Stephen released my hand and stood to face his brother. "I almost lost her once Liam, by his hand; I'm not going to risk that ever again!" Stephen put his hand on his hips.

"What if I went with her?" Patric spoke softly looking at me. I shook my head.

"It won't work Patric," I said, feeling so happy that he loved me so much. He nodded. "Nathanial is smart, very smart and having you there will make him suspicious—*if* he's faking all of this. It has to just be he and I alone," I stated.

"NO!" Stephen rounded on me, but I stared him down.

"Stephen." This time Micah stood and went to put his hands on Stephen's shoulders. "Do you remember what I told you before you and Ana departed for South Africa? Do you remember what I asked of you?" Stephen swallowed.

"You asked me to trust her Micah. You asked me to trust Ana and to listen to her." Stephen was staring at me. Micah nodded.

246

"Yes and did you do that?" Micah scolded.

"Not really." Stephen bowed his head.

"No you didn't and while your efforts to save your brother were unselfish and very kind, you put yourself in a position that would have most likely taken you away from your family and from Ana. You went behind her back and you negotiated without her knowledge; you didn't *trust* in her." Stephen turned to Patric.

"If she comes to the ranch, how quickly can you get to her if she needs you?" he challenged. Patric looked at me, our eyes locking.

"In less than a heartbeat Stephen," Patric said quietly. Stephen ran his fingers through his hair and rubbed his face. I wondered if he would want to marry me at some point. It was an odd thought considering the scene in front of me, but there it was nonetheless. I heard Patric laugh and shake his head, but Stephen was staring at me, his gaze hard and frightening in its intensity. I smiled, feeling slightly embarrassed that Stephen had heard my ponderings. I wasn't expecting or needing him to ask me for that matter; I was just wondering. Stephen held my gaze for a moment longer then turned back to his brother.

"Fine, but you are to be on the ranch every moment that she is there; he doesn't have to know!" Stephen said disgusted.

"Of course." Patric looked at me. "When?" he asked and I turned to Liam and Micah.

"Ana, how do you feel about tomorrow?" Liam came to take my hand.

"That's fine," I said. Truthfully, I wasn't that concerned. It didn't matter to me either way; even if Nathanial was faking this whole amnesia thing, that just proved to me how damaged he truly was and then maybe Patric should consider committing him to some sort of instituition. Patric laughed. I could handle Nathanial and this time I didn't have a mark that he could detach; it wasn't a fair fight last time.

"And you think he's going to fight fair this time Ana?" Stephen stared, the oceans in his eyes mimicking the stormy sea outside. I shrugged. I could handle Nathanial. Stephen snorted and I glared at him.

"Yeah, because you did so well against Saden, Stephen; who in this room kicked his ass?" I said, getting slightly pissed off at his lack of confidence in me. Stephen smirked and I rose from my seat, staring him down. Liam cleared his throat.

"I don't think that anyone needs to prove just how good a fighter they are." Liam stood next to me as I continued to hold Stephen's gaze, my arms crossed. I was going to pound on him the minute we got home. Stephen winked at me and I pursed my lips. Coward. "Ok, so it's settled, tomorrow Ana will go see Nathanial and Patric, you will be there and Micah and I will also be in the area." Stephen started to speak, but Liam cut him off. "You can be with us Stephen, but you are not going anywhere near that ranch." Liam's tone was commanding and his words were final and I liked it when he occasionally scolded Stephen. I smirked and Stephen raised his eyebrows, he was going to kill me. We stood ready to leave, but I saw Liam take Stephen aside and speak quietly to him. Stephen looked at me and nodded.

"Ana?" Liam came to grasp my hands. "Would you mind staying with me for a bit; I want us to talk before tomorrow?" I looked at Stephen and he mouthed the words "you are so dead" then winked and shimmered away.

"Sure Liam," I said, watching as Patric and Micah also started to leave. Patric smiled at me.

"Come to the main house Ana," Patric called as his form and Micah's disappeared, leaving Liam and me alone. Liam led me outside and we stood watching the storm roll over the cliffs and out to the sea.

"That was an interesting idea you had tonight Ana," Liam said, watching the clouds shift and transform as lightening ignited deep within.

"Not really, it just seemed to make the most sense," I spoke quietly.

"You're putting yourself at risk." Liam turned to stare at me.

"You think he's faking," I replied, not looking at him.

"I'm not sure Ana. My gut tells me to be wary because of what he's done in the past, but the very idea that Nathanial would carry his desire to harm you into his Afterlife, to continue to try to manipulate and hurt you; it's beyond me. That is not the Nathanial that I know, that I have known for a very long time." A clap of thunder exploded in the sky and I turned to watch the lightening that ignited the boom.

"Do you think he will try to kill me Liam?" I asked and I was amazed at how calm my voice sounded.

249

"I don't know Ana." At least Liam was honest. He laughed. "How are those powers of yours; full strength yet?" He glanced at me.

"Seem to be," I said, thinking about how I was currently feeling when I was with Stephen. Liam sighed.

"You don't have to show him everything Ana; if it's too painful, if at anytime you feel something is wrong with Nathanial, with his reaction, you leave. Do you understand?" It was my turn to laugh. "What?" Liam cocked his head.

"Nothing, I was just thinking about the last conversation you and I had before you left me with Carlo; it was similar." I said, resting my head on his shoulder. "I didn't know what I was going to do without you Liam, not only when you left the ranch, but when I thought you had died in that fire; I was so lost." I felt my throat tighten and I grasped him tighter. Liam squeezed me back.

"You know the first thing my brother said when he called me from West Papua?" Liam asked, staring at the sea. "He said, 'Liam, I've met the most amazing and special being; she's extraordinary'." I smiled.

"I bet he never thought that he'd be assigned to take me out at one point." I laughed. Liam shook his head.

"What a bizarre journey Ana. I've learned so much from you, so much about myself and about what it truly means to love and be loved. Even now, even tonight, I could see your capacity to want us all to heal from the things that have happened to us, from the choices that we felt that we needed to make. You want Nathanial to heal as well and I am in awe of your compassion." I shook my head.

"Well Liam, if I'm being totally honest, I do have some ulterior motives I guess." Liam turned to stare at me and I laughed at his surprise. "I want him to know what he did. I know it's selfish and retaliatory, but that's the truth. But I also want him to see just how much I loved him, how I fought for him and that he was happy at some point I think. You have to have all of that stuff to help you heal; you have to come to understand the more turbulent parts of yourself in order to see and appreciate the calm and the stable. They work together pushing us forward and taking us back, like the moon to the tides…" Nathanial's image swam before my eyes and the breath caught in my lungs.

Stephen

I was strumming on my guitar waiting for Ana to get back from Liam's. I was not happy about this plan. In fact, I thought it was one of the more insane things that my brother had rallied behind in quite some time. I was also thinking about what I had read in her mind; she'd wondered if I would want to marry her.

"Hey." I looked up to see Ana standing next to me. I hadn't heard or felt her arrive; I must have been distracted. "So let me have it." Ana came and sat next to me on the couch. "I know you're angry." She stared at me. I put my guitar down and turned to study her. I shook my head.

"I'm not angry Ana," I said, taking her face in my hands and gazing into her eyes. "I just don't want to lose you; you have no idea what it was like for me to see you kneeling on the ground in front of him, hearing your screams as he tried to kill you; you have no idea," I said, my tone forceful. She swallowed.

"You're right Stephen, I'm sorry; it was wrong for me not to consider your feelings in all of this. I won't go. I don't have to go tomorrow. I'll do whatever you think is best. I trust you." She leaned her head against my chest. My heart tore. I wanted to tell her to stay, that I didn't trust Nathanial and that he might hurt her, but I also knew that if anyone would be able to tell just what was going on with him, Ana would be the one to do it and honestly I'd rather we knew what we were up against. An enemy you knew was easier to fight and none of us knew Nathanial at the moment, except Ana.

"You should go," I said quietly. "You can figure this out better than all of us Ana, but I will tell you this, the minute you start to feel that something is off, that something is not right, you get yourself out of there and you summon Patric. Do you understand me?" She smiled.

"You sound just like your brother, you know that?" She touched my lips.

"Yes… well, I consider that a compliment considering just how brilliant my brother is." I laughed, but Ana frowned.

"You're brilliant too Stephen and I would trust your insights regardless of whether or not Liam was your brother—most of the time." She ribbed me and I pulled her back against me. "Hey, I forgot to give you your birthday present!" She sat up. "It's been over a week since you're actual birthday; that's totally stupid!" She rose from the couch and headed down to our bedroom. I liked that I considered it "our bedroom" now; it made me feel safe and comfortable. She came back carrying a long white envelope. "I was going to get you a card but I had, I have so much to say that I would have to give you a hundred cards just to get through everything that I want to tell you…" She bit her lip and handed me the envelope. I stared at her; god, I loved her.

"Thank you Ana." I slid my finger along the seal and opened the flap. Instantly, my heart filled with so much joy and love, I thought it might just explode. She had gotten us tickets to a concert, the very same concert that we'd gone to see for my birthday when she was staying with me in Indonesia. Memories came flooding back, memories of us at dinner, of touching her for the first time while we sat in our seats and images of us in the alley before we were attacked. I also remembered that I had asked her a question, a question about how she was feeling about me. She never answered. I looked back up at her and she smiled.

"Yay! Happy birthday!" She laughed. "Maybe this time we can actually enjoy our evening without having to fight off Demons and maybe I won't have to threaten to beat up some woman who's taken to groping you over my dinner plate!" I sat back and fingered the envelope.

"Yes, I distinctly remember you getting very amped up over her behavior." I studied her.

"Well, she was gross, and so were you!" She raised her eyebrows. "I mean the two of you were acting as if you weren't in a public place. And, I clearly remember you referring to me as 'your date', now what

253

woman would want to watch the man they are with, be fondled by some slut? You didn't make a very polite date." She sat on the edge of the chair, her eyes sparkling. I chuckled.

"So you were jealous were you? Odd for you to be jealous over someone who was supposed to kill you, don't you think?" I smiled and swung my leg up on the couch, remembering. She cocked her head to the side watching me.

"I wasn't really under the impression that you were ever going to kill me Stephen; of course that was before you actually *tried* to kill me in the alley and then when I returned from Idaho, and then again on the overlook when I went back to Idaho and then when I found you in New York…perhaps I underestimated your desire to knock me off!" She laughed and touched my shoulder. I sat up and pulled her over to the couch.

"You underestimate my desires all the time, but not to kill you." I smirked and kissed her gently. "So that night in the alley when I asked you why you'd gotten so upset at dinner; what were you going to say?" I kissed her cheek and smoothed her hair back so I could get to her neck. She sighed.

"Umm…well I guess I would have told you that I sorta had developed a thing for you." She laughed softly as I stopped mid-kiss to look at her.

"What?" I said, trying not to laugh; her mind was serious.

"I know it sounds stupid considering our arrangement at the time, but you were the only thing keeping me safe and the only friend I had to talk to really. I mean, I know that you didn't consider us friends, but I did..." She trailed off and bowed her head. "You turned your study into an extra bedroom for me. You took me to work and to practice and let me come to your art shows; we went shopping together and to the grocery. I used to think that if people saw us, they would think we were the most attached couple on the planet." She chuckled. "I guess I started to see so many different sides to you, sides that you let me see, that I developed feelings for you; a crush, if you will." She laughed and sighed. "Plus, you're like super handsome, so that only served to make things that much more intense!" She kissed my cheek. "But beyond any of that Stephen, I cared about you, about your life, about whether or not you were happy or sad; I cared very deeply." She looked into my eyes and I swallowed. I had no idea that she had been so fond of me for so long; I would have never guessed the degree of her feelings. "I thought you were a pretty cool guy when I met you in West Papua, slightly scary and intense, but cool." She touched face.

"I was mesmerized by you," I whispered. "I called Liam the minute I returned from that first dinner."

"I know," she said, gently wrapping her arms around my waist. "He told me tonight. Maybe I wasn't the only one who had a crush." She pressed her lips to mine and moved her mouth in a way that I was sure was illegal. I groaned. She kissed down my throat and I felt her unbutton my shirt, running her hands over my chest. She undid the last button and gently let my shirt fall open as she traced her tongue along my stomach. I trembled. Her hair spilled over my skin and I ran my fingers through the strands, letting her scent move through me.

"It seems that you've gotten you abilities back." I panted softly as she unzipped my jeans.

"So it would seem." I felt her smile as she shifted me so that she could pull my pants down over my hips. I obliged, trying to catch my breath. "Are you comfortable?" she asked, her voice rough and sensual. I swallowed and titled my head back as she moved her mouth slowly down in between my legs. I was quivering with anticipation. It had been a while since we'd done this and the sense memory of what it felt like to be in her mouth, was overwhelming.

"Yeah," I murmured, gasping slightly as her tongue found the tip of me. She pulled away kissing along the pulse in my groin, which was thundering so violently that my legs and hips were aching with need.

"Hmmm…you're blood smells so good." She laughed and playfully bit down on my inner thigh. "Do I smell this good?" She pressed her lips fully against my pulse and I felt her teeth begin to skim along my flesh. I groaned loudly and wound my fingers into her hair.

"Better." I gasped as I started to thrust against her mouth. She ran her hand over my chest, pushing me back gently into the couch. I tried to steady my breathing, but the closer she came to taking me, the more I wanted to thrust and the more I wanted to come—my body was igniting. She bit down and the release of blood made me growl and pant and heave. She hadn't taken from me in quite some time and the connection between us was electric; she had my blood in her veins and that's where it wanted to be. I needed to be coursing through her body. She pressed harder and drank greedily from me, moaning in her pleasure. I opened my eyes and took to watching her as she fed. I was

256

so turned on seeing her body move and her lips become slick with my blood that I started to thrust, climaxing over and over as I watched her drink. She moved her hand over me, running her fingers up and down, feeling how solid I had become. She started moving in rhythm, her mouth and her hand pleasuring me at the same time. I was beside myself. I was panting and groaning and thrusting; I was out of control. She withdrew her mouth and her hand, rising up onto her knees. I watched as she pulled down her jeans and positioned herself so that she was hovering above me now, her hands gripping the armrest of the sofa. She spread her legs and I felt her run herself over the wound in my groin. "Jesus Christ Ana!" I groaned loudly as she started grinding hard against me. This was too much; she was too much. The feel of her, her scent, her movements, I was unraveling. She started breathing heavy as she thrust and pulsed against the wound in my leg and I became stunned into watching. She was rubbing my blood into her and the heat and friction from her motions were driving me to violence. I wanted her in the worst way, in the most violent way, but I couldn't move; watching her get off on me was unbelievable and I hadn't even hypnotized her into doing this. Her body was ready to climax; I could hear her and feel how hot and wet she had become. I focused on her face and her body as she gasped and groaned, moving herself roughly against me.

"God Stephen!" She cried out as I willed more of my blood to release from the wound. I was captivated and I didn't want her to stop. She spread her legs fully and rubbed faster and faster until she screamed, releasing herself to me.

Ana

I was watching Stephen in his trance. It was slightly creepy if you
didn't know what he was doing. He sort of shut his body down so he
could rest and recharge, but he kept his eyes open; it was way weird.
He did look peaceful, if you could get past the whole looking dead
thing. I felt better that our intimate relationship seemed to be back on
track. I was feeling more powerful and not nearly as weakened as I
had since coming back to Ireland. I hoped that was a good sign. I
would need all my skills today. I really hoped that Nathanial was telling
the truth; that he in fact had seen the pattern in a dream and set
about making a bracelet. That he wasn't sinister or malicious in
anyway, that made me very uneasy. The idea of him faking, sort of
reminded me of that old movie *Gaslight* with Ingrid Bergman, where
she starts to loose things like jewelry and Charles Boyer's character
goes nuts and starts to isolate her from everyone; he makes her think
she's crazy. It made for a good movie, but not such a good reality.

I shifted in the bed, gently trying to get up. I didn't know how long
Stephen wanted to recoup, but I was getting hungry. I padded down
the hallway to the kitchen and started coffee and made some oatmeal.
I was sitting sipping my coffee when the familiar blast of someone
shimmering, halted my motion. Liam stood in the kitchen.

"Good morning Ana." Liam smiled.

"Morning." I stood to hug him. "Can I get you anything?" I asked.
Sometimes Liam drank coffee or tea.

"Coffee is perfect Ana, but I can get it—sit." He turned to grab a mug from the cabinet and set about fixing his drink. "So, how are you doing today?" He eyed me as he came to take a seat at the table. I frowned.

"Actually, I'm ok." I said. I was surprised at how little anxiety I was feeling about talking to Nathanial.

"Good, that's good." Liam smiled, but I couldn't help but notice how nervous *he* looked. Liam shook his head. "I don't know Ana, I'm starting to feel uneasy about this whole plan. I've seen Patric this morning and he as assured me that he will be within both ear and eye shot of you the whole time; he's an expert at making himself invisible…but I don't know." His voice grew soft and I reached to touch his hand.

"It's ok Liam; I actually have a plan." I smiled as he stared at me.

"A plan?"

"Yep. I mean it's nothing as sophisticated as something that you or Micah would come up with, but I know Nathanial and I know when he's lying to me. I don't plan on showing him anything right away or even telling him how we know each other, not yet at least. I need to gauge him a bit," I said, frowning again. Liam laughed.

"Ana, that sounds *exactly* like something me or Micah would attempt; you are a very insightful being." He sipped his coffee looking around. "Where's Stephen?"

259

"Resting or meditating or whatever it is your species does when they get tired." I joked, eating a spoonful of my oatmeal. "So where are you guys going to be today?"

"Buenos Aries at one of Patric's restaurants. We'll be waiting for you there." Liam's tone became solemn.

"You're going to have to keep Stephen calm you know; he's trying to pretend that he's ok with all of this, but he's really on edge." I smiled gently.

"Are you saying that I'm a terrible actor because my past professional behavior would indicate otherwise?" Stephen said, leaning in the doorway watching Liam and me. I nodded as he came to kiss me.

"That's exactly what I'm saying." I laughed, reaching my hand up to touch his face. Liam stood and handed Stephen a piece of paper.

"This is where we are meeting. I'm headed there now." Liam turned back to me.

"You may want to include a map with that address." I laughed out loud, remembering when we'd landed in South Africa.

"Don't get cheeky." Stephen playfully growled, tucking the paper into his jeans. Liam bent to kiss my forehead.

"We'll see you soon Ana." He nodded at Stephen and left.

"So you have a plan do you?" Stephen poured himself a cup of coffee and leaned against the counter.

"Yep." I finished off my breakfast and stood to put my bowl in the sink. I looked at the clock. I was supposed to meet Patric in about thirty minutes.

"I love you, you know," Stephen said, staring at me; his eyes were so clear and fluid this morning.

"I know and I am very, very grateful." I hugged him as he sighed and shook his head.

Patric

Ana was due any minute and Nathanial was still out riding Bastion; he'd been gone all morning with the horse. I had told him that Ana was in the area with Liam and she wanted to stop by for a visit, that she wanted to apologize for passing out when Nathanial had given her his gift. He didn't think that she needed to apologize, but he seemed happy to know that she was coming by. Nathanial was sticking to his story about the dream and the Bonder symbol and from what I could tell, he was being honest, however in the last week I had detected a slight bit of anxiety and edginess coming from the depths of his mind and that was disconcerting for me.

I leaned out over the railing and watched as my brother galloped expertly from the mountains and over to the stables. He'd always looked godlike to me but now his energy spoke of an angel rising from the bowels of hell, both reborn and ancient in his knowledge and depth.

"Pretty crazy right?" I jumped whirling to see Ana standing behind me; she looked mystical in her glow and her energy seemed to match that of my brother's. She was following Nathanial as he rode back behind the main house to the stables. He turned and I saw him look right at Ana, his hair blowing wildly behind him as he cantered past us.

"How are you?" I asked, taking her hand and pulling her toward me in a hug. She smiled and bent her head.

"I'm good. Everyone keeps asking me that." She looked at me and I felt something cool and metal around her wrist, Nathanial's bracelet. I eyed her. "It's a gesture Patric." She shook her head. "I didn't want him to think that I didn't appreciate the gift and it is very beautiful." She gently fingered the carved pattern. "So, you're going to be around today then?" She stared at me, the depths of her eyes warm and luminous. I cleared my throat; god, I was still so attracted to her.

"Yes, you won't be able to see me, but I'll be around." I smirked and stepped back a few paces. She sighed.

"Well, maybe I'll go and meet him in the stables. I see he's riding my horse." She laughed and started to walk down the stairs.

"You might want to mention that to him; he's been under the impression that much of this place is his." I chuckled as I watched her wave and head down the path behind the house.

I was ready and I was ok; I could do this. I just wanted to talk to him, feel him out a bit. I took a few moments to shut my mind down completely, erecting the most solid of my walls and closing down my memories. I peered into the stable and saw Nathanial taking the bridle and saddle from Bastion. I breathed deep and took a step forward.

"You know that Bastion is my horse," I said, slowly approaching him. He smiled slightly at me as he carried the saddle into the tack room.

"No, I didn't know that." He stood with his brushes and stared at me. His eyes were so odd, pale but deep at the same time. Bastion was nuzzling me and I reached to stroke his flanks. "You have a way with animals I can see." He handed me a brush. Nathanial was never an animal person and my wolves were always very cautious around him, especially Kuckuc. We stood on opposite sides of Bastion grooming him. I could tell that Nathanial was watching me. "So how are you feeling Ana?" The way he said my name made my heart skip a beat; it sounded as if he had known me forever. I recovered quickly.

"I'm fine and I'm sorry that I'm such a basket case whenever we meet." I had said something similar to him during our very first meeting over two years ago. His eyes flashed and again my heart jumped. "I wanted to apologize for losing it like that. I'm very sorry," I said, studying him as I took the courier brush from the grooming kit. "The bracelet is beautiful and it was so nice of you to take the time to make me something so personal." I lifted one of Bastion's hoofs and set to cleaning out the mud and grass.

263

"It looks nice on you." Nathanial was standing in front of me and I saw his eyes linger on my wrist, my left wrist. The bracelet sat directly on his scar. I had no idea why I had chosen that wrist to adorn, but for some reason, I had felt compelled to place the cuff there; it just seemed right. Our gazes met and I stood facing him.

"So how are you?" I asked as he cleaned out his brush. He smiled and took a deep breath. "This is a good place to relax a bit, feel more centered don't you think?" I said, gazing out of the window in Bastion's stall.

"Yes it is." He was looking down averting his eyes. I watched him for a moment before continuing.

"So you're feeling well then?" I asked again leading Bastion into the stall and locking the gate. He had disappeared into the tack room, but I knew he heard me.

"I suppose." He was behind me and I rounded to face him. His arms were crossed over his chest and I couldn't help be reminded of when I had first seen him in that horrendous camp in Peru; a god amongst children was how I had described him and it was still true.

"Patric's been helpful? Supportive I mean?" I started walking toward the door and Nathanial fell in step, his stride matching mine just like he had always done when we walked together. He glanced sideways at me.

"Yes." His tone was hesitant.

"But…" I said, inferring for him. He smiled as we left the stables and I started heading down to the field where I had sat for so many days after first coming here, where I had cried so many times alone and with Patric.

"But my brother doesn't seem too inclined to answer some of my questions." Nathanial stared at me as I sat down in the grass, the wind blowing my hair softly around my shoulders. I motioned for Nathanial to sit. His eyes narrowed for a moment, but then he lowered himself, keeping a bit of a distance between us. That was fine with me because he was releasing his scent. Somehow other than really enjoying his fragrance, it didn't seem to be luring me to him, at least not yet.

"What kinds of questions?" I asked, lying back and staring at the deep blue horizon over the mountains. I turned my head to look at him; he was also staring at the landscape, his hair blowing like dark satin across his back. He didn't answer. I saw his body tense. "Nathanial?" I spoke softly. He turned his face to me and saw that his eyes had grown a bit deeper. He was either thinking about something, remembering something, angry or hungry. I sighed, hoping for all but the latter.

"Questions about you. About how you know me." His voice was rich and deep and still sounding unfamiliar to me.

"Well, Patric knows that I don't like having people speak for me or tell my story; it's my fault really. I asked him not to discuss things about me with you." That wasn't true but it seemed an appropriate thing to say. "You can ask me anything Nathanial. I can't guarantee that I will know the answer or if I will want to tell you the answer, but you can always ask." I said calmly. This might be interesting. He stared at me.

"So you may not tell me what I want to know, is that what you're saying?" I detected a hint of agitation. I shrugged.

"It may not be my place to tell you Nathanial," I explained, watching him closely.

"Patric says that we were friends." He turned back to the horizon.

"Yes, we were," I said. I could play this game. I knew he was testing me out; I just didn't know the intentions behind the test, if he knew what was going on or if he genuinely was trying to regain his memories about his past life.

"How did we meet?" he asked, not looking at me. Here it was and I had to make a quick decision as to how to word what I wanted to say.

"I met you one day after class in Indonesia," I said, closing my eyes and feeling the sun warm my face and I thought I caught a hint of vanilla and sandalwood waft through the air...Patric. Silence. I waited. I could wait all day.

"Was I in class?" he asked, frowning slightly and I turned over to watch him.

"No, but you were a professor," I said. I had always liked the fact that Nathanial taught. He was an amazing teacher and was so passionate about learning that you couldn't help but get excited to listen to him.

"Your professor?"

"No, we're in slightly different fields of study although you're brilliant enough to teach any subject with expertise." I laughed and turned back to watch a cloud pass over the sun. I felt him shift as he leaned back onto his arms.

"You think I'm brilliant?" he asked, bending his head low.

"Very much so; I have always thought that Nathanial, and not just as a scholar." I smiled at him. His body seemed to have relaxed a bit since we arrived in the field.

"What did I think about you Ana?" He raised his head and stared at me. My heart stopped for a minute. That was an odd question. It required me to have to tell him what I thought his feelings were about me and that had always been a very difficult concept for me. I had thought that Nathanial loved me, but there was always a part of me that also thought his feelings were coming out of our Bond only, that perhaps we if we had just met as humans, he wouldn't have been interested. "Ana?" Nathanial broke through my thoughts. I sighed. I was going to be honest.

"That's a very difficult question for me to answer Nathanial. It's really painful for me to discuss the way you felt about me back then, with you as you are now. You don't know me or remember me or remember anything that you felt during that time and I would never be so arrogant as to speak for you. I can only tell you what I thought you were feeling; it may not have been the case at all…" I trailed off, my throat catching. I was right; it may not have been the case that Nathanial loved me, that he ever loved me. I kept telling everybody that, but no one believed me; they all insisted that Nathanial loved me desperately and more than just as his Bond, but maybe not. Maybe he just thought he did when in fact his feelings were simply an extension of our metal and stone. I thought that he had cared for me, but now I wasn't sure. I wasn't sure if he had ever loved me; if he had ever been in love with me. He was waiting for me to answer. I took a breath. "I think you cared about me Nathanial." I was speaking very slowly and hesitantly. "But I loved you, I fell in love with you." I felt tears begin to veil my eyes. My chest ached.

"But you don't think that I felt the same Ana?" He was staring at the mountains.

"No." There was such a truth to that word; it was a secret that I had tried to ignore, a feeling that I had always thought to be right and true. I had loved Nathanial purely and separately from our Bond; I would have loved him without the metal and without the blood. I would have saved him regardless of what he was or what he did. I believed in the power of the sacrifice from his mother. I believed that she knew him to be good and kind and deserving of love, deserving of forgiveness and redemption. Nathanial's head turned swiftly toward me and his eyes found mine. I let him hear. It was easier, slightly less painful for me. He lay back in the grass and rolled on his side, his hair falling down over his shoulder. His face was close to mine.

"You don't think that I loved you Ana?" he asked again this time his tone was rough and I checked his eyes through my tears. They were changing colors. I swallowed.

"No, not in the same way that I loved you, never in the same way that my heart loved you." I let the tears roll back into my hair. I felt as if I was speaking to a ghost, finally telling someone who was long gone, my deepest secrets, trying to let them know that I hadn't forgotten them and trying desperately to make them not forget me. I choked back a sob. Nathanial leaned over, reaching to stroke my face; this time he didn't pull away. He smoothed back a strand of hair. The gesture was so tender and so familiar; one that he'd done when we first met and on several occasions after, always reminding me that he remembered, that he knew who we were to each other. I felt my left arm grow very hot and my wrist suddenly felt numb. His fingers traced the tracks from my tears; they were falling swiftly now. I closed my eyes seeing all the images of our time together, feeling every hurt, every touch, every kiss, every tender and violent moment. I saw and felt everything and when I opened my eyes, Nathanial was staring at me, *my* Nathanial. His eyes were deep midnight blue with stars moving around the rims and in their depths. "Nathanial?" I choked on the word, not believing what I was seeing. Suddenly his eyes grew dark and embers ignited behind their shadows; his body tensed. His hand stopped caressing me and I heard him growl, low and deep. Frick, Frick, Frick! I shoved him off of me and scrambled to my feet. He was crouched, ready to lunge and just as he did, I felt someone grab me and pull me into a storm of wind and cold.

Stephen

I kept checking my watch. Three hours, ten minutes and six seconds. What the hell was taking her so long?

269

"She'll be here Stephen, try to relax." My brother sipped his tea and pressed my leg as I bounced it violently under the table. I glared at him. Suddenly Micah's phone sprang to life and I jumped.

"Patric?" Micah answered before I could grab the call. "We'll be right there." Micah pocked the phone. "They're in the park across the street." Micah said. I was blurring before he finished the sentence. I saw them immediately. Patric was holding her face, his body close to hers. It made me slightly uncomfortable to see him touching her like that. Almost on cue, Patric stepped back and took her hand, releasing his more intimate hold on her. My brother and Micah appeared and we all walked toward them. She touched Patric on the shoulder, dropping her hand and closing the distance between us. I got to her first and picked her up in a violent embrace. She felt in tact.

"Stephen! I can't breathe!" She gasped and I dropped her to the ground.

"Sorry love." I said, taking her more gently around the waist. She smiled and held her ribs. I kissed the top of her head.

"Ana? How are you?" Micah took her hand; we all could see that she'd been crying. I released her so she could hug Micah.

"I'm fine. I'm ok." She smiled and he pulled her close as she laid her head on his shoulder.

"Patric?" Liam turned to Patric. He looked at Ana, then at me.

"He tried to attack," he said and my blood boiled.

270

"He was *about* to attack," Ana corrected him. Looking at Micah. "He didn't actually attack, Patric got us out of there."

"Ana, do you want to tell us what happened?" Liam asked, his eyes roaming over her face and trying to read her mind; her wall was up.

"I do, but can I please eat something? I'm really hungry." She frowned and I laughed. Patric stepped forward.

"I should get back. Nathanial's never actually engaged in any sort of aggressive vampire mode of behavior and I need to check on him." Patric eyed Ana. She stared back. He was wondering if she thought Nathanial was faking his memory loss.

"I'm not sure yet Patric," she said and my eyes widened. She read his mind? Patric laughed and threw up his hands as if to say, I shouldn't be surprised by Ana anymore. He shook his head and disappeared. I turned to her.

"What the hell was that?" I asked, stunned.

"I don't know." She smiled as we started walking back toward the restaurant. Liam was staring at her. "I get flashes sometimes, not necessarily thoughts but inclinations I guess…" She frowned.

"Since when?" I held her hand. Liam was listening rather intently.

"Umm just here recently; like in the last week or so when I noticed that my powers were resurfacing." She smirked at me. She was remembering the night of our party; she'd been pretty much good to go since then, powers, sex, all of it had returned in full force. I laughed softly. I heard my brother filter the information and I really wished he wouldn't listen so much. He glanced at me then down at Ana's wrist, the wrist with her bracelet. I hadn't noticed she was wearing it. Liam was sorting out a possible connection to Ana's resurgence of her abilities, new and old and when Nathanial had given her his present. It had been in our house since she'd gotten it. I looked at Liam. Did he think it was possessed or something? I had never heard of such a thing; it sounded like witchcraft. *Or Demonic powers,* he answered. Great. I sighed and stared at Ana's arm.

We let Ana eat before we all started drilling her about Nathanial. I knew that my brother was anxious to see and listen to what she said. He was very adept at reading between the lines of how others responded, what kinds of questions that someone asked; they all told him a story and all were potential insights into just what kind of being you were dealing with; he was a genius. Liam chuckled softly and I grinned. I sat and listened calmly as Ana recounted her conversation with Nathanial and I watched my brother and Micah. They were processing everything.

"So then I sort of had all these flash backs of everything that had happened between us and my arm started to hurt and that's when I opened my eyes and saw him; his eyes were the same shade they had been when we first met, not like after he'd tried to kill himself. They were midnight blue." She sipped her water and I felt my brother tense and so did Micah, but not for the reasons I would have thought.

"I see," Liam said, studying Ana. "And what arm hurt Ana?" I stared at him. What an odd question; who cared?

"Uh, my left arm…" She was looking between Liam and Micah. Both Liam and Micah's eyes flashed and I wasn't following; they were shut down mentally. "Why?" she asked, fingering her wrist. Liam took her left hand from across the table and touched her bracelet. Suddenly his hand was shocked, sending a small spark of electricity in the air between the metal and his finger. I creased my brow. What the fuck was going on?

"When did you put this on Ana?" Micah asked, his eyes growing dark.

"Just before I went to talk with Nathanial at Patric's." She looked worried now. I rubbed her back.

"Can you take the bracelet off please?" Liam's tone was sharp and I stared at him. Ana moved to pull the cuff from around her wrist, struggling to release its hold on her, my heart stopped.

"It's stuck." She frowned, still pulling against the metal. I turned her arm over, careful not to touch the actual bracelet. I gasped. The two ends of the cuff were embedded in her flesh… like some sort of metal tattoo.

Chapter Ten

Stephen

"Jesus Christ Liam, just how much more is he going to put her through until he ends up killing her?" I yelled at my brother. It had been three weeks since Ana's meeting with Nathanial and that god-forsaken bracelet still had not released itself from her wrist. He'd tried to Bond her again and now the thing was welded to her flesh just like her mark had been.

"We don't know that's what he tried to do Stephen; we have no idea why Ana's bracelet is not able to be removed. It could have something to do with her and not Nathanial." Micah spoke softly. I threw up my hands.

"You think Ana wants to be re-Bound to Nathanial, Micah?" I rounded on him.

"No Stephen I do not; I just don't think it's wise to rush to any judgment or concern at the moment over something that has yet to reveal itself." Micah touched my shoulder. I shook my head. I could live with her amulet, her permanent Bonding with Patric and it was a gift from Ana's Noni, but this, seeing his mark on her, seeing them entwined together again; it was a lot to handle.

"If you can't handle the events of Ana's life Stephen, then perhaps you should remove yourself from that life." Patric stood facing me, his eyes flashing. I growled.

274

"You'd love that wouldn't you Patric?" I snarled as a sudden surge of anger enveloped my body. "That's not what I meant and you very well know it." I took a step forward and he matched my stride.

"Enough, both of you." Liam glared at me. "I agree with Micah. I don't think we need to worry Ana about any of this until we can observe things a bit more. However, I do not think it wise that Ana spend any more time with Nathanial, at least none where they would be alone."

"He knows where we live Liam. What's stopping him from shimmering into our house and trying to kill her," I said, still glaring at Patric.

"We can protect the house Stephen and Ana doesn't even have to know; let her go about her life as it is right now." Liam studied me. He'd been questioning me for the last three weeks about why I was spending so much time at the club lately. Why I was spending so much time away from Ana. I couldn't explain it or justify it. Every time I held her hand or ran my fingers up her arm, I felt the heat from that thing— that cursed metal. It made me angry and slightly sick. I hadn't been intimate with Ana since seeing it embedded into her skin and I had had no desire to do so. I felt horrible and I couldn't explain why my emotions were so angry or why I would pull away from her in such a cold way. I was being cruel and I knew it. It was Liam's turn to snarl and I heard Patric growl. Micah stood. He glanced at Liam and I could see they were having a private conversation.

"I think it's time that Patric and I took our leave." Micah nodded at me and at Liam. "I'll be in touch Liam." My brother shook his hand, composing himself as Patric and Micah shimmered away. Liam was pissed.

275

"Are you insane?" Liam rounded on me his eyes flashing and his face flushed. "Have you lost your mind?" He crossed the room and stood toe-to-toe with me. "Do you not think that I can't see what it is you are doing? What it is that you are contemplating doing?" He brought his face close. I turned my back to him. I wasn't in the mood to argue with him. "I don't give a damn what you aren't in the mood for Stephen." He grabbed my shoulder and I shoved him violently off of me. His eyes grew wide. I had never, ever shoved my brother. I had never acted aggressive or violent towards him; I just would never behave that way. "Do it." His tone was black. "Go home and get it over with. You clearly have no motivation to fight against your flaws, your jealousy, so just be done with it," he spoke very softly and slowly. "Know this Stephen, the instant that you come back to yourself, the moment that you realize your mistake, it will be too late. You will have run out of chances, redemptions, forgiveness; she will not return to you, she will not save you and she will be yours no longer. You are weak and just like Nathanial you love Ana in selfishness and with barricades that she keeps trying to break down because she loves you." His words stung and I wanted to strike him. "You are my brother and I will always love you, but I warned you; I warned you months ago that if you hurt Ana, if you cause her heart to break, that our relationship is forever altered." His face changed and I could see a dark shadow fall over his eyes. A surge of anger and violence rose up and I felt myself begin to crouch. "What's the matter with you?" Liam hissed at me. "Are you serious?" He stood with his hands on his hips. A curl of nausea hit my stomach; I felt so sick. "Get the hell out of here Stephen." Liam snarled at me. "Make sure Ana knows that she can come here once you're done with her!" He turned his back on me and I left.

276

Ana

A familiar panic had started creeping into my heart over these last
weeks, not over the bracelet surprisingly, although I was puzzled and
concerned, the panic was over Stephen. He'd all but moved out of the
house. He stopped touching me, stopped kissing me, stopped looking
at me and I could sense what he was thinking. He hated the bracelet; it
made him sick and repulsed and the fact that I couldn't take it off just
seemed to make him angry. I knew what was going to happen. I felt it in
my bones and in my soul. I told myself that at least this time there was
no baby, no hospital; at least this time I saw it coming. I had already
packed my backpack, taken off my ring and I was sitting on the couch
waiting for him.

I heard him shimmer into the kitchen and I braced myself. I had been
through worse, much worse. He came through the door and I stared
as he took in the scene. My heart was beating so fast and I was having
a bit of trouble swallowing, but other than that, I was holding strong.
He looked pale and his eye color was off, cloudy. I didn't wait for him
to speak. I handed him my ring. I didn't want it; I didn't need it. I had all
the memories of Stephen that my heart could handle. I didn't need
jewelry to remind me of how much I loved him. I kissed him gently on
the cheek.

"I love you…always." I breathed softly and pressed my forehead to
his face, my throat swelling. I kissed his lips and shimmered away.

No one knew where Ana was. She'd been gone for over two months and she hadn't contacted any of us and neither me or Liam or Micah were able to track her mentally; we couldn't get a sense of where she might be. However, Stephen was being extremely helpful; odd considering that it was because of him, that Ana had left. He seemed confused most of the time, confused as to why Ana had gone in the first place, then he would get angry and then sad. I wasn't beyond wanting to beat the crap out of him whenever we were in the same room and it looked like I wasn't the only one. Liam was beyond angry with Stephen; I had never seen the two of them so at odds with one another. Liam was also finding Stephen's behavior puzzling and I would watch as he tried to process his brother's rollercoaster of emotions and mood swings. He was trying to make connections, draw threads; Ana, Stephen, Nathanial, the bracelet, Liam would flash images up in his head constantly and I could see what he was inferring. He thought the bracelet had something to do with his brother's insane actions toward Ana, but the bracelet wasn't affecting her. In fact, it seemed to have helped to resurrect her stalled powers and given her a new one; she could read emotions and intents behind emotions. I couldn't help but notice what a similar talent it was to Nathanial's as a Bonder. Liam and Micah were both concerned by that observation. I was just really concerned with finding Ana. She must be devastated and hurting yet again, and I didn't want her roaming around the world feeling alone and rejected. I didn't care what was going on with Stephen. I could not believe that he had done this to her again. I just couldn't believe it. How much of an asshole did you have to be before someone gets to beat the living shit out of you? Of course, I wasn't beyond that behavior myself…it was strange just how often all three of us continued to hurt Ana and to betray her; how much longer could she possibly keep any of us in her life? She had to be at her breaking point.

Nathanial had been subdued since his meeting with Ana. He seemed to feel bad at almost attacking her, but yet again, there was an undercurrent of contemplation with the event. He would replay the images over and over in his mind and I would see him focusing on one particular part of their conversation, the part where she'd told him that he'd never loved her in the same way that she'd loved him, that she didn't believe that he had ever really loved her at all. He'd play it like a movie, listening, stopping, rewinding, playing it again; it was unsettling as was his emotional climax when he replayed the image. He would grow violently angry, then be overcome with grief and despair, then anger again…not unlike Stephen in his emotions…I stopped mid stride.

Ana

Catharine and Andrew were kind enough to let me stay in their home in Greece. Thanks to Andrew, I had gotten a job waiting tables at a family restaurant and I was surprised at how happy I was to do the work. It was a wonderful little place right in the heart of Mykonos and I enjoyed helping to cook and talking to the customers, most of who spoke English and were tourists from the States or Europe. I tried not to think about Stephen; just like Nathanial, I had to let him go. I would be ok. I was lucky really, to have so many people in my life that I had loved and whom I thought, for at least some of them, had loved me back. It just never seemed to be in the right way, the way that would stick. I thought about calling Liam, but I didn't want him to tell Stephen that I called and what if Stephen was there when I did call…I sighed— too much drama right now. I left the house and headed down through Chora, the capital, on my scooter. Andrew had a collection of Vespas and he'd told me to take my pick. They were perfect for zipping up and down the narrow streets and I could carry my backpack with groceries quite comfortably. I hardly noticed my bracelet anymore except when it hurt. Sometimes when I would be carrying out plates to a table, one of the customers would compliment me on its design and I would remember that it was embedded into my skin. I wondered if anyone had figured out what was going on with Nathanial. The whole idea of him faking his memory loss was slightly creepy to me as was the idea that he was trying to get to me by pretending to not know me—how bizarre was that? Why would he want to pretend to forget me, forget us? If he was faking, I was sure that he knew how much it hurt me to have him speak to me like a stranger, and if that was the case, then he was just being cruel.

Patric

I waited for my brother to return from the vineyard. He and I were going to have a little chat. I wanted to know what was going on and I wanted to know now. I checked the clock on my desk. He should have been back over two hours ago. I picked up the phone and called Eduardo.

"Hola Eduardo. ¿Dónde está mi hermano?" I waited, my blood running cold. "Sí. Gracious." I hung up. He never showed up today.

Ana

The café was busy tonight. Every table was packed and Milos, the owners' son and me, were waiting and busing every table just in time for the next customers. It was getting close to the winter season and lots of tourists came to the island for its mild winters, lots of tourists. I was finishing up an order when Milos tapped me on the shoulder.

"There's a customer that asked for you." Milos said, handing me a ticket. I stuck it on the reel and stared at him.

"Which customer?" Only the regulars knew me, and none of them came here at six on a Friday night. Milos pointed into the crowd.

"A table outside, the only two top left. He asked for you by name." I couldn't see where he was pointing and I sighed. "I haven't taken his order yet; you want to trade tables?" he asked, smiling.

"Sure, sure," I said as the bell for my next order rang. "I'll get him in a minute." I shouted as I grabbed my plates. I dropped the order off and headed outside to the patio. It was packed. I scanned the crowd

281

and found the tiny table set back from the rest of the diners; it was my favorite table and usually where I ate my lunch after my shift. Someone tapped me on the shoulder and asked for more water. I smiled and told them I would be right back. I turned and headed to my table. I was looking for my pad and trying to find a pen.

"I'm so sorry you had to wait. Let me just get a pen…" I found my pad and looked up. There was nobody there. The customer must have left. On the table was a thin, black, silk scarf; at least it looked like a scarf or some sort of tie… I picked it up. Something about the way the material looked, was familiar. I frowned and scanned the patio.

Patric

"What do you mean Nathanial's gone?" Liam asked as I stood in his kitchen. I sighed, rubbing my jaw.

"He didn't show up to the winery today and no one has seen him since yesterday. I was up North and didn't get back until this morning," I said, feeling uneasy. "I'm guessing that you haven't heard from Ana?" I asked, knowing the answer. Liam shook his head. I had told Liam about my suspicions over Stephen's behavior and Nathanial's and even Liam couldn't ignore the connection. "How is Stephen?" I asked sarcastically. Liam exhaled and threw up his hands.

"He actually tried to hit me the other day. I found a bunch of Ana's things burning in the fire and I asked him about it. He nearly took my head off." Liam was clearly upset and the sudden division that had occurred between he and Stephen, it was hard for him. Moreover, the suddenness of the breakup between Ana and Stephen was also throwing Liam. According to him, Stephen was poised to ask Ana to marry him, soon, and him just suddenly pulling away from her, hurting her after he'd worked so hard to move past his issues with Nathanial, it just seemed strange. Liam rubbed his face and we stared at each other. We were waiting to hear from Micah; he'd returned to central Ontario, the home where some of our ancestors had settled over the centuries. He was trying to find out how one could create a Bonding through a tangible item, like jewelry. The powers needed had to be ancient and very dark to lure someone into a Bond without them knowing, without them having gone through the marking ritual that came with accepting the Bond; it was inconceivable. I couldn't imagine where in the world my brother would even have access to this knowledge; it was beyond me.

"Do you think Stephen knows what he's done?" I asked, trying to distract myself from my own brother. "I mean with Ana and their relationship; do you think he feels things happened suddenly?" Liam sighed loudly, clearly frustrated.

"Honestly Patric, I have no idea. He seems convinced that separating from Ana was justified because he's unable to deal with Nathanial; to me, that's bullshit. I know my brother and I know just how in love with Ana he is, just how he breathes for her, how he lives for her; he was devastated, wrecked when they weren't together. This, what he's done, it makes no sense." A thought occurred to me, a very dark thought.

"What if it does make sense?" I paced the room. "What if the Bond that Nathanial has created, what if it somehow affects Stephen and his relationship with Ana? What if it was made to affect her closest relationship, her intimate relationship?" I studied Liam.

"Made to isolate her? Make her leave?" Liam was following my logic. "I still don't see how Nathanial would know how to craft such a piece of weaponry; the skills and powers needed would be beyond anything that we could ever know. I'm just not making the connection." Liam shook his head. "Still…knowing that Ana is alone, that she's left Stephen, that both of our brothers seem to be experiencing similar emotional upheavals; there are too many threads that connect…" He turned to stare at the window. I felt like we were going in circles and if I was being honest, I just didn't want to believe that my brother was that damaged, that his Afterlife was proving just as fucked up as his Bonder life had been, especially toward the end. "I know Patric." Liam sighed and touched my shoulder.

"Liam, have you tried to talk to Stephen at all about Ana? Maybe if he called her, if they spoke, if she heard his voice, she'd come home. We could protect her better if she was closer." Liam shook his head; he looked defeated.

"I've tried Patric, god I've tried. If that thing on her wrist is really the cause of his problem then her coming back won't make things between them better. Her heart will just continue to be shattered by him…" I winced. I knew Ana was strong, but I just wasn't sure how one person could continue carrying so many wounds and not eventually bleed out. She *was* bleeding and she had been I thought, since the night at the University, since Nathanial had been attacked on my orders. I bowed my head, wondering when I was going to lose Ana for good.

Ana

I had taken to walking the beach in the evening on my nights off. I was feeling slightly depressed as the season turned closer to winter; weeks and weeks had passed since I'd left Ireland and I missed Stephen. The bracelet was running so hot these days that I often had to soak my hand in ice water to try to quell the burning; that too was also making me slightly sad. I didn't understand what was going on with Nathanial and I was feeling a bit on edge. Why would he give me this stupid thing? If he wanted to talk, I would talk. He didn't need to go to such extreme measures if that's what he'd done. I sighed and climbed the stairs back to the house turning to gaze up at the moon, it was full and had a slight red glow to its face. How apropos. I noticed that my steps felt somewhat cushioned on the stone stair. I looked down to see tons of flowers lining the walkway. I stooped to pick one up. Moon Orchid, they were native to Indonesia not Greece. My heart kicked up and I looked around. The beach was quiet, only the sound of the tides pushing and pulling onto the shore. I held the flower in my hands feeling another surge of heat rush the skin of my left wrist. I winced from the pain and clenched my jaw; I wanted to scream.

Stephen

I rolled over and touched the pillow next to me, pulling it to my face. Her scent seeped into my bones and made my chest ache with grief. I didn't know what was wrong with me. I was so angry. I could feel it coursing through my veins. I also felt sick. I was nauseous all the time and weak. I hadn't fed in weeks and I had no desire to take blood from anyone or even use my spare supply. The very thought of having anyone but Ana, made we want to vomit. I stared to sob violently.

"Stephen." Liam was standing over me. "You need to stop now and listen to me." His voice was soft and I tried to breathe. "Something is happening to you that isn't in your control; what happened with Ana, it's not what you wanted, I know that now. You need to fight this Stephen. You have to fight for Ana." He touched my hand and pressed something cool into my palm. "I don't know why this is occurring or how to stop it, but I do know that you can fight, but you have to want to Stephen; its praying on all of you worst qualities, your jealousy, your insecurity, your anger. What's happening is corroding who you truly are, who I know you to be. You have to fight. I can't do it for you, but I can stand beside you as your brother." I opened my eyes and stared at my hand. Ana's ring was gleaming in my palm; it was pulsing and luminous. I gathered myself and sat up staring at the silver band. I felt a sudden surge of power for the first time in over a month, a power that was mine, but that also seemed to be coming from some external source. I stared at my brother, his eyes were glowing and they shared the same pulse as both the ring and my heartbeat.

"What can we do?" I asked, reaching for my phone. Liam nodded.

"See if you can reach her and we'll go from there." Liam stood, but stopped to put his hands on the wall. "Stephen, Nathanial is missing." My heart froze. I swallowed and hit Ana's number and waited.

Ana

Frick! I had lost my phone. Every item that I usually carried in my backpack was now strewn across my bedroom floor. I knew I had it yesterday; I thought I had it yesterday. I sighed and rummaged through my purse for the hundredth time. This totally sucked! I had no idea what Liam or Stephen's numbers were; they were all stored on my damn phone! I ran downstairs and checked on the sofa and the chair, in the kitchen and on the deck table—nothing. Frick! I guess I could always shimmer to Liam, but I wasn't sure if I was ready to actually see Stephen yet. Maybe I could try summoning him; I wasn't that proficient at that skill yet. I needed to get to the café.

Stephen

"She's not answering," I said, but my brother was already pulling out his own phone. He was thinking that Ana was probably upset with me; rightly so and she wouldn't be inclined to answer my call. I waited as

Liam let the call ring and ring and ring. He pocketed his phone. It wasn't like Ana not to take a call from Liam; he knew it and I knew it. I felt a surge of anger well up inside of me as I thought about Ana and I fought it back, picturing her smiling face in my head and holding the image of us dancing together close to the surface of my mind. The urge quelled and I took a deep breath. Liam's eyes narrowed as he read the tenor of my emotions. "I'm ok," I said curtly. He nodded slowly.

"Hopefully she'll call back," he murmured. He turned to me. "Have you tried to track her Stephen? None of us have been able to get a read on her, but you gave her your blood and venom for the Change; you should be able to locate her." Liam sounded urgent. I shook my head. My powers seemed to be diminished slightly since she'd left; I could feel it in my soul. I had tried once and couldn't even conjure her face behind my eyes. "You just did Stephen. Try again." Liam came to stand next to me and I breathed deeply, the nausea rising in my stomach.

Ana

God I was exhausted. It was after two in the morning and I was just getting into the house from work. There had been a birthday party and one rehearsal dinner and the café was floor to ceiling packed. I threw my purse down on the counter and climbed the stairs to my room. I needed a shower. I turned on my stereo and started the water. After twenty minutes I felt my eyes begin to close while I was standing so I exited the bathroom, put on my sweats and turned down my bed. Something flashed on my pillow. I bent my head closer. A tiny diamond sat in the center of the pillow. I plucked it from the fabric and held it close to my face. I didn't own any diamonds. I looked at it again and saw that it looked more like a tiny star than a diamond; colors were shifting and moving deep inside the orb and I gasped reaching to touch the back of my neck. The skin was smooth. Fear ran like liquid ice through my veins. I sat on the edge of my bed, my mind racing; the black scarf, the Moon Orchid, the jewel, the bracelet; he knew, he's known all along.

"Not all along. I've been slowly piecing things together." I closed my eyes smelling his fragrance, it was predatory and slowly, I turned to face him.

Stephen

I had been trying for hours to locate Ana, but like Liam, Micah and Patric, I couldn't get a read on her location. It was odd and frustrating. Ana didn't have the ability to prevent herself from being tracked; that was one asset unique to only Demons and vampires. Both species could also prevent someone they were with, from being tracked by others—at least for a period of time. If Nathanial had found her, that's what he'd most likely done. I had taken to feeding from my storage supply of blood and amazingly, the influx of nourishment seemed to be keeping my surges of emotions steady and the anger at bay. I was just grateful that I could have Liam around without trying to decapitate him. We still were waiting for Micah to return from Canada and having nothing to do, not being able to help try to figure things out, it was driving me crazy. Also, I was full of anxiety about what had happened between Ana and me. She didn't seem surprised when I had come home that night; I hadn't even said anything to her about ending the relationship, she just knew. Honestly, I was having trouble remembering why I had made the decision in the first place. Thankfully, Liam was not shy about reminding me of my flaws when it came to Ana. He had no problem sending massive amounts of guilt down upon my already shattered heart. The fact that Ana seemed to expect that behavior from me was disturbing; it was almost as if she'd been just waiting for something to happen and for me to walk away like I had done before.

"Do you blame her?" Liam was glaring at me. "Really, I'm starting to think that Micah had the right idea of convincing Ana to stay away from Nathanial and Patric because of their behavior towards her and now I think that adding you to the list might not be such a bad idea," he scolded. I sighed.

"I know," I whispered, staring into the fire. I heard him snort. Liam may have agreed to help me fight against whatever that damn bracelet had managed to do to my personality, but he was still incredibly angry with me for not fighting early on, for just assuming that ending things with Ana is how I truly felt and for being so easily manipulated into leaving the woman I claimed to love so desperately. According to Liam, I didn't love her enough. A gust of wind blew through the house and Liam and I stood. Micah's form shimmered into the living room.

"Have you heard from her?" Micah asked, tying his long hair back. He looked exhausted.

"No, she's not answering her phone," Liam said quietly. Micah shook his head.

"Well, if that thing my nephew gave her is in fact a handmade Bond, she's in trouble." Micah's tone was matter of fact and I stared at him in slight shock.

"What did you find out Micah?" Liam asked before I could speak.

"Enough to make me know that Ana is in danger. The bracelet is most likely a form of vassalage, an enslavement of sorts. It was a strategy used centuries ago by demons who wanted to acquire more than one Bond. With the exception of Ana, it is unheard of that Humans can be Bound to more than one demon; it just doesn't happen. Our species have coevolved and the process is part of our unique relationship with each other. Greed is a very dangerous trait and so is jealousy and revenge." Micah's eyes shifted to stare at me. "Demons have their own battles with such deadly attributes and apparently having one Bond wasn't enough for some or desiring another demon's Bond was also an impetus for such enslavements to occur. It's not common practice amongst our kind and if it's discovered that a Human has been subjected to such treachery and subjugation, the penalty is death for the demon." Micah sounded numb and I could see just how sad he was to learn that his own flesh and blood had managed to turn into a being so full of jealousy and revenge, that Nathanial's soul was corroded, possibly beyond repair. Micah's eyes met mine and he nodded slowly.

291

"Micah. Do you have any idea how Nathanial would know about this, this form of Bondage? Is it common knowledge for your kind? Is it something that is inherently known?" Liam took Micah's hand and smiled gently. Micah sighed.

"For any other demons I would say that no, it's not inherently known, but for my family it is part of our history." Micah swallowed and bowed his head.

Ana

I watched as Nathanial came drifting into the room. My heart sank. I didn't want this knowledge, the knowledge that he had tricked his brother, his uncle, and me, not after they had worked so hard to save him—after everything he'd done. They wanted to restore him, to give him a chance at a new life. I leaned back on my bed. Nathanial came to sit on the edge and I was surprised at how natural this scene was, how familiar. I stared at him. "What's happened to you?" I asked, my tone weak and sad. "You used to be so strong, so kind—what happened Nathanial?" I wasn't even sure if he was capable of answering the question rationally; I didn't know how far gone he was. He didn't answer. Tears began to stream down my face and I swallowed, not wanting this to be it, not wanting to leave this world knowing that Nathanial was lost to me, that his love had been no more than a shadow. I didn't want to fight Nathanial.

"Well that will make things easier Ana," he said quietly. I turned to stare at him. His eyes were black. It was odd, I had always referred to Nathanial and my relationship like a revolving door, that we kept going around and around never on the same side at the same time; at least not long enough for us to gain our footing, but maybe I had been wrong in my analogy. Maybe we weren't revolving *around* each other, maybe we had been on a collision course *toward* each other, destined to crash and burn and the very love that I had always had, would ignite and die right along with us.

Stephen

Micah was struggling. The history of his family was something that he had kept from Nathanial and Patric for their entire existence and now he was about to let the secret go. Liam and I stared at him, waiting. Micah sighed.

"Patric and Nathanial are not twins; they are half brothers," Micah whispered. I looked at Liam and his eyes were wide. "We decided never to tell them because their mother, my sister, didn't feel that it should make any difference. The ordeal of their birth was unusual even for Bonders; she carried both of them at the same time, but considering how Nathanial was conceived, perhaps not that unusual." Micah sounded sick and devastated. "Their mother was raped and enslaved by a Bonding that she never agreed to. She was already Bound to my brother in-law and she was happy and in love. She became the object of obsession by a very powerful and unstable demon, something rare for our kind considering my sister was a Bonder herself, but it happens. He wanted no one but her and when he learned that she had already found her Bond, his obsession peaked and their lives collided in a very violent way." I couldn't speak; this was beyond horrible and I hated to see Micah recounting what were obviously very painful memories. "She was already pregnant with Patric, but apparently only by a day or two when she was attacked; amazingly, she conceived Nathanial and carried both children to term. We managed to kill the demon responsible for her rape, but my sister refused to terminate the pregnancy; she loved them both before they were even born." He choked on his words. "Her forced Bonding was slowly killing her and she knew this; she knew she wouldn't get enough time with the children that she loved. She made us promise to raise them together as twins as full brothers and to never tell them how Nathanial had come to be in this world. She wanted him to never use his father as an excuse for making bad decisions or for not being accountable to who we all are, separate from our parents." Micah drifted over to the window. "I had hoped that none of Nathanial's birth father's traits had passed on to him, that my sister's overwhelming capacity to love and forgive would be the main force in his life, and it was for a period of time. It appears that that time is now over." Micah turned from the window to stare at us, his eyes full of tears. I smelled a new fragrance in the room and I turned to look behind me. Patric was standing still and quiet against the wall.

Ana

He let me cry. He let me sob and grieve for everything that I had gained and lost and found and lost again; he let me scream and shake him and cry some more. He didn't say a word, he didn't move or touch me or hold me; he sat on the edge of my bed cold and frozen, waiting.

Stephen

I watched as Patric moved slowly across the room to his uncle's side and with one touch from his nephew, Micah fell apart in his arms. Liam and I stared at each other and drifted outside, the intimacy of the moment was too much for our eyes and too private for the two of us to be watching.

"Do you think he's already killed her?" I asked, staring at the moon, feeling shell-shocked.

"No." I turned to Liam as he spoke.

"How do you know? She could be dead Liam," I asked, watching him as he closed his eyes.

"My heart tells me otherwise Stephen. My heart tells me that she's alive and that she's deciding what to do."

"Deciding to do what?" I was hesitant, a surge of jealousy rose suddenly and I gritted my teeth, forcing it back down. I wasn't jealous; this wasn't me feeling these things, I repeated to myself.

"Deciding on whether or not she has enough courage to fight Nathanial and to kill him," Liam said, his voice distant; he sounded as if he was in some sort of a trance. Well, if nothing to this point had put Ana over the edge, killing Nathanial definitely would. Liam opened his eyes and stared at me.

"Give me your phone," he commanded. I reached into my pocket.

Ana

I wiped my face and stood staring at him. He also stood, his eyes pulsing with black fire. I heard a buzzing noise from somewhere in the room, from where Nathanial was standing. I watched as he reached into his pants and pulled out a phone—my phone! He looked at the screen and smirked. I suddenly felt sick. He held it to his ear.

"Hello Stephen."

Stephen

"No, Nathanial, I'm sorry to disappoint you, but it's Liam." Chills ran up my spine. My brother's voice was icy and black and his entire being had shifted from poised and controlled, to rigid and he loomed large and menacing against the backdrop of the night sky. "I wouldn't advise you to hang up Nathanial, particularly since I think you may want to know just how your plan to acquire Ana has backfired," Liam spoke calmly. "No, I am quite aware that you have her with you and I have never underestimated your capabilities to reek havoc on the lives of so many different beings at one time." Patric and Micah had appeared on the deck. "However," my brother continued, "in your unhealthy obsession of Ana, you have managed to overestimate your own talents with the darker traditions of your species. You were arrogant in what you thought you knew Nathanial." Liam waited. He was baiting him. "Oh I don't think that would be something you would want to attempt; Ana is not who you remember her to be Nathanial." He must have threatened to harm her. Bile moved into my mouth. "Besides, you've already effectively killed her with your little gift, which I am guessing was not your intention. You believe that you love Ana, Nathanial, and I'm sure you had no intentions of making her suffer a long and painful death. I am sure that what you truly want is for the two of you to be together again, for the two of you to have the life that you think you deserve." My heart stopped and I whirled to hear Micah sob gently against Patric. The forced Bond had killed their mother, even after the demon that enslaved her was killed. Ana was now dying. I gasped and Liam's hand shot out to silence me. "That's right Nathanial, your forced enslavement of Ana is killing her as we speak; it was the same enslavement that killed your mother and now it's destroying the life of the woman you want. A rookie mistake I would call it, if we weren't dealing with Ana's heart and her soul. I commend you for keeping the sudden influx of heritable knowledge to yourself; that takes quite a bit of knowhow and I can only guess that during your transition is when you developed such insights into how you could regain your Bond with Ana." I thought I heard Nathanial yelling. I wasn't so sure it was the best idea to get him angry while he had Ana. "Yes, in fact I do know how to prevent Ana from dying Nathanial." I took a step back; he did? I couldn't see his mind. "Let me speak to her first, then I will decide if we can negotiate."

Ana

Nathanial was yelling and his form was shifting back and forth. Whatever he was being told wasn't making him very happy. I thought about jumping out the window, but I was pretty sure he would be able to get to me before I even had one foot out the damn thing. Plus, there seemed to be a weird energy pulsing into the room. I would head toward the door and suddenly I was met with an invisible force that kept me from taking any more steps; it was the same with the area near the window. Nathanial must have created some sort of shield around us. I heard no more yelling and I turned to find Nathanial holding out the phone to me. I stared at him and took it from his hand.

Stephen

I held my breath as my brother waited for Ana to take the phone.

"Ana?" Liam said. Then I heard him take a deep breath and utter a single word into the phone. "Fight."

Ana

Liam's voice hung in the air around me. I looked up from the phone and stared at Nathanial. He was breathing hard and staring at my wrist. A deep bloody fissure had begun to spread over my skin cracking and splitting his scar open under the bracelet. Fighting Nathanial as a Demon had been enough of a challenge, fighting Nathanial as a new Vampire was something wholly unfamiliar. The only thing I kept conjuring was Saden and Stephen, Saden and Stephen. I had fought them both and both were exceptionally strong and experienced. I closed my mind and stepped back from Nathanial. He was growling and his eyes were darting back and forth between my now bloody arm and my face. He was debating. Something that Liam had said to him was making him hesitant to just come at me; he was thinking and for me, that was the only window I needed.

Stephen

Upon hearing Liam's last word to Ana, a picture of her flashed in my mind. She was in a room somewhere... a darkened room and I could smell and hear the ocean. It was early in the morning, like here, but the sun was already coming up where she was. I opened my eyes and scanned our horizon. We were about three hours from the sunrise.

"Greece," Patric's voice thundered through the air. He'd been following my thoughts, seeing my vision. "She's In Greece!"

Ana

I shoved every memory I had of Nathanial, good and bad, from my mind. *That* Nathanial was gone. That was not the Nathanial standing before me now, not the Nathanial that I needed to fight and not the Nathanial that I might have to kill. I scanned the room. I couldn't get out, at least not right now. I needed to stall until I could figure out how to push through the stupid resistance Nathanial had erected in the room—it had to be mentally done; I needed to find the gaps. I needed to make him slip. He growled and stared at me, his teeth barred.

"Nathanial!" I spoke loudly and clearly. "STOP!" He was crouching. "It doesn't have to be like this." I was wondering if what happened to

Carlo would also happen to Nathanial. If he got my blood, would he too be destroyed or did our Bond still offer him protection. I didn't think I was in any position to find out. He rocked back on his feet, ready to spring, his bloodlust out of control. I looked at my wrist and I looked at him. "STOP Nathanial or I'll rip it off!" I yelled. "Stop or I will tear this thing from my arm before you can even blink!" I held the metal between my fingers as pain surged deep and hot through my arm and into my heart. He snarled, but stopped moving. I was fighting two wars here, one with a Vampire and one with a Bonder. I was hoping to appeal to the Bonder first. I backed toward the window, testing the barrier. I was definitely closer than I was before, a foot or two maybe. He took a step toward me and I held up my arm and pulled. He gasped and heaved forward and I took another step back.

Stephen

Patric was blurring and I was on his tail. The streets were dim and narrow and all of the houses looked the same, but he seemed to know where he was headed. Images of Ana kept flashing in my head; she was bleeding, she was standing by a window, she was yelling. We weren't able to shimmer right to her; for some reason her exact location was blocked. My brother and Micah flanked me as we raced up and over the cliffs and over the sea. The sun was creeping up over the mountains, the night horizon giving way to a deep red sky. I closed my eyes. I could smell her; her scent was all around me and I quickly scanned the cliff where we were. A large house loomed to my right and I shifted my face to catch the wind. Ana! I whirled around and headed down the ridge, Patric in tow. The four of us stood, lined up outside the house, looking up. A single light was burning on the top floor. All at once we merged our powers and shimmered inside.

Ana

"Do you think I'm stupid?" Nathanial growled as he stepped closer to me. "Do you think I can't see what you are trying to do?" He kept moving forward. "It won't work Ana; I don't care if you pull the Bond off." He was bluffing; he had to be.

"You want me to die Nathanial? Is that what all of this is about, you want me to suffer and to die?" I said, not moving.

"If it has to come to that, then yes. Sometimes we don't have a choice." His stride lengthened and we were standing toe-to-toe.

"We always have a choice Nathanial," I said quietly, matching his stare. "Even if you can't see it at the time, it's always there." My eyes narrowed as I saw his body tremble slightly. His arm shot out and he grabbed my left wrist sending a shock of pain and nausea through my body. I clenched my jaw as he pressed harder into my flesh.

Stephen

We could hear them; they were in the last room down the hall. I saw Patric nod and then I watched him suddenly blend into the air; he disappeared, but I still felt him next to me. I rose off the ground as Liam and Micah stayed behind me. A curl of anger shot through me, a shot of disgust at Ana and I stopped moving. Why was I here? Why should I save her? She's always wanted him; she's always loved him. Why should I risk my life to save her? Liam appeared at my side and stared hard at my face. I swallowed. I had to fight this; I could fight this. The anger swelled and I steadied my body against its surge. We appeared in the doorway; Nathanial had his back to us. Liam took a step forward, but was thrown backward against the wall. Nathanial laughed and turned to face us; Ana's blood dripping from his hand.

"Ana, it appears that you have some friends who came to witness our little reunion," Nathanial spoke as Liam appeared next to me. He waved his hand and I saw Ana double over, gasping. I started to move forward, but Micah pulled me back.

"So you have no problem with Ana dying I'm guessing," Liam spoke, his voice again full of ice and darkness.

"I have no problem in the slightest Liam." Nathanial turned back to Ana and waved his hand again, sending her body to the ground convulsing. I moved again and this time Liam's hand shot out preventing me from trying the barricade. Nathanial stared at me and I

303

felt the anger rise in my chest as I looked between Ana and him; Nathanial laughed. I looked to my brother for help, but he was watching Ana. She was still and quiet as she lay there on the ground.

"I don't believe that for a minute Nathanial; you are not the master of anything much less of lying and you're not fooling anyone. It would destroy you if Ana were to be killed, especially by your own hand. Of course, I have already informed you that you have put that path for her in motion. Whether you kill her tonight or the next day or never, that Bond you have falsely created will take her life. It's over either way and you've lost Nathanial. You will lose Ana forever and there will never be a chance for you to redeem yourself to her. You have killed your Bond, your love and you, Nathanial, are the only one responsible for that choice."

Ana

I heard Liam's words. That totally sucked! I was going to die anyway? Holy frickin Christ! Nathanial had me down on the ground and I couldn't move, all I could do was watch and listen as Liam tried to negotiate for my life—or what was left of it. Stephen was staring at me; he looked puzzled. I felt anger coming from him, anger towards me. I was surprisingly calm, maybe because I felt that either way things would be over soon. I knew how they would end ultimately, so really knowing was somehow making what I needed to do easier. Nathanial growled and yanked me up to my feet by my hair. I felt the roots pull and rivulets of blood begin to drip down my head. I gathered myself, my whole self, memories, anger, passion, despair, hope, forgiveness, courage, fire and love and I looked once at Stephen and once at Liam and I pulled all the forces from the center of the earth and the center of my heart; I rose from the ground in one quick motion taking Nathanial with me and I twisted and flipped out of his grip and I held him parallel by his shirt. He growled and tried to grab me, but I leveled him to the ground, sending his body crashing back down to the floor. I heard a crunch of bones as I propelled myself downward from the air. I dropped one knee down on the left side of his chest, right over his heart and felt the air leave his lungs. He tried to lunge as he got to his feet. I ducked and spun kicking him to the left side of the temple sending a splattering of blood across the room. Everything was moving in slow motion and I felt outside of myself, like a shadow of mist and cloud that floated above the earth. He lunged again and I stood still, rearing back and kicking him square in the chest sending him crashing into the mirror against the wall. He sprang to his feet, his eyes on fire and he blurred, bouncing off the walls; I stood in the center of the room waiting. He landed behind me and grabbed my head holding my ears between his hands. I dropped to my knees, closed my eyes and breathed. He started to twist my neck and I opened my eyes, thunder filling my soul. I raised my hands, leapt from the ground, flipped over Nathanial and slammed him down onto to his stomach grabbing his head and snapping it back. I heard another crunch of bones as his neck shattered. I had him, but I had to finish it. I was crying and screaming; it sounded distant and faded. Nathanial was heaving under me, his blood spilling from his head in a furious black stream. I looked at Liam.

Stephen

Patric suddenly appeared at Ana's side and he stepped forward towering over his brother. I couldn't breathe. I felt a sudden shove and I fell forward into the room. I watched as Liam slowly approached.

"No Patric. Not you; it can't be you." Liam was staring at Ana. Patric looked at Ana and he shook his head. Nathanial had started to gurgle and the smell of death seeped into the room. Ana was crying, but her grip on Nathanial was firm. I felt numb. Liam was saying something privately to Patric and I could see that my brother was trying to calm his grief. "Ana, you have to make a choice now. You will die if someone else kills Nathanial. You have to be the one to break the Bond if you want to live. You have to decide." Liam was standing next to her. I watched Ana and everything that I had shared with her came flooding back from the first night she appeared at my apartment, to her curled up on my couch sipping her tea; I felt *her* and I felt me *with* her. A surge of jealousy and anger fought to surface but it didn't matter; I didn't have to be any of those things. I could choose to love Ana like I had always wanted to love her, unconditionally, purely and without barricades. I watched her. She was fighting, at war with herself, wondering if it mattered if she lived if this is how it was going to end. It did matter. I walked slowly forward. She was sobbing as Nathanial lay bleeding beneath her.

"LIAM!" she cried. "LIAM!" My brother stood behind her waiting. Her eyes found mine and we stared at each other.

"Ana," I said quietly. I showed her our life. I showed her images of me watching her as she painted along side me. I showed her images of me singing to her and I showed us lying in bed laughing and kissing. I showed us dancing. I showed us standing on a porch of a house with hardwood floors and fireplaces and us on the couch eating pizza and watching a movie; I showed her a life, her life, the life she wanted and the life she deserved. She sobbed and gasped and I saw my brother wave his hand and Nathanial was still; he wasn't suffering. She looked back at me and then she made her choice.

Part II

Chapter Eleven

Stephen

"Why don't you think it's a good idea for me to see her Liam?" My brother was standing in my house pissing me off. It had been a few months since Nathanial's death and Ana was in Idaho at Liam and Micah's insistence. I knew for a fact that Patric had already been to see her at least once and so had my brother and Carmen and Micah. I was the only one my brother was keeping tabs on. I had promised him that I wouldn't bother her the first few weeks after the incident, but that was ages ago and I was now getting angry. I had tried to shimmer to her but for some reason, my ability to get to her was being blocked.

"You know exactly why I don't think it's a good idea Stephen." Liam watched me. I shook my head.

"I'm not going to pressure her Liam; I'm not expecting her to want to pick up where we left off. I'm not that insensitive!" I threw up my hands and Liam snorted. "NOT ANYMORE!" I shouted. "Besides, what happened, what I did, it wasn't me; I would have never done that to her…" Liam stared at me.

"No Stephen you're wrong; all of those things you were feeling, they *were* you, they *are* you, they were just amplified and Nathanial used the worst parts of who you are to try to destroy your relationship and he succeeded. I won't let you use Nathanial's witchcraft as an excuse for the fact that you did not choose to fight against those feelings, no matter where they were coming from. You let them take hold just like you did with Colin and Laura; your jealousy over our brother led to you taking his life and almost taking the life of the woman you loved and an unborn child. You made a choice with Ana. You have made many choices with her that have nearly broken her down beyond repair. I don't trust you at the moment and I'm thinking that neither should Ana." I was devastated. I wasn't the same man I had been in my Human life; I had atoned for those sins. I wasn't the same being and I loved Ana. I wanted to be with her, he had to know that. "I do know that Stephen, but I also know that Ana needs to grieve and to heal and to decide how she wants to move forward. If she wants you, then I will of course support the both of you; if she doesn't, then I will support that decision as well." Liam raised his chin surveying me.

"You don't want me to be with her?" I asked softly; his words were burning in my heart.

"I didn't say that. I said that I don't trust you to be with her at the moment; I don't trust you not to hurt her."

"What do you want me to do Liam? What do I have to do to prove to you that I love Ana, that I won't leave her bleeding and hurt anymore? What do you want me to do?" I was desperate and sick and sad.

"I want you to leave her be Stephen. I want you to listen to me and do as I ask and let Ana heal, really heal, however long it takes then that is how long you wait. If you love her now, then you will love her tomorrow and next month and next year and a lifetime from now. If you love her, you will let her go for the time being."

Patric had brought me Bastion. He'd been to visit last week and he
brought me the horse, my beautiful, beautiful horse. I didn't have a
barn at Noni's to board him, but one of the elders let me keep him in
his pasture and in his family's stables. I'd been riding him every day
for hours since Patric left. I was working a bit at the youth center,
mainly just to stay occupied. If I stayed idle too long, I started to have
massive panic attacks and I would collapse sobbing, no matter where I
was. It happened at the grocery store yesterday. Liam and Micah had
successfully removed the bracelet and my arm was mostly normal, but
I still had the scar from Nathanial, his first scar. Nothing could remove
that and perhaps that was ok.

Liam had told me that I needed to not contact Stephen for a bit, that
he was unhappy with his brother and how things had transpired
between us; he'd asked me to just concentrate on moving through this
whole process. Honestly, I was fine with not seeing or talking to
Stephen, not because I was angry with him but because I just didn't
have the energy for it; this last time with him I thought was enough. I
knew that we didn't work, it was too good to be true, to last.
Happiness with him was fleeting and I had to focus on getting my life
back, whatever that life was going to look like, I had no idea. I was
thinking of heading to the coast of southern California. I had spent a
year out there when I was a teenager and I had loved the whole vibe.
Or maybe I would go back to Italy. I still had friends and some family
living in Naples; I could start over there. Right now, I just needed to get

through the day and the night, through the hours and minutes and seconds. I just needed to survive and not give into the grief.

Stephen

I felt as though I was going through some sort of withdrawal. My body ached, my heart ached, my head ached. I wanted her, I needed her and I couldn't go to her, couldn't touch her or smell her. I hadn't left the house in weeks and I still hadn't seen her since Nathanial's death; it had been months. I was going to have to beg, to plead for my brother to lift the block he'd put between Ana and me. I would get on my knees if I had to.

"I don't think that will be necessary Stephen. Although, as your older brother, I wouldn't mind seeing that." Liam stood over me. I was lying on the floor in front of the fire, drinking. "Jesus Christ; do you really think getting plastered is the best way to keep your sanity Stephen?" Liam stooped to pick up the two bottles of whisky I had on the floor; they were empty. I moaned. "Oh get up!" Liam kicked me not so gently in the ribs. "God you're pathetic and melodramatic!" I stayed down glaring at him. "I'm going to see Ana today and I'll ask her if she wants to see you." Liam stood staring at me as my eyes widened. I tried to sit up.

"When? When are you going?" I licked my lips. Liam sighed, cringing as I tried to stand. He rolled his eyes and offered me his hand. "Thanks." I staggered over to the couch collapsing from the effort.

"This morning. She's been working and this is her day off today." I hated that my brother knew more about what was going on with Ana than I did. "That's too bad." Liam scolded. I ignored his tone.

"Where's she working?" I rubbed my face.

"At a youth center. Patric brought her Bastion and she's been riding a bit as well." Liam stood in front of the fire, his hands on his hips. "Stephen, I'm not making any promises; I have no idea how Ana is feeling and I don't want you to get your hopes up. She may not be in a place to even be able to think about resuming any sort of intimate relationship with you."

"I know," I said, sighing and rubbing the back of my neck.

"Do you?" Liam said, rounding on me.

"Yes!" I replied. "Yes I know Liam; I know that she's hurting. I know that she's devastated. I know that she's grieving. I know Ana too, maybe even better than you do. I lived with her and I loved her…I still love her." I stared into the fire seeing her face.

"I'll contact you when I return." Liam turned and we looked at each other.

"How long are you staying?" I leaned my head against the sofa, my chest heaving.

"However long she needs me." Liam came and stood behind me. "Pull yourself together will you? The last thing Ana needs is to feel guilty about your liquor benders and wrecked mental state of mind. Clean

313

up and feed as well; I don't want your bloodlust ruling your behaviors if you are to see Ana, she's vulnerable."

"Christ Liam. What kind of guy do you think I am? I'm not going to try to seduce Ana when she's grieving. I'm not that hormonal." Liam snorted. I was actually, but he didn't need to know that. Liam rolled his eyes and left me to my fantasies.

Ana

I pulled Noni's jeep into the drive and immediately I saw Liam leaning on the railing of the porch. I let Zanuck out of the car and sprinted up the stairs into his arms. He held me close and kissed both of my cheeks.

"I thought today was your day off?" he asked, pulling back to study me.

"It is. I was just out with the wolves at the stables," I said, unlocking the door and holding it open for him. He smiled. "How about some tea?" I asked, putting the leash and my purse on the hooks in the kitchen.

"Tea would be wonderful, thank you Ana." Liam pulled out a chair. I could feel his eyes on me.

"How's Lucie?" I asked, turning on the kettle.

"She misses you and would like to come and visit. She loved the books you sent to her and the new camera; that was quite an extravagance Ana." Liam scolded and I smiled.

"She's good isn't she?" I said, pouring the boiling water into our mugs. "I mean she has an eye… like Stephen." My throat constricted a bit.

"Yes she does." I handed Liam his cup and sat down next to him. "How are you Ana?" Liam took my hand. I looked down and shrugged.

"I have good days and bad; seems like more bad than good at the moment, but I hear it gets better." I laughed lightly.

"Hmmm…yes I think that it does get better; we heal but we don't forget do we?" Liam's eyes met mine and I nodded. Liam understood; he'd lost his youngest brother, he'd lost someone that he'd loved too. "Stephen would like to see you."

"Oh." I swallowed. "Why?" Even though he helped me with Nathanial that night, I had resigned myself to not ever having a relationship with Stephen again, maybe not with anyone ever again. Liam cocked his head.

"Ana, I think it would be a very sad day in this world if you no longer allowed yourself to be loved or to love, ever again." I bowed my head. I heard something slide on the table. I glanced up to see that Liam had placed my ring from Stephen in the middle of the space between us. I stared at Liam pushing the ring back towards him.

"I don't think I'm ready yet Liam. Maybe I could call him first? I mean, if he was ok with that…" I murmured. I couldn't get my head around seeing Stephen or even attempting to discuss what had happened between us. I didn't want to be an obstacle for him anymore; I didn't want to be something that he had to be at war with himself over; I just wanted him to be happy.

"Stephen won't be happy without you Ana. Never have you been an obstacle for him or anyone who has ever been lucky enough to love you. You are not the cause for Stephen's war with himself anymore than you are responsible for what happened with Nathanial or with Alec or with Kai or with Noni. You have never been, nor will you ever be, an obstacle for anyone Ana." Liam's eyes flashed. I felt very sad.

"Why do you think he keeps leaving me? Why do you think that I can't seem to hold onto anyone?" I had never actually asked those questions out loud; they seemed too pathetic for anyone else's ears but mine. But now, after everything that I had seen and done and experienced, I felt safe asking Liam, he would be honest; he had always been honest. I wiped my face. I was crying, again. Liam stared and then looked down.

"Ana, my brother is a fool. He's only ever loved one person in his life and she betrayed him; he's immature and he's a fool." He raised his head. "But he loves you more than I have ever known any being to love anyone Ana, even me. It is his very same fear that he is not enough to hold you, that his sins and his falls from grace, if you will, are too much to ignore, too terrible to forgive and he can't imagine how anyone with such a capacity to love, would choose him to create a life with, to love him unconditionally. Now, as far as you not being able to hold anyone, I have evidence to the contrary. I know for a fact that Patric loves you so much that he's willing to step aside and let you be with Stephen if you so wish. I also know that Nathanial loved you

316

deeply, that he was happy once and that you changed his life in the most significant way, in a better way. All of these souls were or are better for having loved you, even Nathanial. The Nathanial that died, that was not the Nathanial that you knew, however he is still accountable to his choices and the fact that he couldn't see beyond his own obsessions, beyond his greed and jealousy, has nothing to do with your capacity to hold onto him. You saved him Ana and not just in body, but also in heart and spirit; he *chose* to dishonor that redemption and so too did Stephen, to a point. The difference is that Stephen acknowledges where he's gone wrong and I truly believe that he wants to be everything that you deserve. He's learning to accept himself and to realize that he is not his past; it doesn't have to define him. It is in the choices he makes now, that can truly speak to who he is and who he has the potential to become. Stephen is yours to hold onto Ana, if you so choose. He is waiting and so is his unconditional love."

Stephen

Liam had been back for two weeks and he said that Ana was going to call. She hadn't. She wasn't ready to see me; I understood, but I just wanted to hear her voice, to have her hear mine. I was so lonely for her. I hadn't rested in months; my mind and my heart were hurting and rest wasn't an option for me. I had no idea how long I could hang on without seeing her or talking to her; I was pretty sure that I had reached the end of my rope. My nerves were shot and my overwhelming need for her was reaching a breaking point. I stretched out in bed wondering what she was doing and how she was feeling, wondering if she missed me, if she was thinking about me, about us. My phone buzzed and my breath stopped and my heart stopped. I picked up the call.

"Hey." I closed my eyes upon hearing her voice. I couldn't speak. "Stephen?" I swallowed.

"Hi Ana." My voice was tight and I wanted to tell her to come to me, to let me hold her.

"You know what I'm listening to?" she asked and I suddenly could hear a familiar piece of music from over the phone. "It's the disk you made me for my birthday. You came to Noni's to see Nathanial and me, I guess, and you gave this to me before you left…" I knew the CD. I had recorded my own versions of the songs she liked for me to play. I didn't even remember giving it to her; so much had happened in between. "It's really beautiful. You sound really beautiful."

"I'm glad you like it," I whispered. We listened for a while, both of us quiet and in our separate worlds. I wanted those worlds to merge, to collide and become entangled, igniting in their fusion, bonding us together. I wanted her to let me love her.

"I know," she said. I sucked in a soft breath knowing that she had heard my thoughts. "Will you stay on the phone until I fall asleep?" I took a deep breath.

"Yes Ana, I will stay with you."

Ana

I was sitting in my old apartment in Dublin. I had wanted to come back to Ireland. I needed to come back. There were things here I needed to see and retrieve. I had been talking to Stephen once a week for the last month—it had been four months since I'd seen him. Patric told me that I was being silly now; that I had kept Stephen waiting long enough, that it was time to at least see him. I loved Patric. He was my best friend and so were Liam and Carmen and Micah...and Stephen. Patric was right; I should at least see him. I didn't have to make any decisions about what I wanted right now, but it would be nice to lay eyes on him, to see him smile. I sighed and looked around my room. The scattered remains of the painting were still on the floor. I stood and walked in front of the frame, lifting the torn pieces of canvas, holding them together. Nathanial's face stared at me, his eyes beautiful and deep, and his face solemn and glorious. I traced my fingers along his cheek and let the tears fall. Stephen's gaze met me and it seemed to radiate through the very space between us. I saw Liam and Carmen and Micah and Patric and my dear sweet Lucie; all staring at me, all waiting.

Patric

Riding was all I seemed to want to do these days. Four months had passed since my brother's death and there were few things that offered me any solace like riding my horse, besides visiting with Ana. While she always seemed more than excited to see me, she had a difficult time meeting my gaze. She was closed and contemplative whenever we were together and I was curious to know just what she was thinking and feeling. I had not told her that Nathanial and I were half brothers or about the horrific circumstances that surrounded my brother's conception; it didn't matter. I thought about Ana quite a bit. I knew she was struggling with what she wanted from Stephen and I knew she was untrusting of herself and of him at the moment and I also knew she was contemplating starting over somewhere completely new, somewhere on her own. I just wanted her to be able to heal and to finally find some peace in her life and in her heart; she deserved that more than most.

I brought Descaro into the stables and set about grooming him; it was a meditative ritual and one that I greatly appreciated and needed. An hour later I walked slowly back to the house; it was odd being there alone now. I had never minded living or traveling by myself; I wasn't the most social being, even as a child. I would spend hours just walking or playing by myself, and it was only when Nathanial would follow me, that I succumbed to his company. I pulled my hat down a bit and gazed at the setting sun. Maybe I should start over someplace new as well. A fragrance passed over the wind and I turned my head. Ana was standing behind me smiling gently.

"I like the hat," she said, walking slowly, closing the distance between us. "It's very dashing." She laughed and hugged me.

"It's very Human-male, don't you think?" I said, holding her close. She shrugged.

"Maybe, but it suits you all the same." She tossed her hair back and I touched her gently on the cheek.

"What are you doing here?" I took her hand and we started walking along the riverbank.

"Is it bad timing? I don't want to be intrusive." She looked worried. I shook my head.

"Seeing you is never bad timing or intrusive; I was just wondering that's all." I looked at the water. She released my hand and dropped her gaze to the ground.

"Thanks," she whispered. "Patric, there's something that I need to say to you, something that I should have said to you months ago and didn't." She looked out over the mountains, her face smooth and sad.

"What Ana?"

"I'm sorry. I'm sorry for what happened with Nathanial and I'm sorry that you had to see...that you had to watch me..." She shook her head and swallowed. "I'm sorry that I killed your brother." Her voice was a whisper and her eyes were unfocused. "If I hadn't put on the bracelet, if I had just left it alone, if I hadn't brought it here that day...things might have ended differently; we might still have him here with us. I took him away from you, from us." I turned away from her.

"No Ana." I studied the sky thinking of my mother. "Nathanial took himself away from me, from us; he fell so many times Ana and each time you were there to catch him, to remind him of who you believed him to be and every time he chose wrong. He kept choosing wrong. He was on a collision course to destroy himself and you. You had to save yourself Ana and in a way, you also saved Nathanial." I looked at her. "He's at peace now; he's finally at peace." She started to tremble. I pulled her close and stroked her hair as we watched the sun sink behind the mountains, painting the sky blood red and igniting the horizon with fire.

Chapter Twelve

Stephen

It was now May and still, I had not seen Ana. It had been nearly six months since Nathanial's death. We'd been talking on the phone a bit, but she'd given no inclinations that she wanted to see me. I was back playing at the club and doing my usual routine of hanging out with my band mates and Cillian, but even he could see that I was depressed. Liam too had taken to coming by more often than usual and just staying and talking; I knew he was concerned. I had stopped asking if he'd been to visit Ana; I didn't want to know. I was taking Lucie out for some informal photography lessons and I enjoyed our time together. She missed Ana and had been to see her several times in the last few weeks; Lucie talked about her all the time. The two of us were currently in Howth taking pictures of the harbor full of boats.

"When Ana and I were sailing she would think about you lots uncle Stephen; 'specially when we'd be on the beach and the water was real blue and clear, your face would pop into her head." Lucie dropped my hand and held up her camera to take a picture of a father and daughter standing on the stone wall; they were gazing out at a ship coming into port. I stared at Lucie. "Maybe she'll take me again this summer. Can I ask her?" Lucie jumped down from the wall and handed me the camera so I could see the picture she'd just taken; the image was mesmerizing. She'd zoomed in and captured the father glancing down at his daughter as she studied the ship out on the sea. He was in profile, but you could clearly see the absolute love and devotion reflected in his eyes. My heart ached. Lucie was waiting for me to answer.

"Sure you can ask her; you can always ask although I'm not sure what Ana has planned for the summer, but I'm sure she would love to spend time with you." I patted her gently on the head.

"Maybe you can come with us? Do you like to sail?" Lucie swung our hands as walked along the wall.

"I haven't really been sailing, not in a very long time…" Liam had taken Colin and me once. It had been nice, the three of us together laughing and just being brothers; I fought to regain that memory after my Change and I was glad that I could conjure those images clearly whenever I wanted. I felt very lucky.

"Me and Ana, we slept under the stars one night," Lucie said as she made me twirl her around as if we were dancing.

"Really? We're you camping?" I asked; I didn't know too much about their sailing expedition.

"Nope. We stopped at a place in Italy or maybe Spain; I can't remember, but they put a huge bed up on the roof and it had a fireplace and lots of candles and it looked out over the ocean. Catharine and Andrew were on the next rooftop, but I think ours was the best; we had the best view." Lucie laughed as I scooped her up. "Ana thought about you then too; she was wondering if you would like a place with a bed on the roof!" She giggled and took her camera out. "Would you have liked sleeping outside?" Lucie touched my face and turned me toward her. She was so much like Ana in her affections that it surprised me that they weren't related.

"Uh…I guess; it sounds nice, different." I laughed. The only way that I would ever consider sleeping on a rooftop would be if Ana were with me. Lucie laughed. I would have to censor myself better; she apparently could wiggle herself into my mind and that was no place for a four-year-old.

"I'm almost five uncle Stephen!" She held up five fingers and looked at me like I was stupid. "I'm hungry. Can we go and get mommy to make some rice and chicken and salsa?" Ana had gotten her hooked on that meal and now she wouldn't eat anything but. I smiled at her, thinking of how nice it would be to spend the night under the stars with Ana, holding her, loving her; it would be a dream. My throat tightened and I shimmered us back home. I wasn't going to stay at Liam's, but Lucie insisted that we paint for a bit before she had her meal. Personally, I wasn't in the mood to have my brother studying me every five seconds wondering when I was going to completely fall apart but for Lucie I would endure.

"So how's the club?" Liam asked as I spread out a large piece of canvas paper and handed Lucie some finger paint. I shrugged.

"Ok I guess; the same." I watched the colors bleed together, swirling and twisting as they collided on the paper.

"Have you been playing much?" He was fishing for clues into the status of my mental health; how stupid did he think I was? Liam laughed.

"It depends on what day I talk to you Stephen." Liam joked. I sighed.

"I'm playing a little, just filling in every other weekend right now." Lucie took my hand and put it into a large puddle of dark purple paint. Something about the color made me think of Ana. A flash of me running a purple scarf over her arm rose in my mind and I closed my eyes.

"Ana!" Lucie shouted. I shook my head; god this child was too advanced. "No, Ana! She's with mommy!" I opened my eyes and whirled around to look through the glass doors. Ana was standing with her arms around Carmen and she was laughing. My heart raced and my lungs contracted. I stared not wanting to look away. She finally turned to look outside and our gazed met. She smiled gently and waved. I couldn't move.

"Oh for Christ's sakes!" Liam stood from his chair and slid open the door. "Hi Ana!" Lucie was furiously wiping her hands up and down her jeans and screaming in excitement. "Lucie don't you dare hug Ana with paint all over you; go wash your hands." Liam instructed, but Lucie was already sprinting from the deck into the house. I watched as she ran, crashing into Ana's outstretched arms. Immediately Ana's face and white tank became splotched with purple paint and I heard my brother sigh. She didn't seem to mind. "Well, are you just going to stay out here all night or are you actually going to greet her?" Liam headed inside and left me still sitting on the deck. I took to also wiping my hands on my jeans and stood walking through the door. Ana watched as I came into the house, eyeing me over Lucie's head and smiling.

"Hey," she said quietly. I saw Liam kiss Ana's cheek and take Lucie from her. A heartbeat passed and I suddenly realized we were alone; we stood facing each other. Her hair was lighter and streaked with auburn highlights from the sun; it was also longer, flowing down past her mid back almost to her waist. She had beautiful color in her cheeks and her eyes sparkled warm and deep, their bronzed glow pulsing out capturing the depths of my entire being. She looked down and I realized that I hadn't spoken yet.

"Hi," I murmured. She hooked her thumbs in her front pockets.

"You look good," she said, gazing across the space between us.

"You look beautiful Ana," I whispered. "How are you?" Of course I had been talking to her on the phone, but seeing her in person added a whole other element to how I was feeling. I would have never been able to anticipate the overwhelming surge of love and passion that I was currently experiencing. I was desperate to crash into her as Lucie had done and to hold her until the dawn of my next lifetime and for every lifetime after.

"I'm ok, you?" Neither of us had taken a step closer and I was wondering why. It's not like we didn't know each other; we weren't strangers. I loved her. I was in love with her. I moved toward her slowly. I nodded. "Is that the sign for 'ok'?" She joked and tossed her hair back.

"I'm ok." That wasn't the truth and she should know. "No, actually that's not true; I'm not ok, not for the last five plus months. I'm not ok Ana." Her eyes widened and she swallowed. I continued to walk

327

towards her until I was standing directly in front and could reach out and touch her if I wasn't such a coward.

"Oh. Well do you want to talk about it? I came to see you and Lucie, but really I came to see you Stephen; we can talk if you want." She studied me. "Or not...whatever you want..." She trailed off and her gaze became intense and I knew she wasn't going to let herself get sucked back in. I had left her too many times and for reasons that were out of jealousy and selfishness and she wasn't expecting me to be compelled to enter into a relationship again; I was pretty sure she was feeling exactly the same way. She sighed. I wasn't answering. "This was a mistake." She turned her back to me. "I shouldn't have come; I don't really have anything different to say and I guess neither do you." She grabbed her purse. My words were caught in my throat. She started shimmering and I lunged for her, grabbing her arm and pulling her violently back. We collided. The world stopped and I held her in my arms gazing into her eyes. I felt as though we were falling back in time, spinning together, embedded in our grasps, bonded in our love, merged in our souls. I took her hand and raised her palm to mine, locking our fingers together.

"Marry me." I pulled her closer. She gasped.

"What?"

"You heard me; marry me." She tried to look down, but I held her gaze firm.

"Stephen," she whispered. I shook my head.

"Do you love me Ana?" Her eyes filled with tears. I took her face in my hands and shook her gently. "Do you? Do you love me, because I love you. I would die a hundred deaths to keep your breath in this world and then I would die a hundred more. I am a man asking you now, a man who has been redeemed and by your grace, I have found my own. I am a man whose soul cannot live in a world without you by its side. I am a man who loves you, who needs you, who wants you, and who is asking to let me love you; marry me." She closed her eyes and tears cascaded down her cheeks.

Patric

I was torn. I had made a decision early on, after the night Ana and I had spent together, not to interfere with her heart. I loved her and I had had more time with her than I deserved, still…I thought it only fair that she should know that I was willing to give her a life too, one that I was certain would make her happy and safe, one where she would feel loved and have the freedom to be exactly who she is and who she wanted to become. I was ready for that opportunity. The choice was hers, but I thought that I had every right to state my case, to tell her just how in love with her I had always been; she should know. I closed my eyes sensing her. She was at Liam's. I shimmered.

I heard Liam clear his throat and I watched Stephen close his eyes and take a very deep breath; he was trying not to attack his brother. I had to admit, Liam had terrible timing.

"Ana. I'm so sorry to interrupt but Patric is here. He'd like a word." Liam stared at me and I stared back. What the hell was Patric doing here? Liam raised his eyebrows; he knew something. I touched Stephen's face.

"I'm sorry. We'll…we'll…just hang on," I said, completely flustered. Stephen stepped away and I could see worry fill his eyes. I was worried too, but I was guessing not for the same reasons. I hoped that Patric was ok. I followed Liam down the hall and into his study. Patric was standing, leaning against the desk. He looked fine, slightly on edge, but fine nonetheless. Liam stared at Patric and then at me. He smiled.

"Take as long as you like Ana, I'll be here when you're done." I thought that was an odd thing to say and I frowned as Liam closed the door. I looked back at Patric and he was shaking his head.

"He asked you to marry him?" My mind was so discombobulated; I was having trouble focusing.

"What?" I was saying that a lot tonight.

"Stephen, he asked you to marry him." Patric rubbed his face, his tone quiet. I inhaled.

"Yes." I still wasn't sure that's what happened, but it definitely seemed the case.

"What did you tell him?" Patric turned his back to me.

"Well, I didn't quite get a chance to answer." Duh, I thought walking to stand in front of him.

"What would you like to tell him?" Patric stared at me.

"I'm not sure; I'm just trying to process at the moment. Patric, what's going on? Why are you here at Liam's?" I was slightly confused by his presence. He sighed.

"Are you at liberty to leave? I'd like to talk to you for a while." His voice was rough. I sighed.

"Patric, this isn't really the best time. I mean I kinda left Stephen out there and he's…well he made quite a few declarations that deserve attention," I said, reaching to touch his hand. "How about we talk tomorrow. I can come see you or you can come see me ok? Whatever you want." Patric studied me for a moment. He moved to touch my cheek, his finger gently tracing down to the corner of my lips.

"Will you promise me something?" He took a deep breath.

"Of course, anything," I said.

"Don't make any decisions about the course of your life Ana; let's talk first." We stared at each other and I could see his eyes soften as I held his hand. I nodded. He moved closer, bringing his face even with mine. "Tomorrow then," he whispered and felt the familiar pull from

Patric, the pull that had always been there since our very first meeting, the pull that grasped me and hung on tightly, desperately. I hadn't felt it to such an extent in a very long time and it was slightly overwhelming. I swallowed as he bent his head and brought me closer. I tasted his scent on my tongue, the sweetness of vanilla making my mouth water. Sandalwood and musk enveloped the air around us and my heart kicked up a notch. Patric and I had always had a very intense relationship, very passionate and deep in our connection. Something about the way we first came together, the events leading up to what had happened between us, seemed to have created a profound trust and an unspoken intimacy that only he and I shared. It took us a while to get there, but somehow we'd become bound in both our love and through our own ritual. He breathed deeply on my lips and then disappeared.

Stephen

Liam and I were standing on the deck and I was deciding if I should throw myself off now or wait until Lucie went to bed. Liam laughed.

"You're quite melodramatic these days. Where the hell is that coming from?" He gazed at me sideways.

"Why is he here?" I said, feeling slightly disgusted.

"You know why he's here Stephen," Liam said quietly. I huffed.

"I thought you said that he wasn't going to interfere, that he's stepped aside because he loves her so much that he wants her to be happy. That's what you said." My tone was petulant.

"He has the right to change his mind Stephen. I don't make Patric's decisions for him anymore than I do yours. He's changed his mind and he wants Ana to know." I gripped the railing feeling the wood splinter in my fingers.

"I just asked Ana to marry me Liam; don't you think his timing is just a bit ill intentioned?" I said, gazing out at the sea.

"He had no idea that's what you were going to do and neither did I for that matter. Had I known, I may have suggested you wait a bit until you and Ana had had a chance to talk and reconnect." Liam followed my gaze to the sea.

"You think that I shouldn't have asked her; you think I was overzealous in my declarations?" My tone was sharp.

"I think you have an issue with patience. Ana wants to talk Stephen, talk. Do you really think her emotional state is one that is able to make what I am sure is for Ana, one of the most important decisions of her life? In your desperation to have her back, did you even consider her feelings in any of this?"

"Jesus Liam, I can't win with you!" I turned to him. "First you tell me to leave her alone, to let her heal, to pull myself together, to come to her knowing myself, knowing my faults. You tell me to love her unselfishly. I do all of those things and still you tell me that somehow, I've still fucked things up. What do you want from me, please tell me and I'll do it. Please tell me what it's going to take for me to be worthy in your eyes, to have the woman I love; tell me Liam because I am shit out of ideas at the moment." Anger and frustration were boiling over and I felt lost...and scared.

"Stephen?" I turned to see Ana standing in the doorway; she looked upset. I sighed. A sudden pressure filled my head and Liam's voice entered. *Trust her Stephen. Trust that where you go, she will follow. Trust in her love for you and let her find her way back to you. Trust her and wait; if you love her, wait.*

Ana

I watched as Liam drifted back into the house and saw Stephen turn his back to me as he gazed out at the water. I started to speak but he cut me off.

"I'm sorry Ana; I know that you are still trying to process a lot of what's happened. I shouldn't have overwhelmed you like that. I shouldn't have asked you..." he murmured. My heart dropped, shattering.

"Oh. Well, that's ok Stephen..." I suddenly felt very awkward; he wasn't even looking at me. I wanted to tell him that I was glad that he'd asked me, that he'd said all those beautiful things. I wanted to tell him that I loved him and that I just needed a bit of time, but not because I didn't want to marry him; I just wanted to be a bit more whole first, a bit more put together, but now it seemed irrelevant. He said he shouldn't have asked. He bowed his head and sighed, hearing my thoughts. "I should go," I whispered. "Maybe I can call you this week…" My throat tightened and I tried to swallow. I heard the waves crash against the shore and felt the spray from the sea blow against my skin. Stephen nodded, his back still to me. I turned to look into the house. Liam was standing, watching. I waved slowly and he waved back and I faded slowly away.

Patric

I wasn't entirely sure what to say to Ana; she already knew that I loved her and that I was in love with her. I guess I just needed her to know that I too wanted to be with her, that Stephen wasn't the only one willing to give her everything and beyond that, I wanted her to know just how much she'd given to me. I had never had anyone love me so much and sacrifice so much for me, not since my mother's death. I didn't deserve Ana. I was sitting on the bank of the river, feeling the breeze and thinking about Nathanial. The grass stirred and Ana was suddenly sitting beside me, her legs crossed, stretched out in front of her. I bent my head.

"You're getting very good at that," I said, playing with a tiny flower. She chuckled softly. "I guess maybe I should have proposed first." I laughed gently.

"I didn't think you were the monogamous type Patric. I had no idea that you wanted to get married." She touched my hand softly. I glanced sideways at her.

"I don't know; I could be, with the right person." I smiled, but my eyes deepened as the intensity of my emotions rose.

"And you think that person is me?" She met my gaze.

"I know that person is you Ana." I ran my fingers across hers as she pressed her palms into the earth. She sighed and relaxed back in the grass staring at the sky.

"I had no idea that you felt so committed to me Patric, that you wanted that kind of life with me." She closed her eyes and breathed deeply.

"I do," I replied, staring at her face and watching her chest rise and fall in rhythm with her breath.

"You know, I have moments during the day sometimes when I can feel the entire world stop and I think for a minute that he's still here, that maybe when I leave the house or leave work, that I'll see him leaning against my car waiting like when we first met. Then, I go out and see that he's not, that the space is empty and then I'll remember; my heart will remember and the world starts spinning again and I can't seem to hold on. I don't want to hold on…" She choked and tears fell down her face. Gently, I pressed my fingers to her amulet, calming her. Her body shook and I moved back turning my face to hers. I reached to touch her, running my fingers down over her lips and to her throat.

She sighed softly. I leaned over her and waited for her to open her eyes.

"Ana," I whispered. She swallowed and met my gaze. Her hand drifted and I felt her slowly trace her finger over the shape of my lips. I turned my face into her hand, kissing and breathing her in.

"I can't marry anyone right now Patric," she spoke softly, her eyes bright and brimming with tears. "Not you or Stephen; I have to heal. I have to find a reason to hold on again. I have to learn to be in this world without him and I'm not sure how to do that just yet."

"I know Ana. I know and it's ok," I spoke, feeling a renewed strength in the truth of my words because it was ok; I understood what she was feeling.

"I'd tell you to wait, but that seems cruel." She dropped her hand and turned her head. "I don't want you to wait, you or Stephen. I want you both to be happy, find people that you can love and who will love you as much as you both deserve." She rolled and stood taking a deep breath. She took my hand.

"So what happens now?" I asked, not wanting to let her go, knowing that I would never find anyone else that I loved as much as Ana and I was pretty sure that Stephen wouldn't either.

"We all try to heal, to move forward, start over I guess." She stepped away.

"Where will you go?" I stared at her. She frowned.

"California maybe or back to Italy; I haven't decided."

"Does Stephen know?" I reached to take her hand back. She smiled gently.

"I don't know. He felt bad about asking me to marry him and said that he shouldn't have asked at all; I'm guessing he's tired of the rollercoaster as well." She laughed, but I could feel her heart breaking while she spoke.

"It's his own rollercoaster Ana; it has nothing to do with you." She needed to know that.

"Maybe, maybe not, it doesn't really matter anymore; we were never going to work the right way. I've always known how difficult it would be for us to be together." I suddenly caught an image in her mind, a revolving door. My brother staring at her as they moved slowly around each other, his imaged faded and morphed and in his place Stephen stood also orbiting around her, never on the same side at the same time. She wiped fresh tears from her face and took a deep breath. "I'll let you know where I'm headed," she said. "Who knows, maybe I'll find a cool West Coast coven to hang out with." She laughed quietly. I pulled her close and held her tight. She wrapped her arms around my neck and hugged me. "I love you; you have to know that right?" she spoke softly in my ear.

"Yes," I whispered back, kissing her cheek. She turned her face and our lips met. Her mouth moved strongly against mine, and a surge of heat and energy passed between us. I held her face and kissed her greedily, not wanting her to stop, not wanting her to let go. She started to pull away but I held her against me. "Stay with me Ana; stay with me just for tonight." I breathed against her skin.

"I can't Patric; that would only make things harder and more confusing and that's not fair to either of us." She kissed me gently on the cheek. "I'll call you when I've decided where I'm going." She stepped away. "Please try to stay out of trouble; I don't really think my emotional state is allowing for me to access my powers right now. I won't be able to kick anyone's ass for you if you piss people off!" She laughed and I smiled.

"I love you," I called to her as she stood facing me.

"And I love you." She waved, blew me a kiss and shimmered away.

Seven months later…

Chapter Thirteen

Ana

I dropped the last of my Christmas presents off at UPS and checked my list. I was pretty sure that I had gotten everybody; Lucie was the most important. I had even managed to get a permanent address for Cillian and I sent him a rare bottle of cognac that I found. It was ridiculously expensive, but I knew that he would appreciate the gesture. I scrolled down the list stopping at the only name not crossed off, Stephen. I had never called him; I didn't think it was necessary and I had talked to Liam before departing Idaho and told him exactly the same things that I had told Patric the last time we'd spoken. I didn't think Stephen ever expected me to call. I had something for him; I was just laboring over whether or not to send the gift. One of my friends located a complete set of hand-carved Chinese paintbrushes. They called to tell me that the owner of the set was looking to hand them down to someone who would take care of them. I made a good case for Stephen and the man gave me the set with a beautiful leather case to boot.

"Ana! Aren't you done yet? I'm so fucking hungry, come on!" I smiled and glanced up at Dale as he came down the sidewalk carrying two cups of coffee. I studied Stephen's name one more time and folded the list and put it back in my purse. "Let's go, the taco truck moves every hour and I don't feel like making running around downtown Mill Valley, my second workout of the day!" Dale griped and I shook my head. Dale and I worked together at the Muir Woods National

Monument. We were both in charge of the wildlife education program and we spent most of our days hiking with students and leading groups through the park. I loved my job and I loved Dale; he was one of my closest friends here in California—and he was human, so was his partner Rich. They had adopted a little girl last year and for some reason Dale had taken to behaving more like his four-year-old daughter and less like the forty-year-old man that he was.

"I'm ready, let's go!" I said, pulling him down the street toward his beloved taco truck. We got our food and sat down on a bench, trying to stay warm.

"So next week is Christmas, what are you going to do?" Dale asked, eyeing me over his food. I knew what he meant. For months now I had been debating on whether or not I would visit Liam and Lucie in Ireland. Liam of course had invited me a month ago when he'd called; I had yet to get back to him. Both Dale and Rich knew quite a bit about Patric, Nathanial and Stephen. Dale had been in a relationship many years ago with a Bonder but he had never been Bound himself and he was very supportive of me and so was Rich. I shrugged. Dale laughed. "You know, Phoebe gives better answers Ana." Dale shook his head.

"I guess I could go and see Lucie; that might be nice." I took a bite of my lunch.

"Lucie. Sure, that would be nice." He raised he eyebrows. I sighed.

"Stephen is dating other women Dale; I think that door has now been officially closed." Liam had alluded to this fact when we'd spoken last month. He didn't come right out and say anything specific, but I knew

342

what he was getting at; it was fine, that's what I had wanted for both Stephen and Patric. I had asked them to move on and to heal.

"Dating doesn't mean married." Dale sipped his coffee. "What about Patric? What's he up to?" I frowned. I hadn't actually heard from Patric in at least five months. I'd called a few times and left him messages, but he'd only called once and we didn't talk very long. I guessed he was over things as well.

"I haven't heard from him in quite some time," I said, turning to look at the mist that had now rolled in over the water.

"Want me and Rich to fix you up? How long has it been, like seven months or something?" He laughed and took my hand.

"That's sweet but no thanks. I'm good." I sighed. The very idea of dating just made me slightly sick and sad; ugh, I was not ready to even think about being with a man right now.

"Well then, it's settled. You will be spending the holidays with us, and Rich's crazy parents. Phoebe loves you and she'll be so excited to know that you'll be available to read her every Fancy Nancy book in her collection." He touched the tip of my nose.

"That sounds wonderful, thank you Dale." I smiled and held his hand.

Stephen

"So how are you?" Carmen asked as she stirred a pot of pasta, Lucie and I were coloring on the kitchen table.

"Good," I said, smiling as Lucie traced between my fingers with a crayon.

"How's Sara?" Carmen untied her apron and bent to kiss Lucie on the head.

"Good." Sara and I had been dating on and off for about two months; she was beautiful, fun and just what I needed to get over Ana. Carmen snorted. "I take it you don't like Sara," I mused, handing Lucie another sheet of paper.

"I really take no interest in your love life Stephen; you can date whomever you like." She drained the pot and poured the pasta into a tiny bowl stirring in a bit of Parmesan cheese and olive oil. It was one of Lucie's favorite meals and one that Ana used to cook for her along with their chicken and rice concoction. Lucie's palette was limited to just those two dinners and had been for the last seven months. Carmen sliced up some tomatoes, avocados and grapes and set both bowls down in front of Lucie. I would hardly call my relationship with Sara a "love life", but whatever. I cared about her and maybe that could grow into something more. "Are you bringing her for our holiday party?" Carmen studied me, her hands on her hips. She reminded me a bit of our mother. She rolled her eyes.

"I haven't decided yet, maybe." I shrugged. Sara was adaptable and was used to hanging out with vampires on a daily basis; for a Human she was quite easy going.

"Estúpido hombre," Carmen mumbled under her breath. I chuckled as I saw Liam standing in the door.

"DADDY!" Lucie leapt from her highchair sending noodles and grapes flying. "Woops!" She giggled as I reached to catch the falling bowls. Liam scooped her up, kissing her cheeks. He turned to Carmen and kissed her gently on the lips. I turned away. I wasn't much for displays of affection these days.

"Stephen, I haven't seen you in awhile." Liam pulled out a seat and held Lucie in his lap.

"Yeah, been busy I guess," I said, wiping off the table with a rag that Carmen handed me.

"Doing what?" Liam bounced Lucie on his knee.

"Stuff," I said, leaning back in my chair. "I started teaching a bit in the evenings."

"Guitar?" Liam asked, his eyes roaming over my face.

"Yeah and a bit of painting." I rubbed my eyes. Liam frowned.

"Since when?" He knew that I was never one to teach; I didn't have the patience.

"Since a few months ago," I mumbled. Sara had convinced me; she taught ballet and the art studio needed someone for music and painting.

"I see." Liam was quiet as he read my thoughts. "Well I'm glad. You have a lot of talent to share," he said, nodding his head.

"Liam? Did you send my present to Ana?" Carmen turned to stare at Liam and I felt my heart begin to thud.

"I did. She should get it tomorrow." Liam's tone was soft, but it had a slight edge. I had no idea where Ana was these days and I hadn't bothered to ask so he didn't need to worry about me knowing, it didn't matter. Carmen snorted again and I stood up.

"I'm off," I said, taking Lucie and hugging her.

"We'll see you for the party then?" Liam stood and our eyes met.

"Yeah. I'll see you next week." I waved and shimmered from the house.

Ana

It was chilly and raining and I slogged into my house carrying my mail and tracking water and mud onto the porch. I shrugged out of my coat and kicked off my boots and ran to light the fireplace. I had stopped using my powers with fire. I hadn't used them since Nathanial's death. It was a ton harder to get a fire going without them these days. I got the flames ignited and started to strip off my clothes

346

and change into a pair of sweats—new sweats and a pullover. I curled up on the couch and opened my bills. There was a small padded envelope at the bottom of the pile. The mailer was Irish and I found Carmen and Liam's name on the front. I pulled open the flap and withdrew a small dark, green velvet pouch. There were two exquisite hand-carved, turquoise and silver hair clips wrapped in golden tissue paper. Carmen always wore something nice in her hair and I had wished that I could find something pretty to do with mine; she knew. There was a small note enclosed in the envelope with two words scrolled on the crisp, white paper: *Please come.*

Stephen

I wasn't really in the mood for a party, but Sara begged me to go and she was excited to be out at Liam's for the first time. My brother and Carmen had only met her once and I thought that was enough. Sara wasn't my girlfriend, not officially and I didn't see the point in having her get to know my family in any intimate way. The music was blaring as we climbed up the walkway to the front door. Liam hated traditional holiday parties and liked to make it more of a nightclub type atmosphere than anything Christmas related. I would just as soon be in a bar somewhere. Sara took my hand and I felt the heat from her blood begin to warm my skin and I stopped, pulling her body toward me.

Ana

I couldn't for the life of me understand why I was here. I had left Dale and Rich's before things there really got underway and for some reason decided to shimmer over to Liam and Carmen's. After getting Carmen's present in the mail, I felt bad for not having seen her in so long. I peered into the kitchen and found her at the stove. She whirled and squealed when she saw me. I moved, hugging her.

"ANA!" she shouted.

"Shhh!" I laughed. I had no idea if Stephen was here and I only wanted to stay for a minute.

"No way Ana. You're not going anywhere. I haven't seen you in so long." She kissed my cheeks and held my face. "You look thin." She surveyed me frowning. "Usted necesita comer más," Carmen scolded, using her very formal dialect that only came out when she was in "mother mode".

"I'm eating plenty, I promise." I pulled back to look at her. "You look beautiful!' I said smiling. "And your gift…Carmen, the clips are also beautiful." My eyes misted over and I spun around to show her the way they looked in my hair. "Thank you for thinking of me." I grasped her hands and she started to cry.

"I've missed you Ana."

"Me too." I sighed. We wiped our eyes and laughed.

"Now come and see Liam and meet some of our friends—you know most of them already." She started to walk towards the door. I didn't move. We stared at each other. "He's not here yet. I'll let you know." She bowed her head. I followed her out into the packed living room. Lucie screamed and darted from somewhere under a table, smashing into my leg and almost knocking me off balance.

"Hey beautiful angel! How are you, love?" I said, picking her up and kissing her.

"Good!" She laughed. I tickled her.

"Just good? Just good? Is that all? You're not stupendous or glorious or *Supercalifragilisticexpialidocious*?" I asked, swinging her around.

"YES! That one! I'm that one!' She laughed and nuzzled her face in my neck.

"I'll be right back Ana." Carmen touched my shoulder and bolted to catch a vase that someone had almost knocked over. I carried Lucie over to the couch trying to relax. I didn't see him anywhere.

Stephen

I pressed Sara up against the door. Probably not the best place to make-out, but it was working for me. I heard the bell sound from inside, but I also heard Sara moan and that was more important at the moment.

349

Ana

The doorbell rang and for some reason it appeared that no one was moving to answer it. I stood up and held Lucie on my hip and walked to open the door. The glass screen was in place and I could plainly see Stephen kissing a woman with long, dark red hair, his hands moving up under the back of her shirt. I heard a small hiss as Carmen appeared at my side; at the same time Stephen's eyes opened and we were staring at each other. He stopped moving and the woman whirled around to see me, Carmen, Lucie and now Liam, staring at her. I stepped back a few feet, feeling slightly sick and let Carmen answer the door while I took Lucie back over to the couch. I was ok, this is what I had wanted for him; I was ok. *It didn't matter.* I watched as Stephen and the red head came into the house, they were holding hands and I swallowed. I was fighting desperately to keep it together and I felt Liam staring at me. They all walked over to me and Lucie and I stood, steadying myself.

"Hey Ana," Stephen said and his eyes searched mine. I smiled weakly.

"Hey." I hugged Lucie close as I tried to remember how to breathe.

"Um...this is Sara." Stephen put his arm out and the woman moved gracefully forward and extended her hand.

"Hi Sara, it's so nice to meet you," I said, trying to warmly greet her, grasping her hand and smiling broadly now as I fought not to choke. She was beautiful and perfect. Coming to this party had to be one of

350

the stupider ideas that I'd had in a quite a while. Liam put his arm around my shoulder and I felt a surge of calm wash over me. Carmen stepped forward.

"Let me show you where to put your coat and purse Sara." Carmen took her hand and led her to the stairs. Sara and Stephen smiled at each other and my chest shifted uncomfortably as a memory of Nathanial and Adrianna flooded my mind. I saw Stephen wince and I turned to Liam, fingering my amulet.

"I just stopped by to thank Carmen for her gift," I said as Lucie played with my hair, "and to thank you for the beautiful photo album; it's so special." Liam had placed tons of photographs of Lucie and me in a stunning portfolio and I cherished it dearly. I watched as Stephen went to get himself a drink.

"Of course Ana, it's the very least I could do." Liam tried to smile, but I could see just how sad he was, his eyes searching mine and finding nothing but pain and utter despair.

"It's ok Liam. I wanted him to find someone; I'm ok. It's not the same as it was with Nathanial…it's not the same…" I tried to reassure him as Stephen returned and I turned toward him. I felt so sick all of a sudden, so grief-stricken; my soul actually felt detached from my core.

"It was good to see you," I said, trying desperately to hold on, not to fall apart. "You look well." He nodded and I saw him glance to his side as he watched Sara and Carmen descend the stairs. Another image of Nathanial suddenly flashed into my mind; the image of him at the camp, when I saw him look over my shoulder at Adrianna, his eyes

351

never returning to my face. Oddly, I was experiencing the same feeling of crushing sadness, this time though it was at my own doing. I tried to shake the memory and Liam squeezed me closer. "Well, um, I guess I should get going." I handed Lucie to Liam and swallowed thickly. "Tell Carmen thank you again and I'll call her soon." I was going to lose it; I could feel it. Stephen wasn't looking at me. He was staring at *her*. I nodded to myself, trying to accept, trying to close the door now once and for all. It was over and I felt the threads that had managed to somewhat hold Stephen to me… break. I grabbed my chest, trying to filter oxygen into my lungs. Stephen's head whipped back and he stared at me, fire in the depths of his eyes. I reached up to kiss Liam and Lucie and I turned to smile at Stephen. "See ya," I said. Sara had returned by his side.

"Yeah," he replied and we gazed at each other. I was falling slowly, disappearing into the very eyes that knew me, that had loved me and who had given me so much to be grateful for, Sara was very lucky and I hoped she would take good care of his heart. I shimmered away.

Stephen

"So wait, let me get dis straight. Ya go ta da party and Ana is dere and not only is she dere, but she opens da door ta find ya wall-fuckin' Sara? Holy shit dude…I don't know what ta say!" Cillian was leaning against the bar; we were drinking. I rolled my eyes.

"I wasn't…we weren't…we were just kissing, Jesus," I said, sipping from my glass.

"Whatever; ya haven't seen her in like seven or eight monts now and dat's how she finds ya." He shook his head. It wasn't the first time Ana had found me with someone else and it had happened with Nathanial as well. Patric seemed to be the only one of the three of us that she hadn't found screwing someone. Cillian shook his head.

"Don't mean he hasn't been enjoyin' himself!" He laughed. I eyed him.

"What do you mean?" I swirled my drink. Cillian shrugged.

"Notin', he's just been livin' it up a bit dat's all, but he's always been like dat, it's not new." I sighed. I guessed we were all moving on. I wondered if Ana had.

"Nope." Cillian stared over the bar at me, his eyes flashing.

"How would you know?" I said. I doubted that Cillian and Ana were in touch.

"Wrong again mate!" he chortled, but then his face smoothed. "She sent me a Christmas present, da first one I've gotten in a least a century. I called her." He stared at me as he cleaned the glasses. I looked down.

"When?"

"About a week ago. I suck at tankin' people fer shit, but Ana didn't seem ta mind. I saw inta her mind a bit; she's not been wit anyone at all in over seven monts and it appears dat she has no desire ta so… How

353

someone as hot as Ana can go witout sex fer dat long, I'll never know, but whatever." He put another drink down in front of me. He raised his eyebrows.

"What?" I said sharply. He laughed.

"Would ya like ta know where she is or are ya content in yer current status of tryin' ta forget her by focusin' on slender red heads?"

"That's not what I'm doing," I replied.

"Oh? Well excuse me. I had no idea dat tings were gettin' serious." He crossed his arms over his chest. "In dat case den perhaps I should try ta get Ana back on da horse or da vampire, as it is in my case." He raised his chin. I shrugged.

"If Ana feels compelled to sleep with you, that's her prerogative Cillian. I don't give a shit who she is and isn't fucking these days." My words sounded too harsh and Cillian took a step forward his eyes narrowing.

"You're a bloody asshole you know that Stephen? You're a goddamn prat. You're not *in* love with Sara and you don't *love* her, so you can sit there and try to convince me that you're now free and clear of Ana, that you don't spend every waking minute of every day, thinking about her, grieving over her. You can try and drink her away, you can try and fuck her away, you can date red heads, brunettes, blondes, vamps or Humans; it won't matter. It didn't work for Nathanial and it sure as hell won't work for you." Cillian's voice was dark and low and gone was his usual thick Irish accent; he sounded ancient, commanding and terrifyingly wise. "You love Ana and she is all you've

354

ever wanted and all you will ever need and you're dying without her."
Cillian sipped his drink.

"How about just a one night stand? You could do that...you wouldn't even have to go on a date if you didn't want," said Dale.

"DALE!" Rich scolded as we sat down for dinner.

"What? I'm just saying; Ana's a modern woman. She's progressive and open minded. Lots of women have one night stands," Dale said and Rich sighed.

"Ana? Are you interested in having meaningless sex with a perfect stranger?" Rich glared at Dale while he spoke to me. I laughed and braided Phoebe's hair.

"Uh...I'm not big on strangers seeing me naked; I'm probably not the right kind of woman for a one nighter." I covered Phoebe's ears.

"Nonsense! You are the perfect woman." Dale laughed and Rich huffed.

"I'm not sure that's a compliment Dale!" Rich griped.

"Guys, it's fine. I'm fine, really. I don't think the dating world is missing me. I'm happy to just have the two of you." I smiled at them.

"Ana, and me too Ana!" Phoebe tugged on my hair.

"Oh my goodness, of course you, especially you!" I kissed her gently.

I finished my meal at Dale and Rich's and headed home. Maybe I should think about going out at some point; it didn't have to lead to anything, just something to make me feel human again. I ran from the car onto the porch just as the rain started to fall. I slid into the house and nearly collided with Cillian as he stood in my hallway.

"Gotcha!" His hand shot out and caught me just as I was about to fall forward into his chest.

"Cillian!" I stared at him. "What are you doing here?" I suddenly became nervous. "Has something happened?" He was still holding my arm.

"Nah, everytin' is fine love. No worries. Just tought I'd pop by fer a visit; it's been awhile since my ass has traveled ta da States." He looked around the hall. "I like yer house!" He smiled and I motioned for him to follow me into the kitchen.

"I don't have any whisky, but I have wine or tea? What can I get you?" It was slightly odd having Cillian in my kitchen, but it also felt familiar. He laughed.

"Tea is good." I eyed him and frowned. He laughed again loudly.

"I'm tryin' ta clean up a bit, ya know, old age and all dat!" I rolled my eyes.

"Why?" I said, grinning and putting on the kettle.

"Tryin' ta get a good lassie ta take me in; most don't appreciate a drunk vampire now do dey?" He smirked. I cringed.

"Since when do you go for the 'good girls' Cillian? Are you having some sort of crisis of conscience?" I took out my favorite mugs and poured us some tea. He smiled as I sat down across from him.

"Maybe or maybe I've just seen how lucky some of my mates have been when dey find someone ta love." He raised his eyebrows and I laughed gently.

"But you've also seen how fucked up it can get, better to keep tings simple I think." I shook my head.

"Is dat why ya've taken to a life of celibacy, trying ta keep things simple?" He eyed me.

"Hey! What makes you think I haven't had sex?" Cillian spat his drink out. "What? You don't know! I could've been coming back from…from being with someone just now." I pursed my lips, defiant. He laughed and wiped his mouth.

"Ya *could*, but ya're not! I happen ta know dat ya were just wit yer two Human friends, da ones wit da kid, so you're not foolin' anyone." He smiled at me.

"Well…if I wanted to, I could," I said, frowning.

"As one who has always expressed an extreme attraction to ya, I don't need no convincin', love." Cillian leaned forward his eyes flashing.

"Why are you so concerned with my sex life Cillian?" I eyed him. Why was *everyone* so concerned; that was probably the more accurate question to ask.

"Cause ya're a vibrant, intensely passionate woman and ya should be out dere enjoyin' life." He put his mug down and watched me.

"Uh…well thanks, I guess." I smiled at him, but suddenly felt that familiar crushing sadness that still hit me sometimes. "I'm not ready Cillian," I said softly.

"Yeah, I know Ana." He matched my tone and his voice shifted, changed to something deeper and more passionate; he reached to touch my hand. I nodded and swallowed. "He still loves you Ana; he still loves you very much." Cillian raised my face to look at him. His accent had disappeared. Cillian sounded old, like my Noni, old and sacred in his wisdom. I glanced at him, slightly startled by his change in demeanor.

"He's done what I wanted Cillian and so has Patric, I'm guessing. They both offered me their hearts and I had to turn both of them away; I can't ask for either of them to take me back now, not when I told them that we all needed to move on from each other; it doesn't work like that." I bowed my head. Cillian sat back.

"I don't really give a shit about what Patric offered you; he's not a brother to me and personally I think he'd make a piss poor husband. I care about Stephen and I care about you Ana." He rubbed his face, continuing to speak in an unfamiliar voice. "The door's not closed Ana. I can see that you've been trying to shut it, to lock it, but it's not doing what you want love and do you know why? Because you know

358

what you want, because you still love him, you never stopped loving him and even though you may have contemplated a life with Patric you knew that it was really Stephen that you wanted; even before Patric came back, you knew. See, I have a very unique talent Ana, one that most of my kind don't have. I can see soul memories. I can see just what it is that you have always desired. I can see the entire journey that your heart and soul have made and I can see each and every decision both conscious and unconscious. I can see them all and I see each and every collision of your heart, your mind and your soul. I know that it was that night in the alley right before you and Stephen were attacked, that you made your choice. You didn't realize it then, but I can read it just as if it were a book. I've read Stephen as well; his was way before yours actually. His came when he saw you holding the body of that dead girl and wishing you could take her place. Maria was her name, and his choice was fused from that point on." I stared at Cillian in complete disbelief. "The great thing about this gift of mine is that it allows for me to see, to actually read people like maps, all the roads they've taken and not taken. I can see all the choices made and unmade, all the loves lost and found and lost again, but there are always threads that connect. They may diverge, they made fray, they may even become severed at some point, but I can see the route just before the break and I can see where they were headed. You and Stephen, your threads are on a collision course. They are not a revolving door Ana. The two of you have been on opposite sides of the map, meeting and crossing every now and again, but always moving forward towards each other at full speed. I've been watching and waiting since I first saw you on that couch, the day we met. You can't stop it, neither of you can; it's time to let Nathanial go Ana. It's time to let Patric go. You're holding on too tight and trying to stop a moving train. Let them go now. They will always be threads on your map, but those threads have run their course. You keep trying to weave them into your life when they are already there. You haven't lost them Ana, they are part of your story and of your journey, but their books have ended and Stephen's is waiting to begin. Let them go." I was gasping and sobbing violently, choking and heaving onto the table. Cillian picked me up and held me against him as he whisked us away.

Stephen

I picked up Ana's ring and laid it on my chest feeling its heat warm my skin. Cillian was right and he knew that I knew he was right. Of course I still loved Ana, of course I did, there would never be a single heart on this earth that could ever take her place—ever. I reached across to turn up my stereo, trying to drown out my internal monologue. Familiar lyrics filtered into the room and I sighed. There were way too many things that Ana and I had shared over the course of our relationship. I closed my eyes. It was dark when I came to and I could hear the same song playing again. I shifted on the bed and felt someone next to me. I stared and focused my eyes in the dark. Ana was lying curled up on her side, facing me.

"Hi," she whispered. I stared at her. I had come out of my trance hadn't I?

"Ana?" I reached to turn on the light on the nightstand. "What are you doing here?" I asked, still not sure this wasn't some figment of my overactive imagination.

"I don't know, I just thought I would come and hang out. California isn't much of a happening place these days." She smiled gently. I turned on my side so I could look at her fully. "Cillian brought me." She bit her lip. After I married Ana, I would see if I could also marry Cillian. I smiled to myself.

"Oh. California huh?" I asked, looking down. "Do you like it?"

"Yeah it's fun. I like my job, but I like Ireland better," she murmured. I shifted closer to her, feeling the warmth of her body. "How are you?" She looked at me, but she was also moving toward me.

"Good," I said. We were so close together now. A current of energy passed back and forth between us and I felt charged with heat and passion and love. Our faces were aligned. "What about you?" I whispered, my lips barely touching hers. She breathed gently on my mouth and I tasted her scent.

"Stephen?" Her lips moved just barely grazing my own. The energy surged.

"What?" My body began to tremble as I breathed her in.

"Yes," she said and my eyes opened. She'd said "yes". I pulled back to stare at her.

"Yes?" I was breathless.

"Yes, if you haven't already asked someone else…" She bit her lip again and I laughed.

"No Ana, I haven't asked anyone else." I held her face. "Are you sure?" I swallowed, not believing.

"Yes." She didn't hesitate. "Yes, Stephen." I stared at her, zoning out a bit. I kept picturing our wedding and what she'd be wearing and where it would be.

"Stephen?" she asked, pulling me from my daydream.

"Yeah?"

"I haven't had sex in like eight months, can we focus here for a minute?" She laughed and kissed me gently. I looked at her and raised my eyebrows.

"Really? Eight months?" I cringed, thinking that perhaps I should have exercised more restraint.

"Yes! Why does everybody seem so flabbergasted? I don't sleep with anyone just for the sake of having sex. I mean I could, but I don't!" She glared. I laughed and moved to kiss her. She pulled away. "How many?" she asked, eyeing me.

"What?" I asked, grinning.

"You know what; don't pretend. How many?" She tossed her hair and took my pillow and laid back.

"How many did I sleep with or how many did I date?" I said, baiting her. She rolled her eyes.

"Sleep with!" she said. I moved and hovered over her, bringing my face close.

"None," I said, my eyes flashing and I bent to kiss her, still not believing that she was here with me.

"None?"

"None." I had not slept with Sara; I had never wanted to—ever.

"Dates?" she asked.

"A few."

"Blood?" She thought she had me.

"None," I said smirking. "I stocked up when you left." I winked. She flipped me over and laid herself against me.

"Hmmm…so you're as close to virginal as you can get for your kind." She kissed my throat.

"Virginal? Love, I haven't heard that word associated with my name for well over five hundred years!" I growled playfully and rolled her back underneath me. She twisted.

"Something's pressing into my head," she said. I rose up and let her lift her head. Her ring was on my pillow and I picked it up, holding it in front of her.

"So what do you think? Do you like this or would you fancy something a bit more traditional for an engagement or wedding ring?" I cocked my head to the side and sat up.

"I'm not much for traditional. I love this ring; it's perfect," she said, taking it from me, but I frowned. "What?" she asked as she slipped it back on her finger.

"I don't know, I was thinking that maybe we should get you a new one, something different," I said, pursing my lips. I secretly had been designing wedding bands for us for a while now and I knew someone who would be able to make them for us.

"New? I don't need 'new' Stephen." She stared at me.

"I know love, but just let me do this for you, for us. You can still keep your ring and I'll keep mine; I want to do this for you." I took off my band and slipped it on the ring finger of my right hand. "See?" She twisted her mouth and did the same.

"Ok," she said hesitantly. "But nothing expensive and no diamonds." She hated diamonds.

"Got it cheap and cheap!" I laughed and she nodded forcefully. "Now, where were we coming down on that whole sex thing?" I asked, pushing her gently back down on the pillows. She laughed.

"You haven't had any sex and I haven't had any sex and we're both long overdue!" She grabbed the front of my shirt and pulled me on top of her.

"Right; let's remedy that." I bit her playfully on the neck then she bit me, not so playfully and I came undone.

Ana

I had a ton of furniture and stuff in my house in California and lucky for me, Dale and Rich were taking it all to furnish a rental property they owned. Stephen and I were on my floor packing up my books and clothes for me to take back to Ireland.

"So it seems like you have a nice set up here," he said, eyeing me from the bookshelf. He'd just gone to lunch with Dale, Rich and Phoebe and they'd gotten along really, really well. I heaved a bunch of clothes over my shoulder and laid them on the couch.

"Yeah, I like it here," I said, checking my phone. I had been trying to call Patric for a few weeks. I wanted to invite him to the wedding, whenever we set a date. I was pretty sure he wouldn't come. Stephen smiled and came over to put his arms around me.

"He'll call." He kissed my neck. "Speaking of the wedding. Any ideas of where you want to get married or when?" I had never seen Stephen so excited about anything before. He'd become quite a bit hyperactive in the month since we'd decided to make it official and he was constantly asking me questions about my dress, what food I wanted and what guests I was inviting. Carmen too had become enthralled with the idea of a wedding. She and Liam were married over a century ago. Weddings between Humans and Vampires were pretty rare, but they did happen and I was glad that all of our closest friends were happy and excited for us.

"Um…well where do *you* want to get married?" I didn't actually have to get married; I could be quite happy just living with Stephen, but it was a dream come true for him apparently, and I enjoyed seeing him so happy. He frowned.

"I want you to be happy too Ana." His tone was soft.

"I am, more than you know." I touched his face. " How about May? It's about four months away, that will give me time to get a dress." I hadn't even begun looking yet; the last two dresses I had gotten were for weddings that never happened. I was a bit gun shy. Stephen chuckled.

"How about at the end of *this* month?" he asked, kissing me deeply and making me gasp.

"What?" I asked, trying to catch my breath.

"This month; let's do it now." His hand moved to grab me around the waist. My arousal toward Stephen was causing me some concern, just here in the last few weeks. While I hadn't been using my powers with fire or fighting thank god, it appeared that since our reunion, my desire to be with him was amped up full force and not in any sort of Vamped out kind of way, just pure, unadulterated passion. I was keeping myself in check, mainly because I didn't want to come across as some hormonal teenager, but also because I actually did enjoy doing other things with Stephen, like talking and going for walks and watching movies and dancing; having sex just seemed to be overwhelming those other things at the moment. Stephen laughed hearing my inner monologue. He walked me backwards pushing me up against the wall; he wasn't making things easier. "You want to know a

366

secret?" he whispered in my ear as he kissed down my neck. I couldn't really answer so I just nodded. "I think that I'm addicted to you." He kissed me full on the mouth and I felt his body surge with a flood of heat. His breath was coming heavy on my lips.

"Why, are you having withdrawals?" I panted; he was unbuttoning my jeans. He laughed again.

"I was," he said, shoving up my shirt and shifting my underwear over to the side. I inhaled as he moved his fingers between my legs. He continued to kiss me.

"You're not now?" I gasped as he pressed me harder against the wall.

"Depends." He pushed two fingers inside me and I groaned.

"On what." I breathed into his ear.

"On whether or not you stop trying to censor your desires around me." He smiled as he bit down on my neck. "I mean, if we're going to be married, you should feel free to jump me anytime you want."

"Right ya're mate! I say da only ting marriage is good fer is da quick and easy access ta sex; dat's if ya marry someone who actually still wants ta have sex with ya after da weddin'." Cillian had suddenly appeared.

"WHAT THE FUCK CILLIAN!" Stephen shouted and moved to block me from Cillian's view. "GET THE FUCK OUT OF HERE!" Cillian laughed and winked at me. I was trying to breathe and trying not to laugh. I guess I should have been embarrassed, but at this point, I really didn't care what Cillian walked in on anymore; we'd both seen way too much of everything.

"Right again Ana, way too much; altough I don't quite have a good view of ya love. Maybe if Stephen just stepped a hair ta da —" Stephen growled loudly. "Ok. Ok. I was just comin' ta let ya know dat yer 'items' are done." Cillian using air quotes was funny to observe and I snickered. Stephen whirled around to stare at me and I bit my lip.

"Fine. Now GET OUT!" Stephen threw up his hands and Cillian snapped his fingers and left us alone. "There is no way he's coming to the wedding. No fucking way!" Stephen moved to let me rearrange myself and I laughed.

"We've already invited him you fool," I said, buttoning my jeans. "What items are done? What's he talking about?" I said, moving to put my arms around Stephen's waist. I was already in the mood again and I kissed his neck and his bottom lip. He sighed and let me kiss him on the mouth. He was still upset.

"Our rings are ready," he said and I stopped my movements.

"Really?" I frowned. "Why was Cillian telling you?" Perhaps Cillian was a jeweler at one point, he was two hundred years older than Stephen and had done just about every career and job one could possibly do.

"He has and he's only a hundred and fifty years older." Stephen laughed. "Cillian is also an amazing silversmith; he made our rings." I stared at him.

368

"Cillian? Cillian the guy who can't go anywhere without a drink or a woman in his hand or on his lap; Cillian made our wedding rings?" After our conversation last month, I had a much deeper respect for Cillian, still, I wouldn't necessarily peg him as the artistic type. "Well that's a interesting bit of information," I said, returning to kissing down Stephen's neck.

"Apparently not interesting enough to distract you," Stephen murmured. I pulled away.

"Sorry, I'm too much." I smiled and cringed. I didn't want to overwhelm him. Right as I spoke, I smelled his scent release. I stared at him and he winked at me throwing me over his shoulder and carrying me down to the bedroom. He threw me down on the bed and pinned my arms over my head.

"Now, what's your decision about marrying me this month and not waiting?" With one flick of his finger he'd unhooked my bra and was lifting my shirt over my head. He was running his hands over my chest and stomach and I could feel my blood begin to warm; it was taking the breath out of me. I saw his eyes flash and felt my brain go mushy. He was trying to hypnotize me. He laughed. "Right ya're," his words echoing Cillian. He kissed down my stomach and back up to my chest; he was working me up. "Don't make me wait four months Ana." He moved his tongue over my breasts, lingering and watching my reaction.

"Fine, this month!" I gasped and suddenly he pulled away.

"Good. Now, no sex until the wedding night!" He laughed and threw my shirt at me. I sat there, incredulous.

Chapter Fourteen

Stephen

I had been trying to find Patric. It was important to Ana that he at least called her and if he could, come to the wedding. It was important to me as well; while I was never Patric's biggest fan, he did help to save my life and Ana's and I shared some sympathy for him over losing his brother. He was proving very difficult to find. I had contacted Micah who Ana had also invited and he hadn't heard from Patric in over three months. The last he knew, his nephew was living it up in Ibiza, Spain. He'd turned his businesses over to several friends and had basically fallen off the map. I wasn't in the mood for anymore global trekking and Ana was waiting for me at home; I had been gone the whole week. My trips weren't completely futile. I had managed to find the lodge where Lucie and Ana had their bed under the stars; it had been in Italy. I booked the best rooftop suite for the first leg of our honeymoon. Ana had given me complete autonomy over our plans post the wedding and I couldn't be more thrilled. She was not however, happy about my abstinence policy. I just thought there was something intensely erotic about holding off for a while and letting the desire build. I wasn't completely abstaining, that would be impossible, but it was such a turn on getting her worked up and then cutting it off. I liked teasing her.

I landed in the living room; it was after eleven at night and there were only embers in the fire. I headed down the hall to the bedroom. Ana was in bed on her laptop with the stereo softly playing. I hung in the doorway watching.

"You're back." She grinned as I came to lie next to her. "Any luck?" She closed the computer and put her head on my shoulder.

"Sorry love, but I did see Micah and he told me to tell you that of course he'll be at the wedding." She sighed.

"Well thanks for checking; I know it was a lot of effort." She smiled at me and I kissed the top of her head.

"It wasn't, but you're welcome." I turned up the music a bit.

"So when do I get to see our rings?" She rolled so that her stomach was flush against mine. I ran my hand over her back.

"Maybe next week." She kissed my chest. I laughed softly.

"Do you have them here?" she asked as she slid up my shirt and ran her tongue down my stomach. She was trying to distract me with questions.

"No way," I said, letting her unbutton my pants. "Liam has them." We were having the ceremony at Liam and Carmen's at least for right now; we kept changing the location. The wedding was just Micah and Cillian and Liam, Carmen and Lucie. I knew that Ana had hoped Patric would be around to attend, but we were a little less than two weeks away and that was looking more and more like a pipe dream. Ana had now managed to pull down my jeans and was starting to tease me with her tongue. I cleared my throat. "You seem to have difficulty following

371

rules I can see." I breathed hard as I felt her start to take me into her mouth. She stopped short.

"You just said no sex before the wedding; you weren't specific as to what sex we couldn't do…" She purred. I laughed and pulled her up toward me. Jesus, I had the stupidest ideas.

"I'm sorry, you're right I didn't specify. No sex at all; that would be all inclusive." I brought her mouth to mine and kissed her suggestively.

"Stephen seriously, this is the most ridiculous thing that I have agreed to. I mean, you've been with thousands of woman and you've been with me like, a bunch; what's the big deal?" I wasn't quite seeing how me having been with a lot of women had anything to do with what I had proposed.

"Tell me something," I rolled Ana onto her side and stared, "does it bother you that I've slept with a few women in my five centuries?" I smiled.

"Sometimes. I mean it used to bother me more when I was living with you in Indonesia; I guess because I didn't really know you that well yet and I felt like I was intruding into a life that I wasn't a part of or didn't belong." She folded her hands on her stomach. I stretched out next to her.

"I liked having you there; I liked coming home and seeing you on my couch reading or sleeping. I felt almost normal, civilized." I laughed gently.

"What were you thinking the first night I showed up?" She turned to stare at me as she traced her fingers gently over my chest. I chuckled.

372

"I thought you were by far the most reckless Human that I had ever met. Most people and most women do not go into a vampire's home unless the evening is about to take one of two turns." I raised my eyebrows.

"Which one did you want it to take?" She studied me. I had never discussed with Ana what was going through my mind that night she came to me; it had been one of the most bizarre nights of my entire existence and it would end up becoming the most significant evening of that same existence. "Well first, I wondered just how the hell you knew where I lived." I leaned over on my side so we were face to face.

"Rene," she said simply. "Apparently, you used to have quite the weekend blowouts at the apartment." I shook my head; that was true. "So after you let me in, what were you thinking?" She touched my face. "I mean, you must have been surprised to see me; I just made your assignment to kill me, that much easier." She pursed her lips.

"I was surprised to see you. Of course I read your mind immediately and I saw what transpired between you and Nathanial; it would make my job easier, having you away from him, but I was also acutely aware of what you could do and I was intrigued. Both Liam and I were shocked that you had survived that fall from the deck, or should I say jump?" I stared hard at her face remembering when Liam had told me that he'd heard Ana had sacrificed herself to save Patric and Nathanial. I was in awe and I had been extremely shattered thinking that she had died; it didn't seem right. "And we were stunned to learn that you fought against both Alec and Devon and won. So, I wasn't quite sure what to think about you at that moment." I touched her gently on the lips.

"How was it that you came to be the one to offer to kill me? I mean, I'm sure there were a ton of other Vampires from other covens that could have executed the plan; why you?" She kissed my fingers. I wasn't really comfortable discussing my assignment back then; it made me feel sick, especially now, especially since I was less than two weeks away from making Ana my partner, my wife. I sighed.

"There was a meeting of sorts once we'd all heard of Devon's demise; several of the larger covens met and we counseled about what to do with you. The Bonders were doing the same, but they were more hesitant because of Nathanial's ranking amongst them. We had no attachment to you, no relationships to you and you had none to us except through Patric and none of us ever felt that he was truly part of our species. We took advantage of the Bonders indecisiveness and planned to…" I bowed my head.

"It's ok Stephen; it's fine now, we're together and it's good. I want to know." She kissed my hand. I swallowed.

"We made a plan to kill you." I couldn't look at her.

"And you volunteered?" She smiled. I shook my head.

"Liam was the dissenting opinion." Ana frowned; she'd always been under the impression that it had been Liam that had ordered her to be killed. I shook my head. "He didn't think it necessary for you to be murdered, that from your history, it didn't appear that you were in any way trying to use your powers to defeat us or to cause us harm, that you were using them to defend yourself and the ones you loved. He was adamant that our coven wouldn't participate in any plan to take your life." She looked confused. I sighed again. "While I'm part of

Liam's coven, with my history and my particular skill set, I was considered, apparently, unparalleled in my abilities. They wanted to make sure that you wouldn't survive and that they sent someone who had the capacity to defeat you should you try and fight back." I laid back and put my arms behind my head.

"What do you mean 'someone with your history'?" Ana asked. I closed my eyes.

"I'm the worst kind of my species Ana, at least I was for quite some time. I was known for my severe brutality and my capacity to enjoy watching my enemies suffer. I was always a fair fighter, but you would never win. I would torture and tease and then I would deliver the blow and make sure that you saw it coming. You would know that you were about to suffer and die." My voice turned flat. "I was by far the best vampire to send to finish you off." I turned my face to look at her. She was biting her lip.

"Why didn't you just kill me as soon as I came in? You gave me a chance to talk to you; we talked for a while and you listened to me, why?" I shook my head.

"Because from the moment I met you, I knew there was something very special about you; I could *feel* it. I could feel what was happening to you when you saw Nathanial and Patric down at that first dinner when we'd met; I witnessed how angry you were with both of them, but I could also see how very sad you felt; you thought that it was because you weren't enough for either of them to have made a different choice, that it was because of you that Nathanial left and that Patric used you. It made you so sad. Then, I saw you that morning with that

375

horrible murder; I've told you this. I saw you with Maria and with the mother and the father and I saw memories that you were having. You were wondering if your parents would have been sad if you had died and you thought about yourself as a mother. I was beside myself at the intensity and depth of your emotions and then I felt you get angry, very, very angry—mainly with Patric, but also with Nathanial…when you showed up at my apartment, I was torn. I knew what I was supposed to do, what I had been told to do, but seeing you, listening to you and feeling how hurt and upset you were, your heart was breaking and I just kept thinking that that wasn't right; your heart shouldn't be shattering—it seemed wrong. After everything that you'd done, after fighting so hard for others and for yourself, I think I wanted to *know* you and I wanted you to know me." I smiled gently and breathed in her scent. I laughed. "And then you hugged me! I remember watching you lean in and thinking, 'this girl is crazy' and then I felt your arms around me and the warmth of your skin; I felt your heart beating against my chest and like so many times after that night, including now, I felt as if I was drowning in my desire for you," I whispered moving to lean over her.

"Oh." Her eyes searched mine. I smiled and kissed her slowly. "You didn't want to Change me then right?" I pulled back.

"No," I murmured smoothing back her curls.

"And that night with Carlo, when he'd bitten me, what were you thinking." I blinked; that was the most horrific night of my five centuries on this earth.

"I was thinking that the way he died, it wasn't brutal enough." I rolled onto my stomach, tucking my pillow under my chest.

"But they asked you to Change me; Nathanial and Patric, they asked you? You were the only one who could do it right?" She turned on her side.

"Yes."

"And you didn't want to," she stated. "You didn't want it to be done that way."

"No."

"Were you glad that it didn't take? I mean were you glad that I wasn't Changed?" Christ, she was asking such hard questions.

"I was relieved that you were alive," I said, remembering how angry I was with Nathanial and Patric for keeping me in the dark about her condition.

"That's not what I asked you," Ana said quietly.

"I was incredulous that it didn't work."

"Stephen," she scolded.

"No, I wasn't glad that you weren't Changed. I wanted you Ana and I wanted us to have that connection and for me to have been the one who gave you your Afterlife; it can be a very sacred bond if the two people are already connected. You were already sharing bonds with Nathanial and Patric and I wanted something between us, something that was tangible and ritualistic. I wanted you to be mine in every sense of the word." I knew that my words sounded a bit possessive, but that's how I'd felt at the time.

"And now?" She studied me, her eyes fluid and deep in their concentration.

"And now what?" I frowned.

"And now do you still feel the same? Do you want us to be connected in that way? I mean, I think that there was some definite transfer of things from you to me that night and I do have your blood and venom in my system, whatever my body didn't manage to kill off, but do you wish now that I could be yours in a more pronounced way?" I knew what she was asking.

"It doesn't matter Ana; your body, for whatever reason, won't allow for you to be Changed, so it doesn't matter how I feel." I sat up suddenly feeling frustrated.

"It does matter Stephen. It matters because I want what you want." She leaned forward and turned my face to hers.

"What?" I was puzzled.

"I *want*—what *you* want." She emphasized her words. "I want to be yours, in every sense of the word." She echoed my words back to me. I shook my head.

"Ana, that's very sweet, but I don't need that anymore; I have you and you have me and that's all that's important." She shook her head forcefully.

"No," she replied.

"Ana."

"No!" she said again forcefully.

"It won't work Ana. Your body won't allow for the transition to take place; it's protecting you, your life and I really don't think we should be messing with that do you?" I stood up and ran my fingers though my hair.

"You don't know it won't work; my body is different now, different from what you did. I could have a different composition, one that will allow for things to happen." She seemed somewhat desperate; I didn't know why.

"Ana." I went and sat next to her, rubbing her back. "Why is this so important to you? It's not to me; I love you. I love that you're Human or something close…" I laughed. "You don't need to be like me or Liam or anyone else for that matter."

"Because," she said and I stared at her.

"Because?"

"Because then I could help you better, protect you…" She trailed off and could see her struggling not to cry. I held her face.

"Protect me from what love?" I stared deep into her eyes, searching.

"From being killed, from you being taken away from me." I watched as her eyes spilled over.

"Ana." I pulled her into my chest. "Ana, my love, my life, my soul; you don't need to protect me from anything. I'm not going to be taken away from you." She was shaking her head in my neck.

"You don't know that. You don't know." Suddenly I could see her mind replaying the images from that godforsaken fight we'd attended; her mind was focusing on the violence and then on the night she'd found out that I was staying to fight for Saden. She was overwhelmed with grief.

"I do know. I do know and I can promise you that no one is going to try to take me away from you. You don't need to end your life so that you can protect me, that's not a good enough reason and I won't let you argue for that side."

"No one knows the future Stephen; you can't predict that no one will ever try to harm you. You're not immune to the evils of the world any more than anyone else." She was staring at me and her eyes were moving very quickly over my face. I sighed.

"You're right Ana, no one can predict the future so why worry about it; why take your life away for something that no one has the insight to predict? Plus, we have no idea if it would work and the very idea of making you suffer through something like that again and not having the damn thing work—it makes me sick. I won't put your body through that again." I met her gaze.

"What about Liam?" She pulled back and wiped her face. I cocked my head.

"What *about* Liam?" I didn't like where this was headed.

"Maybe he could help; maybe he knows if it would stick now, maybe there's a test or something." I almost laughed at her train of thought.

"A test? No Ana, there's no test." I touched her arm.

"Well you don't know!" She looked at me. "There might be. Couldn't we just ask? I mean what's the harm?" She crossed her arms over her chest. I sighed.

"Ok, we'll ask but when the answer is 'no', this discussion is over—agreed?" I touched her cheek.

"And what if the answer is 'yes' are we agreed to try it?" She met my stare. I blinked again; an odd sense of nervousness began to creep into my heart. "Stephen? Are we agreed to try the test if there is one?" she asked me again. I exhaled.

"Yes." I swallowed. She nodded.

"Good; *now* the discussion is over." She climbed back into bed and held out her arms to me.

Ana

I was going to beat Stephen to the punch. I had to see Liam first. I knew that if Stephen talked to him before me, he would try to convince Liam to lie and to tell me that there was no test, I wanted to hear it for myself and I knew that Liam would be honest with me, no matter what. Stephen was still in his recovery trance early the next

381

morning, so I called Liam as soon as I got up. He was at their store taking inventory; I grabbed my purse and popped over.

I loved Carmen and Liam's sex shop; it was part art gallery and part adult store, but somehow they blended seamlessly into a very sophisticated experience. The walls were covered in original De Kooning's and Pollack's, but Liam also offered space to local artists and photographers. Some of Stephen's work graced the walls as well. I wished I had something to display; I frowned as I wandered into the store. I heard Liam laughing.

"Have you ever tried to paint?" he asked, looking up from behind the counter.

"Yeah, but I'm not very good. Unless splattering paint on Stephen's very expensive hardwood floor counts as talent." I smiled. Liam glanced at his watch.

"It's five in the morning Ana. Why are you up so early?" He eyed me and I shut my mind; I didn't want Liam to get ahead of me in what I wanted to ask him. I shrugged. He laughed. "I'm guessing that my brother is still 'sleeping' and you have something you would like to discuss without him knowing?" He was writing some checks from a big book.

"No, he knows, I just wanted to talk to you first," I corrected and Liam grinned.

"Very good strategy Ana." He closed the book and leaned forward on the counter. "Now, what can I help you with?" He cocked his head. I took a deep breath.

"So, ok; I have Stephen's blood and his venom in my system. We know that Stephen's attempt to Change me didn't work because my body is wonky." Liam laughed gently. "Ok, but we also think that my body allowed for the venom to heal me, but not allow for the transition to occur right?" I asked trying to catch my breath.

"So it appears." Liam eyed me closely and I could tell that he was trying to get into my head.

"Right, ok; so wouldn't it be correct to assume that after the venom healed my body that that same body would no longer have those restrictions, that it would essentially be a new body?" I met his stare.

"Are you trying to get pregnant Ana? Liam came out from behind the counter.

"What?" I wasn't following.

"Are you and Stephen wanting to try for a baby again?" Liam asked softly. I hadn't even thought about that; that was interesting…but not why I was here.

"Uh no." I pursed my lips.

"Alright, I'm sorry for interrupting, please continue." Liam's body was now rigid. I had his attention, but I had also lost my train of thought. Frick!

"Um…so that body would be different?" I asked.

"Possibly." He put his hand behind his back and I started playing with one of the racks of bras in front of me. This was such a weird place to be having this discussion.

"So if that's what we can infer, then couldn't we also infer that my ability to actually allow for that Change to occur now, might be a possibility?" Liam's head snapped up and his eyes narrowed. "Liam? Wouldn't it be a possibility?" I asked again.

"Ana, what are you asking me?" His tone was quiet. I sighed.

"I'm asking if there is any way for us to test if my body is in fact different than it was before and that it may be better conditioned to undergo the transition again?" I picked up a garter and started twisting it in my hands. I checked the price and immediately put it back.

"Yes." I looked up not quite sure that I had heard correctly.

"Um what?" I blinked and stared at Liam.

"Yes, there's a way to see if your body has changed enough to handle another attempt." Liam was so quiet.

"Really?" I moved forward to stand next to him. "I mean, you know this?"

"Yes." He smiled gently. "I'm guessing you would like to know what it entails?" He leaned back against the counter. I nodded. "Well, it's pretty straight forward. You get two different types of venom in your system, preferably one from the vampire who originally injected you and then we wait to see if you body rejects the one venom and keeps the other. If you have the venom from the original bite, in your case we have two, Carlo and Stephen, then your body in theory, should reject the competing venom and absorb Stephen's into your blood because he was the one to change you—or so we thought. You would start to produce a very low amount of your own venom, which I'm guessing you don't do now." He raised his chin.

"Does it hurt?" I cringed; it sounded simple but…

"Yes."

"A lot?"

"Yes."

"And where do we get the competing venom?" I asked. Liam smiled.

"A volunteer."

"Liam I need to talk to—" I whirled to see Stephen standing behind me. Upon registering the scene, his eyes darkened. He was pissed and he charged into the room. "Damn it Ana!" He stood with his hands on his hips.

"Damn it Stephen," I mocked and stuck my tongue out at him. Childish, yes, but I'd beaten him and he knew it.

"Did you just stick your tongue out at me?" He looked incredulous. Liam laughed. "You are so dead; you realize that right?"

"Relax Stephen, Ana and I were just having a little chat. Don't be a sore loser. She knows you and she just beat you at your own game."

Liam smirked and Stephen threw his hands up. I leaned to give Liam a kiss.

"Thank you," I said.

"I think we should all pick this up as a family discussion Ana, before we make any decisions; you will honor that?" Liam smiled.

"Of course Liam." I liked that he considered me family. I heard Stephen sigh exasperatedly. "Oh shut it." I turned to him. "You and I made a deal and you lost so get over it already. God, no wonder you have the reputation you do; you hate losing!" I laughed. "I'm going back to bed, it's frickin early." I kissed Stephen on the cheek knowing that he was going to rant upon coming home. He pulled me against him.

"'Rant' doesn't even begin to express what I will do when I get home." He growled softly.

Stephen

"So what's this all about?" Liam asked as he moved back behind the counter. I picked up a lacy black negligee and thought about how good Ana would look in this. "Stephen, focus please." Liam snickered and shook his head. I waved my hand.

"I don't know. She's got some ridiculous notion that someone, somewhere is going to try and kill me and she thinks she'll be better able to protect me if she's more like us," I said, pulling a pair of black, silk underwear and holding them up to the slip.

"What's ridiculous about her wanting to protect you? She loves you." Liam stared at me. I shrugged.

"It's not necessary," I said, wandering around the store.

"It's what you wanted, at least a while ago; you wanted to keep Ana with you for your entire existence. You've changed your mind?" Liam surveyed me.

"She'll have a very long life Liam; she doesn't need to be turned into a vampire in order for us to experience a lifetime together."

"Hmm…but what if she wants *you* forever Stephen, have you ever considered that? What if Ana doesn't want to part from *you*? What if one lifetime isn't enough for her to be with you? It's an incredible gift that she's considering offering to you, one that hardly any Human feels compelled to make unselfishly. Usually the motivations are for immortality, not love, not friendship, not respect, not wanting to protect and fight for the individual. Our species, by our very evolutions together, have never been destined to co-exist. Humans hate us, they fear us and typically we have no use for them other than as prey. Ana is devoted to you and while she acknowledges who you are as a vampire, she also loves you as a man. Somehow the two of you have managed to defy the rules of Nature and adapt to co-exist in love and friendship and now you are to be joined in marriage. She wants you Stephen, she has chosen you to start her life with; does she not get a say in how she would like to live that life? Does she not get a choice in what gifts she would like to offer to the man she loves?"

"What about me, don't I get a say?" I challenged.

"Of course, but I think you are scared. I think you are frightened by how much Ana loves you and just what she is willing to do to have the sacredness of your bond made complete. Ana would never dream of doing anything that involves the two of you, without making sure that you both were of the same mind. If you truly do not want her to pursue this, she won't. However, being scared of getting everything that you have ever wanted, having the life that you have been desperately grieving for since that night in the barn, since Collin and Laura, is not the right reason to not allow this to happen, if it can. You need to be a bit introspective Stephen and understand why you are coming to the resistance that you are, then we can proceed or not." Liam spoke evenly.

"Fine!" I said, throwing down the lingerie on the counter. "I'm taking these, on the house and you better put them in a box!" I growled.

Ana

I didn't feel like waiting for Stephen to get home and yell at me, so I called Carmen and asked if she would go dress shopping with me. We'd changed the location of the wedding for the umpteeth time and had finally decided on Bali. It would be warm and we could do the ceremony on the beach; that's what I wanted. I always felt connected to the sea, but since living and then falling in love with Stephen, that connection just intensified.

"So do you want blanco?" Carmen asked as we stopped into a posh boutique in Dublin.

Uh...no, no I don't really look good in white." I cringed. Carmen laughed.

"Color then?"

"Yeah, let's try color," I said, fingering a beautiful gauzy turquoise dress from atop a high display. It moved with an ethereal fluidity and the fabric seemed to glow even under the boutique lights. The color also seemed to shift as it melted in between my fingers. Upon first glance, I thought it was turquoise, but now as I studied it closer, I could see swirls of marine blue woven deep within the fabric. I knew that color; I loved that color, it was the color of Stephen's eyes. "Carmen?" I whispered. She was already at my side, watching. She turned to me and we gazed at each other. I nodded and she nodded.

I let Carmen take the dress back with her; it was a bit too big in some areas and too small in others, but she'd assured me that it would be a perfect fit with a few alterations. I rode the rail back to Bray instead of shimmering. I wanted some time to think. Carmen seemed fine with me wanting to test my body, but I also knew that it made her scared. She didn't want me to have to endure any more pain. It was just a test; once it was done we wouldn't have do anything if Stephen didn't want us to and it might not work. It would just be good to know—for several reasons. I was thinking about why Liam thought I had come to see him; he thought I might want to try to have a baby. That had stopped me cold. I hadn't even been considering that as part of my life with Stephen. What had happened before was so painful for me and for him, I wasn't sure if we needed to put ourselves through that again. I didn't have an acute desire to be a mother and I knew that Stephen wasn't feeling the urge to be a father; it was good that we were on the same page as far as children went, still...

I arrived home to find Stephen lying on the couch reading the paper. He folded it casually and stared at me.

"Been out?" He took his drink off the coffee table.

"Yep, with Carmen," I said, hanging up my raincoat.

"What'd you do?" He stirred the ice cubes.

"Dress shopping." I came to sit on the recliner.

"Did you get anything?" He studied me as he sipped.

"Yep, but it appears that I also need to get bigger breasts so I'll be scheduling that surgery for the end of the week." Stephen choked and coughed. I smiled and walked into the kitchen. I grabbed some cereal and a bowl and sat down to eat.

"What are you doing?" Stephen called from the living room.

"I'm eating!" I called back, trying to swallow.

"Well bring it in here would you!" I sighed and pushed my chair back. I carried my bowl and curled up in the chair next to him.

"What?" I stared at him as I munched.

"You found a dress?" He was trying very hard to be mad about what happened this morning, but I could tell how excited he was to hear about my shopping excursion.

"Yup." I swallowed. Stephen frowned and I saw him look over to the desk where he'd left me his credit card; apparently I was supposed to use it for whatever I wanted or needed for the wedding or anything else in my life. I had a hard time understanding that Stephen didn't delineate between "his money" and "my money" and he was always pointing out that I was fine with making my money his but not the other way around. I was a bit wonky when it came to money, probably because I didn't really have any. I would feel better merging our finances when I starting working again. Stephen sighed.

"Liam's invited us to dinner this evening," he said quietly, reopening his paper. Lucie and I were the only ones who ate of course and it made me feel a bit better about having Carmen prepare a meal, if Lucie was going to eat as well.

"That sounds nice. What are you going to do today?" I asked casually, wondering when he was going to get to his rant. He glanced at me sideways.

"Then you are going to be disappointed, I'm afraid." He skimmed the paper.

"What? No rant? I was promised via a growl this morning, that there would be some sort of rant-like behavior. I believe that you alluded to the fact that a rant would be tame compared to what you would be displaying. Lost your nerve have you?" I smirked and flicked his paper. I could see him bite his tongue, trying not to laugh or lunge at me.

"The latter," he said and before I could even blink, he had knocked me backward in the chair, toppling me to the ground. He pinned me, I landing solidly on top of my body; I was still in the recliner. I stared at him.

"Good god, that was uncalled for," I said, trying to roll him off. He wasn't budging. Clearly my strength in fighting had yet to return. He shrugged.

"Like you so aptly pointed out, I don't like to lose so while you may have beaten me to Liam, I will very easily beat you in a bit of grappling—so it appears." I shook my head.

"That's not fair, you know my strength in fighting hasn't returned; it's not a fair fight! I can kick your ass when I'm one hundred percent!" I tried to heave him off, but it was like trying to move steel and iron. "Frick!' He laughed.

"Hey, I'll take whatever advantage I can get. I saw what you did to Saden; I'm not prepared to witness *that* side of you quite yet. Perhaps we should save that for the wedding night!" He bent to kiss me and I turned my face. "Oh come on don't be a sore loser!" He mocked me and he tried again. Suddenly I felt a rush of electricity pulse from him and from me, like a shot of caffeine and adrenaline, but one thousand times greater. I thrust my hips high, locked his wrists in my hands and flipped Stephen clear over my head, making him crash onto the floor near the fireplace. I rolled and stood up; he wasn't moving.

"Stephen!" I moved toward him. "Stop it, that's not funny!" I said watching him; I couldn't see his breath fill his lungs. "Stephen!" I stepped forward and his hand shot out grabbing my boot and sweeping my legs from under me. He pinned me again in a full mount

"Tap out!" He laughed. I struggled to throw him off. "Tap out!"

"No!" I snarled and I pulled him closer. I may not have had my physical strength back yet, but I could definitely use my womanly assets to win. Very slowly I started to move my hips beneath him.

"Tap out." He cleared his throat and pinned me harder.

"No," I said, moving my face close to his, still moving my body. He laughed softly.

"I know what you're trying to do and it won't work." He steeled his body.

"Really?" I said, gently grinding against him. Heat began to surge off his skin and I saw his eyes deepen.

"Really." His tone softened. I was almost there. I brought my lips closer to his, letting him taste my scent. He sighed and moaned deeply. I had to concentrate; my body was beginning to react to him sexually. I focused and I took my right arm and my right hip and rolled forcefully to the side, tossing Stephen off. He landed on his back and I pinned him in a side mount.

"TAP OUT!" I laughed as he looked at me, stunned. "Now!" I said, holding him tight. He snarled gently.

"Fine. I'm out, but only because I don't want to hurt you and because I'm so turned on right now that I can't concentrate."

"Well that's not my problem; that, my friend, is no excuse!" I stood up leaving him on the floor. I went to lift the chair and then I walked back to the bedroom to find something to wear for dinner. I noticed the familiar box and silver bow from Liam's shop, lying on the bed. "Hey! What's this?" I called, as I heard Stephen coming down the hall.

"Ahh…that's for you." He sauntered over and stood behind me.

"From you?" I asked, turning to look at him, my eyes full of surprise.

"No, my brother thought that it would be appropriate for him to give you something erotic from his store!" Stephen laughed.

"Excellent!" I said and Stephen rolled his eyes. He handed me the box. I slipped off the bow and lifted the lid. "Whoa," I said, pulling out the black silk and lace negligee and the matching underwear. "These are quite fancy," I said, looking at Stephen. Liam and Carmen only bought the best quality for their store and I knew how expensive these garments were. The material alone costs hundreds and these were pure Chinese silk.

"You like them?" Stephen asked as he stared at me.

"Uh yeah; a lot! Are these wedding night attire?" I had already gotten a bunch of stuff from Carmen and some of my other friends at a surprise bridal shower and I had already picked out what I was going to wear for our honeymoon. Stephen shrugged.

"Maybe or maybe we can get a preview this evening." He smirked. Yeah, like that was going to end well, the damn things would be in shreds before I could even get the straps adjusted. Stephen laughed. "Hmm…that's true. So maybe we'll just opt for the underwear." He grabbed the panties and pulled me on top of him.

"So you're not mad at me?" I asked, wondering what his thoughts were on the whole testing issue. He sighed.

"No Ana, I'm not mad at you. I just think that we need to really consider what you're asking here; I just need some time to make sure this is what is best for you and for us." I nodded.

"Of course Stephen; I don't want to do anything without your support." He smiled softly. "This affects you as well," I said, kissing his neck. "But the test might be ok right? I mean you agreed to let me do the test," I said, pulling away and sitting on the edge of the bed.

"Yeah, I agreed," he said rubbing my shoulders. "But that's it! I'm not ready to make any decisions about anything after that test. Let me ask you something Ana," he turned me so that we were looking at each other. "How are you going to feel if the test shows that nothing's changed? Have you thought about how you will handle that emotionally?" Stephen was so sweet. I had thought about it actually and I was much worse off not knowing. We were going to be together no matter what and for that, I was truly grateful; that was all that mattered. "Hmm…" He moved to run his hands over my back. "I don't think that you should be 'grateful' Ana; it makes it sound like I'm doing you a favor by loving you." He kissed me gently. I smiled and shook my head.

"Maybe you are; I mean look at all of the crazy shit that's happened to you since I arrived at your door three years ago! You haven't exactly had an easy existence." I laughed.

"Ana, I would do all of it again, all of it, if it meant that you would be sitting right here with me now, loving me and wanting to marry me." I blushed. That was really a beautiful thing to say. Stephen sighed and held my face. "Whenever you are ready to actually believe what I say, you let me know and we'll have some sort of a party." I reached, pulling him to me. A small puff of air blew my hair.

"Ana, Ana, Ana!!!" Lucie was suddenly standing in our bedroom. Stephen growled lowly and I ribbed him.

"Hi baby! What are you doing here?" I asked, grabbing her hands as she came over to the bed.

"Mommy wants to know what we want for dinner? I told her something fancy because you were coming and it should be fancier than what we usually cook." I saw Stephen subtlety slide the black lingerie behind a pillow.

"Nothing fancy. What do you want?" I asked pulling her into a hug.

"Oatmeal!" She laughed and kissed me.

"Oatmeal? That's what you want for dinner?" I smoothed her hair back.

"Yes and pancakes with chips!" I smiled.

"Chocolate chips?" I asked, watching as Stephen stood up and went to his closet to pull out a shirt. Lucie nodded. "Well that sounds good to me; maybe we can get uncle Stephen to make us a fancy omelet as well. What do you think?"

"Will you uncle Stephen?" Lucie asked as he stood in the bathroom fixing his hair.

"No," he said, but I could see him smiling. Lucie and I looked at each other and she smiled.

"Will you uncle Stephen?" she asked again, giggling.

"What do I get?" Stephen emerged from the bathroom looking like a rock star. He winked. Lucie looked at me. I whispered in her ear.

"Ana says that she will wear the clothes you bought her!" Lucie exclaimed and I saw Stephen's eyes widen.

"Tonight?" he asked. Lucie stared back at me. I whispered again.

"Only if the omelet is edi-b-le!" Lucie pronounced the word slowly.

"Deal!" he said, scooping her up. An hour later we all left for what I was sure would be an interesting meal.

Chapter Fifteen

Stephen

We all sat in the living room at my brother's discussing this insane test that Ana wanted done. According to Liam, it was excruciatingly painful. I had asked to have it done after the wedding, but Ana said no, she'd wanted it done as soon as possible and Liam had sided with her stating that the recovery time was only a day or two. He was a traitor. We were currently discussing when to proceed.

"How about tomorrow?" Ana asked. "That's like a whole eight days before Bali and we can get it over with." She turned to Liam.

"Hang on." I paced the room. "I mean, I have to get my head around…around biting you like that, in that way Ana; it's not just something that I *do*, it takes some thought!" She frowned.

"What do you have to think about?" She eyed me.

"I don't know…stuff!" I said, my hands on my hips. She waved her hand as if to dismiss me, but I felt a bit of a jolt in my body, like when she would try to move me. I watched her; she hadn't noticed.

"Liam?" Ana turned to him. "We don't technically need him to do the test do we?" I rounded on her.

"What? So you're just going to get some random vampire to bite you then?" I looked to my brother.

"NO, not random." She stood, meeting me toe-to-toe. A shot of electricity passed between us, and my body jolted again. She had to have felt that. I stared her down; she still didn't notice.

"Ana, Stephen's right. He should be in the right frame of mind to do this. Giving our venom is a bit of a exhausting experience and it takes a lot from us physically and for Stephen, emotionally as well." Liam rose and stood between us. "You can wait a day or two, no?" Liam took her hand.

"I can." She eyed me. "How about Saturday then?" She looked at Liam.

"Stephen?" Liam glanced at me. I sighed.

"Fine. Saturday." Liam nodded.

"Good, then we're agreed. As for the two of you..." Liam hesitated. "No exchanging of blood in any way; it can disrupt her system. He stared specifically at me. My brother knowing the veracity of my sexual appetite made me uncomfortable. Liam grinned.

"Right!" Ana was smiling broadly. "Thank you Liam." She stuck her tongue out at me for the second time today. I wanted to bite it off. "So who's going to be the other venom?" she asked and I frowned.

"Well, I would," Liam said hesitantly, "but I think that because Stephen and I are brothers, that it would be very difficult to detect any change." Liam looked over at Carmen and her eyes got wide and Ana stepped forward.

"Uhh, not Carmen; she doesn't need to do that," Ana said quickly. She knew that Carmen was a vicious fighter, but she detested biting people; she hated it and Ana wouldn't subject her to that ever. I watched as Ana crossed the room to hug Carmen. "Oh, how about Cillian?" she asked.

"NO!" I almost shouted. Ana rolled her eyes. It would be a dream come true for Cillian to get that close to Ana, to be able to taste her. I would kill him. Liam cleared his throat.

"That might not be such a bad choice Stephen." Liam spoke and I glared at him. He shook his head. "While Cillian is a bit unconventional in his approach to his existence, he also possesses a very unique venom; his bloodline is rare and it would be easy for us to tell if Ana's body has healed effectively." Liam put his hands on my shoulders. "You don't have to be in the room Stephen; I'm happy to quarantine you when your part is over." Liam laughed. I wished our venom was more like our blood, where we could just extract it into some sort of vile and then administer it, but it wasn't. The venom we produced came in a flood of hormones and pheromones that were released when we were ready to bite our prey; the venom was more of a gaseous substance that you couldn't release into a container. It was the action of tearing flesh and penetrating the skin that allowed for us to access that part of our chemical makeup. I sighed. Christ, that's all I needed to see, Cillian getting turned on as he bit into Ana's body. I was going to be sick. "I'll talk to him Stephen; it's not going to be a drawn out experience so calm down." Liam glared.

"Fine, but if I hear a single moan or groan out of him, his head is coming off!" I went to grab Ana's hand. "Let's go," I said, dragging her with me as I shimmered us away from the house.

"Well that was rude," Ana said, as we landed back in our house. "I wasn't ready to leave yet!" She dropped my hand and turned to stare at me. "I didn't even get to say goodnight to Lucie." Ana frowned and went to sit on the couch.

"I'm sorry," I said, sitting in the chair. I sighed.

"Are you really that upset about Cillian? I mean who cares if he likes it. I'm not marrying him, I'm not sleeping with him; I'm marrying you and I'm guessing in eight days, I will also resume my sexual relationship with you, so what's the deal?" She smiled.

"The deal is, that I have seen Cillian's mind and I know what he thinks about and what he's done and you, my dear, have made one too many appearances in some of his more graphic fantasies." She shrugged and moved to come and sit on my lap.

"I don't really care; the only fantasies I care about appearing in are yours." She laid her head on my shoulder. I laughed.

"You have the starring role." I reached to kiss her.

"Really? So would some of those roles include?" she said as she smiled and touched my lips. I grinned. We had already worked our way through quite a few of them. One that we'd done in South Africa and that I still couldn't stop thinking about and then of course I thoroughly enjoyed being in full vampire mode while we were having sex; it was a whole different experience and tapped into a much

401

darker side of my eroticism, but Liam said we weren't allowed to take any blood. I sighed longingly. There were a few other scenarios that I was very much hoping to delve into with Ana, scenarios that included my affinity for more dominant forms of sex. I pursed my lips, thinking.

"You haven't told me any of your fantasies. What do you want?" I kissed her hand avoiding her question. She laughed and blushed. Ana rarely blushed.

"Uhh...well I pretty much think you've taken care of anything that I could ever come up with on my own!" She bit her lip.

"Hmm...well we haven't done it in a public place as of yet; how does that work for you?" I asked as I smirked and started to kiss her neck. This conversation probably was not the smartest thing to engage in since we were currently abstaining and since Liam had thrown the hammer down on what I really wanted to do with Ana. The more we talked, the more worked up I became.

"It would depend on the place." She laughed. "No bathrooms!" I cringed. I had only done it in one bathroom and I swore that once was enough. "I could definitely do it at the club; not in those rooms, but I could contemplate a bit more of a public realm." She sighed as I let my teeth tease into her flesh. I already had the perfect place in mind.

"The club, hmm...I could really get on board with that," I moaned softly, as I started to move my hand between her legs. We had a big post wedding party coming up and Eamonn was hosting it at his venue. He promised to make it classy. The idea was tantalizing. "So would we be talking about full on sex or just..." I trailed off because suddenly Ana's scent was all over me; it was overpowering and I couldn't breathe. She kissed me roughly taking me off guard. Her body surged with strength and I felt myself begin to move under her as she started to straddle me. "Ana." I gasped.

"What?" She bit down on my lip and then on my neck.

"I thought we agreed to wait," I said, moaning as she lifted my shirt over my head. "Your scent; do you know what you're doing?" I watched as she took her own shirt off and unfastened her bra. Jesus Christ.

"Yes and I don't care, I want you." She flipped her hair back and began kissing down my stomach. "Besides, who the hell waits for their wedding night to have sex?" She had my pants undone, and I thought, no one waits who was smart. Still, I wanted us to wait; I wanted that night to be ridiculously erotic. I wanted it to be rough and sensual and urgent and I wanted to have her blood more than I ever had. She stared at me. I looked back at her. She cocked her head to the side. "Umm...I can kinda hear you." She frowned then smiled. She was getting stronger; she was healing. I cleared my throat, that wasn't exactly information that I would have chosen to communicate out loud, but whatever. She laughed. "Well it sounds like you have quite an evening planned for us. I certainly don't want to ruin any of what you have in store." She kissed me gently on the stomach and hopped off the chair, putting her shirt back on. It was going to be awhile before I could stand.

****

Saturday came before I could even get my around what I would have to do. We had gathered at Liam's and he'd set Ana up in the guest room. She wasn't nervous at all. I had expected Cillian to be beside himself with excitement, but oddly enough when he and Ana saw each other, I could see that they were sharing something and his face softened. It was bizarre to see Cillian so calm and centered, but he seemed to be taking this very seriously.

"Ok Ana, you'll just need to lie back. I can't give you anything for the pain, sorry. The less you have in your blood stream the more accurate we can get a read on your body." My brother kissed the top of her forehead and Cillian took her hand. I was going second. Ana turned to Cillian.

"Can you do it on my right wrist. My left is really fucked up." She laughed and held it up for him to see. He whistled. Not only did she have Nathanial's scar and various other scars from being bitten, but she also had a new scar from that psychopathic bracelet. My brother cleared his throat.

"Ana, Cillian has to bite you both in the wrist and the neck; we have to make sure that enough venom gets into your heart and then your blood stream. Your neck provides us with the best access and the wrist is just in case he doesn't get enough the first time." Liam's eyes were apologetic.

"Yikes." Ana looked at Cillian. "Be gentle please." She laughed, but I cringed.

"Noting but." Cillian nodded to me.

"Stephen, do you want to stay?" Liam stared at me; I knew he was wondering if I could tolerate actually watching Cillian take from Ana, especially from her neck. It was an intimate place for me; at least it wasn't her groin. Cillian snorted and I hit him on the back. "Stephen?" Liam glared at me.

"I'm fine, I'm staying if Ana wants." I found her eyes and she smiled.

"Works for me." She took a deep breath. "Do we have any music or anything?" She looked at Liam and he laughed.

"Uh...I think we can do that." He moved to the dresser and hit a tiny button. A large stereo system pulled out from the wall next to the bed.

"Cool." Ana laughed.

"What do you prefer?" Liam asked, holding a remote.

"Something hard core, like Rob Zombie," she said and Cillian turned to me.

"She has got ta be da coolest chick I know; hell yeah!" He laughed and I rolled my eyes as my brother found the appropriate selection.

"Ready Ana?" Liam asked and moved by the bed.

"Yeah." She looked at me and bit her lip. "WAIT!" She yelled so loudly that all three of us in the room jumped. "Cillian's not protected; my blood can kill him!" Ana looked at Liam. "How did we forget Liam? If Cillian gets any of my blood in him he'll die; he's not protected!" I stared at Liam; how *could* we've forgotten? "Stephen's only safe because my body chose him and I chose him; Patric's safe because we're Bound, but I haven't had anyone else. I mean, I haven't chosen anyone else…besides Nathanial and he doesn't really count, we were Bound…" Her voice became soft. Liam frowned. Ana was sitting up and Cillian was staring at her.

"Dat seemed like a bit of crucial info ta tell me mate." Cillian laughed and looked at Liam. "But it doesn't really matter for me; I can spit venom." Cillian winked and it was my turn to frown.

"What?" I asked, not sure if I had heard him right.

"Spit mate; I can spit my venom." He grinned. I had never heard of such a thing. "I don't know how I do it, I just do; Ana got fire and I can spit venom. Granted, it's not quite as dramatic, but fer today, it apparently will prove very useful." Cillian took Ana's hand.

"Why would you want to spit venom?" I asked puzzled. Cillian shrugged.

"For fun; no, um…I can paralyze people or poison dem if I put it in a drink!" Cillian laughed.

"Like a rattle snake?" Ana asked smiling.

"Just like, but in vamp out mode, I'm way cooler." He winked. I heard my brother sigh and leave the room. He returned a moment later with a tiny vial and handed it to Cillian. I leaned over to Liam.

"Sort of dropped the ball there didn't you big brother?" I laughed quietly; Liam growled. He pulled out a syringe.

"Whenever you're ready Cillian." Liam nodded. Cillian held the vial to his lips and I watched as his teeth elongated. I had only seen Cillian once as a full vampire and he provided quite a visual. I saw the vial fill with a dark gray liquid. There were swirls of black blood cutting through the tiny storm of venom and I could smell Cillian's distinct scent. I wondered what Ana thought about Cillian's fragrance. I glanced over to see that she was watching me, her eyes studying and searching me. I tried to garner what she was thinking and I had to steady myself against the dresser. An image of she and I in my house, of her on her knees crying, of her begging me, pleading, an image of her falling to the ground heaving. The images shifted to she and I in a dark hospital room, of me handing her a ring, of me standing as she cried, of me leaving. I exhaled and closed my eyes. When I opened them, she was still staring. I would never leave her; she had to know this. She had to know. She nodded to me gently and turned away. Liam thumped the needle and hovered over Ana. "Ready?" He smiled at her. She looked to me

"Are you?" she asked and her eyes flashed.

"Yes," I said, moving to kiss her gently on the mouth. "Because it doesn't matter. I'm marrying you and I love you and it doesn't matter." She nodded.

"Ok Ana, lie back now." Liam took her arm and tied a band around her bicep. Cillian came and stood next to me.

"I got totally shafted, ya realize dis; you owe me big time. I mean I get every dance wit Ana at Eamonn's party and I mean every dance," he whispered.

"You'll get what I allow." I growled under my breath.

"Uh...how about what I allow" Ana smiled over at us. "And Cillian can get as many dances as he likes; he's responsible for more than you know." She looked at him and I saw his eyes brim with emotion. What the hell had happened between the two of them? I heard Ana take a sudden breath in as my brother stepped back and tossed the needle into the trash.

"All done. Stephen? You're next." I sighed and moved to sit on the bed. I saw Liam motion to Cillian and they quietly left the room.

"It's going to hurt isn't it?" She cringed.

"Liam said it won't take that long. We should be able to test your blood a few minutes after I'm done." I touched her hand; it was hot. Cillian's venom was already beginning to spread.

"Let's do this." She nodded to me. "Neck first?" I nodded.

"Try to relax," I whispered as I bent my head to her face. "I love you." I pressed my lips to her cheek and then to her jaw, then to her neck. I braced myself and felt my teeth sharpen and venom swirl in my mouth coating my teeth and tongue. I pushed down on her pulse and sliced through the flesh releasing the smallest amount of venom I could. She gasped and swallowed and immediately I moved to her right arm and took her wrist, cutting the flesh with my lips and teeth. More venom released and I pulled back quickly. Her body was trembling and she had begun sweating. Liam and Cillian returned. Cillian grabbed a damp cloth from the bathroom and placed it on her head.

"Thanks," she whispered. It totally sucked that Ana had to experience this. It was such a small amount of venom, but it was enough to cause her extreme pain because there was not only one type of poison in her system, there were two. She heaved and shivered and I pulled the blankets up around her.

"How much longer?" I looked at Liam.

"The longer the better Stephen." I sighed. Cillian stood next to me.

"She's hanging in dere mate; she's goin' ta be fine." Cillian put his arm around my shoulder. Ana's eyes were closed and she was clenching her jaw; she was suffering. I rubbed my face wanting to help her.

"Uhh…I think I'm going to throw up," she whispered and Cillian lunged for the wastebasket just in time. This was too much. I stared at Liam and he nodded. I picked up her arm as Cillian wiped her mouth.

"Ok Ana; I'm just going to take some of your blood from you finger." She nodded and I took one of her fingers and pricked it with my teeth, letting the blood fill my mouth and move over my tongue. Jesus I had forgotten how indescribably delicious Ana tasted; it was unlike anything in the world. Liam cleared his throat and Cillian snorted.

"Well?" Liam moved to stand behind me. I swallowed feeling overwhelmed. "I see." Liam read my thoughts. "Are you sure?" I nodded. Ana jerked her hand away and vomited again.

"Sorry." She looked up at Cillian. "I guess you won't want those dances anymore," she said breathlessly. Cillian smiled at her.

"Please, do ya know how many lassies I've had trow up on me? Tousands, hundreds of tousands; not a deterrent at all love." He pressed the cloth to her mouth and I thought I saw her smile faintly. My brother motioned for me to follow him out to the hall. He leaned up against the wall studying me intently.

"Well, have you decided what you are going to do?" His eyes darkened.

"Not yet," I said, running my hands through my hair. Liam nodded.

"You know she will ask," he said quietly.

"I know."

"You have my support either way Stephen and so does Ana. There's no rush." He smiled slightly. I nodded. "Would you like to tell her?"

"Yeah," I said, feeling strangely high. Liam nodded and held the door open for me.

Ana

"Carmen are you sure this is going to fit; you haven't even seen it on me since I tried it on at the store." I was holding the garment bag and standing in Carmen's bedroom. It had only taken a few days for me to recover from the test and strangely enough, I was feeling more contemplative than anything else. According to Liam, it seemed that when Stephen had tried to Change me the first time, his venom had healed me, at least enough for my body to not allow for Cillian's venom to stay in my system, keeping only the venom that it knew and that had come from the being that had created me, so to speak.

"Here, up, up!" Carmen was lifting my shirt over my head and I heard Lucie laugh. She was on the floor reading. "You're feeling good, yes?" Carmen eyed me. I was paler than usual, but I was feeling really well, considering. I knew she wasn't asking about my physical health though and she nodded gently. I sighed.

"I think most days I do really well. The bad days are getting less and less…" I bowed my head as she slipped the dress over my shoulders. That was true. Over all in the last month I was feeling stronger, some of my powers had returned. I could actually light the fireplace and if I concentrated really hard, I could sometimes hear what Stephen was thinking. I had been going to the gym again and trying to work on getting my physical strength back. They went hand in hand for me, if I felt physically strong, then my mental prowess seemed better able to withstand whatever episodes of grief and anger that arose; my emotional muscles had taken quite a beating. Carmen zipped up the

411

back of the dress and spun me around to face the mirror. My jaw hit the floor. Somehow Carmen, in all of her infinite wisdom and skill, had managed to manipulate the dress so that was fit to my exact body shape; there were no gaps or pulls and the fabric was now molded to my every curve, accentuating them and making them appear strong and solid.

"It's not an illusion Ana." Carmen smiled at me in the mirror. "This is how you truly are." I noticed the neckline sparkled and I hadn't noticed that before. I stood closer to the mirror and saw that tiny marine blue stones adorned the front of the dress. It was cut low and the stones seemed to add a sheer light to the bare skin that was exposed; I looked closer. I knew those stones. I looked at the ring on my right hand. The jewel in the center was the same, the same crystal clear reminder of Stephen, of his eyes. I turned back to Carmen.

"Thank you," I said through my tears. She smiled and wiped her face.

"Look at the back!" She laughed and sniffed. I whirled around. She had taken some liberty with the original design. Carmen had cut out the main panel of fabric and made it open and low—very, very low. My entire back was exposed. The marine stones continued along the sides near my waist where the dress came to a point a few inches above my tailbone. She had changed the straps as well, making them more in a halter style, which I had always liked on myself. I was stunned at the transformation. "I thought you could also wear a flower in you hair." She swept my hair back and pointed right over my ear. "some Irish wildflowers, maybe?" I nodded. I couldn't speak. I took Carmen's hands and stared at her.

412

"Thank you for loving me Carmen and for seeing me as beautiful and special; thank you for making me feel as if the world is better because I'm here." I hugged her close and she cried. I felt something hit my leg and I looked down to see Lucie who had wrapped her arms around my legs trying to hug Carmen and me into her tiny arms. I laughed and picked her up. "Hey Carmen?" She grabbed a tissue for us a both. "Do you think I could talk to Liam for a moment. I know he's busy with the new store..." She stared at me and she pressed her hands to her heart. She saw what I was thinking.

"You should see him now. He's in his study." I put Lucie down and headed toward the door. "Not in your dress!" She laughed.

"Woops." She unzipped me and I put on my shirt and headed downstairs. I heard quiet music coming from down the dimly lit hall and I knocked softly on the door.

"It's open," Liam called and I stepped inside. He was sitting on the loveseat with a stack of what looked like inventory slips piled high. He looked up and smiled. "How's the dress fitting going?" He cleared the papers and patted the seat next to him.

"Carmen should be a fashion designer." I laughed. "She somehow has managed to make me look good in a dress." I shook my head and so did Liam.

"Carmen's work is merely a reflection of the person who will be wearing the garment Ana; there's no magic in what she's done, that's all you." I laughed. Carmen and Liam were a perfect match. "How are you feeling?" Liam studied me. "You're still a bit pale." He touched my cheek gently.

413

"I know, maybe I should get tanned up before Bali." I smiled. "I'm feeling much better, really." He nodded.

"And how are you feeling about the results from our little experiment?" He raised his chin, pondering me. I took a deep breath.

"Um…good. I'm feeling good. I mean, it's nice to know that it seems my body is ok and that's good…" I frowned.

"But…" Liam smiled. I shrugged.

"But I'm not quite sure what to do now." I laughed softly. "I know that Stephen is not sold on the idea of trying to Change me again and I don't want him to do anything that he's not fully committed to; we both have to want that to happen." I smiled.

"I agree and I will also tell you the same thing I told Stephen; there's no hurry with any of this. The two of you are just starting your lives together and I think that you can put this issue on the back burner for a while, no?" Liam cocked his head.

"I guess…" I couldn't explain it, but for the last several weeks, I was having an uneasy feeling whenever I thought about Stephen and his existence and his safety. I knew that I had no reason to feel afraid, no one had threatened him or had tried to attack him or me. Still, I was nervous.

"Ana, have you heard from Patric?" Liam asked and I shook my head. "Perhaps that's serving to feed your anxiety about Stephen. Not knowing where Patric is and not being able to tell him that you're getting married, it leaves things somewhat unresolved as far as your relationship to him goes." Liam took my hand. "Are you worried that if

414

he knew, that he would be angry with you or with Stephen?" Liam's eyes roamed over my face.

"More with Stephen I think." I frowned as an image of Nathanial flooded my mind.

"Ana, Patric is not Nathanial. What happened with him, it's not destined to happen with Patric and while Patric has not been known to ever fight fair, he loves you very much and he knows that if he hurts Stephen, he hurts you." Liam touched my bottom lip.

"You're right, of course you're right," I said quietly. "Anyway, enough about my neuroses." I laughed. "I wanted to ask you something." I took Liam's hand.

"Anything." He smiled. I exhaled.

"I know that you're Stephen's best man, which is beautiful, but I was wondering how you would feel about walking me down the aisle. I just think about how much you've come to mean to me, how much you've helped me, believed in me, supported me; how much you've always stood beside me when I've needed you, especially when I felt so lost and so scared. You stood next to me Liam and you gave me the courage to use all of the horrendous things that have happened in my life, to help me survive and find my own redemption. You've done everything that my father could not and did not want to do and you've shown me that a brother doesn't have to cause you harm or hurt you, that they can love you and protect you...they can heal you." Tears fell from my eyes.

"Ana," Liam whispered. He held my face and I saw his own tears brim in his eyes. "*You* have redeemed *me*." He hugged me close. "It would be the great honor of my existence to stand beside you as you begin the life that I have always wanted you to live, the life you so truly deserve. You are my family and I love you."

Stephen

I stood outside the door listening. I hadn't meant to overhear my brother and Ana's conversation, but I was coming down to talk to Liam about Changing Ana and what he thought about her body being able to handle something like that for the second time. I was captivated by what she was saying and what she had asked of Liam. She had endured so much. Her life before me had also been filled with great obstacles and horrors that she still fought to this day. But that was the thing about Ana, she was always fighting even when she was convinced that she'd given up, still, she fought. She just never saw things in the right way, never saw herself as I saw her or as Patric or Nathanial saw her. We all realized that she struggled with herself and her past and with her confidence in her decisions, but where she saw those things as weaknesses, as failures, we saw them as sources of great power and inspiration. Ana could have taken a very different road in her life, a road that could have led her to become bitter and angry and she would have had every right, but instead, she'd made a choice, probably early on, to let the events of her life make her kinder, compassionate, empathetic, intuitive, loving and forgiving. She talked about Patric having made the most difficult choice; to die for her and for his brother, but I think Ana's choice was the more difficult of the two. It was easier to succumb to the anger and the grief over events in your life, easier to blame and not be accountable, easier to hate. Ana had done none of those things, instead, she'd chosen to constantly work on trying to better understand herself and the events in her life. She'd always been accountable and she never once blamed anyone for anything that had led her to being hurt or harmed; she saw no point. I understood all of this because unlike Ana, I made the exact opposite choice in my life. I chose the anger, the bitterness, the blame and I chose the hate. It corroded me and withered away my heart and my soul. I was never accountable, never sympathetic, and I let hate turn me into a monster, one who relished in hurting others and seeing them suffer. Now, now things were so different, altered in such a way that I could have never imagined. Now there was love and life and laughter and passion; now there was Ana. The door opened and Ana and I almost collided. She eyed me warily.

"Have you been standing out here this whole time?" I took her around the waist, pulling her close.

"Yes." I smiled. She huffed. Liam appeared shaking his head.

"I have to go grocery shopping, you wanna come?" she asked.

"Yeah, I'll be right there." I nodded and she took off down the hall. I came into the office. "So…best man and surrogate father of the bride; not a bad day for you." I hit Liam on the back and could see that he'd been crying. I smiled gently.

"Not a bad day indeed." He smiled back. I turned the globe on his desk. "Did you want to talk about something Stephen?" Liam sat down in his chair. I sighed.

"I want to give Ana everything she wants Liam and I want her to be with me forever." Liam nodded.

"But…" He smiled; he was comparing my conversation with the one he'd just had with Ana.

"But I don't want her to be *like* me. It seems wrong somehow." I shook my head.

"Hmm…well personally I don't see anything wrong with how you are Stephen, besides the usual quirks in your personality. Still, I understand your thought process. May I propose something for you to think about?" Liam stared at me, his eyes flashing. I nodded. "Lucie." That's all he said. I raised my eyebrows.

"What?" I should have remembered to have a drink before I came to talk to Liam. It made it easier to follow him. He laughed.

"Lucie, your niece Stephen. She's the most perfect combination don't you think?" It was his turn to raise his eyebrows. I shrugged.

"Uh…I guess," I replied. Why were we talking about Lucie? Liam sighed.

"Christ you're slow today," Liam said exasperatedly. "She's half Stephen! Lucie's half Human and half-vampire. Carmen and I kept her like that on purpose. She has her own special abilities and her own unique make up and she can do some exceptional things, but she's also Human. She doesn't need blood, but she can have it if she wants, she's not ruled by bloodlust. She can bare children if she so chooses and not have to worry about dying from the difficultly of a pregnancy. She can grow and evolve and change right along with her friends. She'll of course out live them by centuries, but she will still have those experiences of what comes with a Human life. She won't have to endure losing her memories and trying to recall them or having some lost to her forever. She'll age incrementally eventually leveling off, probably in her prime and there she'll remain, but she wouldn't have been frozen at one year old. There are pros and cons of each half to Lucie, but Carmen and I feel it was the better of the two options." Liam watched me.

"Oh." I was absorbing. Liam chuckled.

"Just something to think about. Don't keep Ana waiting." He laughed and pointed toward the door.

****

Ana tossed a bunch of avocados into the fruit bowl and stared at me.

"You're quiet this evening." She smiled.

"Hmm…" I said, watching her.

"Having second thoughts?" She laughed and nudged me with her hip as she opened the refrigerator putting in her ginger ale.

419

"Yes," I said not taking my eyes from her. Panic spread over her face as she stood up.

"What?" she said slowly. I crossed my arms over my chest and leaned against the counter.

"Yes, I'm having second thoughts, but not about the wedding you insane woman." How could she think that I wouldn't want to marry her?

"Oh. Ok. Well…um, you know if you're ever not sure, that's ok too; you want to be sure…" She stood holding her glass and her can staring at me.

"Well thank you Ana I greatly appreciate that, but I think considering that I've been in love with you for quite some time now, that I'll go ahead and go through with this whole marriage thing; I mean, we've already gotten the place and you have a dress…might as well just do it!" I laughed and moved, taking her glass and can and putting them behind her on the counter. I placed her arms around my neck. "No, I was thinking about our situation," I mused, staring at her.

"What situation?" She frowned.

"The matter of Changing you." I kissed her gently.

"You want to try it?" She was kissing me back and I suddenly forgot what we were talking about.

"Hmm…" I pressed her back against the counter and ran my hands under her hair, caressing down her neck. "I was thinking more of a compromise," I murmured in her ear. "The best of both worlds." I

420

sighed and parted her lips breathing into her mouth. She trembled and I smiled.

"What do you mean?" she asked breathless. I moved down her throat and pushed my hands up her shirt, tracing along under her bra.

"I mean, what would you think if you and Lucie were even more similar than you already are?" I laughed kissing her stomach and lowering myself to my knees. She ran her fingers through my hair as I slipped down her sweats. She took a breath in as I traced my tongue over her thighs.

"I thought you said no sex of any kind." She gasped, clearly she was having trouble focusing on our conversation. We were only two days away; I could wait. I moved back up her body trying to calm my insane desires. I cleared my throat.

"Sorry." I kissed her hard and deep. Ana pulled back her breath coming in shallow pulses.

"You want to make me half?" She stared at me.

"Yes." I touched her lips.

"Really?" She kissed my fingers and I had to quell the moan that desperately wanted to escape.

"Hmm…what do you think?" She frowned; she was thinking about Lucie. She didn't say anything. I swallowed and waited for her to process.

"Would I be able to protect you if I needed to?" She was still worried about my safety.

"Yes."

"In the same way that you could protect me?"

"If you wanted to harness that side of yourself, then yes, you could. You would have to learn how to switch back and forth, but you could do it." Full vampires didn't have to think about getting themselves into our full form; it happened automatically and on cue if and when we needed it to. Ana would have to learn how to bring that side of herself to the surface and to control it when she didn't want it to come out unexpectedly.

"Would I still have my abilities with fire and to fight?"

"Yes and they may even be a bit stronger; again you would have to train yourself up a bit." I held her hands. She was quiet again.

"I have a counter offer," she finally spoke and my eyes narrowed; she'd blocked me from her mind.

"Ok," I said warily.

"I'll agree to the half-Change if you agree that if for any reason I suddenly become sick or I'm dying or something; if my life is threatened in any way and there is potential that I may be taken away from you, that you do the whole thing. You Change me fully. That's my counter offer." She pressed her lips together, waiting. "And, and you don't wait to see if I'll pull out of it; you do it and you do it without hesitation or consulting with every member of the family." She knew me too well—it was scary. I pushed back from the counter and studied her.

"Alright Ana," I said quietly.

"You promise?" Her eyes narrowed.

"You have my word." It was a fair compromise. She huffed.

"What?" I asked.

"I don't trust you," she said simply. "I want back up."

"Back up?" I smirked. I felt like we were hashing out some big mafia plot to take someone out.

"Yeah, an assurance that someone will make sure you follow through even if you don't want to." She put her hands on her hips.

"So what you're saying is that you don't actually trust me or my promises to you. Is that what you're saying?" I mused.

"Yes, when it comes to this particular issue, I do not trust you Stephen Byrne." She smirked back.

"Hey, are you taking my last name?" It was totally off topic, but I was suddenly curious.

"No, now can you please focus. We'll get Liam and Carmen and Cillian." She stared at me.

"You're not taking my name?" I felt myself pout. She rolled her eyes.

"No. I like being Italian and I like my Italian last name; it's nothing personal." She was annoyed at my inability to focus on our conversation.

"You could hyphenate it," I said softly. I was surprised at how old-fashioned I was being. It wasn't like me, but I enjoyed the idea of having my name as part of her; it made me feel close to her. She ran her fingers through her hair.

"It's important to you." She had heard my thoughts. I nodded.

"Ok, consider me to be Tessatore-Byrne, but you have to make sure that Liam and Carmen and Cillian know what we've agreed to, otherwise no one will get to know that I'm married to you at all mister!" She pulled me to her and kissed me passionately.

Ana

I was fine with the whole half thing. Actually, since I'd done the test, I wasn't really that concerned with becoming anything other than what I currently was. I needed to be stronger and I would like to feel the surges of energy and power that I had felt before, finally return. I knew that everything I experienced and everything that I could do physically, came from how I was feeling emotionally and on a really bad day, I couldn't do a damn thing. The inconsistencies were the most frustrating. Nathanial's face would sometimes appear in my mind and I would fall apart, still after so much time had passed, I would begin to sob when I would see him in my mind. Patric not calling was also frustrating. I knew that I had probably hurt him by not staying with him that night he'd asked, but if he truly cared for me, if he truly loved me, wouldn't he understand? It was killing me that he was ignoring me; I loved him so much and I missed him. Many times I thought about trying to find him in my mind, but if Stephen couldn't track him, then I was guessing he just didn't want to be found. I hoped he was ok and safe and happy. Currently, I was rifling through my drawer packing for Bali and the honeymoon. I had no idea where we were going and Stephen was not inclined to tell me. I had asked him to let me know what the climate was or where we were going, so I wouldn't be packing my entire closest. It was weird that I was getting married. I had always liked the idea, but never really needed it to be a part of my life, but now that it was so close, I was nervously excited. I hoped that it would be everything that Stephen wanted; I hoped he would be happy. I had sent him out with Cillian for what I was sure was a very rowdy bachelor party at one of Eamonn's clubs. I had just wanted a quiet evening at home. I settled onto the couch and started watching some TV on my laptop when there was a knock at the door. No one ever knocked. I shut the computer and listened as a second knock came. I frowned and stood.

"Who is it?" I asked.

"Delivery for an Ana Tessatore," the man said and I went to open the door. I kept the chain on and peered out onto the front step. The man was standing with a small flat envelope in his hand. "Ana Tessatore?" he asked, holding out a tiny signature pad. I nodded and scribbled my name. He smiled and handed me the mailer. I shut the door and walked back to the sofa. I turned it over and immediately I recognized the handwriting; it was Patric's. I swallowed and slid open the flap unfolding a thick piece of stationary. I started to read.

Dear Ana,

First let me apologize for not responding to your calls; that was incredibly rude and not at all what you deserve. I don't really have an excuse except to say that I haven't quite been myself over these last months, not since you left.

Second, let me offer you my congratulations. Micah tells me that you and Stephen are to be married. A wise choice I truly think, mainly on his part but also on yours. He's good for you Ana and he loves you more than you can know. That being said, I also feel compelled to tell you, that I am also good for you and that I love you deeply. While marriage has never been a particular thing that I ever contemplated until being with you again, I offer you the same as Stephen. I would ask you to be my wife just like I did before you left, if that's what it would take to get you to change you mind now. If that's what it would take for you not to marry him Ana.

I stopped reading. He was asking me not to marry Stephen? I swallowed.

Ana, our connection is unlike any other and I know just how deeply your feelings for me run. I know that you love me and that you are _in_ love

426

with me and I'm asking you, I'm begging you, to please stop and consider the choice you are making. I'm asking you to give yourself a chance to explore your feelings for me. I'm not saying that you and Stephen shouldn't be together. I'm saying that you haven't given yourself a chance to see what I can offer you, what I'm willing to give you and show you. I'm asking you not to close the door on the idea of us just yet. I've seen your mind Ana and I've seen what I do to you, how you react to me when I look at you or touch you. You're on fire when we're together.

I gasped. This wasn't happening.

I understand that my timing is horrible, but it's taken me so long to gather myself enough to ask this from you. I know I have no right Ana. I know this but I also know that we love each other and I don't quite know how else to say what I feel. I want you. I need you and I'm asking you to come to me and let me show you how much you mean to me and just how much you have changed the very core of who I am. Please Ana, please come.

I love you Ana and I truly do want you to be happy, if you can believe that after reading this. I will understand if you don't come. I will understand because I know how much you love Stephen and how you would never want to hurt him. I also know that if you don't come, if you can't bring yourself to see me, I can't be a part of your life. It would be too difficult for me now, loving you like I do. I hope you can understand my side of things as well. I miss you Ana. I miss your smile and your beautiful eyes and your scent and your lips and your skin. I miss holding you and kissing you and I miss making love to you. I love you Ana...I'll be waiting.

Patric

Chapter Sixteen

Stephen

I folded the letter. I was stunned and shocked. I hadn't meant to find it, but I was folding Ana's laundry that she'd left on the bed and it was lying in her drawer; I suppose I shouldn't have read it, but I had and now I knew exactly why Patric had gone MIA. I was waiting for Liam. Of course he would yell at me first for reading Ana's private mail, but I needed him to get past that for a moment and tell me what I should do.

"Stephen, what is so urgent?" Liam appeared behind me. I didn't say anything, but handed him the letter. He eyed me and took the paper. I watched as he scanned the note. He finished. "Where did you get this?" I knew that's what he would focus on.

"Does it matter?" I asked, feeling slightly sick.

"Yes Stephen, it does matter. This is a personal note to Ana from Patric and it is hers to keep or not to keep, to tell you or not to tell you. How is it that you have managed to read something so private?" He checked the date. "This came today?" I nodded. "Where's Ana?"

"She wasn't here when I came home." Granted it was now after one in the morning; I had been out with Cillian when I came home to crash. Maybe she was with Patric?

"I hardly doubt that Stephen. Ana would not leave without telling you." Liam seemed certain.

"What should I do?" I asked, sitting on the bed feeling overwhelmed.

"What do you mean 'what should you do'? You do nothing. This was not yours to read and it was information that was not intended for your eyes Stephen." I rolled those same eyes.

"Did you even read it Liam? Don't you get it? He loves her, he's in love with her and he's asked her to reconsider marrying me! Patric! Patric has written the woman I love a letter begging her to go to him and to be with him, to give them a chance at a life together. Did you read it?" I was feeling desperate and really angry. Liam folded the letter gently and put it on Ana's dresser.

"Yes Stephen, I have read the letter and Patric has said nothing that you didn't already know. You have always known that he loves Ana, very deeply in fact, and I also know that you have reconciled that Ana does also love him, perhaps in a different way than she does you. But this has nothing to do with you Stephen. This is between Ana and Patric and if you cannot trust her enough to let her deal with this, then you do not need to be getting married." I sighed. He was right as usual but still...

"Still nothing!" Liam glared at me. "There is nothing for you to ponder Stephen. Ana will deal with this as she sees fit and I'm guessing that would be letting Patric go from her life because she wants to be with you." I looked at him.

"What if I want her to be sure Liam. What if I want her to make sure she really wants to be with me? Maybe she needs a chance to see what else is out there. I mean, she's young and hasn't been with that many people. Maybe she needs some time to grow and to explore. Who am I to take those options off the table for her." I stood and went to stand near the dresser, fingering the letter.

"Stephen, I would actually find some validity to those words if they weren't couched in your own fear and jealousy at the moment, not to mention your mistrust of Ana, which I'm baffled by. She has never given you any reason to doubt her love for you; she has never betrayed you and your memory of when she rekindled things with Nathanial in Idaho, does not count. I was the one who told her about your past and I was the one who recommended that you not be with her; that was not a betrayal of any kind." Liam was always one step ahead of me. "Now, if you are having second thoughts about whether or not Ana is the right person for you, well then perhaps it is you who needs to do some more exploring and if you are having difficulty trusting her for some bizarre reason, then postponing your marriage might be an option. You should not be entering into such a commitment with doubts and mistrust in your heart Stephen. This letter should have nothing to do with those. If you were already having doubts then all this has done is confirm those doubts; if not, then you are merely looking for an excuse to run. Either way, you need to figure out what the hell is going on with you."

"Something's going on?" I watched as my brother closed his eyes as Ana appeared in the doorway. Her eyes darted from him to me to the top of the dresser where the letter was placed. How much had she heard?

"Enough," she said, twisting her lips to the side, hearing my question.

431

"Ana, I am so very sorry for our intrusion into you private matters; we have betrayed your confidences in us and I have no words to express just how sorry I am." Liam stepped forward and grasped her hand.

"It's ok Liam. I don't feel betrayed. I would share everything with you and with Stephen…" She trailed off staring out the window. Liam turned to me and shook his head; he was beyond upset. She sighed.

"How was your party?" she asked, but her voice was tight. Liam turned and walked toward the door. He touched Ana on the face and then glared at me as he shimmered away. I moved toward her.

"Fine. Good," I said, watching her face. She cleared her throat and took the letter.

"Crazy right?" She laughed gently as she tucked it back into her drawer. "Three years ago, there's no way that I would have ever pegged Patric as the romantic type; his personality was anything but." She swallowed. "So…what would you like to do Stephen?" She faced me. "I mean, I'm ok if you would like to delay things for a bit. I heard what you said and what Liam said and really I don't want to get married to someone who is having difficulty trusting me; it's awkward to say the least. Sometimes people need a bit more time to feel confident in their decision. Marriage is a big deal, it should be a big deal and not something that you should do if you're just not quite sure." She stood by the window. "Seriously though, this is the last time that I'm doing this with you. All of this on and off again crap is getting ridiculous and I don't really have the energy or the inclination to wonder just when and if you are going to take off again." She laughed darkly as she turned back to me. "Do you trust me when I say that I have made my choice, that I love you and that I want to spend the rest of my life with you Stephen?" I walked slowly toward her.

"Yes," I whispered, taking her hand and pulling her close.

"Really? Are you sure? Are you sure that you don't want me to go out and screw around with Patric or Cillian or whomever else I can find to sleep with, or have a life with; are you sure Stephen?" Her eyes were intense and her body rigid.

"Yes." I bent my head and kissed her slowly and gently. She wasn't relaxing.

"Because we can wait. I don't know how long it will take for me to catch you in the number of people I can experience, but if that will make you feel better—" I cut her off as I pressed my lips against hers again.

"No," I murmured as I held her tightly. I didn't want to wait; I knew Ana. I knew her better than she thought and I knew that she loved me and I knew that had she had any doubts, any at all, she wouldn't have said "yes" to me. I did trust her.

"Tomorrow then?" she asked, hugging me.

"Tomorrow." I took her hands and led her over to the bed. I couldn't stop kissing her.

"Ok, but if you freak out tomorrow, that's it!" She pulled out of my hold and glared at me.

"I'll save the freak out part for the honeymoon." I winked and pulled her on top of me, moving my hips gently against her body. She sighed and matched my rhythms.

"You promise?" She kissed me and bit down playfully on my bottom lip.

"God yes." I pressed against her harder.

"Stephen?" She pulled her face back a few inches to stare at me.

"Yes?" I stared back.

"I love you and I want to marry you ok?" She kissed my nose.

"Ok."

Ana

We were having the ceremony right on the beach and Liam and Cillian were already out there checking on the flowers and checking on Stephen. I wasn't entirely convinced that he wouldn't try to bolt just before I walked down into the sand. Carmen snorted as she delicately curled my hair.

"I'd rip his heart out." She growled gently.

"Mommy!" Lucie scolded as she stood on a chair behind me playing with my hair. She was ready to go. I let Lucie pick out whatever dress she wanted to wear and surprisingly she'd chosen one in a similar shade to my own, but she topped her look with a tiny tiara. Carmen's dress was a beautiful shade of pale purple with deep turquoise threads embedded in the organza and fabric. She was stunning and her skin and eyes shone bright and luminous. All of our dresses were loose and flowing and were not fancy or overdone; I wanted to be comfortable and I wanted Carmen and Lucie to be comfortable. I had no idea what Stephen had chosen to wear, but he'd assured me that it was beach appropriate, whatever that meant. I still had yet to see our wedding rings; Stephen wanted them to be a surprise. I hoped he was feeling good. I sighed. I hadn't responded to Patric. I had no idea what to think and I felt slightly manipulated by his letter. He knew what to say and how to say it and he preyed on my feelings for him trying to create doubt in my mind. There was none. I loved Stephen and I wanted to be with him and I had done as Cillian had advised; I had let Patric and Nathanial go. I had made my choice and now it was time to move forward.

"All done." Carmen smiled gently and I knew she'd heard my contemplations. I stood and stared into the mirror. I had no idea who the woman was staring back. She looked strong both physically and emotionally; she held her chest high and she appeared to be confident. Carmen had intricately spiraled each and every curl on my head making them loose but defined; they flowed gently down my back and over my chest. She wove a small cluster of Irish wildflowers into my hair and tucked them securely with a tiny, jeweled pin. I had opted for minimal makeup, but Carmen had insisted that we play up my eyes and she somehow seemed to give them their own mystical glow bringing out the gold and bronze tones.

"Well, I think I know who I will be paying to do my hair and makeup for the rest of my life." I turned toward her. "Everything is perfect Carmen. Everything." I hugged her close. She swallowed.

"Stephen is going to be beside himself," she said softly, gazing at me.

"Is that because most of the women he's been with don't usually wear this many clothes?" I laughed gently. Carmen shook her head.

"No, Ana, he'll be beside himself because today, Stephen is the luckiest soul in this world," Liam spoke from the door and I turned to stare at him. He was so handsome, stunningly handsome. He laughed. "Why thank you Ana." He moved powerfully into the room. He'd pulled his hair back into a long ponytail and he was wearing a loose white shirt and kaki linen pants that flowed perfectly from his narrow waist. He took my hands and smiled. "You are beyond exquisite." He winked as Carmen handed me my small bouquet of flowers; they matched the one in my hair.

"How's Micah?" I asked, smoothing my dress. Liam laughed.

"Well, he's arguing with Cillian over just what to play for you. Cillian is possessive about his guitar and Micah made the mistake of touching it." Liam shook his head.

"What's Cillian going to play?" I asked, wary. Cillian and I had the same taste in music, but I also enjoyed the quieter side of things every now and again.

"Stephen has offered some suggestions and I think you will be pleased." I nodded. "Ready?" Liam held out his arm and Carmen and Lucie stood in front of the large doors. We had a private beach and the villa offered direct access to the shore and my entrance was only a few steps away. I stared out the window. It was a full moon tonight and I suddenly thought about Noni and Nathanial; I wondered if they would be happy for me. I also thought about Kai and how he'd always wanted to be the one to walk me down the aisle. I turned to look at Liam. "It's ok Ana," he said. "Be happy." I swallowed and nodded. Carmen blew me a kiss and swung open the doors.

Stephen

I saw the doors open and watched as Lucie and Carmen descended the stone walkway onto the beach. Cillian began playing and Micah winked at me. I held my breath. The moon shone overhead and it glowed softly, bathing the sea and the sky in its deep luminance. I looked up and my heart stopped. Ana and Liam were walking toward me. Tears brimmed in my eyes. The world stopped turning and as I saw her move slowly across the sand, I saw nothing else. I knew nothing else. I felt nothing else but her. Liam smiled down at her and put Ana's hand in mine. She winked at me and I shook my head. Liam came to stand next to me along with Cillian and Micah; Carmen and Lucie stood with Ana. We faced each other.

"Nice choice of music," she whispered. I had Cillian do a version of the song we both liked, the one that always seemed to be playing when Ana and I were together, the one that was playing the night of the concert. We both turned to face the Seer. Liam had found someone who honored some of the same traditions that Ana's Noni followed and I could see just how much it meant to her to have those as part of our ceremony. Personally, it went on a bit too long for my taste. I was ready to get to the party and then the honeymoon. Really I was just ready to get Ana alone. Christ, it had been so, so long since we'd been together, I could hardly contain myself. Liam cleared his throat gently and I tried not to laugh. He handed me the rings. I presented Ana with hers and she gasped. I had designed ours as two parts of a whole. Her ring was shaped like a half moon carved into a silver band with a tiny marine-blue stone set to the side like a star. Mine held the tides and intricate waves swirled and flowed into the metal. If you held them together, they fit. The moon over the tides, a gravitational pull that was always constant and that pushed and pulled, waxed and waned, rose and set; a perfect fusion of what we both needed. I showed her how they could be joined, then I took her hand and gently slipped the ring on her finger. Tiny silver sparks ignited as the band suddenly melded with her skin and we stared at each other. She took my ring and slid it over my finger and the same sparks lit the space between us. I felt my hand warm then grow hot as the ring solidified itself into my own flesh. I didn't need to wait for the official signal that we were now bound as husband and wife; Ana and I were always headed for this moment. We had always been on a collision course to love each other and no matter how much those courses diverted, we managed to find our way; we had found our way back. Ana stared at me and she cocked her head to the side. An image of Cillian and her Noni filled her mind. They both had communicated just what I had been thinking, both of them at two separate points in her life and she was thinking that now she finally understood, that now everything made sense. I took her face in my hands and kissed her as passionately as I possibly could.

"Dude." Cilliian laughed. "There's a little girl here. Hold off for a second." I felt Ana smile as I kissed her more gently.

"I'm not little. I'm five!" Lucie commanded and Ana lost it, pressing her head into my chest.

"Let's go! Eamonn's waitin' and I have a special surprise fer Ana's entrance as a married woman!" Cillian snapped his fingers and shimmered off the beach. Liam hugged me and then hugged Ana.

"Have fun." Liam winked at me.

"You're not coming?" I asked surprised.

"After reading your mind this evening, I think it best we let the two of you have fun with your friends." Liam laughed and I hugged him again.

"Liam," I said quietly. "I love you." Liam pulled back to stare at me and his eyes changed color from deep sea blue to the clearest, purest waters that I had ever seen.

"And I you Stephen." He nodded. Lucie was climbing up his leg. I watched as he scooped her up and smiled at Ana and me. Then he, Carmen, Lucie and Micah disappeared from the shore. I turned to Ana who was staring at her ring.

"Do you like it?" I held her hand and fingered her band. She smiled and kissed me softly.

"No. I *love* it Stephen; there are no words…" She stared at me. I smiled.

439

"So it's official I guess. You're married now. How does it feel?" I asked as we walked further out to the water.

"Me? What about you? Do you know how many women came back and forth in that apartment of yours? I think I counted at least three in just one evening. How do *you* feel about being married?" She put her arm around my waist. I looked down at her and smiled.

"You want to know a secret?"

"Always." She replied.

"I used to come into your room at night after…well after I'd been out or whatever, and I used to wonder what it would be like to lie next to you, to wake up with you, to make love to you." She stared at me.

"Umm wow that's really sweet and slightly creepy." She cringed and I nudged her.

"It's not creepy." I frowned. "Intrusive maybe, overstepping bounds definitely, but not creepy." I kissed her.

"Ok, how many Vampires do you want coming into your room at night and staring at you while you sleep?" She wrapped her arms around my neck.

"I don't know about vampires, but I would have been quite pleased if you had decided to come into my room at night." I raised my eyebrows at her. She frowned.

"Really?" she asked surprised. "I didn't think you ever were attracted to me like you were with the other human women you dated."

"Hmm…you thought wrong," I said, running my hands down her back.

"Huh." She seemed puzzled. "So if I had tried something back then, you would have been responsive?" She grinned and I laughed.

"What would you have tried Ana?" I smirked and she shrugged.

"I don't know. There were a few times when we were on the couch and I'd be listening to you play. I would think that you probably were a good kisser." She grinned. "Maybe I would have tried to kiss you." She bit her lip. I remembered those times very well and I had been thinking the same thing except a bit more graphically.

"You attempting to kiss me would have been met with a very enthusiastic response." I ran my fingers through her hair and let my hand trace up and down her bare arm. She touched her lips to my throat and pressed gently.

"What about more than kissing?" She ran her tongue over my neck and chills broke out on my skin.

"Well then we would be talking about some very dangerous territory." I breathed out shallowly.

"Why?" She kissed over my ear and bit my earlobe. My body trembled.

"Because I had very little control when I was around you in the first place and for most Human women, sex with a vampire, at least the first time, can be somewhat of a rough experience." I breathed out as she pressed her forehead to mine. She smiled.

"I bet you would have made it nice for me." She kissed my cheek.

"You give me way too much credit Ana." I laughed. "Besides, I don't think I would have had much of a choice back then; I wanted you too much, wanted your blood and your body, it was overwhelming for me." She pulled back.

"And now? Are you used to me now?" She smirked. I turned to look at the water. The waves lapped over our feet and the reflection of the moon shimmered on the surface of each crest.

"No Ana, I'm not used to you," I said softly. I was still having some difficulty getting my head around the fact that she had chosen to be with me, that we were married; it was a whole different kind of overwhelming experience for me. She held my hand. A gust of wind blew us from behind.

"Jesus Christ! Would ya two please hurry da fuck up? I've got hundreds of people, a band, a bar and way too many women waitin' ta give me lap dances. Let's go!" Cillian stood his arms crossed and a smirk on his face. Ana laughed and she reached out to take Cillian's hand, pulling him close. I watched in awe as she kissed him gently on the cheek and whispered something in his ear. He swallowed thickly and closed his eyes and held her face in his hands. It was the oddest sight, Cillian as tender, but only Ana would be able to bring that side of personality to the surface. She turned to me.

"Let's go," she said as Cillian disappeared. I grasped her hand and she looked at me. "So, is that fantasy of yours about the public place still in play?" She put her head on my shoulder. I tilted my head back; apparently Ana and I were very much in tune.

442

Ana

Eamonn had completely transformed the club into a Bali themed party. There were Moon Orchids and Frangipani flowers scattered on the tables and their fragrances wafted sweet and lush in the air. Tiny torches were lit on the walls and the dance floor was now a beautiful white sand beach. I had no idea how Eamonn had done it, but it was amazing. The music was loud, heavy and sensual of course and Stephen's band mates were waiting for our arrival. They announced us, and the whole crowd screamed and yelled with Cillian leading the charge. I looked at Stephen, my eyes wide. He laughed and pulled me out to the dance floor. Cillian's choice for our first dance was unconventional, but very apropos—a Rob Zombie song. He raised his glass to me as Stephen took me around the waist and pulled me close. I looked around the room. There were a ton of people I knew, but most were Vampires I had never met, some that looked pretty rough and slightly scary; Cillian's friends I guessed. Stephen twirled me and I laughed.

"So what do you think?" he asked as I leaned in to kiss him.

"It's amazing!" I had to yell a bit, the music was so amped up. Stephen nodded and smiled. He moved against me. Stephen and I had danced loads of times, but I had never seen him dance like this. He was holding me so close and the way he was moving my body against him was extremely erotic. The rhythms of his hips were slowly grinding against mine in sync with the music, and he was so powerful as he commanded our bodies. His eyes were focused on me and I saw them change color from crystal clear to a warm gold, to a deep silver with gold flecks, the pupils turning vertical. If I hadn't seen it before, it would have totally freaked me out. They weren't the sickly yellow that I had first witnessed when I found Stephen in that awful bar. These were his eyes in their most natural state, the way they were when he was closest to who he was as a Vampire; they were mesmerizing. He was pushing himself against me and grinding my hips and kissing my neck; my senses were over stimulated. I moaned softly. He kissed deeper into my throat and as the music pulsed and rose, so did my desire. I felt his teeth grow sharp and I swallowed trying not to climax right there on the floor. He pushed his lips to my pulse and I felt a sudden prick as his tongue caught the stream of blood coming from my throat. He moved his mouth suggestively against my neck and I heard him growl low and deep as he took from me right there as we danced. If my desire wasn't so revved up, I would have felt self-conscious, but I couldn't feel anything but tremendous need and desperate wanting, violent wanting. He was pulling the blood in time to my heartbeats and the strange rhythm was increasing my passion so much that I felt myself grab the back of his neck and push his mouth harder against me. The heat I was experiencing was lapping over my body and I could feel just how close he was bringing me to my release; I was going to scream. Somehow he had brought us through the crowd without me noticing and I was now up against a wall near the back of the club. People were everywhere, but no one seemed to notice what we were doing; we weren't out of the ordinary here. Stephen withdrew from my neck, gasping and breathing heavy, his lips deep red and swollen and he licked them slowly, his eyes hypnotic, watching me. I wanted more so I grabbed his shirt and pulled him back against me. He laughed.

"Feeling a bit daring this evening?" His voice was slightly different, lower and more sensual and I knew he was ready to go all out. He traced his fingers along the fabric of my dress. "This is really pretty. I don't want to ruin your wedding dress." His fingers caressed down my chest, skimming my flesh slowly, the heat from his fingertips leaving a trail of desire so deep within my body that I was about to tear off my dress and explain it to Carmen later. He smiled and I saw how long his teeth had become; my eyes widened. He pulled me back to a very dark corner and one slightly further away, but still in among the partygoers. He pinned my hands above my head and raised us a few inches off the ground, holding us against the wall. "I think I can manage to avoid tearing this off of you right now, but I make no guarantees for later." He smirked and he ran his hands so that he was lifting up the fabric over my thighs, his body shielding me from anyone's view. I groaned as I felt him slide down my garter. I wasn't wearing anything else and he looked at me shocked. "Looks like you came prepared." His eyes flashed and he pushed up the dress even further. The music blared and I heard him growl loudly. He began grinding against me slowly and the friction was perfect. He held me against the wall and watched as my body started to respond to his thrusts. He moved so that both of my wrists were now pinned in one of his hands. He took his other hand and undid his belt and slipped his pants down a bit over his waist. He knew what he was doing. He hitched one of my legs up around him and suddenly he was inside of me and I groaned. He was holding my hip and pushing hard against me, running his hand up and down my outer thigh and around to my lower back. His thrusting was so perfect that I shoved him deeper, wanting more and he gasped and moaned, his breath in my ear. I was panting as he pulsed harder and faster inside of me. He bent his head

445

and began pulling blood from me again. Stephen moved his fingers around to my rear and he began tracing ever so delicately in a place that I never thought he would want to venture. I sucked in a sharp breath as he lingered close to the tight ring of muscles.

"Stephen." I moaned and tensed, unsure of what he wanted from me; this was new.

"I know." He licked over my throat as he continued to thrust deep inside. "Have you ever done it like this before?" he asked kissing me as I shook my head. I didn't have any clue what the whole fascination was with anal sex; it seemed a bit weird to me. Stephen laughed as we continued to pound into each other. "It's weird if you never considered the possibilities, but I think we can change your opinion. Relax," he murmured as his fingers began pressing down gently from behind. I held my breath and clung to him; he thrust once, deeply and as he did, he pushed a finger into my ass, sliding it in and out in rhythm with his length. I stopped breathing; the arousal was so intense, so painfully, deliriously blissful, that I had no idea what to do with myself. The twin sensations were overwhelming me and my entire body was surging with liquid fire as he continued to slide himself back and forth, filling me. "Now see," he whispered in my ear, "I knew your body would be responsive to this; I want more Ana, so much more. I have so many things that I want to do with you and to you, things that I want to show you, teach you. Will you let me? Will you let me take you like this, fully?" Stephen pushed deeper and I was groaning so loudly that I was thankful the music was almost deafening.

"Yes." I panted, gripping his hair between my fingers.

"Yeah?" He held me against the wall and tried three fingers. Oh god!

"Yeah!" I was beside myself in need; my body was reeling, surging, filling with lava and his fingers, his depth, his entire pulsing length, they weren't enough.

"You want more?" Stephen's voice was rough and full of passion and a deep sensuality that made my heart race.

"I don't know if I can take much more." I gasped, his fingers thrusting, sliding into the wet channel and I clenched around him.

'Jesus Ana; imagine if that were me, if that were my cock inside of you. I can fill you like this, fill you deeply, fully. I want this so much. I want to possess you like this." He hit something with his fingers at the same time, he thrust between my legs and I grunted from the force of the pulsing desire he created in my bones. "I can't wait! Ana! I have to have you right now! Fuck, I want you!" He snarled and withdrew his mouth from my throat as he came; his body shook and I pushed him forcefully against me. I was so close and I didn't want him to break his rhythms. He was slamming me against the wall as he moved himself back and forth inside of me, his fingers creating a scorching heat in my ass. I screamed out as my climax hit, fast and violent. It shook my brain and sent my muscles falling away from the bones. Stephen moaned and slowed his thrusting, letting me come down from the high of having him in me in so many places. He lowered us slowly back to the ground, pulling my dress over my hips and sliding himself gently out from between my legs. I was shaking, but in a good way. I watched as he redid his belt and smoothed his shirt. His eyes returned to normal and his teeth retracted. He looked me over. "Are you ok?" he asked bringing me into a hug, his voice breathless. "I guess that wasn't the most romantic way to consummate our marriage, but I just couldn't wait for romance; I needed to take you." He laughed softly and I thought I saw him blush slightly. "Are you sure you're ok?"

"Uh huh," I said, my own voice not quite steady. He laughed softly in my ear.

"I didn't take too much did I? Are you feeling weak?" He pulled back and ran his finger over his bite marks. I did feel weak, but I was pretty sure that it wasn't from the blood; it was more from wanting him so much and not having been with him in a while and from the whole finger thing. "Hmm...yes, we have quite a bit of missed time to make up for, don't we; did you like that?

"Yeah." I studied his face; he had a few secrets he'd been keeping from me. Stephen laughed. He kissed me gently and deeply. "I'm prepared to share with you everything; all secrets will be revealed. What do you say we get started on that honeymoon of ours?" He pulled me back out into the crowd.

"Really?" I asked getting excited for many reasons now.

"Really," he said, his eyes sweeping over my face. "I love you Ana." He turned in front of me, leading us back to the front of the club. "Let me just talk to Cillian for a minute. He pulled me with him, holding his hand. An odd fragrance wafted passed my nose and I turned my head. It smelled metallic and slightly smoky. I frowned and scanned the room. No one else seemed to notice. I looked behind me and saw some of those rougher looking Vampires standing near the exit in the back. They were all together and nobody was talking to them or had approached them. I frowned again. Stephen was still holding my hand as he chatted with Cillian and a guy in his band. I tried to follow the conversation, but I was feeling uneasy. I scanned the room again and saw that the group near the exit was no longer there; I looked behind me, to the side, and to the front—nothing. I gazed into the crowd—nothing. The smell was getting stronger. I looked at Stephen; he didn't seem to have detected anything and neither had Cillian. Was it just me? Suddenly I felt my amulet grow warm and I looked down to see the outer rim was glowing red. Everything happened in slow motion. I whirled quickly, shoving Stephen to the ground and covering him just as the explosion hit.

Chapter Seventeen

Ana

Glass blew past me, scraping my face. I screamed at Cillian as Stephen and I hit the floor. I waved my hand knocking Cillian to the ground just as a wall of flames erupted behind him. I lay on top of Stephen shielding his body as chunks of marble from the bar crashed down around us. Screaming filled ever corner of the space. I kept down and breathed. I had to get us out of here. I looked down at Stephen; he wasn't moving. A small pool of black blood was seeping out from under his head. Christ!

"CILLIAN!" I screamed. The smoke was heavy and thick now and I couldn't see anything. I steadied myself. I waved my hand and parted the haze keeping it at bay while I searched for Cillian. I found him crawling on the ground trying to get over to me.

"ARE YOU HURT ANA?" he was yelling over the blasts and the screaming.

"STEVEN'S HURT! HE'S BLEEDING!" I yelled back as Cillian reached me. Just as he grabbed my hand, another more violent blast erupted near the back of the club and I saw people go flying through the air, their bodies catapulted like ragdolls. We ducked as a metal door flew past our head. Fire was engulfing the air and I could see that Cillian was beginning to choke. I waved my hand again trying to give him a pocket to breathe. There was a ton of smoke and it just kept coming, thick and heavy. I grabbed Stephen and hoisted him over my shoulder as I rose to my feet. I pulled Cillian up; he was bleeding from his chest. "Cillian!"

"I'm ok; it's just from da glass!" He stared at me as I held Stephen.

"Take my hand!" I grabbed him. "Can you shimmer?" He shook his head "no".

"Dere's someting wit da fire or da smoke!" he yelled. I remembered that problem from before, from the night of the fire when I had to escape with Lucie at Liam's—this was Demon fire. Those weren't Vampires by the exit they were Bonders. I shifted Stephen over to my right shoulder and scanned the room. A wall of fire was now erected over both exits. Two large windows were behind the flames; they hadn't been blown out. No one could get past the wall. I turned to Cillian. The blood on his chest had now completely soaked through his shirt. He looked at me. "I'm fine Ana, I swear." He nodded.

"Ok listen! I can get us out of here Cillian, but you have to stay with me; I don't know how good my powers are right now! You need to stay with me!" I stared at him and he nodded again. Suddenly, another explosion shattered the entire front of the club, the force blowing me back. I crashed to the ground pulling Cillian with me. Stephen rolled and I crawled back to him. Frick! I looked to my side and saw Cillian get to his feet. I pulled Stephen up for the second time and carried him over my shoulder. I grabbed Cillian and started to walk slowly toward the wall of fire. Blood was now seeping into my eyes; I had been hit by something. We were stepping over burning bodies and the stench of charred flesh was making me gag. I turned to Cillian. "We have to go through the fire and we have to go through the window!" I called to him and for the first time I saw fear cross his face. 'It's ok Cillian, I can keep you safe, but you have to stay with me!" He looked at Stephen and I saw him swallow. I didn't even have time to think about what sort of condition Stephen was in; I had to get us out of here. People were running everywhere and I wished they would stay in one place. I could get more out if they just stood still! I took a deep breath and stepped forward toward the wall. Patric's face appeared in front of me and suddenly I remembered that stupid training session he made me do by the river; he'd taught me how to move the wall. I focused. I saw the flames quiver. Frick!

"Uh Ana?" Cillian was holding his stomach, blood seeping wet and black through his fingers; he was looking behind us. Three of the Bonders near the exit were heading our way. Double frick! I turned and waved my hand sending them flying backward. At least that talent was working. I turned back to the wall. *Come on Ana!* I told myself; *you can do this!* I quieted my mind and the base of the wall shifted a bit to the side. I huffed. Shit! I turned back around and saw the Bonders recovering. I looked at Cillian and he stared at me, his eyes flashing and glowing through the haze of smoke. I suddenly became angry. All the grief I had been experiencing turned to the most violent anger I had ever known and I exhaled all the breath I had in my lungs. The wall shifted, not a lot, but enough. I yanked Cillian and ran, jumping full speed, crashing through the window and shattering the glass. We hit the pavement and immediately Cillian shimmered us away from the club as one last explosion blew through the roof. We landed violently on a floor and I heard Cillian groan as I fell on top of him with Stephen between us. Blood was everywhere; Cillian's blood, Stephen's blood, my blood. We were all covered, our faces smeared

452

dark red and black, soot and ash coated our hair and skin. I coughed and tried to stand, rolling Stephen off of Cillian.

"ANA!" I heard someone yell. "ANA!" I turned to see Liam come jumping over the banister, Carmen in tow. Cillian had brought us to Liam; smart guy.

"Cillian's hurt and so is Stephen!" I called to him. Cillian groaned again, his eyes were shut. Liam picked Stephen off the floor and carried him in his arms over to the couch. I did the same with Cillian. Carmen rushed from the room and I heard her rummaging through things in another room. "His head Liam; he hit his head." I motioned to the now congealed blood matted into Stephen's hair. Liam nodded. I laid Cillian on the other couch and he opened his eyes as I tore off his shirt.

"Hmm...dis is quite a dream come true love, but I'd have much preferred us doin' dis in some private bedroom somewhere." He laughed and then winced. I shook my head as Carmen handed me some weird looking salve. I tore off the cap with my teeth as she left to help Liam with Stephen.

"I have no idea what this is Cillian so if it hurts, I'm sorry." I dripped the medicine onto his skin. He gasped as it filtered its way into his wound. He still had some shards of glass jutting out and I worked to try to get as many of the pieces as I could out of the wound. He closed his eyes again. I was doing everything in my power not to listen to what was happening beside to me. I didn't want to know; my brain wasn't processing Stephen at all. I concentrated on Cillian, on making sure that I got every last piece of glass out of his stomach and chest. The gashes were already beginning to heal, his skin pulling itself back together. I swabbed the dried blood from his chest and smoothed his hair back, pulling pieces of what looked like charred skin from the strands. I didn't know how long I worked over him, how many minutes or hours passed; I didn't care. I just wanted to fix him. Cillian was breathing deeply and he seemed like he might be sleeping.

"Ana?" Carmen stood next to me. "You're bleeding, let me look at you." She took my hand and pulled me off the sofa. She led me to the bathroom down the hall and leaned me back against the counter, her eyes roaming over my face. I let her press something cool and moist to my head; it smelled of lemon and honey and immediately my body started to shake. "It's ok Ana; you're ok." She kissed me gently on the cheek.

"Is he…is he…" I gasped, my brain not forming the words. This was my nightmare; it was coming true.

"He's fine Ana, just knocked out. Stephen's fine." She smiled softly as I tried to breathe. She cleared away the blood and the ash and led me back out into the living room. Liam was cradling Stephen's head in his lap and running his hands over his skull. "It just helps to speed up his natural healing process." Carmen whispered upon seeing my concern. I nodded. My body felt tight and I realized that my hands were balled into fists. There was a sudden gust of wind and we turned to see Eamonn standing in the room.

"Ana!' he called and I ran to hug him. "You're ok?" He looked at me, and then over to the couches where Stephen and Cillian were.

"They're ok Eamonn; what about you and the others?" I asked. I hadn't seen anyone that I knew in the chaos.

"We're fine Ana." He was staring at Stephen. "How did you get out?" He looked at me and I saw Liam rise from his position on the couch.

"She fuckin' moved da goddamned wall of fire and jumped trough a fuckin' full glass window holdin' me and carryin' Stephen." Cillian called from the couch. I shook my head. Liam put his arms around my shoulders; he was staring at me intently.

"Eamonn, what happened?" Liam sounded in sheer disbelief.

"Got me," he said. "One minute I'm behind the bar and the next the whole place is exploding; it happened out of nowhere. I turned to Liam my eyes wide.

"What is it Ana?" he asked gently.

"I saw them," I said, looking back at Eamonn. "I saw a group of Bonders in the club when we arrived. I thought they were Vampires; they looked like...they looked like Vampires. No one was talking to them. I saw them before the first explosion standing by the back exit door and I smelled something in the air..." I probably sounded like a crazy person. Both Liam and Eamonn were staring at me.

"What did you smell Ana?" Eamonn asked.

"Like a metallic scent and something that smelled like burning or fire...and my amulet..."I started down at my chest; it was cool now. "My amulet started to glow and burn and that's when I shoved

Stephen down; a second later the place exploded." I frowned. Liam and Eamonn exchanged glances.

"I'll go and see what I can find out about our uninvited guests." Eamonn turned once more to Stephen and Cillian and I saw Cillian give a "thumbs up" sign. "I'll be back as soon as I know anything Liam." Eamonn smiled at me and then shimmered away. My head hurt and my body was still tense and Liam staring at me wasn't making me feel any better.

"I'm sorry Ana." He smiled gently. "Forgive me; I was just wondering how you managed to learn how to move a solid wall of Demonic fire." His eyes narrowed. I sighed.

"Patric taught me," I said quietly. "At Carlo's, we practiced together a few nights while I was there." I bowed my head, feeling a rolling wave of sadness hit me. I hoped to the entire universe that Patric had nothing to do with happened this evening. He wouldn't have to worry about Liam or Stephen coming for him because I would kill him myself first.

"I see," Liam said. I hated when he said that. He laughed softly. I went to sit over by Stephen, taking his hand in mine.

"Why isn't he breathing?" I asked, watching his chest for any sign of movement.

"His body is healing and it shuts down in order to conserve the energy it needs to repair itself." Liam sat in the chair and leaned forward. I saw Carmen bring Cillian a drink; it looked like whisky.

"Right ya're lassie!" Cillian said weakly as Carmen helped him to sit up. I felt Liam's eyes on me.

"Liam, what is it?" I said, my tone slightly harsher than I intended. Liam smiled.

"Do you think that Patric had something to do with this Ana?" he asked, surveying me.

"No," I said without hesitating. "I mean, Patric was probably upset that I didn't respond to his letter, but there is no way he would have risked killing me over that," I said. "No way." Liam studied me again.

"What if he knew that you could escape?" Liam asked calmly. I shook my head.

"Liam, no way! Patric would never leave that much to chance; I mean, I could have been knocked out and then burned to death; there's no way he would have taken such a risk." Liam's eyes went to my chest and he stared intently at my amulet.

"What if he could warn you?" His tone dropped and my heart skipped.

"What?" I asked slowly. Liam sat back and put his hands in his lap.

"What if Patric could warn you before the explosion hit; the scents, the amulet...what if he wanted you to know and to be able to get out." I shook my head again.

"It wasn't him," I said. "This was a group of Bonders Liam; they weren't Vampires; the fire was Demonic, you said so yourself. Patric has never aligned himself with the Demons; it's always been Vampires."

457

"Until now," Stephen's voice cut through the air and I turned to stare at him. His eyes were still closed but he was breathing now. I laid my head on his chest feeling him breathe.

"What do mean Stephen?" Liam was frowning and I moved to kiss Stephen's cheek. He touched my face. I wished he would open his eyes.

"I went to see Patric." He sighed as he spoke and I pulled back to stare at him.

"When?" I asked.

"Early this morning." He licked his lips.

"Why?" Liam beat me to the punch.

"Dude," Cillian called from the other side. "Dis can't be good."

"Stephen?" Liam asked again.

"Well, I originally went to offer a truce of sorts and to tell him that he should be there for Ana on her wedding day, that I wouldn't mind having him there; it didn't go as I had hoped." Stephen finally opened his eyes. Our gazes locked.

"Go on." Liam was glaring at his brother and I could almost feel the anger pulsing from Liam's body.

"He wasn't alone. He was with an odd group of Demons, rough and hardly civilized. He wasn't particularly happy to see me. I tried to explain why I had come and how important it was to Ana to have him with us; that seemed to make him upset. He didn't want to talk about

458

the wedding, he did however, want to talk about Ana." Stephen's eyes flashed as he stared at me. I was rubbing my temples.

"And?" Liam prompted, his eyes growing darker the more Stephen spoke. Stephen took his hand and traced along the metals of my amulet.

"I don't know; he was ranting on about how he and Ana were Bound and that it didn't matter if we were married. It meant nothing and that I was controlling and obsessive and didn't let her make her own decisions, that I had scared her into thinking that I would leave again if she even considered him as an option. He felt it necessary to remind me that I had broken her heart and that he was the one to see the devastation I caused; that she was broken, half dead, when she came to him on the ranch and that it was his love that helped to fix her not mine." Oh this was not good; this was so not good, I thought.

"And?" Liam asked; he could anticipate where this was headed. Cillian snorted.

"And then he said that he didn't wish me any harm, but that he wouldn't be terribly upset if I was to suddenly be removed from the picture." Stephen and I stared at each other. "I asked him if he was threatening me and he shrugged. I told him that I don't take to threats very well and he said he was glad that I was up for the challenge...and then..." Stephen looked to Liam and I saw his eyes grow wide.

"What?" I asked, looking at them both.

"Jesus, fuckin' Christ. Dat's da Patric I remember," Cillian murmured.

"WHAT?" I shouted. Stephen sighed loudly and glanced back to me.

459

"He told me, if what I witnessed with Nathanial, if I thought that was bad, then I had no idea what I was dealing with." Stephen's voice grew soft. I stood. That was it. I had had it. My rope was gone, my patience was gone, my sympathy and empathy were gone; any compassion that I felt, any bond that I had been holding onto with Patric was severed. He knew just how horrific those events with Nathanial had been and not just for me—for him as well; now he was threatening to kill Stephen and possibly me. He was threatening to put me through that again? This was insane; what was wrong with the Arias family? Were they all psychopaths?

"Just ta clarify love," Cillian sat up sipping his drink. "I don't tink Patric actually wants ta kill *you*; I tink it's Stephen he would like ta knock off." Cillian chuckled.

"What time is it?" I asked, smoothing my dress.

"What?" Liam stood, his eyes full of worry.

"What the hell time is it? I asked again.

"It's almost six thirty in the morning Ana," Liam said and I pointed toward Stephen.

"Is he ok?" I asked, surveying him closely. I didn't see any more blood.

"Yes." Liam's eyes flashed.

"And Cillian?" I put my hands on my hips.

"Tanks ta ya love, I've never been better." Cillian winked and sat back sipping his scotch.

"Ana, do you really think this is necessary?" Liam crossed the room to where I was standing.

"Yes Liam, I do." I hated being so stern with him but I was having a difficult time controlling my anger at the moment. I heard Stephen sigh.

"She shouldn't go alone," he said quietly and I knew he was thinking about how Nathanial had lured me using Lucie.

"I agree Ana; why don't I go with you to see Patric," Liam spoke softly. Sometimes it was excessively annoying having so many people in the room able to read my mind. I needed to be cognizant of closing it more often.

"No way. I can handle Patric. He's not Nathanial, at least not the Nathanial that I…" I cleared my throat unable to say the word. "He's fine; it's fine Liam. We're just going to have a little chat." I bent my head and kissed Stephen gently on the lips. He pulled me closer and whispered in my ear.

"You saved me again Ana. I'm starting to feel somewhat inadequate as a husband." He laughed gently.

"Well, I guess we'll just have to remedy that on the honeymoon won't we?" I whispered back and Cillian snickered.

"Shut it." I turned to him. "I saved your ass as well." I went over and kissed Cillian on the cheek. "If I'm not back in an hour, come and get me please." I motioned toward Liam and he nodded.

"One hour Ana," he replied. I nodded and thought about the ranch and how stupid Patric was and left the house in a blast of angry wind.

Stephen

Liam was glaring at me from his position in the chair. I closed my eyes.

"I was trying to do something nice," I said quietly. "I wanted Ana to have everyone there that she loved, Liam."

"Yes, but you also wanted to confront him about that letter Stephen; you cannot lie to me, I know you too well." Liam lowered his eyes. "He killed innocent people Stephen and he could have killed you and he most certainly could have killed Ana or hurt her terribly."

"We don't know it was him," I answered, feeling my brother's concern for me. The room was dim and the silence between our breaths was somewhat calming; I couldn't get my mind to quiet down. I just kept thinking about hearing the blast and feeling Ana throw herself on top of me, shielding me, protecting me. That was the last thing I remembered. I hoped Eamonn could get us some information. Liam and I sat for the next hour watching the sunrise and not talking. Cillian had taken off to catch up with Eamonn. All we could do was wait. Liam checked his watch.

"Give her a minute," I said. Ana was pissed and when she was pissed she tended to rant for a while. Liam sighed.

"Where are you taking her for the honeymoon," he asked softly. I laughed. I was positive that Ana wouldn't want to go anywhere after this mess. She'd be upset and I wasn't entirely sure that she wasn't angry with me. Liam snorted.

"Sicily first, then Corsica, then Rapallo…" I smiled, glad that I hadn't made our reservations in Sicily until tomorrow.

"Cheers," Liam said sarcastically. I chuckled. "I'm going." He stood and I nodded. I felt a breeze cross my face and I sat up watching as Ana's figure appeared next to Liam's, she looked dazed and very, very worried. "Ana? What happened?" Liam took her hands and led her over to the chair. She stared at me and her eyes grew dark, black almost.

"He's gone," she spoke slowly and softly, looking down.

"Patric wasn't there?" Liam asked, trying to decipher her words. She shook her head.

"No, everything is gone. The ranch is empty; there's no furniture, no horses. The guest house is closed and locked and he's left nothing in his study; he's gone." She ran her fingers through her hair, the anxiety falling over her body was permeating into the very air I was breathing. I frowned. It wasn't anxiety over Patric, but for me. I could feel her desperation and her fear over my life. "I tried to summon him, to try to find him, but I just kept shimmering back to the ranch; he's blocked his location." She swallowed.

"It's ok Ana." Liam stood behind her, rubbing her shoulders. I should be doing that, but standing was a bit difficult at the moment; my head

463

was still healing and the room kept tilting back and forth. "I have individuals who can track Patric even if he doesn't want to be found. He's talented, but I am more talented." Liam's voice was commanding and I got the sense that he shared Ana's intolerance of this entire situation.

"Can you get on that Liam? I don't want any more surprises if we can help it," Ana spoke in an equally commanding tone and I couldn't help but think that Ana just might make a pretty good general for some army; I'd follow her orders.

"You can't follow any orders you imbecile," Liam muttered under his breath as he left the room. Ana cocked her head and stared at me. I held out my arms for her to come to me. She moved and sat on the side of the couch barely touching my hand.

"That's not quite what I was suggesting love." I smiled and she laid her head against my chest and I took to rubbing her back.

"No more doing it in public. We're cursed for sure now," she murmured into my shoulder.

"I disagree. I think you have to do it a lot in public and for things to go wrong each time, in order to be counted as 'cursed' and technically, nothing happened while we were indisposed. I think we need a few more tries." I laughed and lifted her head.

"It was nice what you tried to do Stephen; I know that you were upset about the letter and you probably shouldn't have gone, but I think your deeper intentions were to try to make me happy; at least I hope that was the case." Her eyes narrowed as she studied me.

464

"I only want you to be happy Ana," I murmured and I started to kiss her. It was odd, I was dizzy and slightly weakened and I was upset with myself over Patric, but somehow, I wanted Ana and I wanted her in the worst way. My reaction to her was horribly inappropriate considering the timing and my condition, but I couldn't help myself. She was intoxicating and I felt as if I was experiencing some sort of withdrawal symptoms even though we'd been together just a few short hours ago. I was craving her. I moved my mouth against hers roughly, parting her lips. She cleared her throat.

'Um Stephen, I'm not sure this is the best place to being doing this." She laughed. "And you're still healing…" I cut her off. Her taste was inexplicable and it had somehow changed since I kissed her last. Now, her scent seemed to have merged with the flavor on her lips and her tongue, and it was exactly what I needed, what I wanted, what I had to have. I bit down on her bottom lip, running my tongue over and in her mouth. A flood of chemicals released in my body and the power from the surge made my body clench. What the hell was happening to me? My hormone release had never been that strong even when I was in full form. Ana pulled back and stared at me, her eyes wide. "Are you ok?" She had noticed how tense my body had become. I was ok; in fact I was fine. I wasn't dizzy anymore and my head felt perfectly normal; the weakness was gone and I suddenly felt a rush of power and strength that I had not felt since my fighting days. I wondered if the blow to my head had something to do with all of this. My left hand was warm, very warm. I looked down to see the ring on my finger was glowing slightly, pulsing. I took Ana's hand and was stunned. Next to the tiny moon there were now three small jewels hanging in the metal

465

sky, not one as before. They shimmered and sparkled and had their own pulse that was matching the rhythm of my ring. I stared at Ana.

"How are you feeling?" I asked her quietly.

"I'm a bit angry and frustrated and slightly petrified that you're going to die, but other than that, I'm fine." She was holding my hand and gazing at our rings. She didn't seem surprised by the new additions to her band. I bowed my head.

"You saved me again Ana," I said, memories flashing before my mind. Memories of an alley, of a fire, of an overlook, of Ana offering herself to fight with Saden, offering her life for mine; memories of her letting me go unselfishly too many times, memories of every single time that she had shown that it is me that she wanted, that it was me she loved. I closed my eyes.

"Of course," she said touching my face. "Always." She hugged me. "I love you, you dope." I held her close, kissing her face tenderly. I heard Liam come back into the room. Ana pulled back and I sighed.

"Eamonn called." Liam stood with his arms folded across his chest. "The individuals that Ana saw were definitely Bonders and they do have some connection with Patric, but no one knows for sure if they were acting on his orders. Eamonn has always had some trouble with Demons and even he'll admit that his relationship with many of them has been less than diplomatic. He's caused quiet a bit of chaos and anger with various groups. Still, it's unlikely that they would go to such lengths over some petty gambling debts and bad business transactions." Liam paced. "We're having Patric followed and we'll be able to track his movements; it will just take a bit of time to get a hold of his location." Liam turned to me. "The two of you should continue with your plans." He smiled gently at Ana.

"No way!" she said, standing up and I could feel her panic. "I'm not having Stephen away from you or from other people who can help us; if we're out there alone and Patric really does want him out of the way, I'm not going to be able to fight alone Liam. I won't put him at risk, at least not until you can find Patric." She shook her head and I snickered.

"I do know how to fight love," I said, laughing under my breath. She waved her hand and I was gently thrown back against the couch. I laughed harder.

"No," she said again. "We'll stay in the area for a bit; it's fine." She was biting her lip and her nails. Liam crossed the room and gently took her hand away from her mouth. He held her face and stared into her eyes.

"Ana, my love, you cannot live your life fearing death. It serves no purpose to be afraid of what we do not and cannot know. You have lost so much and have endured so much; do you not believe that your life is now deserving of happiness? Do not let your fears dictate what you do or where you go or how you love; that is no way to live. Yes, Patric is still out there and yes, he is hurt and angry, but you must not hold yourself accountable for fixing him or to spending your entire existence trying to save my brother from Patric's jealousies. Neither of them are your responsibility. All you are responsible for is healing yourself, loving yourself, allowing yourself to be loved and for realizing all that you are and all that you are destined to become. While we are grateful to you for how unselfishly you continue to give of yourself, it is time now for you to begin your life, a life where you have chosen someone who I think, regardless of his many, many faults, wants to devote his entire being to loving you, to making sure that you feel safe and protected both emotionally and physically and who wants to build a life with you—forever." Liam paused. I didn't think it was necessary to point out that I had faults but whatever, the rest of what he was saying was true. Ana looked over at me and I winked. She turned back to Liam and exhaled. Liam took her face back into his hands. "Ana," he said her name with such reverence and admiration that I felt my heart swell. She shook her head.

"Ok," she whispered.

"Ok." Liam smiled and kissed and hugged her. "Good, now I believe the two of you have some packing to do?" He turned to me suddenly. "What's the matter with you?" he asked and I stared at him, confused.

"What?" I asked. Liam frowned.

"You're scent has changed and it's all over the place." He glared. I hadn't noticed I was releasing anything. It wasn't coming from me. I stared at Ana and her face was bright red. I busted out laughing so loud that Liam jumped. He whirled and looked at Ana, her face giving her away.

"Sorry," she whispered, stepping away from him. "I guess some of my powers are a little off at the moment." She cringed and Liam chuckled, but then his face smoothed and he studied her for a moment. His eyes narrowed and I could see what he was thinking. Ana was experiencing another mating cycle. I suddenly wondered if that had anything to do with how I was currently behaving towards her. Vampires didn't

468

necessarily go through any sort of mating ritual. Liam's voice suddenly entered my head. *Yes they do; it just takes a very special bond for you to experience that need, a permanent bond.* Interesting. Ana had taken to biting he lip and several of her nails, again.

"You two go and we'll see you when you get back." Liam smiled at us. I stood and went to pull her hand away; at this rate she wasn't going to have any lips or fingers left for me to kiss. I heard Liam's voice again. *Be aware Stephen, not to the point that you can't enjoy yourself, but your instincts need to be heightened. I can track Patric, that I have no doubt, but I have no idea how long that will take. I will call you as soon as I can get his location.* I nodded subtlety and took Ana's hand.

"Ready?" I asked.

"Yep." She smiled at me and then at Liam and I took us back to the house. We landed and she turned to me. "I've already packed," she said smiling. "Have you?"

"Uh, no," I said. It had been a while since I'd been on any extended journeys; I hated packing.

"Well let's get cracking!" She snapped her fingers and started to move down the hall. I followed, still thinking about what Liam had said, not about Patric, but about vampires having a mating urge. It was odd considering how difficult it was for female vampires to get pregnant by a Human mate; it could be life threatening for them to conceive and to carry a child. I sat on the bed and watched as Ana brought out a large duffle bag and placed it on the floor. She started pulling my shirts and jeans out from the closet and dresser.

"Sooo…" I said casually. She looked up at me from her position on the floor.

"Yes?" She folded a pair of boxers and placed them neatly in the bag.

"You want to talk about what's going on with you?" I asked; the last time this happened it had scared her to death. I had thought it was funny then and I still thought it was somewhat amusing, but now that I seemed to also be experiencing a similar process, I thought it was really, really erotic and exciting. This time she didn't have to restrain herself and neither did I.

"Me? What about you?" She laughed. "You were practically ready to do it on the couch with your brother right in the next room!" She cringed. That was true. She pulled a hat out and a blue sweater from the armoire and held it up. "I love this on you," she said. "You wore it when you brought me the painting." She smiled and folded the sweater into the bag. She remembered the oddest things. She was avoiding me; she was anxious about something, something other than Patric. I studied her, but she was keeping me out. I sighed. "There," she said, hoisting the bag up onto the bed. "What else would you like to bring?" She started rifling through my drawer. She pulled out several pieces of folded paper stapled together. Shit! I blurred to her side and grabbed them from her. Her eyes widened.

"What the hell?" She laughed slightly. "What is that?" she asked as she tried to take the paper back. I folded them together and tucked them into my back pocket.

"Nothing," I said. I had forgotten that I had put those documents in my drawer. I needed to be more organized.

"Nothing?" She eyed me. "Then why can't I see them?" She stepped toward me and I laughed.

"Because they're private." I leaned against the dresser.

"My letter from Patric was private and you read that!" She stared hard at my face. She had a point.

"You're right."

"So?" she said, moving closer to me. I stepped back.

"So, these are private," I said again knowing that I was close to pissing her off.

"What are they, like love letters or something?" I saw an image of Sara pass through her mind. She was crazy.

"No, I'm not as heavily pursued as you, love. I don't get love letters." I smirked and stepped back a few more feet. She huffed.

"Stephen Kieran Byrne! We are not supposed to have secrets, at least not about important things…" She frowned. I had never heard her use my full name before; it sounded nice.

"So we can have secrets about other things?" I challenged, distracting her.

"Well, I mean, I respect you as an individual; I'm sure there are some things that you like to keep to yourself sometimes, but I hope you know that you can talk to me about anything, if you wanted." She frowned again and I saw an image of the fight she'd seen in South Africa and how she witnessed just how excited I had gotten watching.

471

It was disturbing for her to think about me in terms of what I used to do and how she hadn't known about that side of my existence.

"That's very kind Ana, but I have no need to have any secrets from you—" She started to cut me off, pointing to the papers. "These are a surprise," I said, "and you will just have to wait." I took the papers out from my pocket, waved my hand and they disappeared.

"How'd you do that?" she asked, staring at me. "And what kind of surprise."

"My god, you ask a lot of questions!" I said, laughing and pulling her back to the bed. I held her hands. "I'll answer the one about the disappearing papers if you answer me one," I said raising my eyebrows at her.

"I don't want to know that badly." She smirked and turned away. I shrugged.

"Ok, but it's a teachable little trick and quite useful," I said baiting her.

"Yeah, at children's parties!" she said sarcastically. I laughed.

"I can also bring them back," I said, watching her. She turned slightly to look at me. I waved my hand again and the papers reappeared. She pursed her lips.

"Humph. Big deal, I can move a wall of fire," she said, tossing her hair back. "You're just like a fancy magician."

"What!" I said, tackling her down on the bed. "A magician? How dare you compare my extraordinary vampire skills to some quack that Humans are fooled by; I'm insulted." I kissed her neck. "I can make you disappear too you know," I whispered in her ear. "I can send you anywhere I want, without shimmering with you." I bit her gently on the ear lobe. "And, I can *make* you do anything I want, but of course you've already experienced that little talent." I winked and kissed her mouth. She pushed me back.

"Well I can do that!" She rolled from underneath me and I laid back; something was bothering her. She was resisting me physically. She was also trying to suppress what was happening to her as far as her current mating cycle. I could tell she was trying to force it back. "Hey, can we go early?" She stood and went into the bathroom bringing a change of clothes with her. This was ridiculous; now she didn't even want me to see her change? What was going on with her? She emerged in jeans and a long sleeve t-shirt. I sighed.

"Yes we can go early," I said, rising from the bed. I zipped up the bag and put my hands on my hips. Ana grabbed her pack and I saw her check for something, something that looked like a circular case, birth control maybe? I frowned, that didn't make any sense. She took my hand and I felt a pulse of anxiety course through her fingers. I stared at her. She swallowed and smiled at me. My eyes narrowed, but I shimmered us away wondering what secrets she was keeping from me.

Frick! Stupid mating cycle! There was no way that I was having sex now, no way. I was trying trying to figure out how this was going to work; it was our honeymoon and we should be intimate—a lot. Frick! Stephen had done an amazing job with our first stop. He'd found the same villa that Lucie and I had stayed during our boat trip and booked us the most beautiful rooftop suite, equipped with a roaring fireplace, a gorgeous full view of the Mediterranean Sea and a huge bed under the stars. Frick! Currently we were sitting outside at a small café and I was having a late lunch; I couldn't remember the last time I had eaten and it felt good to get some nourishment into my body. Stephen was staring at me trying to read my thoughts; I kept him out, which I hated to do, but I just wasn't ready to talk about what was bothering me; I was running out of time. I was sure he would wonder why I was suddenly not interested in him physically. Something was going on with him as well; since the couch at Liam's, Stephen had been very affectionate, even more so than usual. He was kissing me and caressing me, even out in public and his scent had shifted. Now it was deep and had more musky notes to it; I couldn't detect any of the ocean fragrance that he usually emitted, that scent had been replaced by something rich and spicy. It made my mouth water. I wanted him and I knew he wanted me; I just couldn't. I pushed my plate back and took his hand.

"Finished?" he asked, smiling.

"Yep; that was wonderful, thank you," I said, smiling back. He rolled his eyes. He thought it bizarre that I always thanked him when he bought me meals or groceries or anything else. I just appreciated him.

"Shall we walk for a bit?" he asked, standing and still holding my hand.

"Yes." I pushed my chair back and we started to stroll through the narrow streets. The air was warm and the sun felt nice on my skin. I could hear the ocean and the seagulls and smell the saltwater; it felt amazing to be here with him. We walked out to a small jut of rocks over looking the water. Stephen pulled me close and we stood staring out at the horizon. He swept my hair back from my face and traced his finger from my temple to the corner of my mouth.

"Hey," he said softly as he turned me slowly toward him.

"Hey," I said just as softly.

"I love you Ana." He brought his lips close to mine and kissed me gently. I breathed deeply, savoring his taste and his scent; they seemed to be coupled now.

"I love you too." I let him pull me closer. We stayed out on the rocks for the rest of the afternoon, just walking along the shore and talking about different things that had happened in our relationship. There was something that I had wanted to ask him.

"What are you thinking about?" he asked as we walked back to the street. I took his hand

"That night when I came back to the apartment after leaving to go to Idaho, when Noni's vision sent me back to you. I was just wondering if you were actually going to kill me that night?" I had no idea why it mattered to me now, but I had always wanted to know. "Because you looked like you were going to attack me." I smiled and Stephen chuckled.

"Hmm…I did, didn't I?" He tucked me under his shoulder. "You kissed me," he said quietly and I could see that he was remembering. I nodded. "No Ana, I wasn't going to attack you. I didn't know what I was going to do, but I wasn't going to kill you." He kissed the top of my head.

"And what about that night on the overlook when I had Noni? Did you know that group you were with had killed her and those children?" I asked. Stephen took a deep breath.

"I didn't know. I had no idea. I was just trying to find you Ana. I wanted to talk to you; well, I wanted to yell at you for letting my brother convince you not to be with me. When I saw you on the ground, your face was covered in blood and you were so broken. I had no idea what you had just seen coming from Nathanial's, but I could tell that something was very, very wrong with you. I was so angry, angry with you and me and the world; I was just angry. I watched you let Noni go; I watched you pick up the body of this woman who had cared for you, who had given you some semblance of a life, who had loved you. I watched as you dropped her from your grasp and I could see it in your eyes that you thought I was going to harm you, that I was waiting to kill you and then you put your head on my shoulder and my world stopped spinning." His footsteps halted and we were standing on a little side street, alone. He stared at me. "Talk to me Ana. Please. I know something is wrong. Tell me." He sounded urgent and I could see the pain in his eyes from not knowing. I sighed and leaned back against the stone wall.

"I'm scared Stephen." I bowed my head.

"About what?" he said, taking my hands.

"About losing another baby, about losing you again, about watching you leave me alone and scared in some hospital bed; I'm scared." Tears fell onto my cheeks. He closed his eyes and held me close and tight.

"That was one of the worst mistakes that I have ever made in my entire existence Ana and you have every right to be frightened, but I will never leave you again, not now, not ever. No matter what happens to you, no matter what you experience in your life, we are a family now, you have a family and we will go through whatever we need to, together. You are the most sacred being in my life and all I want is for you to let me love you and let me take care of you when you need me to. I want you to let me stand next to you or behind you or to lead you when you can't find your own way. Don't be afraid Ana; don't be frightened, live." Stephen opened his eyes and I saw a single tear move down his beautiful face.

Chapter Eighteen

Stephen

I thought it best to take things slow with Ana on this trip. She was scared and she needed to work through that a bit. I was patient; my body however, was a completely different story. I couldn't stop touching her. Her skin felt amazing and every time I reached for her, my body tensed in utter pleasure. We were currently out at a club in Corsica having dinner and dancing and Ana seemed in good spirits. I had not heard from Liam since arriving weeks ago, so I did call last night. He said they were close to finding Patric and not to worry. We were sitting in a booth near the back of restaurant; the club was above us and we could hear the pulse of the music and watch people hovering over the ledge on the next level.

"So where did we come down on that whole half-Vampire thing?" she asked as she ate her food. I choked slightly on my drink. I hadn't thought about that in quite some time. I thought she might have forgotten about it, I had. "I mean, that's what we agreed to right?" She sipped her wine.

"Yes," I said hesitantly.

"So when?" She moved closer to me and I eyed her.

"When what?" I asked, smiling slightly. She sighed, clearly agitated that I was playing stupid.

"When do I get to have this done?" She glared.

"What's the hurry?" I touched the tip of her nose. She shrugged.

"No hurry; I was just wondering that's all." I felt her touch my leg and I bit my tongue to keep from running my hand up her dress.

"Hmm…well maybe I'll think about it for your birthday, seems apropos for a Halloween birthday combo doesn't it?" I laughed and took a deep breath; my hormones were releasing again. She studied me.

"That's months away." She frowned and she absently started to caress my thigh. I cleared my throat.

"I thought you said there was no hurry? What's seven months?" I took a sip from my drink and passed her hers. She smiled.

"This is the best trip I've ever been on; I'm having so much fun. Thank you for doing all of this." She took my hand and squeezed. She was bizarrely appreciative. I laughed.

"It's my pleasure, love." I pulled her close and attempted to kiss her gently. Immediately upon our mouths touching though, my body had a very different idea. Christ! I wish Liam had told me about this sooner; I could have been better prepared. This was bad timing. Ana was feeling hesitant and yet her body was in mating cycle mode; I wanted to be respectful of her emotional state but *my* body was in mating cycle mode—frustrating didn't begin to express our current situation. I pulled back a bit and swallowed.

"I'm ready to go." She sighed. It was late and we'd been hiking and shopping all day. Of course I wasn't allowed to buy her anything, but still she let me take her into the stores. I grasped her hand and shimmered us back to our villa. We were right on the beach and the caretakers had lit the fire for us and set out various bottles of champagne and decorated the room with fresh flowers and tiny votive candles. I would leave Ireland for this, I thought, as I put another log on the fire. I turned to see Ana on the couch staring at me.

"What?" I asked, sinking down next to her.

"Nothing; I was just thinking how handsome you are." She smiled and touched my face. I laughed. "But I'm guessing you've heard that lots over you five centuries. You're old!" She smirked.

"You don't like older men?" I fingered one of her curls twirling it around in my hand.

"I do like older men, like maybe fifteen or twenty years older, but five hundred is pushing it a bit don't you think?" she replied and I shrugged.

"I have a lot I can show you." I smirked and leaned over to kiss her. "And thank you for saying I'm handsome, that's very sweet." I breathed gently in her ear and she turned her face towards me.

"Are you happy?" she asked, tracing her fingers over my palm and looking down.

"Happy is too simple a word Ana," I said, reaching to lift her chin.

"Are *you* happy?" I asked caressing her face. She smiled and started kissing me deeply. I laughed. "Would that be a 'yes'?" I whispered easing her back against the couch.

"Yes." She ran her fingers through my hair and my body tightened at her touch. "I'll be right back!" She pushed me off and headed to her bag and then to the bathroom; I groaned. "Just give me a second!" she called. I stood and uncorked a bottle of champagne and opened the veranda doors out to the sea. I was about to pour two glasses and just as I tilted the bottle I saw Ana emerge from the bathroom, I missed the glass.

"Shit," I said, moving away from the flow of liquid. She laughed.

"Hey, that happened before, on the night of the concert, you spilled your drink then too." She smiled. She was standing before me in the black lingerie set that I'd gotten for her, at least I think that's what she was wearing, there was no way that I could have ever anticipated that it would look like that on her body. All of her curves were accentuated and the underwear was cut high up on her hips and left very little to the imagination. Her legs were strong and muscular and she leaned back against the couch watching me. The top was completely see-through, but you had to look hard; there was a subtlety to the fabric that teased at what was underneath and it slid on her skin, the color adding a depth and sensuality to her already mystical looks. Her shoulders were shapely and defined and I could see just how much fitter she'd become in the last month. Ana was never one of those featherweight-type women. She liked being muscular and curvy and strong; she was all of those things and so much more.

"Do you like it? I think you have pretty good taste." She smiled and walked slowly over to me. I was speechless. She took a glass and sipped it slowly. "That's pretty strong!" She laughed. I still hadn't said anything. My physical reactions were running rampant and I could feel

481

every nerve in my body responding to how she looked and how she smelled; good god her personal fragrance was so heady and intoxicating that it was signaling my body to do things I was sure, were illegal in most places. I stood, holding my glass and trying to control myself; I didn't want to be rough with Ana, not tonight. Tonight should be calm and tender and slow; there would be plenty of time for us to explore other intimacies—we had lifetimes. I wanted to hold her close to me and I wanted to feel every inch of her skin and taste every part of her. I wanted to savor her and love her in the way that she needed and wanted. I took her glass from her and set it on the bar. Pulling her close, I wrapped my hands around her waist and held her against me.

"Um, you haven't said anything in like an eternity, you alright?" She laughed lightly.

"Yes." I let my eyes focus on her. I had the capability to calm her down and I wanted to make sure that she was feeling relaxed before I initiated anything intimate. I filtered my way into her mind and I was surprised to see how at ease she really was; the only thing that seemed to be on her mind was us and sex. She was quite amped up at least internally; externally she seemed to be easing herself into things. I watched as I ran the back of my hand up and down her shoulder, feeling the softness of her skin against mine. She smiled gently. I moved my hand to touch her thigh, letting my fingers skim across her hip and over the back of her leg. She was slowly unbuttoning my shirt. My body was pulsing out of control and waves of hormones were coursing through my system; I had never experienced anything like this before. I wanted to be with her urgently, violently. I took a deep breath trying to steady the onslaught of desire and unquenchable hunger, not for her blood, but for her body. I was craving her like

482

some sort of drug that I had been away from for too long. "Ana?" I murmured as we kissed, "I need you." My voice was urgent and tight against the hammering of my heart. She kissed me forcefully and I groaned. "Please," I said, kissing her back. "I have to have you." I was walking us backward holding her and shrugging out of my shirt. She was breathing hard. "Please," I said again, laying her on the bed. She arched her back as I ran my lips over her throat and chest, lowering the straps to her top. I brushed her hair back and let my lips move over her cheeks and her neck and finally over her mouth. Each kiss, each taste was making me want to devourer her and I groaned deeply with need. I slid her top over her head and pressed her chest against my body. Her scent absorbed into my blood and I trembled as my body reacted with such physical and emotional pleasure, that I was breathless. I lowered her underwear and pushed her arms up by her head, weaving our fingers together as I held her down gently. She started to move under me and I closed my eyes wanting to feel more; I needed to be inside of her. I let my pants fall away as I laid my body on her, moving slowly and matching her rhythm. I gasped as I slid myself deep inside of her and I felt a torrent of desire and passion and hunger, rise forcefully in my body. Ana breathed heavily as I kissed her and her body began to find it's own throbbing cadence. It was perfect. She was warm and her skin surged with heat and scent and I began tasting her sweat, running my mouth over every part of her body as I thrust. I moaned as her hips upped the friction between us and she whispered my name. I held her hands, pressing her harder into the bed and grinding against her. My desire was peaking, but the surge was so addictive that I held off, not wanting to stop, not wanting to end this feeling. Ana groaned and I needed more. I moved her faster against me, flipping her on top. I let her grind herself against me working her up into a deep passion. She spread her legs wider and we began making our rhythms faster and harder. She groaned again and started riding me violently. I had wanted things to be gentle, slow, but her body wanted something more, something rougher and I was happy to oblige. She came and I moaned, saying her name as I let myself go, filling her with my release. I pulled her down on top of me and I kissed her biting down on her lip and drawing a bit of blood. I held her against me, staying inside of her, not wanting to break our connection. I buried my face in her neck and breathed softly against her skin. I ran my fingers gently over her back, feeling her relax, her muscles melting at my touch. I don't know how long we stayed like that, hours maybe; I didn't want to move and I wanted the world to stop. I wanted stay locked together, loving each other, knowing each other.

I felt Ana sigh contentedly and she smiled, rolling off of me as I pulled her up and back against the pillows, kissing her greedily. The breeze from the sea wafted into the room gently caressing our bodies. Ana's skin erupted in chills and I pulled the covers over her and nestled her closer against me. I heard her breathe deeply.

"Was that...was that ok for you?" I asked softly, I hoped that she hadn't felt pressured. It was a tad too quick for me, but I just couldn't help myself.

"Hmm...better than ok," she said her brown eyes sparkling as she gazed at my face. "What about you? I know that was much more tame than what you usually experience." She pursed her lips. I shook my head. If she could only understand just what it was like to be me and to be with her having these moments of passion and desire, she would never worry about pleasing me ever again. "Really?" She looked at me and I guessed she'd picked up on some of my thoughts. I smiled.

"You have no idea," I said, kissing her gently. She tried to stifle a yawn. I laughed. "You should rest; we've had a very long day." I smoothed her hair back. I wasn't particularly tired, but I could definitely enjoy reliving the past hour, zoned out.

"Mmm…" she murmured and I felt her body begin to relax; she was asleep in seconds, which for Ana was rare. She'd been a constant insomniac since she'd shown up at my door three years ago. I watched her for a while then I sat back and let my mind drift.

Ana

I smelled coffee and eggs. I stirred and rolled over, keeping my eyes shut, burying myself in the down comforter and relishing how interesting my body was feeling. I felt strong and solid and very, very turned on, weird, but not unpleasant. I stretched and turned on my stomach looking into the kitchen where Stephen was cooking, he had the radio softly playing. It was nice that he made me food when he didn't eat himself. I heard him chuckle.

"Whatcha doing in there?" I called propping myself up on my elbows as I tried to tame the mass of tangled curls on my head. Stephen turned and nodded in time with the music. I laughed. He carried a bamboo tray over to the bed and I wrapped the sheet around me flipping over and leaning back against the pillows.

485

"Breakfast Madame." He sat back with me and handed me a napkin and fork. I stared at him. His eyes were almost translucent, but the color was so bright and blue that it served as a startling juxtaposition. His skin glowed, burnished and bronzed and the highlights in his chestnut locks were now a lighter more coppery brown, probably from the sun or because he was some otherworldly being. I sighed, feeling slightly plain. Stephen shook his head in disapproval of my commentating and pushed the plate toward me. "Eat please." He laughed. I finished quickly, partly because it was so good and partly because I wanted him. I waited for him to return from the kitchen and he sat on the edge of the bed. "So what do you want to do today? We have a boat, we can sail or we can rent a car and go for a drive. Whatever you want." Clearly he hadn't been listening to all of my inner monologues.

"Neither," I said, moving toward him slowly. He raised his eyebrows.

"Ahhh…so no tourist activities today then?" He let me kiss him as he spoke.

"Nope," I said as I started to slip off his shirt. He laughed, but I suddenly stopped. "Hey, you know what?" I asked, kissing him again. "We haven't been outside; you know, in the water." I winked at him. He looked out the open door and smiled.

"Hmm…we have not." He surveyed me.

"Do you like the water?" I asked. I had never seen Stephen in the ocean before; maybe he wasn't a fan.

"If you are going to be there, then I'm a fan." He kissed my hand.

"Have you ever been with anyone…you know, in that way?" I asked as I bit my lip again, trying not to recall how many women I had seen Stephen with throughout our times together.

"Uh, no actually I haven't." He frowned.

"Are you sad?" I laughed at the expression on his face. He seemed disappointed.

"No, I'm just thinking why we haven't done this sooner." He smirked and I pushed him back and kissed his mouth hard. "I thought you wanted to go outside," he asked, breathless as I tore off his shirt and let my sheet fall down off my back.

"I can't wait," I said, kissing down over his stomach. I undid his pants and slid them off.

"Hmm…apparently not." He moaned softly as I took him into my mouth. Suddenly I heard a faint buzzing noise and I stopped moving and so did Stephen. I rose up and looked at the night table. His phone was ringing. "Jesus fucking Christ; I am going to beat Liam's head in." He reached to grab the phone just as it headed toward the edge of the table. "Liam." Stephen's tone was curt and I had to bite my lip to keep from laughing, but then I remembered why Liam might be calling; Patric. I held my breath. "No, not the best timing as usual." Stephen spoke and looked at me as I gently covered him back up with the sheet. It seemed inappropriate for him to be talking with his brother lying half naked. Stephen rolled his eyes, but smiled. I watched as his face smoothed and his lips pressed into a fine line. His body tensed. It seemed as if Liam was talking nonstop. "I see," Stephen finally spoke. Good grief, he and Liam needed a new catch

487

phrase. "Why don't I let you explain it to her Liam; you are less likely to taint the scenario with your personal bias. Are they there now? Fine." Stephen sounded disgusted and I frowned. "We'll be home shortly." He cut the phone off and exhaled running his hands through his hair. Panic loomed dark in my bones.

"Why do we have to go back Stephen?" I spoke quietly. Stephen stood from the bed pulling up his pants and buttoning his shirt. He was angry. He moved over by the doors.

"Ana, it's better if Liam speaks to you; I'm actually too pissed to talk about this right now," he said and his tone made my heart sink. I got up slowly and started to gather my things. It took me less than an hour to pack both of our bags. Stephen didn't speak the entire time. I kept swallowing trying to push back the fear that continued to rise in my throat. I went to stand next to him, not sure if he wanted to be touched right now. I gently put my hand on his shoulder and he shimmered us away from our perfect night and almost perfect morning and away from the entrance into our new life together. I wanted to throw up.

****

We landed in Liam's living room and I quickly saw that there were two people that I had never seen before, two Vampires. I put my pack down and looked at Stephen. He was staring at them and I distinctly heard a low snarl erupt from someone. Liam cleared his throat.

488

"Ana, I'm so very sorry about all of this." Liam stared at me and I could see that he was agitated. What the hell was going on? "Ana, this is Miguel and Juan. They are Carlo's brothers." My knees weakened, but I held it together and immediately shut my mind down. I stared at them. Miguel looked as if he'd just come from one of Saden's fights. His face was scarred and what appeared to be fresh wounds barely healed, decorated the flesh up and down his arms. He was glaring at Stephen; clearly they knew each other. The two Vampires looked identical, twins maybe, but they also looked just like Carlo. They had the same strange brown eye color. They kept their distance and I wondered if they knew that my blood would kill them; it would melt them from the inside just like it had done their brother...was that why they were here? I braced myself against the couch. "Ana," Liam continued, "it appears that Patric has gotten himself in a bit of trouble, shall we say." Liam stared at me intently. "He's being questioned in regards to the events surrounding Carlo's death." I nodded. Liam sighed and I tried to swallow. "Patric has told Miguel and Juan that he was responsible for killing Carlo, that he set you up that night, that he knew Carlo had followed the two of you to the restaurant and he knew that Carlo was going to try to get you alone; that Patric planned for that to happen and that he was anticipating that Carlo would shape shift and that he would try to take your blood and that you would try to kill him. He didn't know about your rare blood type of course and as he's telling it, he was relying on your abilities with fire to at least get the ball rolling and then he could finish Carlo off." Liam paused and a wave of complete and utter despair filled my body. "Clearly he must have had some concerns over your safety and that's why he went to find Stephen and Nathanial to aid him and you just in case." My blood started to boil and I stepped back from the room. I was seething and in shock. No, this couldn't right; he couldn't have done this to me again, not after everything we'd been through, not after everything he saw when I came to the ranch. He had to be lying for some reason. He had to be. I heard both Liam and Stephen exhale loudly. My anger boiled over.

"What do you want from me?" I addressed the brothers. My voice was icy. Miguel stood and moved toward me. Suddenly I heard a fierce growl erupt from behind. Stephen was looming larger than life and his entire form had changed; he looked like a dark angel rising from a hellish fire. I turned back to Miguel and met him in the middle of the room. "I killed Carlo. It was me. He wanted me and I refused him and killed him, but not before he tried to rape me." My heart was pounding, but not out of fear, out of sheer, violent anger. "I have no idea what Patric is talking about. I am not accountable for his life and his decisions. It was my life on the line that night, not his and I fought your son-of-a-bitch brother and I won!" My voice was black. "If Patric had a plot to take Carlo out then good for him; the world's better off and if you want to come for me then let's finish it! Let's finish it now!" My fists were balled and I could feel the center of my core ignite and my hands surged with flames. I couldn't believe this was happening again. Miguel growled and I growled back, louder and stronger and I stepped forward. He stared at me.

"Ana." Liam stepped between us. "That's not necessary." He sounded nervous. For the first time, I actually ignored Liam. I pushed passed him and stood in front of Miguel; Juan stood as well.

"What-do-you-want?" I said, commanding them. Juan stepped forward.

"We want to know how much you want to save the life of someone who you just found out betrayed you, Ana." Juan smirked and I lunged, knocking him to the ground and slamming his head onto the floorboards and pounding my fist into the side of his face; I was unleashed.

"ANA!" Stephen yanked me off of Juan as Miguel started to crouch.

"I wouldn't do that if I were you." Liam stood before him, raising himself off the ground and looking utterly terrifying, his fangs barred and his eyes glowing yellow. Stephen held my arms behind me as I tried to lunge again.

"Stop it!" Stephen said, his fangs were also out, but his eyes were the color I knew. "Stop now." He held me against him tightly. I looked at him, desperate and my heart breaking.

"You need to go. I will discuss with Ana the situation with Patric and she will make her decision. I will inform you of what that is; there will be no need for you to return to our home," Liam hissed and I felt chills run up my spine. The two brothers gathered themselves and disappeared quickly. I shook myself loose from Stephen and stood in front of Liam, my arms crossed. Liam lowered himself back to the ground and eyed me. I was waiting for him to yell; I didn't care. I had every right to be angry. What I had just heard, it was unfathomable.

"Is it true Liam?" I asked, not relaxing my posture. "Is what they said true?" I raised my chin and glared.

"I don't know Ana; I can't speak for Patric. I can only say that the situation is indicative of his pattern. I can say that I would not be surprised to learn that he used you and put your life in danger yet again." Liam and I stood staring at each other. "He knew about how strong your powers had become and he knew that helping you recover from Stephen and from Nathanial would be to his advantage. I was suspicious when I had heard that Carlo had requested you; when Stephen and I went to meet with him and Patric appeared, my suspicions just became that much more heightened. While Patric was overseeing Carlo's coven he was not garnering the respect he wanted and Carlo was still very much an influence over his brethren. The strategy is classic Patric." I had stopped listening.

"So they want to kill him?" I asked.

"Apparently. Unless you can tell them that you do not believe that Patric had any plan to kill Carlo using you, that he had not influenced you in any way and that you killed him on your own volition without Patric's help." Liam continued to stare at me.

"Why does it matter what I say? Who the hell cares? And what's to stop them from killing me? I mean I killed Carlo, why not come after me?" Liam laughed darkly.

"Patric has not learned his lesson. There was already a plan in the works to take Carlo out, even his own brothers were in on it. They had agreed on a strategy and it seems that Patric in his infinite quest for power, went out on his own. He disobeyed the consensus of the coven and he proceeded against their wishes. They have no beef with you Ana or with Stephen, although it appears that Miguel wouldn't mind fighting with my brother again." Liam turned to glance at

Stephen who was standing so still and quiet that I had forgotten he was there.

"When you say that Patric 'hasn't learned his lesson' you're referring to me; when he took my blood the first time when he was supposed to bring me to Carlo after Nathanial's attack at the University…is that what you mean?" My head was hurting now and so was my stomach.

"Yes." Liam and I faced each other once more.

"Where is he?" I asked, feeling numb.

"He's being held." Liam replied, his eyes narrowing.

"Held?" Was he a prisoner?

"He's at the coven's house in Argentina. He's not allowed to leave until they hear or don't hear from you." Liam was watching me.

"How do we know that they just won't kill him regardless?" I studied Liam's face

"They won't," he said simply.

"You know?" I met his gaze.

"Yes. I've run a coven for many centuries Ana and I know that's not how things are done. If you testify that it was you and you alone that made the decision to kill Carlo, then Patric will be banned from the coven for his renegade behavior, but he will be allowed to live." I turned back to Stephen.

"Do you want to stay here?" I asked, shifting my gaze to Stephen; I wasn't prepared do anything yet until I laid eyes on Patric and asked him myself.

"No." Our eyes met and I nodded.

"Liam?" I walked over and took his hand. I didn't want him to be angry with me.

"Of course I will accompany you Ana and I'm not angry with you." He smiled gently.

"Fine, let's get this over with; I have a feeling that Juan isn't going to be the only one that I lunge at this morning." I already felt defeated and diminished.

Stephen

Ana was completely shut down. I couldn't even gauge the tenor of her emotions. She was stoic and solemn as we arrived in Argentina and she stood quietly by my side as Liam went ahead to talk to the rest of the coven. We waited in a large living room on the couch. I kept glancing at her out of the corner of my eye, but her vision remained straight ahead, staring into the fire. I had no idea if what Patric was saying was true and after witnessing the way Ana had reacted to Juan. I hoped for his sake he was lying, but for what reason I didn't know.

494

"Ana." Liam returned with another member of the coven. Ana rose from the couch. "This is Marco; he was an advisor to Carlo and to Patric. He'd like to hear your side of the story. You won't be allowed to speak to Patric alone." Ana moved to shake his hand and he looked surprised, but returned the gesture. "Patric will be in shortly." Liam and Marco stood together and Ana drifted over to stand by me. She was pinching the bridge of her nose and her eyes were closed. I should have killed Patric when I had the chance. I hated what this was doing to her. If he had in fact betrayed Ana, I couldn't imagine how she would recover from this, how she would ever let herself trust anyone ever again. This just might destroy her completely. I saw Patric enter the room and I gently touched Ana's hand. She kept her back to him, which I thought was odd. I stood and stared as he came to stand next to Marco. Surprisingly, he looked calm for someone whose life was depending on how generous Ana was feeling today. He didn't speak. Marco was watching Ana and I could see that he was trying to get into her mind, see if what she was thinking and what she would be saying were consistent. He was shit out of luck. Ana placed her palms on the mantel and stood hovering over the fire, still not turning to face Patric. He was staring at her, his eyes intense and bright.

"Tell me the truth Patric," Ana spoke quietly and evenly, "and don't you dare lie to me; I don't care who's in the room."

"What do you want to know Ana?" Patric's tone matched hers, but there was a slight edge to it, something dark and very sad.

"Did you try to set me up that night we went to dinner? Was that the whole reason for me coming to that ranch was so that you could assess how strong my powers were so that I could help you kill Carlo, because you needed me?" Her voice was strong. I held my breath. Truly, I was pulling for Patric at this moment. Perhaps Ana had rubbed off on me; perhaps I too wanted to believe that people would make different choices, better choices.

"Yes," Patric spoke and I exhaled. Shit. I watched Ana's body. It trembled once then steadied. I wanted to go to her and hold her, but that's not what she needed. She kept her back turned.

"You know what's funny?" she said, her voice a bit higher and tighter than usual.

"What Ana?" Patric studied her.

"You've never believed in yourself Patric. I mean, yes you were always confident, overconfident, which to me is just a sign of insecurity, but you never saw yourself the way I did. You didn't need me at all. You didn't need my powers for anything. You could have done this on your own without me because you are strong and you are smart and you are talented; you didn't need me. But here's the even bigger kicker." She took a deep breath and I could see she was struggling. She turned around slowly and I watched their eyes meet. It took my breath away to see the intensity in their gazes. "I would have helped you Patric. I would have helped you because seeing you alive was truly the best gift, the most beautiful thing for my heart to bear witness to; I would have helped you had you just asked. I would always have helped you; you know this. I told you that night that we went to see Nathanial when he was dying and I had to save him; I told you—I told you then that I would have done the very same for you...always

Patric, always I would have saved you." Ana's voice choked and her body started to shake. I swallowed; she was in hell. " You put my life in the hands of someone who had the potential to kill me. He almost raped me Patric and you have the nerve to tell me time and time again that you love me, that you are in love with me, that you want to offer me a life and happiness and peace. Well how can any of that be true? How could you spend day after day with me pretending? Even after Carlo's death, you stood by my side and declared your love for me. We spent the night together and I told you that I loved you and I told you just how important you have always been to me even after that night in my room, after Nathanial left, after you took what you wanted from me and you left me alone and bleeding—I forgave you. I defended you. I grieved for you when I thought you had died. I don't understand." This was heartbreaking for me witness; the extent of Ana's pain was now so tangible there was no way that a single soul in that room could not feel her devastation. She continued and I watched as she moved closer to him. "Is it me? I mean, is there something inheritably wrong with me that made both you and Nathanial think that killing me was a good plan? Well let me tell you something Patric, both you and Nathanial seem to be misinformed about how to go about killing someone. Between the two of you, between what I had to endure with your brother and all that I had to endure with you, both of you have already killed me many times over." She was shaking and I felt all the air leave my chest upon hearing those words. She studied Patric as he bowed his head and I could see that he wanted to speak; Ana knew as well. "I don't want you to say a single word, not one word. I don't want you to explain or to try to tell me why you felt compelled to betray me; it doesn't matter. After everything that we've been through Patric, after everything that you and I have seen and done together, after both of us have grieved for Nathanial; there is not a single thing you can say to me now that will ever make any of what you have done, make sense. I can't even wrap my head around it and yet it seems familiar somehow..." she trailed off, her voice distant. "Did you know about the explosion Patric? Were you behind killing all of those people and almost killing me and Stephen and Cillian?" I looked at Patric and his body was shaking. Christ, I didn't have to kill him; he'd done that all by himself. Patric raised his head and stared at me. "Patric?" Ana moved to stand closer to him, her hands behind her back, she reminded me of Liam.

"Yes Ana." Patric met her gaze and for the second time, I witnessed Ana's body tremble. I was pretty sure she was going into shock.

"Because you were angry? Because you were angry with me for not answering your letter? Because I didn't come to you like you asked? You killed innocent people, took innocent lives, almost took my life, because you were angry?" Her voice rose.

"I wasn't going to let you die Ana or Stephen," Patric spoke quietly and I heard Ana growl lowly, I stood.

"Oh, well how very kind of you Patric; what do I owe you for that?" Ana moved a step closer and I saw Liam mirror her stride; he was nervous. "Jesus, Micah was right about you. You're a child, a brat and I'm really struggling to see how what you did isn't so different than what Nathanial did." Ana threw up her hands and tiny blue sparks ignited on her fingertips.

"The difference is Ana, that I would never harm –" Ana cut Patric off.

"BUT YOU DID HARM ME PATRIC!" she screamed. "HOW ARE YOU NOT SEEING THIS? CARLO ALMOST KILLED ME!" She was in his face now. Patric was shaking his head, tears streaming down his face.

"It wasn't supposed to happen like that; things went wrong…" He gasped and I saw Ana's jaw drop.

"THEY WENT WRONG? THEY WENT WRONG PATRIC? ARE YOU HEARING YOURSELF?" My whole body tensed with her pain, her anger. I hadn't seen Ana this intensely upset since Nathanial's death; she was beside herself, she was hurting so very much it was soul shattering. She took his hand and placed it over her heart. It was an odd gesture. "Do you feel that Patric? Do you feel that? That's my heart; it stopped beating the day I saw you die. It stopped as I buried my face into the ashes of what I thought were the remains of your body. Do you feel it? It started to beat again the day I saw you in Argentina alive. Do you feel it? It stopped again when Carlo bit me and it stopped again before we arrived here today. My heart has always beat for you Patric, from that very first night in my room, to right now; it still beats for you because I love you and because it still holds out hope that you will make a different choice, that you will honor the gift that I gave to you without you even asking. It holds on Patric, it holds on even now in this moment, it's waiting." Patric sobbed as Ana dropped his hand and stepped away; her heart tore. I felt it break and crumble. She turned to Liam and Miguel. "What do you need from me to spare his life," she said defiantly, collecting herself. "Tell me what you need so I can take my husband and my brother in-law and leave." I had never heard Ana call me her husband before; if we weren't in such a traumatic situation, I would kiss her. Miguel was gazing intently upon Ana and his stare was making me uncomfortable. He moved forward.

"I don't need to hear any more Ana. Patric will be banned from this coven for disobeying orders and for taking matters into his own hands, but his life will be spared." Miguel's eyes did not leave Ana's face.

"I have your word?" She stared him down and I saw her eyes flash and tiny embers ignited in their depths. Miguel took a small step backward.

"Yes Ana, you have my word." Wonderment crossed his face. If he only knew what Ana was capable of I thought, smiling to myself. Ana looked to Liam for confirmation and he nodded.

"Fine." She moved and stood in front of my position on the couch. She offered me her hand. "Let's go." I held her close as we stood in the center of the room. "I've always loved you Patric," Ana spoke quietly. "I've always believed in you. You have a chance again to make things right with your life. I don't know what else I can say or do for you anymore. You betrayed me and while I truly believe that you do love me, you have devalued that love and friendship we shared. I will always be grateful to you for giving me the very best parts of yourself, but you have also shown me your very worst; still…I forgive you," Ana whispered. "I forgive you Patric and because of that… I will not break our Bond." She fingered her amulet that was now glowing bright blue in the center. She bowed her head and she shimmered us away.

Ana

It was after five when we arrived back at the house and I was hungry and exhausted. I didn't want to talk. I grabbed a bowl of cereal, ate and then changed into my sweats and curled up in bed. Stephen was kind enough to leave me alone for a while. I closed my eyes and tried to pretend that it had all been a dream, that everything that happened with Nathanial, that everything with Carlo and Patric, even all the craziness with Stephen, that it was all a very bizarre dream. The only thing that I wanted to be real was my love for Stephen and his love for me... that had to be true. I closed my eyes tighter and swallowed, shaking my head back and forth trying to clear the memories, all the memories from my head and my heart. Nathanial's face appeared in the darkness and for just a moment I reached out trying to touch him; his image swirled and faded and I began to cry.

Stephen

I was worrying my wedding band and Liam was pouring us some drinks.

"How is she?" he asked, handing me a scotch. I nodded and sipped slowly.

501

"I don't know, she's sleeping. I think she's emotionally drained. She was thinking about Nathanial a bit when we got home." I said resting my head back on the sofa.

"I had hoped it wasn't true," Liam said quietly, running his hands through his hair.

"Me too," I said.

"I was proud of you today." Liam smiled and stared at my face.

"Oh really?" I asked sarcastically.

"Yes, really," he said, coming to join me on the couch.

"Why?" I closed my eyes.

"Because I know how difficult it was for you to hear some of the things Ana had to say today; it would have been hard for anyone Stephen, but especially for you." Liam turned to look at me.

"Why especially for me?"

"Because you love her so very much and she was in so much pain today; it was palpable." Liam shook his head.

"You felt it too?" I said, remembering how it had filled the room so rapidly, sucking the very breath from my body.

"I'm sorry that you had to cut your honeymoon short. Maybe you can take another trip here in a few months, finish seeing some of the places on Ana's list," he mused. I leaned forward staring at him.

"By the way, the next time you feel the need to call at eight in the morning, do a little mental reconnaissance and just make sure it's appropriate, will you?" I said, remembering what Ana and I had been in the middle of experiencing when he interrupted us today. He laughed.

"You better get home, possible make-up session might be a good way to take her mind off of today, it works for me." He chuckled and I left immediately. The smell of burning eggs greeted me as I landed at home. I frowned and walked into the kitchen. Ana was standing over the stove looking quite perplexed. She turned and pouted.

"I wanted an omelet, but I couldn't get the eggs to fold right and I burned the bottom and now the pan is all charred." She held up my sauté pan and sure enough it was now so black that you couldn't even see the silver-plating beneath. I cringed and then smiled, taking the pan from her and throwing it in the recycling bin. "Well that sucks. It was a nice pan." She frowned. "I'm sorry." I pulled out a chair and motioned for her sit down. I opened the window and placed another pan on the burner and set to making her some dinner. "You haven't had much in the way of nourishment lately." She held a piece of kiwi in her hand. I had restocked my supply of blood thanks to Cillian and I was using that until...until Ana felt like going down that road again with me; I couldn't remember the last time I had taken from her, it had been awhile.

"I'm fine," I said, stirring the eggs and adding in onions, tomatoes, spinach and olives. "Do you want any meat in this?" I asked, trying not to think about Ana's blood.

503

"No thanks," she said and I could feel her eyes on me. "Hey," she spoke from the table. I turned staring at her. "I'm sorry about today. I mean, I'm sorry that you had to sit there and listen to me say that I loved Patric, but you know it's not the same thing right? You have to know that now?" Her voice sounded slightly urgent as if she was desperate to convince me just how much she loved me. I folded my arms across my chest.

"You don't need to apologize to me Ana. You needed to say those things to him and he needed to hear them, and yes I know that you love me and I know that you will always love Patric and that you will always love Nathanial, that's just one of the qualities that makes you so extraordinary; you have very bad taste in men, the worst of any woman I have ever met." I laughed and she glared at me.

"So that would make you a very bad choice then." She stood and came to hug me close.

"A very bad choice indeed." I tugged on her ponytail. I finished her omelet and sat next to her while she ate.

"So do we really have to wait until my birthday to try the whole Change thing?" She sipped her water.

"I thought you weren't in a hurry?" I kissed her hand and took her plate over to the sink.

"Hey, are you ever going to tell me what the surprise is, you know with those papers?" Her mind was all over the place.

"Uh...yes.," I replied. I was debating on whether to tell her after her transition or before. Liam had suggested that I tell her as an Afterlife birthday present. I had thought that was bizarre and stupid, but now it seemed like a nice idea.

"When?" she pressed. "Oh, you know what?" My god, I couldn't keep up with her tonight, she was slightly manic.

"What?" I loaded the dishwasher trying not to laugh.

"We should take Lucie back out sailing this summer, maybe in May, give Liam and Carmen another summer of alone time," she said and I could hear the smile in her voice.

"What about our alone time?" I said, hoping to get her to focus on just one thing this evening, us. I closed the dishwasher and turned to see her grinning. She rose from her seat and came to put her arms around my neck. I stared into her eyes. I hoped she was doing ok; it was such a god-awful day for her today and she still wasn't letting me into her mind. "Hey," I said hesitatingly as she started to kiss me.

"Mmm?" She moved her mouth gently against mine and I had to concentrate on what I wanted to ask.

"How are you Ana?" She pulled back.

"I'm good." She took a deep breath and stepped back twisting her ponytail in her hands. "I mean, I guess I feel a bit numb and sad and disappointed and all the usual stuff that I've been feeling over these last several years; it's not really anything new." She frowned. "But I also don't want to let what happened ruin the life that I have with you now. It's not fair to you or to me. What Patric did, it was…it was beyond belief and I guess if I really gave myself time to feel all of those emotions, I would probably fall apart, but it's not necessary for me to

505

do that now. Falling apart doesn't change what happened. It doesn't make Patric able to have made a different choice and it just takes away all of the energy that I could be putting towards continuing to heal from all the other crap that's occurred; this was just an added bonus." She shook her head and sighed.

"Hmm...so what's with you and the growling?" I eyed her smiling slightly.

"What?" She pursed her lips.

"The growling. You growled at Saden and then today you really growled at Juan, right before you lunged at him. Since when do you do that?" It was an interesting trait that I had noticed the first time in South Africa and I thought it was an odd reaction for a Human to be able to access. Then today, her energy behind her growl was so intense and vicious that it had given me chills; she sounded like a vampire.

"Oh. Well, it sometimes happens I guess; when I get mad, it just sort of comes out." She pushed her bottom lip out frowning. "You scolded me!" She laughed and pointed her finger.

"No I didn't," I replied. *Had* I scolded her?

"Yes you did. You pulled me off of Juan and then you told me to 'stop it'! You scolded me!" Her eyes widened and flashed. I chuckled.

"Ahh...yes I did, but I would hardly consider it a scolding, more of a preventative mediation, if you will." I pulled her back into my arms. "Plus, I would have much preferred you'd gone after Miguel than Juan."

"I know, what's with the two of you?" She kissed my cheek.

"I beat him in a fight," I said, kissing her forehead.

"Why didn't you kill him? Isn't that what you do?" She kissed my nose.

"Um, not all the time," I said, feeling slightly uncomfortable; I didn't want Ana thinking that I was some murderous being who just killed for sport, at least not most of the time. I kissed her ear.

"Oh. Well he should be thankful and not such a prick." She kissed my neck. All of this subtle physicality between us was getting me worked up.

"I don't think it works like that." I spoke as I moved my lips over her throat; the scent and the feel of her blood throbbing were making my mouth water uncontrollably. Oddly, I felt another rush of hormones flood through my body. I thought I had come to the end of whatever mating crap that I had been experiencing, but apparently not; my body was tensing again as Ana moaned softly. Now I had to contend with both of my addictions, her blood and her body. I had no idea if Ana was feeling comfortable with us engaging in the more violent intimacies that my bloodlust tended to bring out, but that's where we were headed if I didn't stop things. Every muscle and tendon in my body tensed with desire and I clenched my jaw as she pressed herself against me. "Ana," I said, gently pushing her back. I cleared my throat.

"What's wrong?" she said, staring at me. I felt my teeth shift and the colors in the room began to change, shit. I bowed my head and looked down, not wanting to frighten her. She lifted my head and our eyes met, mine now fully transformed, the pupils vertical and the color

507

glowing. "Oh." She stared and then smiled. "Feeling a bit frisky are we?" She laughed and I raised my eyebrows at her, slightly incredulous with her reaction. Ana grabbed my hand and pulled me out of the kitchen and down the hall. I shook my head; she was a dream come true. I took a deep breath not wanting to come at her with too much force. She hadn't taken from me in a while and I wondered if that were something she would want to do. I wanted her to have my blood; it was an intoxicating experience. Ana was amazingly adept at biting; again, an odd talent for a Human even one as uniquely skilled as Ana. She was slowly removing her clothes and I watched in awe as she undid her hair and stood before me in a very erotic bra and underwear combination. My teeth pushed through and I let myself fully transform. She moved to take my hands, wrapping them around her waist. Ana stared at me intently, as my breath became shallow. She traced her fingers along my mouth and I bit down on one of her fingers, sucking the blood slowly from the tip. The sudden influx was like heroin to my system; I had been in withdrawal and now my body was getting what it craved and what it needed. I licked up and down each of her fingers, biting them in turn. My body began to tremble and tense as the blood mixed with the hormones. It was like nothing that I had ever experienced before; the feelings were almost too powerful and too intense for me to handle and I had to stop for a minute and try to catch my breath. I gasped softly and pulled her close, panting in my anticipation. She swept her hair to one side revealing the soft skin of her neck and her scent released. I groaned loudly. I pushed her back onto the bed and hovered above her. She arched her back so that our hips were slowly grinding against each other.

"Ana, is this ok? Do you want me to do this?" I asked, my voice low and rough and changed. She smoothed my hair and touched my face gently.

"I would love for you to do this Stephen." She smiled. I exhaled and bent my head low; for some reason I felt like going slow. I wanted to savor this moment between us and I wanted to make it passionate and sensual for her; it didn't need to be rough or violent. I wanted to take from her as I moved inside of her gently. At least that was my intention. I rose up, taking off my shirt and pants and shuddering as she ran her hands over my bare chest and stomach. I slid off her bra and underwear and laid her back against the pillows kissing over her body. She sighed softly. We stared at each other as I gently pushed myself between her legs and felt how perfect she was, how perfect we fit together. I closed my eyes as my body surged with both of its wants, blood and body. I could have them both. I bent my head pressing my mouth to her neck and grazed the flesh as I thrust slowly. She groaned softly in my ear. I felt the first rush of blood pass over my lips and Ana gasped and so did I. She tasted different. Not bad different, but unbelievably, overwhelmingly delicious. Her flavor was sweet, but also rich, luscious and spicy. Ana's blood had always been my weakness and her flavor had always provided me with the taste of something otherworldly, but now, for some reason, I was beyond myself in what I was experiencing. My mouth watered fully and I pushed harder inside of her as I plunged my teeth deeper into her neck. I took and took and took as I thrust faster and harder between her legs. I was drinking so much that my body was shaking from pleasure and energy. Ana was gasping and moaning and I sucked harder, pulling as much blood from her as I possibly could. I came over

509

and over again, each release getting more violent and rough. I pushed her head to the other side and bit her again, tearing the new flesh and letting the heat of fresh blood fill my mouth. I moved my tongue in rhythm with my hips, pushing in and out and back and forth wanting Ana to come. Her body was coated in sweat and I licked that up as well, mixing the flavorings together. I growled as I released again. Ana dug her fingers into my back and I knew she was close. I wanted more friction so I picked her up and lowered her to the floor. She moaned as I pulled her blood and pushed myself forcefully against her.

"Stephen," she whispered. I couldn't pull away from her neck; I was feeding fully now, something that I had never done with Ana. "Stephen." She groaned. "I want you to do it now; I want you to Change me now." She spoke in my ear. That got my attention.

"What?" I breathed heavily, my lips dripping and my hips pulsing.

"I want you to Change me, to make me half. I want you do it now." She stared at me; her eyes were on fire.

"Ana." I groaned and licked up her spilling blood. "That's…I don't know if I can." I was so engaged in what was happening, I would need to really concentrate on not making the full transition; it was very difficult to turn someone half. I slowed my movements and hovered over her.

"Please." She touched my lips and kissed me deeply. "Please Stephen." She pressed her fingers into my back and brought my face down to her neck. I tasted her blood and I tasted my blood; they were one in her system now and had been since that night at Carlo's; our own unique blending of everything that we both were and are. "Stephen," she whispered again and I steadied myself.

"Are you sure Ana? Are you sure this is what you want?" I kissed her neck and I could feel a different surge start to swell deep within my body; my venom was rising, churning—it wanted to be released.

"Yes. I love you and I want you to do this." Her scent was now filling the room and I started to move deep within her. I groaned in pleasure.

"God Ana; I want you to be mine. I want you so badly, are you sure?" I asked again as I thrust and ground against her on the floor. She arched her back high as I felt her come against me. She gasped and moaned and called my name. I opened my mouth and pressed my lips against her flesh, feeling my teeth become slick and coated with venom. My blood rose to the surface of my lips and it slowly released itself through the skin. I growled deep as I pushed, wanting her again. I wanted her so much. I braced myself against her and held her down. She was still grinding me inside her. "Ana, stop moving," I whispered in her ear. I waited for her to climax again and then come down. I closed my eyes, filled my mouth with her blood and then bit down, releasing my venom deep inside her veins. My body rocked and I gasped and suddenly I came. I came so violently that I stopped breathing and the only sounds were of my simultaneous releases; venom and desire. Ana sucked in a sharp breath and I felt her body convulse as the poison entered her system. I pushed deeper into her veins and felt a wall burst inside my body; I couldn't stop, couldn't stop sucking her blood and I couldn't stop the surge of my own blood and venom. I groaned loudly and forced myself to pull away; Ana heaved once, then her body remained still under mine.

511

Chapter Nineteen

Stephen

My head was in my hands. I had Changed Ana completely; I knew it. I could feel it when it was happening and there wasn't anything I could do to stop it. My body wasn't my own. It wanted her, it needed her and I was out of control. She was so cold and pale and she wasn't breathing. She hadn't even screamed or thrashed; her blood didn't release through her skin. I had never seen anything like what happened to her. She looked dead. I heard the door open as Liam entered the room, his face stoic and curious.

"Would you like to explain how this happened? I thought you had agreed to wait so that you could take your time, you could make sure things were done correctly, Stephen." Liam lowered his eyes to gaze upon my face. I ran my hands through my hair.

"It just happened Liam; I don't know, it just happened." I wasn't sure if he needed to know exactly the circumstances of how things transpired. Liam sighed.

"Was it an accident?" He frowned and stared at Ana.

"No."

"Did she ask you to Change her while you were together?" he asked and I knew he understood exactly what we'd been doing.

"Yes."

"Well, there's not much we can do about it now. You think you gave her too much venom?" He stared across the bed at me.

"I'm not sure. It felt…it felt out of control and it just kept flowing out of me." I sighed and took Ana's hand; it was icy.

"Is that what happened to you the last time you tried to Change her after Carlo? Were the feelings similar?" Liam touched Ana lightly on the cheek.

"No," I said emphatically. They weren't even close to the same kind of experiences. This came out of so much passion and love and need to be a part of her and the last time, that was to keep her from leaving me forever, to save her life or give her a chance at a new one; that was done out of complete and utter despair and terror. Liam nodded.

"We'll just have to wait," he replied. "When she wakes up we'll test her blood for coloring; it should come out red then change to black, if she's half…all black if she's whole," he said quietly. I swallowed. I felt sick and guilty and I just wanted her to be ok. I wanted her to just be Ana again. Liam patted my shoulder. "She will always be your Ana, Stephen and she has a family now to help her get through whatever she may be facing. She'll find her resilience and she will thrive just like she's always done throughout her entire life; that *is* Ana." I grasped my brother's hand tightly.

"Thank you." He nodded and left me in the dark alone… waiting.

Ana

Oh my god, I was so tired. I felt like I had been sleeping for years. Apparently the events with Patric had taken their toll. My body must have just collapsed and needed to rest. I stretched or at least I tried to stretch. My muscles felt like jello, wobbly and weak. Crap! Was I sick? I didn't feel sick. I felt tight and achy like I did after a really hard workout, but I didn't feel sick. I took a deep breath and opened my eyes. Stephen was sitting in a chair by the bed and his eyes were open, but they weren't moving; he was zoned out. Maybe I *had* been sick or not feeling well or something; wouldn't I remember? I tried to shift but my body collapsed back on itself and I gasped; I was so weak. A heavy darkness penetrated the room and there seemed to be a dull haze filtering in the air. I rubbed my eyes; the haze didn't disappear. I tried to turn my head, but my neck felt wobbly, like it wasn't attached to my spinal cord. Why was I in bed and Stephen wasn't with me? Why was he sitting in a chair? My mind felt heavy, like I was trying to process things behind some veil or mist. I wondered if I should wake him up; he didn't look particularly comfortable. I took a deep breath and tried to reach my hand out to touch his leg. Immediately upon making contact with his body, tiny sparks shot out from my fingertips and Stephen startled, jumping up from the chair.

"Ana!" He looked at me, but I was staring at my hand, my left hand. My ring was ablaze in a brilliant glow and the three tiny jewels that had appeared after the explosion were twinkling deep within the metal universe that was my wedding band. I turned my eyes back to Stephen and glanced down at his hand. His ring was also ignited, pulsing strong

514

and bright through the dark. His glow was a beautiful sea-blue color, mine a silver illumination like the moon. "Ana," he whispered and moved to hold me against him. "Ana." He began kissing me gently on the cheeks. I felt my skin warm from his touch. "How do you feel?" he asked softly as he lay me gently back against the pillows.

"Uh...I feel mushy," I said. That was the only way I could describe how my body was currently feeling; I felt mushy. "Was I sick or something?" I asked, trying to pull my knees up as they kept falling straight. Stephen frowned and reached to turn on the tiny bedside lamp. The sudden influx of light made my eyes sting and I shut them.

"Mushy?" he asked, his tone sounded worried.

"Uh huh." I rubbed my eyes again; the haze was still there. "And I can't see that well," I said. "Did I get sick?" I asked again. Just then the door opened and Liam entered the room. That couldn't be good. Liam laughed softly. Stephen turned to him.

"She says she feels mushy." He raised his eyebrows. "And she can't see very well." Stephen then stood and whispered something to Liam, which I heard quite clearly.

"Don't remember what?" I asked, picking up on their conversation. They both turned to stare at me. "What don't I remember?" I was getting nervous. Had Patric done something to me? Liam came and sat on my bed.

"Ana, what's the last thing that you remember?" Liam asked as he pulled open my eyes wide and shown a light over them; I cringed and pulled away.

"Well, I remember that I don't like people shining bright lights in my eyes Liam," I said, rubbing my eyes for the third time. He chuckled.

"Beyond that?" he said putting the light away and taking out a small needle. I eyed him.

"I remember seeing Patric and telling him stuff; I remember coming home and eating a bowl of cereal and getting into bed and I remember burning Stephen's nice omelet pan and I remember talking to him…" My mind was racing as hundreds of images came rushing forward. It was so sudden that I had to steady myself against the onslaught of memories. "Uh…we kissed and then…" I saw a very graphic image of Stephen and I on the bed and on the floor moving roughly against one another and I saw him taking blood from me… and I saw me talking to him. I was asking him something, something important. My breathing became rapid as I flipped through the pictures in my head. "I asked you something." I looked at Stephen, trying to hear the conversation in my mind. I saw him take a deep breath, exhale and then plunge his mouth into my throat…Holy shit! I gasped and my eyes widened. "OH!" I cried out. "OH, YOU CHANGED ME!" I pointed at Stephen accusatorially. "That's why I'm in bed; that's why I feel mushy! You Changed me!" Stephen looked reproachful.

"Um Ana, with all due respect love, you asked me to Change you." He bowed his head and looked up from under the thick frame of his eyelashes.

"YES, I DID AND YOU LISTENED TO ME!" I had no idea why I was shouting. I wasn't angry, but I was suddenly hyper. Suddenly I started laughing hysterically. Liam turned and looked at Stephen. Then I

516

started crying then laughing again; my emotions were all over the place. Liam waved his hand gently over my heart and I instantly felt my body and mind calm; the pictures in my head drifted and I settled back in the bed. "Sorry," I murmured.

"It's quite alright Ana; it's to be expected. I just need to check something. May I have your finger?" I raised my left arm. "HOLY SHIT!" I shouted and Liam jumped. My scar on my wrist was gone. Nathanial's scar was gone. The skin was smooth and unblemished. I held it up to Liam. "LOOK!" I shouted again. Jesus, what was wrong with me; I was totally spastic. Liam swallowed.

"I see Ana, that's…that's really amazing." Liam laughed and I heard Stephen snort loudly. I frowned—I thought it was amazing and weird that I didn't have that as part of my body anymore. I started to cry. Stephen came and put his arms around me.

"I'm ok really." I sniffed. I looked at Stephen as another wave of mania hit. "HEY! DID YOU SEE YOUR RING?" I shouted. Stephen jumped as I looked at the silver band on his finger. I tried to speak quietly. "Did you see it glow?" Stephen's eyes widened and he looked at Liam.

"What the hell's wrong with her?" he asked. Liam chuckled.

"Nothing; you were the same way, except you thought you were ready to fight anyone and everyone; it was too bad that your muscles hadn't rebuilt yet when you decided to try to take me on." Liam eyed Stephen.

"Oh, that's why I'm mushy?" I asked and Liam nodded.

"Give it a few weeks." Liam smiled and Stephen stared. "Your finger Ana?" I gave Liam my hand and he pricked it quickly smearing a few drops of blood onto a thin slide. I couldn't make out the color; it looked like it was red or black, the haze was still in my eyes. I watched intently as Liam stood and motioned for Stephen to follow him into the hallway. I frowned.

"You know I can hear you!" I called as I pulled the covers up over me and sunk back down into the bed, waiting for them to return. I felt Stephen bend his head low next to my head.

"Oh I know you can hear us; even half-vampires get pretty decent hearing." I pulled my head out from under the quilt.

"REALLY?" I shouted again and Stephen laughed. "I'm half?" I tried to calm my voice.

"So it appears," Liam said.

"WHAT-DOES-THIS-MEAN?" My voice was so loud. "Sorry," I whispered. "What does this mean?" I asked quietly.

"You'll go through a bit of healing process. It will be much shorter than if you were fully like us, but a process nonetheless. You will need to recondition your body a bit; it's been weakened considerably and the more you can do during the rebuilding process, the stronger you will be. You will also need to learn how to control the different sides of yourself Ana. You can access your vampire side when need be, but it can come out even if you get the least bit upset or excited. All the powers you had before should still be in tact, but they too may need a bit of reconditioning; they will most certainly be stronger and it will take some practice learning to harness those capabilities. You don't need blood to survive, although you may find yourself craving it from time to time; while it may be uncomfortable to experience, it's certainly not intolerable and Lucie seems to do just fine. This is a journey just like anything else in your life and it will take some setbacks and some frustrations until you can start to see some adjustment and adaptability. You must be patient with yourself and know that we are all here to help and support you." Liam smiled and I nodded, my eyes wide. He laughed. "Oh and the haze will lift in a few days." He stood. "And your emotions will also level off, although they tend to emulate your true nature without the constraint that our pasts and our own burdens tend to suppress in us over time. Perhaps this amount of…joy, shall we say, is more truer to form for you." He laughed. I nodded.

"Right on," I said. Liam shook his head and turned to Stephen.

"Have fun," he said. "Oh and we'd like to have a little celebratory dinner for you at some point, if that's acceptable?" Liam asked.

"What are we celebrating?" I asked, rubbing my eyes. Stephen pulled my hand away gently. Liam looked surprised.

"You haven't told her yet?" he asked, staring at Stephen.

"Uh no, but thanks for bringing it up Liam." Stephen shook his head.

"Told me what?" I looked back and forth between them. "What?" Stephen sighed.

"I'll tell you later love." He smiled and I frowned. Liam laughed and then nodded to both of us and left us alone. Stephen came to sit next to me on the bed. "How are you truly, Ana?" His tone was serious and I tried to match his mood.

"Truly, I am pretty good. I mean besides the mania and the mushiness, I feel normal. Will you workout with me when I feel better?" I asked, laying my head on his shoulder, my neck lulling to the side. Stephen laughed and propped me up.

"As soon as you can hold your own head up, we'll hit the gym," he said and I turned my face to kiss him. I pulled back stunned.

"Oh my god," I said, kissing him again, this time full on the mouth. "You taste so good! Have you always tasted like this?" I asked, not caring for him to answer. I was trying to move to so that I could bring him down on top of me, but my body wasn't cooperating. Stephen cleared his throat.

"Hmm…why thank you Ana. Why don't we just go slow for a bit until you get your strength back?" His eyes flashed. I wondered if it would be a different experience making love with my new heightened senses; it would probably be overwhelming like it always was when we were together. I stared at him and I saw images of us appearing in his mind. We were on this bed, but we were fully engaged in having sex and his pictures were really graphic. I laughed, but I was also now, really turned on.

"You want to have sex right now!" I laughed and tried to maneuver my body so that I could lie back.

"What?" he asked, dumbfounded.

"I saw what you were thinking just now and you were picturing us right here!" I said, grinning coyly at him. He cleared his throat again.

"Hmm...well we're just going to have to wait for a bit," he said, leaning over and smoothing my hair back.

"Why?" I asked as a sudden swell of passion crashed over me and I tried not to gasp in pleasure. Stephen eyed me.

"Because you're mushy." He joked. I bit my lip.

"So. I'm more likely to let you have control," I said, my voice changing. Stephen's eyes grew wide.

"Um, that may be love, but really wouldn't you rather wait to experience things when you are feeling stronger?" He moved to pull back and I grabbed his shirt, kissing him with a violence that I didn't think my body was capable of expressing. He gasped and I groaned savoring how delicious he tasted. "Ana, I feel like I'd be taking advantage of you." Stephen breathed heavily as I traced my tongue over his lips.

"I want you to take advantage of me." I exhaled softly into his mouth and he groaned.

"Jesus Ana." He kissed me back and I could feel his barriers breaking down. I wasn't feeling weak anymore; I was feeling powerful, wonderfully powerful and I wanted him in the very worst way. I wanted him urgently and my body was surging with pleasure and desire and need. I felt hungry for him. "Ana!" Stephen heard my thoughts and he tore off my shirt and ran his fingers between my legs. I moaned as he caressed me deeply. My body was overheating and I relished in the pleasure he was giving me. I pushed his hand away and moved him so he knew what I wanted. "God Ana." He gasped and started to lower himself down the length of my body. He pushed my legs wide and I felt his tongue enter me. He pushed back and forth and I thrust against his mouth, my body dictating what I wanted and needed. Everything was happening with so much force, so much desperation, it was intoxicating. He pulled and teased and he held me off until so much desire had built that I screamed for him to let me come. He did and I gasped as he kept me overflowing with my release. I exhaled and immediately my body felt replenished, renewed. Stephen was breathing hard and trying to recover from my onslaught of physicality. He pulled himself back up next to me and stared, wide eyed.

"Sorry," I murmured, stretching and flexing my limbs; they were already feeling less mushy. He was still staring. I kissed him softly and pulled him down next to me. "You ok over there?" I asked, laughing quietly.

"I think so." Stephen took a deep breath and rubbed his face. "That was interesting." He laughed, still staring at me.

"Oh please, that was nothing!" I said, ruffling his hair. "You do that sort of thing to me all the time!" I was now laughing really hard.

"It's different when you do it," he said, smiling slightly.

"Why?" I asked, biting my lip.

"Because of who you are and how you move and feel and *taste*—it's different." His eyes filled with emotion and I stared deep into his eyes.

I could have stared at him for hours or days or months, but I was suddenly hungry. Stephen grinned. "Can you stand?" he asked. My legs felt a bit weak, but not from my muscles being mushy; they were weak from him. He shook his head. "Try being me for once," he said, pulling me gently to the edge of the bed. He shook his head, still overcome by the suddenness and ferocity of our coupling. I stood, leaning on his shoulder. My legs felt ok, wobbly, but ok. I walked down the hall to the kitchen not quite trusting my own strength. He pulled out a chair and watched me as I carefully lowered myself. He turned to the fridge. "Well, we have cereal and cereal; I'm afraid we are in dire need of a trip to the shops my dear." He turned back to me, his hands on his hips.

"I like cereal," I said.

"Good thing." He laughed and pulled a bowl down from the cabinet and handed me the box and the milk. I munched quietly for a while feeling slightly giddy and high. I kept staring at my left wrist. "Ana?" Stephen had been watching me.

"Hmm?" I poured another bowl.

"Are you ok?" His tone was soft and his eyes sparkled.

"Yeah; I guess it's just weird that I don't have…I mean I don't have anything left…." My voice suddenly choked and I swallowed. "It's just weird that's all." I chewed slowly.

"He's in your heart Ana; he'll always be in your heart. You don't need metals or stone or jewels or even scars to remember Nathanial and to remember how much he loved you and how you loved him. He's with you, always." Stephen held my hand and I nodded blinking back some tears.

"So when do I get my surprise?" I asked, steadying the upsurge of emotions in my chest.

"Ahh...yes well, how about next week sometime? Give you a chance to rest a bit and then we'll go." My eyes narrowed.

"We're going somewhere?" I asked, finishing my cereal.

"Uh yeah, sort of." He smiled sheepishly. I shrugged.

"Ok. What should we do now?" I put my bowl in the sink and washed it quickly. I blinked. "Hey, the haze is gone!" I tried not to yell.

"Well that's great!" Stephen mocked me and I stuck my tongue out. "Classy," he replied. "Why don't we go for a walk?" He stood and offered me his hand.

"Classy," I said and I reached up to kiss him.

Stephen

If I didn't know Ana better, I would have guessed she was on crack. She was bouncing off the walls and I couldn't get her to focus to save my life. Cillian wasn't helping either. We were all at the gym and he kept encouraging her behavior by mocking me; it was like trying to wrangle in a bunch of children. Lucie would have been better

524

behaved. I was trying to get Ana to work on building her strength. Bizarrely, she didn't seem to need any help; she was insanely strong, so much so that she'd managed to throw me clear across the gym in one hit, slamming me up against the wall and blurring to me in seconds to level me to the ground. I was so stunned by her force and speed that I didn't even see it coming; that was a dangerous talent. Cillian was whooping and hollering from the side of the ropes as Ana and I stood toe-to-toe in the center of ring.

"Cillian shut it!" I yelled and held up my gloved hands. Just as I turned to look back to her, Ana decked me clear across the face with a right hook. I hit the mat and she started wailing away on my head with blows so powerful that I had to grab her arms and toss her off more violently than I wanted, but she was beating the shit out of me. "Ana Sofia Tessatore! You cannot sucker punch someone young lady!" I scolded her as she lay flat on her back. Cillian was booing.

"Ya do mate!" Cillian called from the side.

"Not helping asshole!" I said, waiting for Ana to get up. "Are you alright?" I asked, suddenly concerned that I may have hurt her; she was still part Human.

"You just don't like losing; you're a sore loser!' she said, getting to her feet. "I could kick your ass before and I can kick your ass now and you're a sore loser!" She pressed her glove into my stomach. I heard the music crank louder.

"Go again Ana; kick him in da balls!" Cillian yelled from the stereo. Ana nodded.

"Let's go. Winner gets anything they want in bed!" She smirked and I shook my head; yeah, she was on crack. I nodded and met her in the center. Cillian rang the bell and Ana rose from the ground and kicked me square in the chest, I grabbed her foot, spinning her rapidly and landing on top of her.

"This could all be over very quickly," I whispered as she tried to flip me off. Her ground skills needed some work. "In fact, if you tap out now, I promise to be gentle with you tonight." I growled lightly in her ear.

"Never!" she gasped as I held her down tightly. Suddenly I felt a jolt of electricity course through me, stopping me cold. Ana heaved once and sent me hurdling backward over the ropes towards the wall. I tried to stop my fall, but my body wasn't responding. She'd shocked me somehow and I couldn't move. Shit! I was going to hit the concrete at full speed. Just as I saw the wall start to meet my head, Ana was in front of me, her back pressed up against the stones. She stopped me just as we would have collided. She spun me without touching my body and held me against the wall fifty feet above the ground. "Give up," she said, her tone dark.

"What did you do to me?" I asked, eyeing her.

"Give up and I'll tell you." She laughed and hung in the air with her arms crossed over her chest; she looked terrifying and beautiful and I wanted her.

"She has ya mate! End it now or she'll have ya for dinner!" Cillian hollered from the ground. Ana moved her body close to mine and she bent her head to my ear.

"Give up now and I will wear anything you pick out for me and I might even consider doing what it is you wanted the night of our wedding," she whispered, her breath moving softly across my skin. Jesus, there was something so intoxicating about her that it was all I could do not to take her right now; too bad I had to teach her a lesson about cockiness. I laughed and grabbed her forcefully and sent her flying back across the other side of the gym. Her body catapulted through the air and I followed right behind, leveling her to the ground with my knee. I had her.

"Ahh love, he's got ya but ya're still by far, da hottest fighter I have ever seen and ya made dis loser work for his win! Cheers lassie!" Cillian rang the bell and Ana huffed. I bent my head and kissed her gently.

"Now as far as picking out something for you to wear, I don't think that Liam's shop closes for another few hours. If we leave now we'll have plenty of time to browse *and* do what I want in bed." I laughed, took off my gloves and helped Ana to her feet.

****

Ana wasn't talking to me. I found her anger amusing, but clearly I couldn't laugh. We were standing in the middle of Liam's shop and I was looking at the items on the walls. I kept sending Carmen to the back to find more erotic assembles.

527

"You cheat!" Ana said eyeing me as I held up a pair of crotchless panties and smiled.

"I don't cheat love, I strategize. You being the practiced diplomat, I would think you would get that concept." I put the underwear on the counter next to the already large pile of items we were purchasing.

"Stephen, those don't have any crotch; they're not even underwear." She huffed.

"Easier access love." I winked as she rolled her eyes. Carmen came out from the back carrying a blood red bra and panty set—*blood* red red. Ana eyed the garments and I could tell that she liked them. Hell, I loved them. "On the counter." I pointed and Carmen laughed.

"Stephen, are you ever going to let Ana come out and play. Lucie is begging us to see you!" Carmen started wrapping up the clothing. I had been keeping Ana to myself quite a bit lately. I was enjoying helping her and answering her questions about how and why she was experiencing things with her body and her mind. I liked being there for her. Plus, Ana was insanely turned on these days. It had only been two weeks since her Change and her arousal hadn't quelled one bit. She had gone through patterns like this before, but now she was giving herself over to her instincts more and she was comfortable doing so; I was just happy to go along for the ride or to be ridden. I laughed to myself.

"Uh, hello!" Ana stared at me. "You do know that I can hear you right?" That was taking some getting used to. I smiled at her and took the bags from Carmen. "How about tomorrow night?" I asked and she eyed me. She wanted to know why I hadn't told Ana yet about her surprise. I shrugged. Carmen sighed.

"Tomorrow then." Carmen blew a kiss to Ana and we strolled out of the shop.

"I don't need all of that stuff you know. I know you were you using the excuse of me losing at the gym, to buy me things." She sighed and looked down at the full bags.

"Actually, these are all for me; they have nothing to do with you love," I said, smiling and shimmering us back to the house. We landed and immediately Ana took the bags and headed for the bedroom; I followed.

"Ok, so, what would you like for me to wear?" She pulled the tissue off and spread the lingerie out on our bed. I knew exactly what I wanted her to put on. I raised my eyebrows and pulled the blood red bra set from the pile and handed it to her. She smiled and shook her head. "I'll be right back." I watched as she went to the bathroom and shut the door and just as I sat down on the bed, I stopped. She was thinking about something, something that I hadn't even considered before and certainly not in any sexual scenarios. My arousal heated my body and I felt myself contract and grow hard; I wondered if she would ask me. She stood in the doorframe watching me as I let my eyes roam over her body. The blood red color of the fabric against her olive skin made my body clench with deep arousal. There was nothing about her or the way she looked that didn't scream sex and sensuality. I waited for her, waited for her to ask. She moved over to me and her fragrance swam through my pores igniting every ounce of self-control I had. Ana as a Human was intoxicating and addictive; Ana as a half-vampire leveled me to the most basic and primal animal instincts that I had. She pressed her body against me and lifted my shirt up over my head. My skin was burning.

"Stephen?" she purred, running her fingers over my chest and stomach, digging her nails gently into my flesh. The tiny bursts of pain made me groan in pleasure; I wanted her to draw blood.

"Yes?" I panted and I tilted my head back letting her stroke my throat with her tongue.

"I want to take from you," she whispered into my neck. I groaned. "I'm craving you." She licked the artery that was now pulsing. Ana hadn't actually been craving any blood since her transition, not any Human blood, but I had been able to sense a distinct affinity for my blood; it was in her mind a lot. "Would you like that?" Her voice had shifted and she was speaking low and rough. She pushed me back onto the bed and pulled my arms up and curled my fingers around the slats in the headboard, pinning me. I couldn't answer, my arousal was so intense that I was biting my lip trying not to release. She pressed my fingers with one hand and moved her other down between my legs. I heaved my hips, thrusting involuntarily against the heat of her palm. She was dominating me and I wanted more.

"Yes Ana, I want you to take from me." I panted as she slid my pants down slowly. She ran her fingertips up and down feeling the pulse of me and how hard I was. She moaned.

"As a Human?" she whispered and I gasped. This is what she'd wanted. She wanted to feed and to have sex in her vampire form, something she had yet to experience. My body trembled as she worked me into her mouth, pushing in and taking me out, letting me feel the heat and moisture of her tongue and her lips as she sucked deeply. I growled low and ground myself around in her mouth.

"No." I snarled as I felt myself begin to orgasm. I grunted as I came running my fingers through her hair. She ran her tongue over me, tasting my release.

"No?" Ana asked moving to lie next to me, her legs falling open and her back arched; her desire was so close, she was so aroused and I wanted again what she'd done in South Africa. I wanted to watch her come, but not as a Human. Immediately, my fags pushed through, my eyes changed and my body coursed with adrenaline, making my muscles tighter and fueling them for what I wanted. I ran my hand over her mouth and let her bite one of my fingers, letting my blood help to initiate her transition. She pulled and sucked as I nourished her. Her teeth were sharp, razor sharp, not fangs, but something close. I checked her eyes; they had shifted to the most mesmerizing color, still deep and luminous brown, but now in the center was the most startling color; a clear marine blue shone from within. She was ready. I wanted to start slow. The experience was overwhelming and I wanted her to be able to satisfy both of her hungers as much as she wanted. I moved myself over her, floating just a few inches above her body; I needed both of my hands.

"Let me guide you Ana," I whispered. "Let me show you." I kissed her deeply and I slid open her legs even more. I put my wrist to her lips and at the same time I slid my blood-coated finger as deep as I could go, fucking her with my hand. She groaned as I pushed in and out feeling her. I pressed my wrist to her mouth. "Bite Ana." I moaned. She didn't hesitate and instantly she began to feed, sucking in perfect rhythm with my finger inside of her. She pulled and released and I pushed and moved, massaging her, caressing her. I had never had another vampire take from me before and my own experience was beyond anything that I could ever imagine. My body was pulsing and shaking. I was releasing bellows of pleasure as I watched her drink from me. I wanted to see the whole thing. I shifted and guided one of her hands away from my wrist and slid it down between her legs. She groaned and her hips arched, suddenly she flipped me on my back not breaking our connection. I was stunned as I felt her mount; she drilled me hard, still feeding, still taking. I grunted in pleasure as I watched her dominate me. She pinned my one arm down and kept the other on her mouth as I cranked up the force behind my thrusts.

"Harder!" She moaned, pulling her mouth away and forcing me down into the bed. I had never been ridden like this before; it was intoxicating. "Harder Stephen!" She groaned. I didn't want to hurt her, but it seemed that the friction wasn't enough. I flipped our positions, grabbed onto the headboard, wound her fingers over the slats and proceeded to fuck her as hard and as rough as I possibly could. I heard the wood splinter under my grasp and the bed trembled beneath the violence of our coupling. My muscles surged with strength as if this is what they had wanted to do. I wound my arm under Ana's knee bringing her leg back almost to her shoulder; Christ, she was flexible and I decided at the moment to ask for what I really wanted, what I knew would make her pleasure so unfathomably spectacular that she might always want it to be this way.

"Ana." I panted as we thrust powerfully against each other. My fingers began circling her rear, feeling the tight ring of muscles contract. "I can make the penetration what you need; I can get deeper, harder like this," I begged her and she groaned as I shifted out from between her legs. "It will hurt for second." I ran myself over her channel, lubricating her with my arousal. "It will only hurt for a second Ana and then it will feel so good to you." I steadied myself. Anal sex in the missionary position was an extremely powerful act and the notion that I would get to see her face while we did this, I pulsed and dripped with desire just thinking about it.

"Ok," she whispered and I nodded. Thank god.

"We'll go slow." I let her feel where I was and immediately she tightened. "Relax and don't clench." I guided her as I gritted my teeth against the unbearable amounts of need that were coursing through me. Inch by inch, I entered her, feeling the unending length of how much she could take me and the tightness of how I was being held. "Bear down Ana!" I grunted and growled as I spread her legs, bending her knees back toward her chest. "God yes." I shoved and my breath disappeared. "Oh fuck. Ana my god." I started to thrust desperately, urgently as I filled her completely. I wanted to be both places and I took to massaging her clit as I pistoned in and out of her rear.

"Stephen!"

"Does it feel good Ana? God you feel so good." She gasped at the new depth this position allowed; I pounded into her as my orgasm exploded. The headboard shattered, the bed collapsed, Ana climaxed and every painting on the wall crashed to the ground in a colossal heap of glass and wood.

I pulled back slowing our movements to a quiet passion until we both could catch our breath. I felt Ana's body begin to shake under me and I looked down alarmed; she was laughing—hysterically.

"Uh…Ana? Are you alright?" I asked unsure about this sudden display of emotion. All she could do was nod and laugh as she pulled me into a hug. I buried my face in her neck and relished in having her hold me so close. I kissed her gently as I slid myself out, careful of her delicate tissues. I felt odd, not bad odd, but wonderful odd. My body felt strong and solid and something deep coursed and pumped through my muscles making me quiver. The air in my lungs expanded and I felt as if I would never need another drop of oxygen again. Ana's scent filled my entire being—she was my air supply. My heart pounded as my blood surged with heat that I could feel. I flexed my arms, my fingers and my legs; every tendon was fluid and firm. My entire soul had been awakened. I pulled back to stare at Ana, to stare at my best friend, my lover, my partner, my wife. She was smiling.

"Hey! Can we go to IKEA and get a new bed?" she asked, her wonderfully weird sense of humor returning. I laughed out loud and kissed her passionately.

Ana

I checked my watch. I was supposed to be at Liam and Carmen's for dinner in less than an hour and I still was waiting to get my exam. I had called Stephen and told him to go on ahead and I would meet him there. The office was insanely crowed today. Liam and Stephen didn't actually know if I should still be getting my period once my Change had taken place and I wanted to check with Dr. Connelly just in case. My periods were always horrible and I was proactive about making sure that things were ok health-wise and I had been cramping a lot these last few days.

"Ana!' Dr. Connelly came into the room and I was surprised again at how much he resembled Alec; it was the emerald green eyes. "It's so good to see you!" He grasped my hands and kissed my cheek. I had already talked to him on the phone so he knew what had happened to me physically. "My goodness you've had quite a few things going on!" He surveyed me over my chart and I couldn't help but wonder if he could see my memories of Nathanial and of what happened. He smiled gently and took my hand. "So you're not feeling too well?" He motioned for me to slide down the table.

"Just crampy and some spotting; we weren't sure about my whole reproductive cycle once I had been Changed. I just wanted to make sure everything was ok." I said, holding my breath as he began to examine me. I felt him poking around and I tensed. Internal examines were always psychologically difficult; I had to fight to not remember the abuse from my childhood.

"Try to relax Ana," Dr. Connelly said softly. I breathed in and out as steady as I could. "You're only half now, is that right?" He changed instruments.

"Uh huh," I said, sucking in my breath.

"That was a big decision." He was trying to distract me and I was grateful.

"It was, but I love Stephen," I said, tilting my head back as a few tears spilled out. Dr. Connelly looked up at me.

"We're almost done Ana. You're doing great," he said and I nodded. I heard him pull off his gloves and gently close my legs. "Well." He pushed his chair back and handed me a blanket to wrap around my waist; I was shivering. He stood and put his arms around me. "So, it looks like you are completely healthy. There is no more scar tissue and the damage to your uterus is repaired. Vampire venom is remarkable stuff really." He laughed. "You should have no worries about carrying the baby to term," he said. I pulled away from him.

"Excuse me?" I said, my heart thundering in my chest. I stopped breathing. Dr. Connelly stared at me.

"Ana. You're pregnant. You didn't know?" His eyes were wide. All I could do was open and close my mouth. "Ok, I guess that's a 'no'." He laughed. "So the time frame of course will be a bit different. I'm guessing you are about two months along, but that doesn't mean that's when you actually conceived; it could be anytime here over the last month even. And you most likely won't have the traditional nine month gestation, more like five, so you're almost halfway through already!" He rubbed my back. "Ana, it's ok. This is great news. I mean, if you want it to be great news, it is." He lifted my face. "You're healthy and the baby will be healthy and you can do this if you and Stephen want. You don't need to be frightened now." He held my face in his hands as the tears came down in a full torrent.

Stephen

I was at the stove with Lucie when I heard Ana come into the living room. Lucie screamed at the top of her lungs and stopped mixing in her bowl. She jumped down from the chair and sprinted to see Ana. I watched as Lucie launched herself through the air and into Ana's arms. I went back into the kitchen and brought out a glass of wine for Ana.

"Oh I'm ok thanks; maybe just a soda." She smiled and kissed Lucie.

"But it's your favorite, that disgusting Riesling crap you drink." I laughed at her and handed her the glass. She rolled her eyes, but took the glass. I watched as she put it on a coaster as she sat down on the couch pulling Lucie into her lap.

"I'm sorry I'm late," she said. Liam waved his hand.

"No worries at all Ana; Stephen was just telling us about your time in the gym over these last few weeks. Ana eyed me.

"Did he tell you that he's a cheat?" she said emphatically.

"No, he failed to mention that." Liam smiled.

"Convenient." Ana glared and then winked at me. Her mind was completely shut down. That was odd. I knew she hadn't been feeling well and I hoped the Dr. Connelly had been able to help. I wished she would let me go with her to these visits; I knew they were hard for her.

"Ana, Lucie; dinner!" Carmen called, laughing from the kitchen. Ana rose, holding Lucie and she stared at me, her eyes penetrating me to my core. She took my breath away. I watched her all through dinner. She seemed fine, but I would catch her every once in a while staring at me again. Her eyes were full of some emotion that I didn't know. I wanted her to open up again. I waited for us to get home before I asked what she was thinking about.

"So, how did things go today?" I asked, sitting back on our couch watching her.

"Good," she said, coming to sit beside me.

"Yeah?" I kissed the top of her forehead.

"Yeah."

"How was Dr. Connelly?" I asked fishing.

"Good," she replied. I sighed.

"Ana." I turned toward her.

"I have something for you." She stood and went over to her pack. She returned carrying something behind her back. I leaned forward curious. "Close your eyes," she said. I obliged. She placed something soft in my hand; it felt like a t-shirt. "Open." I looked down to see a tiny Mixed Martial Arts baby outfit with the words *"Vampires Don't Tap Out"*, scrolled across the back. I held the shirt in my hands not able to speak. I looked up at Ana. "Two months," she whispered. "I'm healthy and the baby will be too Stephen." She touched my face. I swallowed.

"Ana," I whispered. "God Ana." I held her face. "I love you. I love you." I pulled her to me and kissed her. I was overcome with so many emotions. I wanted to know everything that the doctor said and I wanted her to start from the beginning. She humored me and we stayed on the couch most of the night talking. I kept my hand on her stomach. She eventually fell asleep after we discussed that I would be at every doctor's visit from this point on. I carried her to bed. I pulled out the papers I had been keeping in my drawer and opened them. Thank god Liam had convinced me to purchase a four-bedroom house instead of the massive loft apartment that I had wanted to get for us. It was a beautiful home set in the mountains just outside of Galway. It had hardwood floors, a wood burning stove, two fireplaces, deck, and huge wrap around porch; it had everything that she had told herself she would never have, that she couldn't have. I even got her a sculling boat and propped it up in the shed. Liam had found the place on one of his business trips out to the Western part of Ireland and he'd offered the owners money to keep it off the market; he'd had it for over a year. Odd just how much my brother knew. He was one to always say that he didn't have the luxury of knowing the future and yet he knew me and he knew Ana and he had the insight to foresee that we would find our way back to each other, that we would be together.

Ana

I couldn't believe that Stephen had bought us a house. It was insane, beautiful and perfect, but insane. Liam and Stephen had managed to shimmer all of the furniture from Stephen's house to our new place, which was fine with me; Stephen had great style in home décor and all the pieces fit really well with the feel of the house. The baby was kicking constantly now and Dr. Connelly thought that I must have been much further along than we thought. He was planning for an end of June birth; there were only two weeks left in the month. I was feeling pretty good considering I was a half-Vampire carrying a baby that we could only assume would also be half; he or she would be like Lucie and me. Stephen was ridiculously excited and he was coming home everyday with something new for the house or for the baby or for me. Liam and Carmen were also thrilled. They had brought us this beautifully hand-carved crib that Liam had made for Lucie and I couldn't stop staring at it; it was almost too nice. Cillian had also taken to his role as an 'uncle' quite well. He was always popping in and out to help us paint and sometimes he would just come by to sit and talk to me while I folded laundry. He was like a brother to me—a brother and a best friend.

Stephen and I were with Dr. Connelly waiting to do an ultrasound. Stephen was pacing the room biting his nails, a new habit he had started.

"Stephen quit; you're making me nervous," I said as the nurse spread the cold goop onto my stomach.

"Sorry," he said and came over to hold my hand. "Do you want to know?" he asked. I stared at him.

"I thought we already decided that we were going to wait," I said and the nurse laughed as Dr. Connelly came back into the room.

"I know but now that I'm here, I think I want to know. Do you?" Stephen mumbled through his fingers. I reached to pull his hand away from his lips. Dr. Connelly looked at us and smiled.

"Debating I see." He smiled and turned to the monitor. I sighed

"Ok, then we'll find out," I said, glancing at the screen.

"No. I can wait, we can wait," Stephen said and I rolled my eyes.

"Well now's the time to tell me," Dr. Connelly said as he moved the wand over my belly and the baby kicked. I stared at Stephen. He stared at me.

"Tell us," he said and I smiled.

"Ok; you two are having what I am sure will be the most beautiful baby girl the world has ever seen." Dr. Connelly laughed and Stephen exhaled.

"A girl. Wow. God, my god a girl!' Stephen's voice was tight and I could see his eyes brimming with tears.

"And she's healthy and quite active; really active. Ana, you should be going into labor here in about week; how are you feeling?" A week! Frick! I stared at Dr. Connelly. He smiled. "It's perfectly natural that you are nervous Ana. This is a life-changing event for the two you.

Try to relax. I promise you that you are going to be a wonderful mother and Stephen, if he can stop pacing and biting his nails, will make an incredible father. You are going to be just fine."

"And you're going to be there the whole time?" I asked as Dr. Connelly gently wiped my stomach. He stared at me, his green eyes flashing.

"I wouldn't miss it for the world Ana and I'm honored to be with you." He bent his head and kissed the top of my forehead. I turned to Stephen.

"Are you happy?" I asked, reaching for his hand. He nodded and I watched as the tears in his eyes were let loose. He pressed his face to mine and together we cried.

Stephen

Two days after we saw Dr. Connelly, Ana went into labor. Carmen, Liam, Cillian and Lucie were all at the hospital waiting and I was currently thinking about passing out. I had no idea how Ana was doing any of this; it was insane. Unfortunately, the labor came on so quickly that they couldn't give her anything for the pain except some herbs and Healer medicine, which didn't really appear to be helping. I held her hand as she pushed and pushed and pushed; I thought she might die from exhaustion. I was so terrified of losing her.

"Ana, you have to push harder; she's breech," Dr. Connelly commanded. Fear iced through my veins.

"It's ok Stephen," Dr. Connelly said, sensing my emotion. "But Ana needs to push and she needs to push now."

"I can't," Ana was crying and sweating and she was so tired. "I can't push any harder, can't she just stay where she is; I'm really ok with that." Ana squeezed my hand. I lowered my face to her ear.

"If you do this, I promise to do whatever you want in bed for the rest of our lives."

"Stephen, not the best time to be thinking about sex; I think that's how we got into this little scenario in the first place. Plus, I'm never having sex with you again." Ana breathed and I laughed.

"Push Ana," I said and kissed her gently. She nodded and steeled herself one last time." I heard crying; one I knew and one that I had been waiting to know. Ana fell back against the bed and I closed my eyes, too overwhelmed to look.

"Stephen, Ana?" Dr. Connelly rose from the foot of the bed and handed Ana a tiny bundle of moving and squirming material. He laid our baby on her chest and I watched as Ana pulled back the tiny swaddling. There was a mass of dark curls tumbling out over the blanket, curls with coppery highlights that glinted against a fair, olive toned face.

"Stephen! Look at her eyes." Ana stared at me and I stared at my daughter. She was gazing up at me, odd for a typical newborn, but not for us. Underneath a dark fringe of lashes, were two beautiful brown eyes. Copper, bronze and gold flecks lined the rims, but in the very center, in the very depths, there was a glint of marine blue, like a tiny jewel or star radiating from some unknown place within her soul.

"So, do we have a name yet?" Dr. Connelly asked coming to stand next to me as Ana handed me our daughter. We stared at each other.

"Can we name her Maria," Ana asked. I blinked. Of course, of course that's what we should name her. That day down in West Papua when I'd witnessed Ana cradling that young girl in her arms, the day I saw so much of Ana's pain and so much of her love and her desire to heal people who were hurting; I knew then that she was the one. I had watched her kneeling in the dirt holding Maria and wishing that it had been her own life that had ended instead; that's when I knew, that's when I came to realize just how special and unique Ana truly was and that's when my heart had made its choice.

"It's beautiful and perfect, Ana," I said and I held Maria close as she reached her tiny arms to touch my face. I shook my head. She was just like her mother.

"She knows you," Ana whispered, as she rested back, closing her eyes. "She loves you." I watched her as her breathing steadied and became deep and slow. Dr. Connelly patted me on the shoulder.

"She exhausted; she'll be out for a while. We need to take Maria for a bit and check her over." He smiled as I gently handed her to him. She grazed my lips with her tiny fingers as she left my arms. I felt a sudden surge of warmth from her touch and I glanced down at her perfect, beautiful face, Ana's face. Maria smiled softly, her pink lips curving

upward and her eyes flashing bright. I kissed her nose and watched as
she left the room.

****

I stayed by Ana's side while she slept and while she attempted to
breast feed and once we came home and when she was holding Maria
and changing her and putting her down; if Ana wasn't so tired I was
pretty sure she would have decked me for hovering so much. We were
lying in bed and I was holding her hand.

"Hey," I said quietly into the dark.

"Hey," she whispered back.

"So that deal I made you in the hospital; it still stands." I joked, taking
her hand and kissing it.

"Hmm…I think that's how our entire journey together started, with a
deal," she murmured, turning on her side. I rolled to look at her.

"Yes it did and now look at what we've created; look at all you've done
Ana. I am in awe of you." I swept her hair back and touched her cheek.
She laughed softly shaking her head.

"Thank you," she said quietly and I moved closer to her.

"For what?" I asked, pressing my lips gently against hers.

"For finding your way back to me." She kissed me and I could feel that
her cheeks were wet. In my heart and in my soul, I had never left Ana; I

had never been completely lost from her. We both had been bound by different ties. We'd both fallen through our own personal hells and we'd both awakened, awakened, transformed, redeemed and forgiven; we were together. Ana was snoring softly beside me and I heard Maria begin to coo. I rose from the bed and went to her room picking her up gently from her bassinet. She stretched and twisted in my arms and I held her up so she could see the moon. She turned her face to the stars and I saw her exhale softly as tiny embers danced deep within her eyes.

Ana

I was dreaming, standing on the cliffs near my old house in Indonesia. I looked down to the crashing sea below and then up to the moon. The scent of lemon and honey, woods and musk drifted softly over my face. Nathanial took my hand and we stood together watching the moonrise over the horizon. He turned to smile at me and I saw that his eyes were clear and deep; they were midnight blue.

"So, a baby?" he said, watching me intently.

"Yep. Crazy right?" I shook my head.

"No Ana, not crazy, perfect." Nathanial reached to touch my cheek. "A girl?" he asked as I watched stars shoot across the depths of his eyes.

"Yes; we named her Maria. You remember?" I asked, getting lost in the beauty of his face.

"Ahh…yes, Maria. Of course I remember. What a beautiful testament to her life Ana and to you and Stephen." Nathanial took both of my hands in his.

"Patric screwed up again." I sighed. "He betrayed me, again." I turned my face to glance at the sea.

"Hmm…I know. I am sorry that you had to experience that side of him Ana. I also think that you know just how much Patric does love you, that you changed him in the most beautiful way possible, but he makes terrible choices; we both do." Nathanial turned my face back toward him. I watched as his hair blew softly across his shoulders. I reached to sweep the locks back from his face.

"I've forgiven you Nathanial—for everything. Can you forgive me?" I asked desperately searching his face. He smiled gently.

"For what Ana?"

"For not helping you have the life that you deserve. For causing you pain and for making you suffer, for you being so sad for so long." I touched his face.

"Ana, my love, my heart; you are not responsible for my life. I have made my own decisions, chosen my own paths as have you, but neither of us can hold ourselves accountable for anything other than what we have chosen to do. As far as causing me pain…" He shook his head. "You have only ever loved me Ana and I understand now why you had to do what did; you had to save yourself from my selfishness, from my greed and my jealousies; you had to save yourself, but by doing so, you also saved me." Nathanial held me close as I shook my head.

"But you're not here now, you're gone and you're not with me anymore." I gasped. "I lost you Nathanial." My body shook with grief and I buried my face into his chest. He stroked down the back of my head, smoothing my hair.

"Shhh now, Ana it's ok. You haven't lost me. I will never be lost from you. I will always be here to catch you when you fall; I will always be with you and I will always love you. We are bound Ana, not by symbols, but by our love and our friendship and our journeys both separate and together. We are bound, entwined and I will never be far from your memories or from your heart." He held me tight as I sobbed violently. "You have a life now, you have a life that is full of happiness and love and that is all you have ever wanted and deserved, this I know. "You have to honor what you have created for yourself and the only way to do that is to live." Nathanial pulled my face from his body and held it in his hands. "I love you Ana and this is not goodbye; it will never be goodbye for us. Don't grieve anymore, don't cry; don't cry Ana." Nathanial bent his head and pressed his lips gently to mine and as I reached to hold him, he disappeared. I stood alone on the cliff watching as stars moved back and forth over the sky, a warm breeze drifting slowly over my body and ever so gently, I felt the back of my neck grow warm.

Upcoming Titles by I. R. Harris

The Dark Hunger Chronicles

The Legion Series

www.irharrisbooks.com

www.facebook.com/IRHarrisBooks

Made in the USA
Charleston, SC
13 October 2015